LOOKER

LOOKER

Michael Kilian

St. Martin's Press   New York

This is a novel. Although there are some references in the text
to several famous fashion models and other celebrities, the
novel's characters are entirely fictional. They are not intended to
resemble any actual person, living or dead: not any member of
the St. Cecilia Society, nor anyone working in the fashion
industry, nor any resident of New York, Charleston, Savannah,
or any other locale in this book.

....

Design by Karin Batten

Library of Congress Cataloging-in-Publication Data

Kilian, Michael, 1939–
    Looker / Michael Kilian.
      p.   cm.
    "A Thomas Dunne book."
    ISBN 0-312-05123-9
    I. Title.
PS3561.I368L6   1991
813'.54—dc20   90-49207
                                         CIP

First Edition: January 1991

10 9 8 7 6 5 4 3 2 1

For Dianne deWitt
and for Jan Strimple,
my loveliest friends.

CHAPTER

....

1

The old Gullah granny woman was an ancient thing, as old, it almost seemed, as Tawabaw Island itself. She was a bent and bony creature with stalk limbs and black, crab hands who nattered and cackled to herself as she tottered around her decrepit shack at all hours of the day and night between the brief but deathlike naps that were her only sleep.

She had few clothes and went about in most of them— a faded and shapeless cotton print dress that came down to her knobby ankles, a shorter dress over that, and then a soiled and tattered apron. Her head and the tops of her long, flappy ears were covered with a tightly wound cotton kerchief. Her gnarled feet were sheltered from the dirt and muck around her dwelling place by old leather shuffle moccasins so worn they might have been made from her skin. When she went outside to rummage in the nearby swamp grass and moss-laden trees or fuss with the animal carcasses she kept hanging about the place, she wore a ragged black cloak and wide-brimmed hat that once perhaps had been Sunday church finery. She used a stick as gnarled and knobby as she was to support her fragile weight and poke about the weeds and foliage.

When she sat in the sun, it was on a plain board bench by her door. The only other furniture was a homemade rocking chair kept by the shack's clay-brick fireplace, a sagging cot with a ragged quilt, and a rude table heaped with dusty crockery and medicines. She kept animal bones and skins in careful heaps about the floor and, in a box in one corner, roots and herbs and musky swamp plants. Among the gutted carcasses of animals and sea creatures hanging on the shack's outside wall and from the surrounding trees was one of a gray dog so large it might have been a wolf. Some of the island children believed that it was. She had put seashells in the empty eye sockets, and when she had a fire burning outside, the flickering reflection of the firelight made it seem as though the wretched, ratty thing could see.

Throughout the island she was spoken of as a hoodoo nana, an evil hag steeped in the bewitched West African ways of the first slaves. The people of the village just across the narrow inlet that was her moat brought her food and kerosene for her lamp, but otherwise stayed fearfully away unless they were desperately ill and in need of her curatives. Many were just as fearful of the doctor from the mainland who came by on occasional rounds. He had come twice to attend to the old woman when she was shaking with fever and moaning and crying in the night, but she had only screeched and hissed at him, and ignored the pills he had left among the animal detritus and roots and powders on her table.

The old woman sang at odd times, and always when there was a moon or at day clean, as the islanders called daybreak. She muttered Gullah chants when she had a consultation— her consultation of the spirits. She chatted with her biddies, the little chickens who pecked and fluttered about her small, cluttered yard until they fell victim to her religion. She wailed about the long eye of the bukras who wished to make resort developments of her patch and other shore

2

holdings on the island as they had all over Hilton Head and Daufuskie Island, which lay just across the channel.

The islanders humored her in this. She gave them the dread feeling, but in a way they cherished her. It was believed that she cast a strong magic, and that while she lived, the white bukra and his bulldozers would never come near.

Her eyes, set in deep wrinkled holes of bone and skin, were the oldest thing about her, and she could but dimly see, but she could find strange treasures in swamp grass and boggy creek beds that to others were only worthless barren. Her hearing had badly faded and she responded only vaguely to speech, yet she could sense the presence of wild creatures and ken the call of seabirds when something had disturbed them. She could name the sounds of the night.

It was fully night now, as many hours from the day clean as from the sun's last rosy glow above the thick trees that shielded the island from all view of the channel separating Tawabaw from Daufuskie and the mainland. She sat hunched in her rocker, her hands occupied only with themselves, singing softly to herself. The flickering lamplight danced her silhouette against the wall. The air was sweet with the fresh spring heat. It gave her pleasure.

The door swung open. She lifted her head slowly, without startle or fright, as though she expected or at least welcomed the man who stepped inside. He stood a moment without speaking, his searching glance about the shack's shadowy interior his only movement. She smiled, her dark, creased lips widening across her weathered face. She spoke gibberish, then cackled and broke into Gullah, "Heh! You ben don 'em. One day 'mong all!"

"Where is it, Nana?" said the man, his deep voice attempting friendliness, but full of threat and anger.

Her speech lapsed into chicken sounds.

"Where is it? Where's his tote?"

She seemed to be ignoring him. She was talking to herself, to spirits, to ancestors, in words he couldn't understand—words that were simply noise. He had come far, traveling with difficulty through the night, and this is what he found. He began shouting.

She continued her nattering. He strode up to her, hulking over her, intimidating.

3

"Where is it, Nana?!" The question came forth as a bel-
low. He grasped her by her thin shoulders, his thumbs near
her long, scrawny neck. Her head eased forward, almost
as though she were offering herself to his strong hands. He
gripped her hard, then harder, and began shaking. There
was a sudden snap. Her eyelids closed for the last time. He
held her head erect above the humps of her shoulder bones,
as though there were still a few whispers of life within her.

But she had died in an instant. The thread of her existence
had been as frail as those that hung from the edges of her
garments. Gently, he lifted and eased her back into the
rocker. It moved to and fro a few times. She might merely
have been nodding into sleep.

He stood back, as enraged at himself as he had been at
her. He took deep breaths to calm himself, reminding himself of his mission and his hurry. He looked about the shack.
There was not much to search. He went at the task with
swiftness and great purpose, overturning her crude bed and
tearing open its wretched mattress. Finding nothing, he
pawed through her one cupboard, knocking crockery to
the floor. He seized the old pitted poker from the fireplace
and used it to break open her decrepit wooden chest. In
frustration, he jabbed at loose bricks and pulled up loose
floorboards, finding nothing.

The rocking chair jittered with the violence of his effort.
Her head lolled to one side, as though she were turning to
see what he was about.

Eyes. He crashed his way outside. The firelight reached
through the open door and window, its glow limning the
animal carcasses hanging from the edge of the shack's roof
and the tree limbs beyond. He knocked one down with the
poker and ripped it open, revealing only slime and crawly
little insects. He went down the line, repeating the grisly
process. In one, so old the interior had mummified into
something like leather, he found a rusting old tin box and
kicked it open. It contained only shells and pieces of bones.

A dead bobcat, twirling slowly, hung from the thick limb
of a nearby tree. He went up to it and, dropping the poker,
pulled the belly apart with his bare hands. A spattering
moisture fell upon his face and neck and into his shirt,
little pieces of slimy grit that at once began to move. He

4

brushed madly at the terrible multitude of things, causing some to fall down his chest and back. His skin was alive with them.

A dog barked. He jerked around toward the path that led to the distant village, catching a flicker of light in the distance. Standing motionless, he heard muffled voices.

The villagers were fisher folk. It could be a party of fishermen taking early to their boats to catch the night tide. But it might just as easily be people startled from their sleep by his noisy actions. Had he called out when these damned crawlies had fallen into his collar? He couldn't remember.

The dog barked again, more loudly. He hadn't uncovered even a hint of what he'd come to find. If the old nana had it, she could have hidden it anywhere on the island. He hadn't the days it might take now to discover it. He hadn't minutes. He saw the light flicker again. He ran, his feet squishing into patches of muck as he headed for the beach. He'd have to think of another way.

•

In the afternoon, when the sheriff's men from the mainland came by boat in response to the islanders' summons, her body was still in the rocking chair. The sheriff's men took away her remains but left everything else as it lay. So did the villagers, who thereafter treated the shack and swampy plot of land as a haunted place.

The death bringer had left a few footprints in the wet soil leading down along the inlet to the beach. A boat's keel had made a long imprint in the sand, but both traces of his coming disappeared in the next rain and following tides.

A homicide report was clumsily typed and forwarded and filed. There was the requisite autopsy and a coroner's report. But there was little subsequent investigation, there being no one to press charges, and few to mourn.

CHAPTER

....

2

Those who regularly attend the gilded social rites that are
New York fashion shows do so as much to be seen as to
see, and the crowd that was packed into the Terrace Room
of the Plaza Hotel for the presentation of the new Philippe
Arbre fur collection was as richly dressed as the models.
The women ranged from fading young beauties to aging
matrons clinging to the last vestiges of glamour. They glittered with expense, their carefully tailored garments set off
with magnificent jewelry of the sort displayed in Fifth Avenue store windows where price was a mere detail. There
were a few men in the audience, the younger largely in
Italian designer suits and fashionably slicked-back hair, the
older tending to more openly effeminate garb. They were
present either because they were in the business of fashion
or because they were "walkers," daytime companions of
the wives of rich, powerful, and extremely busy husbands
who found fashion shows and afternoon teas a frivolous

6

and embarrassing waste of time. The walkers were as commonplace at these patrician pageants as eunuchs in a sultan's harem, and perhaps as necessary. Yet they seemed somehow inappropriate, like the rouged and peroxided women who hang out at prizefights.

A.C. James was not like them. He ostensibly came to fashion shows because his friend Vanessa Meyers did. She appreciated his company and he was very fond of hers. But he mostly came because he liked to watch the girls.

Vanessa was the *New York Globe*'s fashion editor and these shows for her were serious work. A.C. wrote a column for the tabloid on the city's social and celebrity life, and also contributed commentary on the theater and the arts.

For all its glamour and obvious pleasures, it was a frivolous, even trivial job, the sort often given to worthy but battered old reporters ready for the pasture. A.C. was not even forty. He'd been a foreign and military correspondent, specializing in nasty little wars like Northern Ireland and El Salvador. After he'd been wounded accompanying a British foot patrol in Belfast, his wife, Kitty, had made him take reassignment to the *Globe*'s Washington bureau. When he'd embroiled the paper in too many fights with the White House and the Pentagon, she'd then made him move to New York and accept the post of social columnist and arts critic.

No one had thought it peculiar that she could order him about in this manner. Kitty was not only his wife; she and her brother owned the *Globe*.

She had come to regret this last move. To everyone's surprise, A.C. had taken well to the life of a boulevardier. He found he enjoyed spending his afternoons in museums and taking tea or cocktails with lovely ladies as much as he had the adventure of helicoptering into the deadly mountains of Central America and riding in tanks with the Third Armored Division. He'd discovered there were as many fools and villains in the Upper East Side haut monde as there were among the power elite of Washington. And he wrote about them just as boldly and woundingly.

Now there was no place left for Kitty to make him go except away. They'd been quarreling frequently. Their last fight, occasioned by a cozy four-hour lunch he'd had the previous week with a rather notorious corporate "second wife," had led to his moving into the East Side apartment he and Kitty kept for late evenings in town. She had remained in their big place on the river up in Westchester, smoldering.

A.C. didn't like Philippe Arbre much, and had said so in print. The man was both a fawning social climber and a vicious gossip. He had hurt a lot of people in New York he now considered beneath him. A.C. had written of him that he was reminiscent of Truman Capote and Elsa Maxwell, except that he hadn't Capote's talent or Maxwell's taste. Arbre hadn't spoken to him since.

But A.C. loved Arbre's models. They weren't superstars like Dianne deWitt, Jan Strimple, Margaret Donahoe, Iman, and Laura Dean. Those girls—and all fashion mannequins referred to themselves as girls—worked the top-line shows for the very best fashion houses. Despite the fashion-press hype he had been able to generate with his fawning, Arbre was essentially a second-echelon designer, and in the high season often had to settle for new girls breaking into New York from other cities or older veterans no longer quite right for the perfection demanded by fashion photography but still able to earn a considerable living on the runways. They were nonetheless remarkable beauties, and worked hard for their money. A.C. admired them very much.

A.C. was what the French call *un homme amoureux*, a man who loved women. He delighted in everything about them. He was still in love with his Kitty, and, though no one believed it, had been scrupulously faithful to her—in the sense that he had never actually gone to bed with the objects of his many infatuations. But he was by nature courtly and reflexively flirtatious. His society columnist job kept him constantly in the company of other women, and the resulting relationships were not always platonic. His wife had never understood. The sadness he felt over their quarreling had begun to show in his eyes as much as the wars he had covered did.

Vanessa didn't fully understand his attitude toward

8

women, either, but they were very close friends and she humored him.

They were seated snugly together in the front row of the press section that afternoon at the Arbre show, up against the brightly illuminated risers of the runway and in the full glare of the carefully arranged floodlights.

They were a stylishly attractive couple and drew not a few glances from their social betters. A.C. was tall and slender and tanned, handsome enough despite a few scars and a slightly odd angle to his face caused by some long-ago broken bones. Disdaining the Gucci, Armani, Ralph Lauren foppery so prevalent on the Upper East Side, his journalistic hunting ground, A.C. dressed to suit himself, rather as his grandfather had dressed. In winter weather, this meant dark, conservative, vested suits, mostly from Brooks Brothers. On a bright and breezy June day like this, his style allowed for the flamboyance of white shoes, white ducks, and blue blazer.

Vanessa was neither as beautiful as the models nor as rich as Arbre's clients, but she was pretty and, thanks to a successful and generous husband and her own impeccable taste, as stylish as anyone in the room. Her light brown hair was perfectly cut, and she wore a cream-colored silk blouse, short black skirt, and tan and black shoes. The gold chain around her slender neck was from Cartier and her gold watch from Tiffany's. She wore no other jewelry. Despite her small stature, she had a model's legs, and, as always, A.C. resisted the temptation to caress her knee.

He was distracted by movement at the other end of the room. One of the mannequins was beginning her descent of the runway in a huge sable coat with wide collar and ermine trim. She was a blonde and her long, abundant hair shimmered as luxuriantly as the fur. Her well-formed face was as immaculate as a new white marble sculpture. As she came closer to him now with the sable thrown open to reveal a short-skirted gray couture suit beneath, he noted the springy insouciance of her step and the haunting depth and glimmer of her blue-gray eyes. All runway models performed their promenades like empresses arriving at court, goddesses descended temporarily to earth, but this

9

girl had an especially commanding presence. The chatter among the rich ladies who filled the room fell away as she passed by them. No garment, plastic surgeon, health spa, or three weeks' pounding and painting at Elizabeth Arden could make any of them remotely resemble this spectacular, still young woman.

"Who is she?" he said, turning to whisper quickly to Vanessa, who was scribbling something hurridly in her leather-bound notebook.

"Be quiet, A.C.," she whispered back.

"She's bloody marvelous," he said, perhaps too loudly, for as the blonde came nearer, Vanessa flushed, as much with anger as embarrassment.

The model halted just in front of them, turning to flare the sable coat, a movement as practiced and perfect as a dancer's arabesque. He found himself staring at her marvelous legs from a distance of less than two feet.

She glanced down at him with the briefest flicker of eyelash, as she might at something she had inadvertently stepped on, then, with another swirl of furry hem, she swept on down the avenue of floodlights. He found himself as intoxicated as if he had just gulped a half pint of gin.

She disappeared through an exit to the rear as two more girls appeared at the top of the runway, a change in the taped musical accompaniment to the show announcing their arrival—the richly mournful saxophone of David Sanborn that had served as sensuous background music for the new blonde segueing to a rock beat. Moving in time to it, the two of them nimbly negotiated the first of the descending steps of the runway side by side, not once looking down.

"Please, Vanessa," he said, speaking more loudly against the increased volume of the music. "Who is she?"

Vanessa put down her gold-trimmed Montblanc pen, and slowly shook her head in not so feigned exasperation.

"Why do I bring you to these things, A.C.?" she said. "You never behave yourself."

"It's just that I'm the only heterosexual male here. And anyway, I was only joking."

"No you weren't, sweetheart. As you say, you're a heterosexual. I think you are succumbing to a very serious case of lust."

10

"I've only just seen her."

"Some diseases strike quickly."

He waited impatiently for her return, but fashion shows follow a carefully structured script. Appearing at the top of the runway now was a long-haired brunette in an oversize white fox. As she approached them, it occurred to A.C. that her bearing was nearly as regal as the new blonde's, but her expression was much too smug. It was as though she was contemptuous of those in the audience, as though she doubted they could afford the coat, and was daring them to try to buy it.

"This one looks like she took up modeling just to annoy daddy," A.C. said. "A Bryn Mawr girl, yes? Perhaps Wellesley—and not on a scholarship?"

"Certainly not on an academic one," Vanessa said, nodding at the brunette's rear as she twirled and passed. "That's Belinda St. Johns, *nom de naissance inconnu*. She's one of the better models in the city, but I'd bet my summer place in Bridgehampton that she never graduated from high school. From what I know of her, I'd also bet her IQ isn't much over eighty. Appearances are deceiving, sweetheart, or didn't you learn that when you were working down in Washington?"

"Who's the new blonde? Please. Tell me and I'll buy you a Lamborghini—anyway, lunch."

"Here?"

"At Vagabondo, a quiet, Italian lunch. Please."

The old restaurant, which had one of the last bocce ball courts left in Manhattan, was on the Upper East Side near the Ford Agency and had become a fashionable hangout for models.

"All right," said Vanessa, after making another notation on her pad. "Vagabondo. Her name's Camilla Santee. And she's top dollar. Fashion royalty. At any rate, she used to be."

"What is she doing working an Arbre show?"

"I suppose she needs the money. Santee's been out of the country. She was one of the top girls here when you were in Washington, but four or five years ago she started working exclusively in Europe, and then more or less retired to the south of France. There was some talk she'd gotten

11

married but I never saw anything in *W* or *Women's Wear Daily*. I don't know what brought her back, but early this spring she turned up on the New York runways again, and she's been working her little haute couture tail off ever since. When she was on top, she was making better than eight hundred thousand a year. At this rate, she could be up there again, though I don't know. She must be thirty now. *Trente-et-plus.*"

Someone jarred heavily against the back of A.C.'s chair in the process of taking the seat behind him, a clumsiness not followed by any apology. A.C., smelling a strong odor of bourbon though it was not yet noon, was about to turn and glare at the intruder, but the room lights dimmed and the music changed once more, quickening from pulsating rock to something stranger and wilder, a rapid, electric, melodic pounding.

"That's 'The Great Balloon Race,' " Vanessa said, in sudden recollection. "I can't quite recall the name of the group. I think they're called Sky or something. But Bob Mackie used that same music in his fur show last year. This business is nothing if not original, *n'est-ce pas?*"

Heads were turning back toward the high end of the room where an extraordinarily tall and long-legged black model, with enormous eyes and skin as light as a May tan, stood at the entrance summit in a floor-length white ermine coat held back to display an ensemble of tight black sweater and short, short skirt, black stockings, and high heels of the Times Square mode.

A.C. knew her. He had interviewed her a few months before. Like many models, she was struggling to become an actress, and had won a small role in a low-budget New York film. She played a murder victim but her brief appearance was in a nude scene considered one of the steamiest ever to get away with an R rating.

"Ah, yes," Vanessa said. "The up and coming Molly Wickham. The 'African body'; a Nutra-Creme face. They say she could be another Iman, but I don't think she has the class."

"She gave me a good interview. I think she's very nice."

"I bet you do."

The black girl wrapped the coat about her dramatically,

12

then, head high, started forward down her dangerous course. She wore her hair straightened, long and full, or perhaps, A.C. thought, it was a wig.

"If she makes it without stumbling in those shoes she deserves a ten-thousand-dollar bonus," Vanessa said. "I don't know what possesses Philippe sometimes. He'll do anything for effect. I wonder if we'll see his girls on stilts next year."

The person behind them coughed as the black model approached, intensifying the unpleasant aroma of whiskey. The girl paused a little overlong before them, but otherwise paid them no attention. She was extraordinary to behold, but A.C. had fallen for the blonde—*un homme tombé amoureux*. Camilla Santee. It seemed a professional enough name for a model, but odd—the first part out of a Southern gothic novel, the last name almost something from a western movie.

There were only eight mannequins working in this Arbre show, and Camilla Santee reappeared within a few minutes, the music gentling to David Sanborn again to welcome her back, this time in a sable jacket.

A.C. sighed, too loudly.

"You're wasting your time, A.C. I mean it. Santee has a reputation for aloofness. *Très hautaine.* Even a little mysterious. I've probably told you all I really know about her, and I've been writing about fashion for nine years."

A.C. was no longer listening. He was fixed to his chair as though with arrows. As before, he was staring at Camilla Santee like a man possessed, but this time, without missing a step, she was staring back at him—her look deliberate, steady, serious, and flamingly provocative. The effect on him was electrifying. Perspiration began to moisten his palms, neck, and brow. This was in its way a signal honor, perhaps even some peculiar form of invitation. But it was also a serious transgression. Except perhaps to smile in response to an audience's applause over a particularly winning ensemble, runway models never looked at anyone except those on the platform with them. They kept their eyes averted from their audience, lifting them to gaze off into space during their pauses and turns. On the rare occasions when they did make eye contact with someone they knew,

13

it would be with a quick, almost imperceptible wink. To communicate directly with someone off the runway was as great a sin as a stage actress interrupting an important scene to wave at someone in the seats.

Yet here was this blond vision A.C. had never encountered before performing her routine with her eyes full upon him. He felt quite sexually excited, but at the same time puzzled by this odd and inexplicable occurrence. But for the merest glimpse of him during that pause on her second trip down the runway, she could not possibly have ever seen him before. And even though nearly all the others in the room were older women, and peculiar men in effeminate clothing, he was still just a vague face in the crowd.

A.C. now felt troubled. Something was wrong here. His elation, he realized, was probably going to be very short-lived.

As she approached them now, her stare vanished. Her eyelids lowered. Her pale face reddened. She made her turn in front of them with something close to violence and stalked away with the angry stride of a flamenco dancer. Behind A.C., the man who smelled of whiskey began coughing again, causing the air around them to reek. A.C. turned angrily in his seat, confronting a large, middle-aged fellow with dark curly hair and black-rimmed glasses. There was something vaguely familiar about him, but A.C.'s eyes were still full of the glare from the runway lights and it was hard to see.

Rising, pausing to cough once more, the man then began awkwardly making his way back down the aisle, stepping on the foot of a fashion reporter from one of the women's magazines. She swore.

A.C. sat facing forward again. "I'm confused," he said.

"Well, I'm impressed," Vanessa said. "I've never seen a model do that before. You're certainly not chopped liver, A.C., but that was ridiculous."

"It doesn't make any sense."

"Philippe's probably going to kill her. Everyone was looking over at us instead of at that jacket, and that jacket probably goes for sixty thousand dollars."

"Perhaps it was just our imagination," A.C. said, slouching down in his chair.

14

"Well, we'll find out next time around, won't we, sweetheart?"

Next time came around, but there was no appearance by Camilla Santee. The girls pranced along in the proper order, but the succession began over again without her.

"Arbre's probably beating her," Vanessa said.

"With his handkerchief."

"Be quiet, A.C. This is my work. You may not get along with Philippe, but I have to."

Eventually Santee did return, toward the end of the show, modeling a long silver fox coat with the collar high up against her cheeks. She looked somber. Her eyes met A.C.'s only once, during her first turn, but she ignored him thereafter. He felt awkward, and then depressed. It was the last they saw of her during the show. The other girls joined Arbre for the finale when he came forth to accept the tumultuous applause with a sheepish bow. Santee's absence from this concluding ritual was as remarkable as her prolonged look at A.C. had been.

"I'm afraid I've gotten her into trouble," he said, as the floodlights went out and the chandeliers were rekindled to their full brilliance. They rose to join the stream of two-hundred dollar coiffures and ten thousand dollar designer outfits heading toward the stairs and the Plaza lobby.

"Come off it, A.C.," said Vanessa, gathering up her notebook, program, and black Prada bag. "You were just another guy along the runway, even if you do dress like Commander Whitehead, or is it Jay Gatsby? I think Santee's getting a little strange, that's all. That may be why she retired in the first place."

A.C. fell glumly silent and let Vanessa lead them toward the exit. The aroma of expensive perfume in the crowd was so strong it was almost as unpleasant as the whiskey breath of the stranger in the seat behind him had been. He longed for the clean, clear air of the out of doors and the bright sunlight that had been sparkling over the entire city when he'd stepped out of his apartment building earlier that morning.

Unfortunately, Vanessa had other ideas. "I want to stop and get a few quotes from Arbre," she said.

"I'll meet you in the main lobby, or maybe outside."

15

"No," she said, taking his hand firmly. "I think you'd better come with me. Otherwise you might see her on her way out and go up and say something embarrassing. I'm afraid you might try to apologize or something. *Mon Dieu!*"

"I don't want to talk to Arbre."

"You don't have to. You can just stand there and take in the scenery. I'm sure you'll like it."

Vanessa led him through an opening in a wall of folding screens set up across the foyer outside the Terrace Room. The barrier had created a large, temporary chamber, into which were filing a number of highly stylish women, and men in strange, wide-shouldered suits that looked to be much more appropriate for the next century.

It was the changing room. A.C. had been in them before, but had never felt completely comfortable. It was customary for men and women in the audience to come back after a show to congratulate the designer and his or her girls, but to A.C., it was just the same as barging into a woman's dressing room or bath.

Arbre—a short, balding fellow with curly side-hair, double-breasted suit, and crimson silk handkerchief flowing out of his breast pocket—gave him a dark look, but turned happily to Vanessa. A.C. stood awkwardly by, trying to be inconspicuous and feeling anything but. Some four or five of the girls were standing or sitting about in their underwear—not the "woman of substance" proper lingerie that Kitty and doubtless all her friends wore, but the briefest, flimsiest, laciest, and certainly most expensive sort of "innerwear" that A.C. could imagine. They stood or sat and chatted as unconcernedly as National Football League players in their locker room after a game.

One of them was Camilla Santee, curled up with knees and calves tight together on a folding chair in the corner as she talked with a youngish man in a punk hairdo, polka-dotted wide-shouldered sport coat, zebra-striped pants, and gold slippers. He was consoling her and she appreciated it, giving him in return a small but winsome smile.

A.C. tried to catch her attention, but though she turned once in his direction, the eyes that had stared at him so fixedly from the runway eluded him completely. Carried away in his excitement, he had presumed flirtation, but now, for her, he had ceased to exist. He felt increasingly embarrassed and exposed standing there, and, despite himself, furious. This was not simply an awkward moment; as Santee continued to ignore him, it became a humiliating one. He was immensely grateful and relieved when Vanessa finally came to rescue him—and angry that she had taken so long.

"I should never have gone in there," he said, as they emerged into the normal world beyond the folding screens.

"No one minded."

"They were in their underwear. Some of them, anyway. Camilla Santee, too."

"That will happen when one takes off one's clothes—as I believe you may have noticed on occasion in the past. If this embarrasses you, A.C., you ought to come with me to the shows in Italy. A lot of the models there don't even bother with undies."

"She didn't look at me—not even a glance. I couldn't have been more than twenty feet away."

"But you certainly looked at her, didn't you, A.C.?"

They reached the corridor that led around the Palm Court to the lobby. The restaurant was crowded with expensively dressed patrons.

"When do you suppose Camilla Santee might next be in a show?" A.C. said quietly.

Vanessa glared at him. She was one of his very best friends and he had never before seen her look at him in this disapproving way.

"I'm sure you're just having an odd morning, darling, and that this bout of puppy love will pass by this afternoon. But if you're bent on anything more serious, let me give you the best advice I have to give any man about the fashion business. Never, dearest, get seriously mixed up with a fashion model. Some of them are great ladies. Most are just hardworking kids. But there are some sleazeballs like Belinda St. Johns, and a few are even worse than Belinda."

"I still think she looks like a Wellesley girl."

"Your wife actually happens to be a Smith girl. What became of all your talk about patching things up?"

17

"I called her last night, but nothing's changed."

"And, *vraiment*, panting after the mannequin du jour is going to help?"

He said nothing. They passed through the lobby and then waited their turn to go through the revolving door on the north side of the hotel that led to that stretch of Fifty-ninth Street known as Central Park South.

"Kitty's the genuine article," Vanessa said, leaning close to him. "With these ladies, what you see is seldom what you get. Why haven't you learned that? Mannequins are even worse than actresses that way. I used the wrong word when I said Camilla Santee had a reputation for aloofness. A lot of people have found her downright scary. Fashion models can be a lot of trouble, A.C. If you want to fool around a little while you're waiting for Kitty to make up her mind, go home with one of those married *belles dames d'un age certain* you're always flirting with at parties. You'll have a good time. They'll be grateful. They won't complicate your life for exactly the same reason they would expect you not to complicate theirs."

"I'm not looking to fool around, Vanessa."

"And I am Jacqueline Bouvier Kennedy Onassis."

Stepping out into the midday glare, both put on their sunglasses. There was a row of horse-drawn carriages farther along the curb and two stretch limousines standing with motors running in the street before them, one of them with a rear door partly open. But there were no cabs.

"There's an auction this afternoon at Sotheby's," Vanessa said. "The late Marianne Mills's jewelery. I think I'll go after lunch."

"Junk jewelry," A.C. said.

"Costume, sweetheart, and with a hell of a history. Do you want to come? See who's there? Tell the collectors from the ghouls?"

"Sure."

A.C. heard a soft flurry of sound behind him and turned to see several of the models from the Arbre show descend the red carpeting of the steps in a group and head toward Fifth Avenue. They had changed into street clothes, all in knee-length or full-length pants and bright-colored blouses, and two or three were carrying oversize picture cases. The

18

girls seemed much smaller and more delicate than they had on the runway, walking with light little steps like a small herd of impalas or gazelles. A.C. heard one of them utter a coarse profanity, and then the others laughed.

Camilla Santee was not among them.

"I met a real ghoul the other night," A.C. said. "A woman next to me at a dinner party. She makes her living going through the possessions of dead celebrities and Park Avenue rich ladies for trustees of estates. She decides what's worth auctioning off and what should be tossed or dumped on relatives."

"She could do well performing that service for the living. I can think of quite a few rich bitches who would pay well for judgment like that."

Another of the models emerged from the Plaza, but halted on the steps behind them, waiting her turn for a cab. It was the brunette Vanessa had identified as Belinda St. Johns. She was chewing gum. A moment later, she was joined by the bald man A.C. had seen in the changing room. Philippe Arbre, come to join the mere mortals on the street. He chatted with St. Johns, studiously ignoring A.C. He kept looking at his watch. A.C. guessed he was late for a lunch date.

The doorman, blowing his whistle noisily but futilely, moved away down the street, searching the oncoming traffic for the rooflight that would identify an approaching available taxi.

"I don't understand why there are no cabs on such a nice day," A.C. said. "You'd think they'd be prowling the streets begging for fares."

"We ought to walk," Vanessa said. "In this traffic, we'd get there just as fast."

A vague movement at the entrance caught A.C.'s eye. He turned to see the black model Molly Wickham standing goddesslike just outside the revolving door. It was as though she were still performing on the runway, and waiting for all to notice her before proceeding farther.

She smiled at A.C. in recognition, looked up and down the street, and then, moving quickly, started down the steps. The lead limousine began to move, as though pulling away. A.C. caught a glimpse of a man in the rear seat. He

19

was wearing glasses and leaning forward. Then the limousine halted as a motorcycle came roaring up swiftly on the driver's side.

What struck A.C. so profoundly—and would later haunt his sleep for nights to come—was the brutal suddenness of what happened next. The motorcycle abruptly slowed, pulling almost to a stop just ahead of the limousine. The motorcyclist, a man in black leather with a demonic-looking black crash helmet that shadowed a movie-actor-handsome face behind a clear visor, was looking at them. He reached into his heavy jacket.

There was a muted pop, and then A.C. saw Molly Wickham's head snap back and felt the splash of wetness against his cheek and neck. But he witnessed all this in surreal slow motion and eerie soundlessness, even as the motorcyclist sped away through the traffic and around the corner into the park. Then all sound came back in an overwhelming rush.

People everywhere were screaming. It was as though all the world were wailing over Molly Wickham's savage death. And utterly dead she was. With long limbs akimbo, her graceful body lay sprawled impossibly on the steps. She had a terrible wound in her face and the back of her head was missing. Blood was gushing in surges from the cavity, and there was the bright red of blood and other, darker stains all over the sidewalk. Her long, full wig had been blown several feet away.

A number of people on the street had turned and fled at the report of the gunshot, but many more were now hurrying up to see what had happened. Incredibly, a uniformed policeman was already there. A.C. looked down at the dead girl again, transfixed by the extraordinary innocence of what remained of her beautiful face. He felt an urgent need to kneel beside her, to hold her hand or cradle her body, to make some useless but still important gesture of help. But he could not. Brusque, flippant, cynical Vanessa was clutching him tightly, her face pressed tightly against his shoulder as her small chest heaved with her sobbing.

A few like the policeman were impassive, but the expressions of most of those crowded around them were those of shock, grief, or horror. Arbre seemed utterly bewildered.

20

Belinda St. Johns's face was utterly blank. She had been splattered with much of the gore.

Looking up, A.C. saw Camilla Santee standing on the landing by the door. She was staring down the street in the direction the motorcyclist had gone. Instead of shock, grief, or horror, her face was full of fury.

CHAPTER

····································

3

A sweaty, unpleasant policeman asked them to wait in the hotel lobby. A.C. and Vanessa complied with some reluctance and Arbre and the St. Johns woman did so only after angry protest. Camilla, her eyes staring vacantly, obeyed without a word, taking a seat off to herself. She sat as if she were posing for a somber portrait, her hands perfectly still. She was wearing a simple skirt and patterned blouse, and sandals. A country setting would have been more suitable, a meadow with flowers—perhaps flowers in her hair.

More and more sirens were heard, their sounds rising and mingling until it was impossible to differentiate one from another. Policemen came in and out, including a number of detectives. One of them, a very tall and improbable-looking black man with glasses, light skin, and an odd color to his hair, took their names and addresses. He wore a dark three-piece suit and looked more like a lawyer or professor than a cop. Though he introduced himself simply as Detective Lanham, the others seemed to defer to him, including a lieutenant of detectives and several uniformed sergeants.

Arbre, mopping his head with his large breast pocket handkerchief, became very agitated and demanded that they be allowed to go, complaining that he had an important luncheon engagement. St. Johns joined in his lament, arguing that she had to clean up, had another booking, and was losing large sums of money. In response, the detectives curtly asked them to come to the homicide division to give statements.

"We've done nothing!" Arbre protested. "Why are you arresting us?" His faintly French accent slipped slightly in his excitement.

"You're not being arrested," said Lanham, politely, but with some exasperation. "Look. This is a homicide. Murder One. Whatever else you've got to do—and I've got other things to do, too—nothing's more important. We sure as hell plan to catch this son of a bitch but we have to convict him in court. That isn't always easy nowadays. So please, help us as much as you can."

They were taken to the police station in two police cars—A.C. and Vanessa in one; Arbre and the two models in the other. Once there, Arbre began demanding to see his lawyer. Lanham and another detective, an equally large white man named Petrowicz, explained patiently again that that would not be necessary—that they were merely witnesses, that there was nothing to fear.

They took Arbre into the interrogation room first. It was obvious they wanted to be rid of him as soon as possible.

A.C. waited uncomfortably in the old wooden office chair they had given him, looking around the squad room as old memories of his police reporter days came back to him. They were squalid memories—of murderers, thieves, drunks, wife beaters, dirty people in T-shirts, bloodstained victims, and cops who treated everyone who was not a cop as an alien species. It had seemed high adventure at the time. Now it hardly seemed possible it had been part of his life.

Squad rooms had certainly changed little since then. This one was large, but overly crowded. The desks were heaped

23

with papers and jammed together every which way, wherever there was room. Phones were ringing incessantly. Detectives were everywhere—typing, talking on the phone, standing about together—each wearing a pistol and many holding a plastic cup of coffee, as though it were part of their regulation equipment. There were two men behind the chicken wire of holding cells along one wall. One of them, a black man, appeared to be bleeding, and sat clutching his bandaged arm.

A.C. noticed one difference between then and now. He could remember a time when detectives had mostly worn cheap gabardine suits and even hats. These men were nearly as well dressed as he. One of those working with Lanham had on what appeared to be a Giorgio Armani double-breasted pin-striped suit. Another was dressed like a very wealthy gangster.

Vanessa and Belinda St. Johns carried on a desultory, unhappy conversation to the effect that this was another example of the general miserableness of life in New York. Camilla Santee remained utterly silent, gazing at her folded hands, her extraordinary legs crossed at the ankles.

She looked so very sad, A.C. felt like hugging her. It was the silliest possible notion in the circumstance, but he was consumed by it. He imagined that her trim shoulders would be hard and strong beneath his touch. Her golden hair, however, would be soft and silken, her cheek cool and perfumed.

"*Mon Dieu, si fatigant, ça,*" Vanessa said, in response to something St. Johns had said. Santee looked up, as though the French words were directed at her. Seeing they were not, she withdrew into herself once more.

Arbre, still mopping his head, emerged from his interrogation quite flustered. He barked something at St. Johns and then hurried out. Belinda, looking sullen, was summoned next. Vanessa gave a weary sigh and looked at her nails.

"It won't be so bad," A.C. said lamely. He addressed the words to Vanessa but was looking at Camilla Santee. She ignored him.

"I told myself this morning the day looked too good to be true," Vanessa said.

24

"We'll have a late lunch," said A.C.

"More likely an early dinner."

Belinda St. Johns seemed restored to her natural demeanor when she sauntered out of the interrogation room.

"They're shitheads, like all cops," Belinda said to Vanessa. "All I had to tell them I could have told them back where it happened. Now I've probably blown my booking. These fucking assholes probably cost me five hundred bucks."

She traipsed out through the double doors leading to the corridor. She might have been a prostitute who'd just made bond.

"Mrs. Meyers?" Lanham was standing in the doorway, like a doctor at a waiting room with not very good news.

"Save my place," Vanessa said.

When she had gone, A.C. noticed the large coffeemaker against the opposite wall and the tall stack of white cups. Impulsively, he stood up. "May I get you a cup of coffee?" he said to Santee.

She lifted her head slowly. Her eyes were very wide and melancholy. Instead of speaking, she shook her head just once, and then lowered her gaze. He brought coffee back for himself, though he didn't really want it.

They kept Vanessa nearly twenty minutes. She was all business when she came out, fiddling with the catch on her purse.

"I'm going to call the office," she said. "I can't possibly think why, but I have the strange feeling our beloved editors will be wanting to speak with us."

"Mr. James?"

•

There was nothing in the interrogation room but a long table and four chairs. A.C. was gestured to one in the middle. Lanham took the seat opposite, a tape recorder and a yellow legal pad in front of him. Petrowicz, wearing a green plaid sport coat and tan pants, was at the end of the table, smoking, his light blue eyes studying A.C. carefully.

Lanham clicked on the recorder and then turned to a

clean page of the pad. He consulted a small notebook A.C. had seen him use back at the Plaza, then began to write.

"Arthur Curtis James," Lanham said, consulting the notebook. "Are you by any chance a relation of Mrs. Arthur Curtiss James of Newport?"

"No." A.C. was surprised. That Mrs. James was long dead, and had been many millions of dollars distant from being related to A.C.'s genteel but contrastingly impoverished parents. "That's a different family entirely. They spell their name C-u-r-t-i-s-s. Mine has just one s. And we come from upstate New York, not New England. How do you know about Mrs. James?"

He wished he hadn't said that. It made him sound as if he had presumed that such a man couldn't possibly know about anyone like the Newport Jameses. The detective's expression hardened somewhat, but he remained very polite.

"She had a very famous garden. I do a little gardening in my spare time. Roses, mostly. *Damascene* and *odorata.*"

"What?"

"Damask and tea roses," Lanham said. He spoke in a low, well-modulated tone. One couldn't tell he was black from his voice. He might indeed have been a college professor. There was little coplike about him, except for the eyes. Cops all had a very weary, haunted look to their eyes. They reminded A.C. of a famous war painting of a marine he recalled hanging in the Pentagon when he had worked in Washington. *The Ten-Thousand-Yard Stare.*

"I also grow vegetables," Lanham said.

"Come on, Ray," said the white detective, Petrowicz. He squashed out his cigarette disgustedly and sat back, his arms folded. A.C. remembered good-cop, bad-cop routines. This team was chatty cop, churlish cop, although he sensed that Lanham was on the verge of becoming a little churlish himself.

"Okay," said Lanham, picking up his pen again. "Mrs. Meyers says you and she are with the *Globe* and you were covering the Philippe Arbre show for the paper."

"She was covering it. I was just along."

"Okay, tell us what you saw, please."

"It all happened so quickly."

26

"We don't get many slow shootings," said Petrowicz.

A.C. related the incident as conscientiously as he could, as he might have doped a news story to an editor. He remembered things that he had not realized he had noticed—that the motorcyclist had slowed, but not stopped; that the weapon the killer had used had been a large revolver; that the black girl had not seemed to sense any threat in the motorcyclist; that she had continued to walk toward the curb, and thus ultimately toward his pistol. A.C. recalled also that the murderer had fired from a position slightly forward of his victim, over the hood of the limousine, at an angle that had left all the others on the sidewalk out of the line of fire.

He said he had seen the motorcyclist's face, and that it had struck him as handsome. He couldn't describe it well, though, because of the visor.

"Was he dark or light?" the detective named Petrowicz asked.

"Dark?"

"He means black or white," Lanham said.

A.C. felt uneasy. "I'm not sure. He didn't strike me one way or the other."

"Was he as black as me?" Lanham said.

A.C. refrained from saying that the detective was not very black. "He had a dark complexion. He could have been a black man, but he could have been white. I'm not sure. I'd have to look at him again."

"If we sat you down with a police artist could you help him make a composite sketch?" Lanham asked.

A.C. wanted to help. He felt a strange sense of guilt over the girl's death—as though there were something he might have done to stop the killer. Stepped in the way. Pulled her aside. Something. But his memory of the man's face was fading. If he misdirected the artist, the police might end up looking for the wrong person. A.C. was tiring of all this. He wished desperately to escape, to resume his normal life.

"I really wish I could," A.C. said. "But it was so quick. I didn't get as good a look as I thought. His helmet had a visor. And the sun was shining. There was a glare. No. I don't think I could help your artist."

Lanham removed his glasses and wiped perspiration from

his face. "Okay, you didn't see him clearly. But if you remember anything more, please let us know. I mean anything. That's how murders get solved. Little things. Okay?"

"Certainly. Whatever I can do."

"How come you go to fashion shows if you don't cover them?" Petrowicz asked. He was looking at A.C.'s white shoes and pants. There were splatterings of blood on one leg.

"To see who was there. I write about these people."

"You do the 'A.C.'s New York' column in the *Globe*," Lanham said.

"Yes."

"Did you know the victim, Marjean Dorothy Wickham?" Petrowicz asked.

"As a matter of fact, yes. Well, sort of. I interviewed her a few weeks ago. Marjean? I only knew of her as Molly."

"Can you tell us anything about her? Anything about her background?"

"Just that she said she came from New Jersey. Paterson, I think it was. She said she'd been a cheerleader, and that she'd gone into modeling after high school. We mostly talked about her movie career. She had a small part in a prizefight film they made here. She did a nude scene, a rather violent nude scene. It reminded me of a movie called *Angel Heart*, in which Lisa Bonet did a rather violent nude scene. Lisa Bonet was one of Molly's, er, Miss Wickham's idols. That's all. I didn't have much space. It was just a column."

"Where did you interview her? In her apartment?"

"In a restaurant. That's where I usually do interviews."

"Did she say anything about any of the people she knew? Any boyfriends?"

"No. We didn't go into that. It was just about sex. I mean, doing nude scenes. You know, a respectable ex-cheerleader from New Jersey, breaking into show biz the all too typical way."

"A black ex-cheerleader," Lanham said. "What was the name of this movie?"

"*The Last Round*," A.C. said. "It seems odd, now, because she got killed in it."

"Who produced it?"

"Peter Gorky, I think. Yes. Peter Gorky was the name. He wrote, produced, and directed it. Very low budget. I think she said she used to do commercials for him."

Lanham wrote this down and then leaned back in his chair. He looked to be an inordinately strong man, for all his professorial demeanor. His coat was open but A.C. could see no sign of a revolver.

"Anything else?" Lanham said.

A.C. hesitated. "Well, I remember it seemed odd. She walked past us toward the curb very directly. But there were no cabs. The doorman had gone off down the street to hail one. There were two limousines, though, and I think one of them began to move."

"Cadillac? Mercedes? What?" said Petrowicz.

"Now that you ask, I don't quite remember. It was an odd color, though. White. Or light blue."

"Did you see the license number?"

"I didn't notice. The motorcycle came up and . . . and there was the shooting. I didn't notice anything else. The limousine must have moved off into traffic."

Lanham scribbled down A.C.'s words with a stenographer's efficiency. "Anything else?"

"No, I don't think so."

"Maybe you can explain something to me. This Philippe Arbre gave his real name as Phillip Abramowitz. Why would he go by a French name instead?"

"It's a vanity of the profession, I suppose. Ralph Lauren's real name is Ralph Lipschitz. Oscar de la Renta was born simply Oscar Renta. Geoffrey Beene was Sammy Bosman. Arnold Scaasi? Scaasi is Isaacs spelled backward."

"But they're businessmen, not movie stars."

"It's a peculiar business."

"Are they all Jewish?" Petrowicz asked. It occurred to A.C. that the man was probably Polish, though he had thought him Jewish when he heard his name.

"No. Not particularly. They're all kinds. Just like policemen."

"Alexandra Zuck," Lanham said. He was smiling slightly. It occurred to A.C. that Belinda St. Johns might well be right.

"Sorry?"

29

"That's what Sandra Dee's real name is," Lanham said. "Alexandra Zuck."

"Sandra Dee?"

"Never mind," said Lanham, rising. "Thanks for your help. We'll be talking to you again, if you don't mind. Probably tomorrow."

"Don't go anywhere where we can't find you," Petrowicz said.

A.C. had been brought up according to Oscar Wilde's maxim: A gentleman never insults—except on purpose. Petrowicz was no gentleman. He couldn't help his rudeness. A.C. accepted that. He had been taught to do that, too.

A.C. rejoined Vanessa, feeling like a man released from prison.

"They want us to come in and help with the story," Vanessa said, gathering up her things as Camilla Santee took her turn to enter the interrogation room. "Pasternak said something about an eyewitness account. Double byline. All very grand."

"I'm a columnist."

"Not today."

"The deadline's not until six o'clock. I want to get a drink."

"I thought you were on Perrier this week."

"I need one. I feel a little rattled."

"I feel like throwing up. Maybe a stiff scotch will help."

"Let's wait."

"Wait?" Vanessa glanced toward the closed door of the interrogation room. "Oh no, A.C. You're not going to use this wretched occasion to try to pick up a girl?"

"If you want to go on ahead, fine. I'm going to wait."

"This is not wise, A.C."

"Don't worry. Miss Santee will probably say no."

But to his great astonishment, she accepted, perhaps because the invitation came from Vanessa. The blonde seemed to have been badly unnerved by the questioning, though in her case it had been fairly brief. It struck A.C. that there were tears in her eyes.

He was also struck by her voice when she spoke. He hadn't known what to expect, perhaps a breathless sort of whisper like Jacqueline Onassis's, or the affected tone used by the Upper East Side women who patronized places like Mortimer's. Instead, Santee's was low, gentle, and well modulated, her speech quite formal. But she had an odd accent, not British, but something almost as alien. He sensed it was Southern, but not the magnolia and honeysuckle "ah do declare" Southern accent of the stereotype. Something rarer, and far more aristocratic. Old Virginia perhaps.

"You are very kind," she said, her eyes on Vanessa, after a quick glance at him. "I, I'm at a loss what to do just now. I need to collect myself. Yes. Thank you. I would very much appreciate having a drink."

As they descended the interior stairs of the precinct station, A.C. reached to support her arm, but she moved away.

The nearest bar was the lounge of a Japanese restaurant just down the street.

A stiff drink for her proved to be a slender glass of Galliano. Vanessa, who artfully managed to seat Camilla between them in a circular booth, ordered a double scotch and water. A.C. asked for a martini. He hadn't had a drink since the night he and his wife had had their last fight.

The lunch hour was long over and the restaurant was deserted, with nothing to distract them except the Asian waiter and a cook's helper mopping up in the rear. Vanessa tried saying something cheerful, but when this drew no response, lapsed into flippant commentary on the general fecklessness of policemen, recounting a time when her apartment had been burgled and it had taken the detectives more than an hour to respond.

Camilla wasn't listening. When their drinks came, she left hers untouched for a moment, staring at the tabletop, her mind in some other place. At length she spoke, as though to herself, her voice barely audible.

"Toujours les nègres."

"Sorry?" said A.C.

His query startled her. She looked up, flustered. She tried to compose herself, but he could see in her eyes that she was very upset.

31

Vanessa studied her, gave A.C. a quick look, then downed most of her scotch with several hurried sips, setting the glass aside. She reached for her purse.

"You may have clout at the paper, A.C.," she said, "but I'm just a poor working girl. I'll give Pasternak the great exclusive he's panting for. I'll tell him you were delayed at the police station."

Looking confused, Camilla started to get up with her.

"No, no," said Vanessa, putting her hand on Camilla's arm. "You stay right here and have your drink. I think you really do need it. A.C.'s a good man to have around at a time like this. New York's last gentleman."

With a hasty smile and much bustle, she departed. A.C. caught a glimpse of her through the window, hurrying down the sunlit street.

"I—I know how you must feel," he said, turning back to Santee.

He found himself suddenly afraid, utterly unsure of how she might react to anything he said. She was so nervous. When she lifted her drink to her lips, some spilled. She set down the glass sharply, trembling all over. Then she began to sob.

A.C. handed her a blue silk handkerchief from his pocket. She took it clumsily and pressed it to her eyes, but her crying was uncontrollable. She let the handkerchief drop and put her hand down flat on the table, as though to steady herself.

With a sudden certainty of what to do, A.C. put his hand over hers, curling his fingers around its softness. She returned his grip tightly. With tears pouring down her cheeks, she sagged and leaned close against him. His heart was racing. He put his other arm around her, holding her gently. Her hair was against his cheek, as soft and fragrant as he had imagined.

There were no words to say. Finally, he began murmuring her name over and over, but as he did so, he felt her stiffen. All at once she sat up. The sobbing ceased. A good model has the same exact control over her body and expression as any athlete or actor, perhaps more so. Camilla began to call upon this ability, upon her inner strength, restoring herself. The cold, icy, almost hostile expression returned. She slid away from him, rising from the booth.

"This was very kind of you, sir," she said with studied correctness. "Please pardon my outburst. I really must go."

A.C. pulled a twenty-dollar bill from the wallet in his breast pocket, dropping it quickly on the table. He shoved himself out of his seat. She was already heading for the door.

"Please," he said. "Let me get you into a cab."

"No. I'm fine. I'm very late."

He followed her outside, moving with great haste, catching up to her rapid stride.

"Miss Santee, I . . ."

Her pace quickened further. She walked with her head down, holding her small handbag in front of her. She seemed to be concentrating very hard on something.

"Please, Miss Santee, I only want to—"

Abruptly, her long golden hair swinging wildly around her head, she stopped and turned, standing squarely in front of him.

"Please," she said. "Please leave me alone."

Her hair whirled again as she spun on her heel and stalked away, rounding the corner at the intersection, vanishing.

Common sense dictated that he let her vanish. In a city like New York, people were forever coming in and out of each other's lives this way—briefly together, and then forever gone. Having Camilla Santee in his life would be of little help in his troubles with Kitty. She wasn't offering much prospect of his seeing her again, anyway. With the rejection implicit in her abrupt departure, she had made something of a mess of his pride and dignity. He felt hurt and foolish, and was glad Vanessa had left when she did.

But he was far from feeling sensible. The violence and stress of the afternoon had shaken him terribly, and then having this magnificent woman in his presence—for a brief moment in his arms—had completely unsettled him. In the most intoxicating and addictive and besotting way.

A.C.'s life had been full of women, many of them beautiful. Kitty was considered one of the great beauties of New York society. To say that Camilla was the most beautiful of all was only marginally correct and a pointless measure. Hers was a beauty of perfection, the beauty of a sculpture or painting that somehow lost nothing in being brought to life. It had overwhelmed him. He'd found it difficult to talk to her while looking at her face.

What so irresistibly fascinated him, though, was what sort of woman lay behind those extraordinary blue-gray eyes. Vanessa had rightly warned him that such a lovely face could mask a truly awful person, or a person who wasn't much of anything at all.

But Vanessa didn't know Camilla Santee, not in any meaningful way, and neither did he. He now wanted to, fervently, almost desperately. He had a compelling sense that she was not all illusion, that the mind and heart and spirit of the woman within might be all caught up in the quality of that perfect skin and golden hair. He wanted to find out. And he wanted very much to know what it was that had made her so frightened.

•

Lanham and the other detectives on his team gathered around Lieutenant Taranto, the head of their homicide division, at Lanham's cluttered desk. It would be many hours before they'd be free to go home, and they were already weary. Pushing back his chair, Lanham stood. The lieutenant sat uneasily on a corner of the desk in what little space he could find. All except Lanham smoked. They had refilled their coffee cups.

"Okay, Ray," Taranto said to Lanham. "You caught the case. What do we got?"

The lieutenant was a few years from the twenty needed for retirement. The time showed.

"We got shit," Petrowicz said.

"No one was able to make the perp," said Lanham. "The guy had his visor down. I was going to get an artist to make up a composite, but the result would only look like a man from Mars. We're pretty sure the bike was Japanese. A pedestrian caught a couple of numbers from the plate. One-four-seven. Or maybe one-four-Z. And it may have been out of state."

"You're through interrogating all of the eyewitnesses?"

Lanham nodded, blinking behind his glasses. "Plus the doorman and some of the horse-carriage drivers. They couldn't give us much. The models were no help. The brunette called us names and the blonde said she couldn't remember anything. The designer wasn't much better. He said he had only begun using Wickham a few months ago. Said she got her start doing lingerie ads for cheap outfits in the garment district. Mail-order stuff. The newspaper people were better. Gave us a lead on a movie producer she worked for. And where she came from—Paterson, New Jersey. She may even come from some kind of money. Her address checks out to a new high-rise on Sutton Place, the kind you'd expect one of the Trumps to live in."

"There's only one way a broad like that gets to live on Sutton Place," said Detective Tony Gabriel. He had eyes as dark and suspicious as Taranto's, but was very good-looking in a smooth, well-oiled way, while the lieutenant was flaccid, balding, and overweight. Gabriel was wearing a double-breasted suit that must have cost two weeks' salary, along with gold cufflinks and a Rolex watch. It was rumored they were gifts from ladies he had "assisted" in the line of duty. The division's jurisdiction was known as a "Gold Coast" beat. Its residents could afford to be generous in their gifts.

"We don't know that yet," Lanham said carefully.

"So what do you think, Ray?" Taranto said. His deference was due to more than Lanham's having caught the case. In the New York Police Department, detectives were either promoted along civil service lines—becoming sergeants, lieutenants, and, if they were well connected, captains—or they remained detectives and were promoted through the grades of third, second, and first. As a detective first grade, one of not so many NYPD blacks to hold that position, Lanham earned as much money as the lieutenant and was one of the elite of the department. But without the civil service protection of a lieutenant's or sergeant's rank, a detective-first could be busted back to patrolman without much administrative review. To survive, a detective-first had to perform. And most did. Lanham had one of the

35

highest conviction rates per arrest in the entire police department.

He tapped his pen against the desk top. The paperwork from the Wickham case was already beginning to pile up. "I think we have a professional hit," Lanham said. "I don't think this was some racist crackpot or rejected boyfriend."

"He got her right through the face," Detective Caputo said. "One fuckin' shot." Charley Caputo was Gabriel's partner. He was shorter than most of the detectives, resplendent in a gray silk suit, black shirt, and black tie.

"What bothers me most, boss," Lanham said to Taranto, "is that the perpetrator's M.O. is like one of those terrorist hits over in Italy or El Salvador or someplace. An assassination. I mean, this was a highly public murder, in front of the whole world. I think the perp was trying to make some statement. If he just wanted to kill her, he could have hit her outside her apartment. That's about as quiet a neighborhood as there is in Manhattan."

"Was she involved in radical politics?" Taranto said.

"She wasn't a hippie," said Lanham.

"What about race?" Taranto said. What he didn't need to say was that white on black murders were continuing to be very big news in New York. A dark Puerto Rican girl had been raped and murdered by still unapprehended white gang members in Brooklyn four months earlier, and the story still kept turning up in the papers. The Howard Beach and Bensonhurst murders of blacks by white youths were now very old cases, but still much remembered. Such cases gave the mayor fits.

"Nothing definite on the race of the perp," Lanham said. "But I sure as hell don't think this was a racial killing."

Pat Cassidy, the swing member of the team, joined them. A skinny, nervous, chain-smoking Irishman, he had eyes with rims as red as his curly hair. He hadn't been drinking—that day, at least. He'd been in court at the time of the shooting. Lanham handed him a copy of his initial report, the one that would go downtown. The "fives," the blue flimsies containing witness statements and other pertinent information, remained with the division. So did the "unusuals," reports of anything that might have seemed out of place or that indicated an inconsistency. Lanham planned

36

to take a briefcase full of all these things home. It would be another night in which sleep was of no concern.

"Okay, let's get our shit together," Taranto said. "I put out a citywide on the motorcycle. And a stop at all the bridges and tunnels."

The other detectives let this pass. They all knew they'd never recover the motorcycle with the perpetrator still on it.

"We'll keep the canvass going on the general area," Taranto continued. "What else? Call some shots, Ray."

Lanham looked to Petrowicz. "I'd like you to check out her background," he said. "And find her family if we can. There's this movie guy she worked for, Gorky. But we can get him tomorrow." He turned to Gabriel, anticipating his happy reaction. "Tony, why don't you go talk to the other models in the show, including that Belinda St. Johns. Maybe you can get more than we did."

A hint of a smirk came over Gabriel's face.

"Don't mess with the blonde, though, that Camilla Santee. She's real spooked. I want to let her calm down."

"I can calm her down," Gabriel said.

"No," said Lanham. "I mean it, Tony."

"Let's not have any horizontal interviews," Taranto said, and not in jest. They'd lost a big case the year before to mistrial when Gabriel was found to have screwed a woman who was subsequently called as a key witness. Gabriel had been suspended for thirty days. He'd been lucky.

"I'd like a canvass of Wickham's apartment building," Lanham said. "Leaning especially hard on the doormen. I want to know about all the men in her life."

"Are you going to need me?" said Pat Cassidy, looking at his watch. "I've got to testify in court tomorrow."

"So do I," said Caputo.

"You bet your ass we're going to need you," said Taranto. "I'm putting the whole division on double shift. Downtown's jumping up and down on this one. Murders aren't supposed to happen in front of the Plaza Hotel."

"Check vehicle registration," Lanham said. "A black motorcycle, probably Japanese. License including a one-four-seven or one-four-Z. Possibly out of state. Check out limos, too. A white or light blue stretch. One of the witnesses said a limousine like that pulled away from the curb right after the shooting."

Lanham looked over at his wooden "active" box, which was heaped with files of other pending cases. One was a murder-suicide in an expensive town house in the East Sixties. Another was a cab driver who'd been found shot dead in his vehicle near the Central Park boathouse. Another involved a naked corpse of a man found in an alley. The head had been neatly severed from the body, rendering the case a "cuppy"—a department acronym meaning "circumstances undetermined pending police investigation." It meant there'd been no way of immediately establishing whether the victim had met with foul play. Technically, the head could have been severed after death from natural causes. Before the "git-go" on the Wickham murder, Taranto had been after him to move on these cases. Uniformed force had been alerted to look for the decapitation victim's missing head.

"What do you have in mind for yourself, Ray?" the lieutenant asked.

"The M.E.'s going to do the autopsy at eight tonight. And I'm waiting for the forensics report."

"Downtown wants something for the eleven o'clock news. They're screaming for it. The mayor wants to go on TV."

"Tell them we've got a citywide out."

"Shit," said Taranto. "It would be big fucking news if we didn't. We'll hope for a better tomorrow."

•

At a hasty conference at the *Globe* city desk, it was decided that A.C. would do a special column on the murder. Pasternak, the city editor, planned to run it on page one next to the lead story. A headline reading GUNMAN SLAYS BLACK MODEL had already been dummied across the top of the page.

"Give me some 'Killer stalks the world of high fashion' stuff," Pasternak said. "You know, models screaming in terror, society ladies. Were there any celebrities there? Broadway stars? Barbara Walters?"

38

"Not that I know of," A.C. said, uncomfortably.

Pasternak stubbed out a cigarette and lit another. "All right," he said. "But get in 'the world of high fashion.' You interviewed this girl a few weeks ago, didn't you? Put in some stuff about that. Didn't we have a picture? A nude shot from some movie? Why didn't I remember that?" He shouted for a copy clerk.

A.C. walked quickly away, feigning great purpose. He was just as glad they'd asked for a column. He was too confused and upset to attempt a straight news story. He hadn't written one in years.

Because so much of its editorial content consisted of columns, the *Globe* was joked about in the city as having more columnists than reporters, and it was nearly true. There'd been little ill feeling when A.C. had been added to the columnist list. It was assumed he would have eventually become one even if he hadn't been married to Katherine Anne Shannon.

Every columnist had his or her own cubicle. A row of them ran along the east wall of the newsroom and A.C. had one of the best, occupying a corner with a view of both the East River and the high-rises to the north. Its walls and table surfaces were covered with framed, autographed pictures of famous people—many of them society ladies and actresses. As he now realized, this hadn't pleased his wife much, but he had thought the pictures harmless. After all, the sports columnists covered their walls with photos of athletes, and the film critic decorated his cubicle with autographed publicity stills of actors and actresses. One of the critic's photos was a nude.

On A.C.'s desk was a silver-framed portrait photograph of his wife, Kitty, standing on the lawn of their riverfront house in Westchester with their two children. When her brother, Bill, who was the *Globe's* publisher, came into the cubicle nowadays, he always stared at the photograph, a silent commentary on A.C.'s increasingly painful domestic situation.

A.C. moved the picture out of view as he began his piece, wanting to concentrate on Molly Wickham and what he could remember of her from the interview he had had. She had been frisky, almost flirtatious, smiling frequently and

39

crossing and uncrossing her legs. He recalled that she had dressed provocatively, and had laced her comments with salacious and sometimes scatological phrases.

"Molly Wickham was a happy girl," A.C. wrote, pausing to stare at those six words on the green screen of his computer terminal. He supposed it was true. He resumed typing: "She had reason to be. She had almost overnight become one of the top models in New York, and had recently launched a movie career."

This was exaggeration, but it would please Pasternak and the readers of the *Globe*. She wouldn't have objected.

"But all that ended in one sudden, terrible moment at noon yesterday when she was gunned down on one of the most fashionable street corners of Manhattan."

He paused again and took a deep breath, then went on to describe the shooting in vivid detail. He followed with what Wickham had told him about having been a suburban cheerleader in New Jersey, and how she hoped someday to be a movie star. He recounted the plot of the film *The Last Round*, noting the irony of her playing a murder victim.

It was a good place to end the column, and so he did. With the finality of a musician striking the last note of a composition, he pushed the SEND button on the computer keyboard, instantly transmitting his piece to the news desk and, eventually, the four hundred thousand New Yorkers who would read it in the morning. Then he sagged back in his swivel chair and briefly closed his eyes.

He had thought of possibly including some reference to Camilla, describing her as a mystery woman. If she read it, he might hear from her again, and quickly.

He had dismissed the idea. It was unprofessional. It would certainly displease her, and might get her into trouble—and she seemed to be in that already. Worse, it would please Pasternak.

As though he had been hovering nearby to wait for A.C. to finish, A.C.'s brother-in-law, Bill Shannon walked in, neatly combed and beautifully tailored, looking very much the Princeton graduate he was. His and Kitty's grandfather had been an Irish immigrant laborer who ultimately had acquired a fortune in real estate. Their father had improved upon it, becoming rich enough to buy the *Globe*, among other ego indulgences, when it had gone on the market cheap.

Bill Shannon, a handsome man just past forty, now belonged to the Council on Foreign Relations, and to several of the city's better clubs.

"I hear you had an awful time today," he said.

"It wasn't exactly the way I like to start my day."

Shannon looked at the photograph of A.C.'s wife and children, and picked it up.

"You might want to call Kitty," he said. "She's probably worried about you."

"I doubt it," A.C. said.

Shannon put the picture back, not where A.C. had shoved it but in its proper place near the center of A.C.'s desk.

"Thanks so much for coming in and writing a piece on this," Shannon said. "It's more than I'd be able to do in the circumstance."

"I'm still a loyal employee."

"Yes," said Shannon, turning. "Well, thanks. It's greatly appreciated."

After Shannon was gone, before A.C. could himself leave, Vanessa entered, smoking and looking tired.

"So," she said. "How went the tryst?"

"Please, Vanessa."

"I wasn't sure you'd be back here, though perhaps I was."

"She left. She was very upset. She even cried."

"Actual tears? How sweet."

"As you said, you don't know very much about her."

"But you'll fill me in, won't you, sweetheart?" She stood up, flicking her ashes in A.C.'s wastebasket. "I do love a summer romance. I can hardly wait until her picture is up here on your wall of fame."

"Vanessa, I need a favor. I'd like you to find out her address and phone number for me."

"Shall I arrange for a motel room, too?"

"Please. I just want to talk to her again."

"This is dumb, A.C. Very dumb."

41

A.C. lived not far away, on the top floor of an old, small, but very expensive ten-story cooperative in the East Sixties. The apartment was small as well, but suited him and Kitty well enough as a place to stay over for evenings in town. It also suited him as a man living alone.

When he had first settled in the city after leaving college, this part of Manhattan had seemed a magical, princely land—a place of baronial towers, elegant town houses, canopies, doormen, and sophisticated people leading the most wonderfully glamorous lives.

Now it was simply his neighborhood. He knew shopkeepers and grocers, newsstand vendors, and a number of people who lived on his street. The community life was really not all that much different from a neighborhood in Flatbush—except there were few doormen in Flatbush.

The combination doorman—elevator operator who greeted A.C. was as old as the structure. A.C.'s penthouse apartment had just four rooms, but there was a rooftop terrace along most of its length, reached through wide French doors. Kitty had cluttered it with large potted plants, but A.C. often forgot to water them.

He neglected them again, going instead to the living room's small bar, where he poured himself a large straight scotch whiskey. He took his drink onto the terrace, and seated himself on one of the wrought iron chairs. It was dusty—his maid came only once a week—but he paid that no mind.

The view was airy. His street was one of relatively lowrise buildings and he had a spacious glimpse of the river to the east and of the prominent midtown structures to the south, most notably the Chrysler Building, his favorite piece of architecture in the city. The apartment house directly across the street was much like his own, complete with a penthouse surrounded by all manner of shrubbery. The rest of the rooftops were quite ordinary, a jumble of skylights, air-conditioning equipment, vents, smokestacks, water tanks, and elevator housing set off only here and there by a garden box.

42

There was no one by the penthouse opposite, but on an adjoining building, at a level slightly above A.C.'s, a man was standing. He had on a coat and tie, which seemed peculiar. A.C. had only seen workmen on that roof, though on weekends a woman who lived there sometimes came up to sunbathe. A.C. had seen her frequently enough to feel comfortable waving. Sometimes she waved back.

The man had been staring at A.C.'s terrace. Noticing A.C., he looked away, toward the river, as though he had come up merely to inspect the skyline. Perhaps he was a new tenant, or someone's guest.

A.C. reminded himself to lock the terrace doors when he left. The rooftop of the building next door was just one story shorter than his own. He and Kitty had never been burgled, but no one had ever been shot outside the Plaza Hotel in his memory, either.

His telephone was ringing. He took a sip of the whiskey and then went to answer it. The sun had passed well over to the west, and his living room was getting gloomy.

It became cheerier. The voice on the phone was that of his wife.

"Has anything happened to you?" she asked. "I saw you on the news, at that terrible murder. You were talking to a policeman."

She sounded unhappy and irritated, though he could not tell if he was the cause of her ill humor.

"I'm fine. There was only one gunshot, the one that killed the girl. We weren't hurt."

"You were with Vanessa Meyers, and some blond woman."

"We were all witnesses. The police made us stay."

"You were at the fashion show?"

"Yes. With Vanessa."

There were a number of silver-framed photographs on the marble-topped table next to the phone. One was a studio portrait of Kitty, a striking woman with perfectly gray hair, dark eyebrows, and heavily lashed gray eyes. She had had gray hair even in her early twenties, when A.C. had first met her. She had been a young feature writer at the *Globe*, just out of Smith College. Her father, Patrick Shannon, had still been alive then, holding the posts of both editor and

43

publisher. A.C. had been one of his star reporters, and he'd been very pleased by the marriage.

"A.C.?"

"I'm here."

"I—I want to see you again. I'd like you to come home." He hesitated unhappily. "I want to very much. But it'll be hard tonight. I have to go out again. With this shooting, my regular work got pushed aside. I've got to catch up."

He was lying to himself, and to her. It wouldn't make much difference at all if he walked right out and caught the next train to Westchester. But he wasn't ready. He'd dreamed about his wife and children every night since their fight, but they weren't what he needed at this perplexing moment, not yet.

"We need to talk," she said.

"Yes, we do. But I'm not in great shape to do that right now. This murder really threw me. I was just sitting here trying to get my thoughts straight. Trying to calm down, actually."

She was silent, then spoke, more warmly than before. "Come up this weekend, then. Friday night."

"All right. If you're sure."

"I'm sure."

"I can take Davey sailing. Tell him."

"I will. Please don't make a late night of it tonight. Get some sleep. Take a sedative. And I mean a sedative, not Johnnie Walker Red."

"I will. Don't worry."

"I do worry."

"We'll talk. I love you, Kitty."

More silence. "Goodbye, A.C. Take care of yourself."

She spoke with a distinctive Upper Westchester accent. One would never have known that her grandfather had once slapped mortar against brick. A.C.'s grandfather had talked the way Kitty now did. A.C.'s ancestors had been landowners in the Mohawk Valley two centuries before hers had arrived in America.

He looked at his crystal glass, and took another sip of whiskey. "Goodbye, Kitty."

When he returned to the terrace, the man in the tie and jacket was gone from the rooftop across the street.

44

Camilla Santee's small, cramped apartment was one of several in what had once been a single-family town house on a side street just off Fifth Avenue near the park and the Metropolitan Museum. It was very expensive, but it wasn't much.

She fumbled with her keys as she undid the three locks to her door. She had just had two of them installed, and still had trouble finding the right keys.

The apartment was on the first floor, and there wasn't much light from the window. She went to her favorite armchair, an antique she had bought years before at Christie's, and lowered herself wearily into it, leaning her head back. Before her lay the task of removing her model's makeup. Because she retouched it so often going from booking to booking, it was usually quite thick at the end of a day's work. Now it was a ruin, smudged and run with tears and cracked around the eyes from her anguish. The face that would look back at her from the mirror would be not a little hideous.

She would take a long shower. She wanted only to go to bed. There were two invitations on her entrance-hall table—one to a gallery reception and another to a dinner party. She would decline them. She was in no mood for anyone's company. She had been unspeakably rude to a number of people that afternoon, including the columnist from the *Globe*, an apparently rather nice man who had only been trying to help. An attractive man, the sort of man she had hoped she might meet and marry when, as a young girl fresh from the South, she had first moved to New York.

A married man. She was married herself. She had come back here in a desperate effort to protect her marriage. But now everything was coming apart. She was not a cowardly woman. Cowardice had not been tolerated in her family. But she had never been more frightened in her life.

Her phone began to ring, a harsh, sudden, and insistent sound. Camilla covered her ears and let it continue. She had already called her modeling agency about the next day's bookings. There was no one else she wanted to talk to; there were some she wanted very much never to talk to again.

The telephone rang three times, and then the answering machine clicked on. Because she kept the sound off, she couldn't hear the caller. Whoever it was left only a short message. There was another click when it went off. Then there was silence and gathering darkness.

She would try music. Rising stiffly and moving to her stereo, she searched among her tapes, locating the one she wanted only after a great deal of trouble. It was of a strange, eerie Vangelis piece, "L'Apocalypse des Animaux." There was a slow, sweetly somber passage in it that always reminded her of two ghostly people dancing slowly at twilight. A man she had once loved—a man, as she thought upon it, much like A.C. James—had given her the tape. He had made it for her from a recording, saying he found it of help when he was troubled. She put it on, and poured herself a glass of cold chablis from her refrigerator.

That man was long gone now, like so many she had let slip from her life.

An old man was walking slowly by just below on the street. There were always people there, at any hour. Never crowds, but always someone. He glanced at her window, or maybe another in her building, but kept on. A young girl, wearing high heels and dancer's leggings, came by from the opposite direction. A Rolls-Royce followed, and then two taxicabs. She stood at the window, just beside the curtain, watching. Camilla hated being in this small apartment. She now hated being back in New York, though once she had thought living in this city the most wonderful thing that could possibly happen to anyone.

Again the phone began to ring, the sound more painful. Once more she waited it out, then went into her bedroom, wincing as she turned on the bright lights of her makeup table. The face in the mirror was as dreadful as she had expected, but it seemed almost not to be hers. It occurred to her that she had long ago lost her face, sold it on the market. Her face belonged to whoever paid for it. Her face was whatever the buyer wanted it to be.

46

After removing the last of her makeup, she peered closely once into her reddened, bleary eyes, then snapped off the lights. Kicking off her shoes, she slipped out of her blouse and skirt and underwear and walked naked into her bath, closing the door and the world behind her. She turned on the shower tap as strong and hot as she could tolerate, then stepped inside, letting the steamy water embrace her back and shoulders, tilting back her head so that the cascade ran freely over it. She remained like that until her scalp seemed to go numb, then stepped forward from the stream to work scented shampoo into her long golden hair. Rinsing it out finally, she began to lather her body with the soap she always used, an expensive French brand that was half cold cream.

The feel of it was highly sensual. It had been months since she had slept with a man. She wouldn't care now if she never did again. Her desire was as dead as Molly Wickham's shattered body.

She looked down at her small but perfect breasts, holding them gently. So much beauty, such priceless, expensive beauty, given to her for no purpose.

What was the purpose of beauty? Nature had decreed only one. To assure new life. *Pour la chasse.* As her mother had continually put it, beauty is there to attract the strongest and the best. To assure the ascension of the superior. Yet all the ugly things of the world reproduced, in great, vile numbers. And here she was without issue. She was over thirty now. In a recent photograph, one used in a jewelry advertisement in *W* magazine, she had looked strikingly harsh. It had frightened her so much that she had thrown the magazine away.

Dully in the thudding rush of water, through the thickness of the old-fashioned oaken door, she heard the telephone sound yet once more, a malevolent summons.

As the answering machine again did its duty, she wondered if the caller might be someone from the police. She hated the thought of that, but the police could mean no harm. Not to her. Not yet.

Camilla quickly turned off the shower. Toweling off, she turned her thoughts to her makeup table. Bringing herself

47

back to her full beauty once more was at least a task that would occupy her mind. It was a complicated procedure, growing all the more complicated with each passing year.

She was still naked, though dried and powdered and combed, when the persistent caller tried again. Shaking her head in exasperation, she strode angrily to the telephone and pounced upon the receiver.

"What do you want!" she said.

There was a pause, and then the man spoke her name. It was a voice she knew all too well, a voice she had heard all her life.

"You bastard!" she shouted. The vehemence and volume of her response startled her. "You goddamned monster! You rotten shit! Do you realize what you've done!"

"I did what I had to, what I said I would do."

"You didn't say you would do this! That poor girl is dead. *Sacrée mère*, she was only twenty-one years old!"

"She was nothing to you. She was nothing to anyone."

"She was alive!"

Camilla's breathing was almost frantic. She felt she was suffocating. She wanted to twist the receiver in two, to break it into little pieces, to do the same to him. She slammed it down on its cradle.

Her hands were still shaking as she sat down to attend to her makeup. In her haste, she used only a little, adding just touches of eyeliner and mascara and finishing with a subdued lipstick. Even this she botched, leaving her face barely passable for the street. If she were to show up for a job this way, she'd be sent back for repairs.

Dressing quickly, she was almost to her door when the caller struck again. This time she could not even muster fury. She felt weak and beaten, capable only of surrender. Otherwise, he would keep calling and calling, like some merciless fiend.

She let him speak first, with the frail hope that somehow it might be someone else. But of course it wasn't. The deep, manly, noble Southern voice that in past years had been such a source of strength and reassurance for her was now back to frighten her once again.

"Camilla?"

"Yes." Her own voice sounded dead, like that of some

48

character in a Greek tragedy—Cassandra in *The Trojan Women*.

"What did you tell the police, Camilla?"

"Please, just leave me alone."

"What did they ask you, Camilla? What do they know?"

"I can't believe that I'm talking to you."

"I have to know, Camilla. I need to know what to do next."

"Do next? Go away! Disappear! I never want to talk to you again!"

"It was necessary, Camilla. He's frightened now. He'll stop this."

"You don't know what he'll do!"

"I should kill him now. I should have done that long ago."

"That won't do any good! Hasn't he made that clear enough? If he should die, everything will come out. He's fixed it that way. What's wrong with you?"

There was only his breathing for a long moment.

"I killed the old nana, Camilla," he said quietly.

"You what?"

She was beginning to feel dizzy. She reached to steady herself. Her arm felt incredibly weak.

"I killed her. I didn't mean to. I shook her too roughly, I suppose. She was very old."

"You killed that poor old woman, and now the girl?"

"I didn't mean to! I wouldn't have hurt that old nana. It was because of him! I was sure he'd hidden it all down there with her. He's always going down there, isn't he? I was certain I'd find it. I looked everywhere. I tore her place apart. I even went through some of those old animal skins. God have mercy."

"You didn't find it?"

"Nothing. Not a scrap. Not one old picture."

Camilla remembered mossy trees and dark faces, warm and gentle seawater against her feet. She had loved that old woman, for all her strangeness.

"Has Pierre talked to you?" her caller asked.

"No," she said, after a long, slow breath. "He's probably drunk somewhere."

"Are you going to talk to him?"

"I'm going to see his lawyer tonight," she said. "About the money."

"You talk to him. You tell him I'll do it again."

"No you won't! Do you hear? If it wasn't for Momma, I'd turn you in to the police. I'd do it in an instant. Do you understand that?"

"Don't you talk to me like that, Camilla."

"And there's something else I want you to understand. I think all your talk about family and honor and 'the chivalry'—"

" 'The unwritten law.' "

"I think you've disgraced it! I think you've turned all that into something vile and terrible and disgusting! I hate you now. You have to know that. I hate you!"

"I'll do what must be done." He spoke with pronounced menace and finality.

Camilla screamed, a long, primal echoing scream that emptied her of all feeling. Then she slammed down the receiver so hard that the telephone slid off the table. She crouched down beside it, reaching to the outlet and pulling the cord free. Then she hurried through the apartment, snapping the cords out of the kitchen and bedroom jacks. She hurled herself onto her bed, and once more began to cry.

•

To Lanham, this was the grimmest part of the murder of Marjean Dorothy Wickham and all murders, the scientific disassembling of the body under the statutory requirements of the city, county, and state of New York to legally establish the exact cause of death and to seek, examine, and analyze samplings of tissue and other evidence that might be admissible in court for the prosecution and conviction of her killer.

Lanham had signed the requisite forms as the investigating officer. Now his role was one of witness, observing the entire autopsy in accordance with procedure and authorizing any extra steps or analysis he considered necessary. Some pathologists played music while they went about their ghoulish, lonely task. One favored tapes of Mahler at his most somber. Others liked to joke or chat. Dr. Morris Seidman, a soft-spoken, white-haired man near retirement who had the careful manner of a scientist, preferred to work in silence, speaking only in accordance with the prescribed police routine.

Molly Wickham lay on her back, her remains neatly arranged on the stainless steel table with her arms turned palms up close to her body. Dead, she had the color of a white woman. Her remaining eye was open, staring up at the bright light above as though she were patiently waiting for the postmortem to be over. She retained her beauty even in this ghastly state.

Dr. Seidman spoke into his tape recorder briefly, then turned to the victim's head. He had removed Wickham's expensive clothing and cleaned the flesh. Forensics had recovered the squashed lead slug that had torn through the girl's left eye and skull, assessing it to be a flat-nosed round from a .357 Magnum. Seidman, probing the hole punctured in the bone behind the eye, confirmed the finding. He examined the remaining eye and then looked over the body for other wounds, finding none.

"The woman has had breast implants," he said, pointing to the neat, surgical scar beneath each breast. Lanham nodded.

The doctor then picked up a scalpel from a tray beside him and made a long incision around the top of the girl's head. Pulling the skin away from the bone, he reached for a small electrical saw and began to cut. There wasn't much brain tissue left for him to remove and weigh.

Lanham took a deep breath, exhaling slowly. He steeled himself to remain where he was standing.

After speaking again for the tape recorder, Seidman moved to the torso. He made two incisions—one across the chest and another vertically from clavicle to pelvis—then opened Molly Wickham up like a package, a terrible Christmas present. As he cut free and removed the organs, setting each aside in orderly inventory, it occurred to Lanham, as it had so many times before, that now the victim was truly dead. With the removal of her functional parts, her humanity was gone, surgically removed. She had been rendered a laboratory specimen.

51

Her stomach had been empty, her bladder full. She had had appendicitis, but there had been no surgery to excise the inflamed intestinal appendage, which had simply scarred over. She appeared otherwise to have been in remarkably good health.

"She had sexual relations sometime not long before death," Seidman said. "I find no trace of sperm, however."

"A condom that worked," Lanham said.

"Yes," said the pathologist. "Presumably."

When the procedure was fully complete, Lanham took one last, long look at the medically violated body. Dr. Seidman had taken photographs throughout the autopsy, but Lanham would have no need of them. The details of this scene would be as firmly retained in his mind as on a photographic plate. The images would help him struggle through the long hours of boring, tedious, and frustrating work the case would require. It would help him in the unlikely event he had to shoot someone.

"Thank you, Doctor."

"I'll call you with the lab test results, though I don't think they'll add much."

"No. Thanks again."

Lanham hadn't eaten before coming over, and wouldn't eat now until the next morning. He never had dinner the night of an autopsy.

•

There was a surprise waiting for Lanham when he returned to the squad room. A middle-aged black couple was sitting in the chairs by the door. They were wearing what were probably their very best clothes—in the man's case, a rumpled old brown suit with a purple polo shirt buttoned at the neck, yellow socks, and cracked brown leather oxfords. His hair was gray and he was not well shaven. His eyes were weary and sad, like an old dog's. He smelled a little of beer.

The woman appeared to have once had beautiful features, but her skin was pockmarked and there was an ugly scar alongside her ear that showed brightly white against her

52

brown flesh. She was heavy, and there was a large roll of fat at the base of her neck. Her black dress might once have been expensive, but it was old and faded and let out at the seams. Her feet were in flat red shoes that might have been slippers. Her eyes were glassy. She had been drinking even more than he.

"That's Mr. and Mrs. Harold Wickham," said Petrowicz quietly. "They came in a few minutes ago. They're from Jersey City. They said they've lived in Jersey City all their lives."

Lanham grimaced, then went over to them, introducing himself politely. Noting their clothing again, he wondered if there was some mistake, a similarity of names that had led the couple to think it was their daughter who had been murdered.

"We seen about Marjean on the TV," the woman said.

"On the news," the man said, almost proudly.

There was no mistake. Looking past the ravages, Lanham saw Molly Wickham in the mother's face, saw what Molly would have likely become if fortune had not intervened.

Paterson had been a lie. Molly Wickham, whatever she had been, had never been a wholesome middle-American cheerleader. The price of the clothes she'd been wearing when killed would have bought this couple a closetful of garments—by their standards, enough to last them the rest of their lives.

"You're sure it was her?" Lanham said gently.

"We sure," the woman said. "She left us a few years ago, but she ain't changed none."

"They showed a picture of her," said the man. "She sure pretty."

It occurred to Lanham that they might have never seen her fashion photos, or the movie she had appeared in. They knew nothing of the glamorous young woman who had lived on Sutton Place.

"I'm afraid we have to ask you to make an identification in person," Lanham said. "It won't take very long."

The woman nodded sadly. There were no tears in her eyes, but Lanham knew there would be keening and wailing soon enough. There was always that.

53

A.C. had a date that night. He had regularly had dates with women other than Kitty since he'd taken up his New York duties. He had endless social affairs to attend as a columnist and when Kitty didn't feel up to it, he'd simply take someone else—if possible, a family friend. Kitty hadn't minded, or so she had said.

His date that night was Theresa Allenby, a one-time English aristocrat now married to a wealthy American. She had enjoyed a twenty-year career as a serious actress on Broadway—from teenage ingenue to reigning star. When her success began to diminish, she had retired to simply being a New York rich woman. It suited her. She and A.C. were very close friends.

That night, she was in spirits as happy as A.C.'s were not. Though she was forty-three, four years older than he, she looked as pretty as she had in her first starring role. She was very much in love with her husband, who owned a large chain of movie theaters in New York and New England, as well as substantial real estate holdings in the Caribbean. When A.C. thought about what it might be like to be married to another woman than Kitty, it was often of Theresa.

She was wearing a simple but elegant deep blue Givenchy cocktail dress that went well with her short blond hair and twilight-colored eyes. A.C. had changed into one of his somber Brooks Brothers pin-striped suits, which fitted his mood.

The event they attended was a private preview of an exhibition opening at the Metropolitan Museum of Art—essentially a dreary stand-and-stare cocktail reception in honor of a garishly rich social climber who had donated several million dollars worth of what Theresa called "grotesque jade thingies." They had left as soon as it was polite to do so and dined at Petrossian, a Russian restaurant Theresa favored just off Central Park South. Well aware of A.C.'s strained finances—as were too many of his acquaintances—she picked up the check. The embarrassment made him feel even more depressed.

Now they were at her club—Doubles, in the Sherry-Netherland. There was dancing there at night and it was noisy.

"The famous boulevardier isn't living up to his image," Theresa said, smiling sweetly.

"The famous boulevardier is barely living," A.C. said.

"Was it really that awful, darling?"

"The murder? Theresa, as these things go, it was the worst I've ever seen."

That wasn't entirely true. As a police reporter, he had once covered the murder of a woman who had enraged her lover to the point where he had thrown her off the terrace of his high-rise apartment. She'd been naked, and the building façade had torn away much of her flesh in her tumbling fall.

"Let's dance," Theresa said. "It always works for me."

She was a marvelous dancer. A.C. was not, a fact that was more obvious than usual. After a few turns around the crowded floor, they returned to their table. Several other couples were watching them.

"Cheer up, darling," Theresa said. "New York loves you."

"New York loves no one."

"Well, New York can at least show you a good time. If this won't do it, we'll try somewhere else."

They sampled three other places, and even made a foray down to Club M.K., an erstwhile "hot spot" on Fifth Avenue near the Flatiron Building which featured rooms decorated with stuffed animal trophies and framed antique pornographic photographs.

They ended up at Mortimer's, as they often did. It was crowded, but on the strength of Theresa's theatrical and social prominence and A.C.'s cachet as a celebrity columnist, they were given one of the better tables the management always kept empty and waiting for its preferred clientele. Princess Stephanie of Monaco, insufficiently disguised in dark glasses, was there with another girl and two or three younger men. Elizabeth Taylor and a young man were eating voraciously at a corner table. Several people in the room waved to Theresa. She cheerily waved back.

"I'm sorry, Theresa. I'm a rotten date this evening. Per-

55

haps we should have one last drink and then I'll take you home."

"If you like," she said, "we can skip the one last drink." Her suggestion suited him, and then all at once it didn't.

Camilla Santee was there, seated at a bad table near the kitchen door, her companion an older man with silver hair and a dark, expensive suit. She appeared nervous, constantly brushing her long hair out of her eyes. She appeared not to have noticed Theresa and A.C.

"I don't know who that woman is you're staring at," Theresa said, "but that's Cyrus Hall, and he's one of the most expensive lawyers in the country. Even my husband can't afford him."

"I know. He's a member of my club. She's a model who was at the Arbre fur show today. She was at the police station with us."

"As I think upon it," Theresa said, "perhaps I do know her. Is she French?"

"French? No. I believe she's lived there for a time, though."

"I think it was in Paris. Last year, or the year before."

"One of the fashion shows."

"No, a party. A very grand party. She seemed to be a friend of the host, but I can't remember who it was."

He glanced around the room. Among the celebrated faces, he saw those of Gloria Vanderbilt and her friend the cabaret pianist Bobby Short, who, noticing A.C., nodded and smiled.

"Would you excuse me for just a moment?" A.C. said. "There's something I want to ask Bobby for my column."

"Tell him he was marvelous at the Fête de Famille party last week."

"I'll tell him for us both."

A.C. chatted briefly with the famous couple. He had known Short since meeting him at a White House state dinner years before and was a regular at the Café Carlyle whenever Short was playing there. Instead of returning directly to his table, A.C. then made a circuit of the room, passing finally by Santee's table.

"Why, hello," he said.

Startled, she looked up at him as though he had just announced he was going to murder her.

"I'm A.C. James," he said, "in case you've forgotten."

She responded to his friendliness with the merest smile. Cyrus Hall was frostily civil. He disliked A.C.'s newspaper.

"I haven't forgotten," she said. "I'm sorry about the way I left you today. It was inexcusable. I . . ."

"It was a terrible thing that happened."

Hall looked at his watch.

"Yes, a terrible thing," she said. "Terrible." She glanced down at her hands, then looked back at A.C., the smile vanishing. "Well, nice to see you again."

The silver-haired man put money on the table. He rose, and she quickly did the same.

"Good night," she said, and followed the man through the crowd to the door, leaving A.C. to stare forlornly after her. He returned to his table, feeling—and doubtless looking—rather foolish.

He stared glumly at his drink, wondering if he would ever see Camilla Santee again.

"Did you forget our table was over here?" said Theresa. "Or are you practicing for a job as a waiter."

"I'm sorry, Theresa."

"At the least, I hoped Bobby would cheer you up. He always does me."

"Not tonight."

Theresa reached for her stole and purse. "Normally, darling," she said, "an evening with you is about the most fun there is that's legal, but tonight you've been on another planet, and I think it's time I returned to mine."

"I'm sorry, Theresa. You're a good friend. I shouldn't have done this to you."

"It's all right, A.C. I'll just jump in a cab. They're those yellow thingies with the lights on the top? With drivers who all used to live in Odessa or Addis Ababa?"

"I'll take you home, Theresa."

A.C. always got women back to their homes as promised. It was one of the reasons their husbands trusted them out with him.

When their cab pulled up in front of her apartment house, she kissed his cheek. "Call me when you get back from wherever it is that you are, A.C. Good night."

She was inside her lobby before the doorman could fully open the door.

A.C. leaned back against the cracked vinyl of the seat. The driver, a patient, weary man, was indeed from Russia, according to the spelling of the name on his ID card beside the meter.

"Back to Mortimer's," A.C. said. He had the ridiculous hope that Camilla might somehow return there.

•

Detective Second Grade Tony Gabriel didn't mind working a double shift. He and his partner, Charley Caputo, had spent the evening talking to models. Most of those on the list had been home. As one explained, models didn't go out much at night during the busy season. Working three or four shows a day, plus photo shoots, they needed their sleep. As another had made very forcefully clear to Gabriel, they needed their sleep alone.

Nearly all of them had been as hostile, incommunicative, or otherwise unhelpful. Two of them had husbands, who didn't warm to the detectives' presence at all. But one, a young black woman with skin as dark as Molly Wickham's had been light, was more cooperative. Her name was Penny Hooper, and she said she had been Wickham's friend. She said she wanted the girl's killer caught and blown away.

She and Wickham had double-dated, though not often, for Wickham preferred older white men and Hooper liked her men young and black. Hooper had little to say about Wickham's past, except to note that she had formerly done a lot of work for a free-lance photographer who sold nude layouts to the cheaper men's magazines. His name was Peter Bernstein, she said, adding that he had gotten Molly Wickham work modeling lingerie, and that's where Philippe Arbre had discovered her.

She couldn't recall the names of any of Wickham's recent boyfriends, but did say that one of them was supposedly important in politics or government. Hooper said she had never met the man, but Wickham had been very proud of the relationship. The man was very generous, and had helped Wickham acquire her Sutton Place apartment.

Two of the nine models on the list had not been home and would have to be interviewed the next day. That left only Belinda St. Johns. Gabriel remembered resentfully how insistent Ray Lanham had been about leaving Camilla Santee alone for the night.

St. Johns wasn't home, either, but Gabriel decided to wait. She was an eyewitness, and Lanham hadn't gotten very far with her. Gabriel would do better. He had his reputation to maintain.

He and Caputo sat in one of the division's newer un-marked Dodge sedans across the street from St. Johns's Central Park West apartment building. The doorman had said she had gone out for the evening, but was expected back early. He said he kept particular track of her comings and goings, and she was seldom out late during the week. Gabriel took him at his word. Caputo wanted to go home.

"For Chrissake, Tony. We've been on since eight fucking A.M."

They had started on their third round of plastic-cup deli-catessen coffee.

"Ray said to check out the models. She's the last on the list."

"But he already talked to her."

"Yeah, right. He got her name."

"We're gonna wait till tomorrow on those other two. What's the difference with this one? She may be more talkative in the morning, anyway."

"Since when do you know so much about women, Charley? I want to hit her tonight. I'll bet she's got something Ray couldn't get."

"Tits and ass and a furry fucker."

"She's a looker, all right."

"Not as much of a looker as that Camilla Santee. Why do you think Ray put her off limits?"

"I'd do the same fucking thing myself."

"What do you think, she gave Ray a hard time because he's black? She's about the whitest broad I ever seen."

"Sometimes blondes like it dark."

He lit a cigarette, the flame of his butane lighter limning the shadows and angles of his face, making him look a little sinister. Sometimes Gabriel scared the hell out of Charley Caputo.

"I got a court case tomorrow," Charley said. "I need sleep."

"So sleep."

A black Jaguar sedan pulled out of traffic and glided to the curb in front of them a few feet short of the entrance to St. Johns's building. A long gray Mercedes-Benz stretch limousine came by just as slowly and halted forward of it. The driver of the Jaguar was Philippe Arbre. He came unsteadily around to the passenger side and opened the door. Belinda St. Johns stepped out, laughing. It appeared they'd both been drinking.

The driver of the Mercedes remained where he was, observing the scene through his rearview mirror.

"One of the witnesses said Wickham was walking toward a stretch when she got whacked," Gabriel said.

"But he said it was light blue."

"He said he wasn't sure. Check out the plate, Charley."

Caputo reached for the two-way and called in a license and registration check, speaking softly. Arbre made a big show of smack-kissing St. Johns on both cheeks, then climbed clumsily back into his car and drove away, an easy mark for a DWI if Gabriel hadn't been otherwise preoccupied. St. Johns went up to the limousine and spoke a few words to the driver before going inside, trailing a fur wrap behind her.

Caputo lowered the volume of the two-way when the response to his query came back. The woman dispatcher said the stretch was registered to the Varick Cartage Company.

"Holy shit, Tony. Varick Cartage. Isn't that one of Vince Perotta's outfits?"

"Sure as shit."

"What do you think, St. Johns is one of Vince's bimbos?"

"That two hundred pound nursemaid in the Mercedes isn't here 'cause he's lost."

"Why would a big time wiseguy like Vince let a faggot squire his meat around?"

"Because he's a faggot, and won't mess with the merchandise. A lot of busy guys use faggots like that. It saves on ammunition."

"Ain't Vince afraid of getting AIDS or something?"

"You can't get AIDS from kissing cheeks. If you could, half the Upper East Side would be dead."

The Mercedes turned away from the curb, pausing as the driver looked back at Gabriel and Caputo. Then he hit the accelerator, and sped away.

"Okay," said Gabriel. "I'm going up there."

"Tony. That's mob cunt."

"I'm a police officer, investigating a homicide. If I'm not down in fifteen minutes, wait until I am."

"One of these days you're going to stick your fucker into a meat grinder, Tony."

"This is not that day."

When Gabriel did come down, he was smiling like a buccaneer in a bad swashbuckler movie.

"Time to go home, Charley," he said. "I've found out all we need to know about Marjean Dorothy Wickham."

•

A.C. returned to a Mortimer's that, in his brief absence, had become considerably less crowded. Its luminaries of the night had vanished. Camilla Santee had not returned. A.C. stared at her empty table as he might at a ransacked house.

He went to the bar, finding no place to sit but space enough at the end to stand. He ordered a gin and tonic. He still held out the small, forlorn hope that Santee might reappear.

"Buy me a drink, sailor?"

A.C. looked down into a pretty yet unusual face—bright blue eyes and high cheekbones beneath a wild mane of long, unkempt jet black hair. Smoke from a cigarette stuck carelessly in the corner of a small, perfect mouth clouded an almost chalklike complexion.

Memories rushed into A.C.'s mind that had nothing to do with fashion models and runways—canoeing on a lake in upstate New York, a lawn party in Westchester with girls

61

in white summer dresses, late-night Manhattans after an outdoor jazz concert, a walk hand in hand along the beach at Cannes on a starry night.

"Hello, Bailey," he said. "Where in the hell have you been?"

"In L.A. Where else would I be when I'm not anywhere else?" She inhaled deeply from her cigarette, then clouded them both with smoke.

He was at a loss for anything to say. He had last seen her a year before, in Cannes, and they had parted strangely.

"I got a movie," she said. "Up in Boston. A made-for-TVer for cable. Yet another remake of *The Scarlet Letter*. Do I look like an adulteress?"

"You've always looked like an adulteress. As I realized too late."

She smiled and frowned at the same time, a practiced gesture.

"Golly, A.C. What a shitty thing to say."

He forced a grin. She was being playful. He wished he was in a better mood for it. When she was in the mood, there was no better companion than Bailey Hazeltine.

"For having been in L.A.," he said, "you haven't much of a tan."

"Tan's out. Pallor's in. Everyone's wearing hats and using number five hundred sunscreen. The last audition I went to looked like it was for *Night of the Living Dead*. Where's my drink, sailor?"

Bailey was the younger sister of a man who had been A.C.'s best friend in prep school and college. She had started drinking at a very early age and hadn't stopped since.

"What would you like?"

"A double Tom Collins."

"I'm not sure they make those anymore."

"You can get anything here. That's why I come."

A.C. tried to get the attention of the bartender. He was in conversation with two young men in Italian suits.

"I changed my mind," she said. "Let's go someplace."

"This is someplace. Gloria Vanderbilt was here."

"She isn't now. Someplace else."

"We can go to Billy's," he said, naming an unpretentious restaurant in the East Fifties with a very chic clientele.

62

"Why do I know Billy's?"

"Greta Garbo lived around the corner."

They got a cab immediately, one of several patrolling south down Lexington Avenue.

Bailey sat far across the seat from him, sitting sideways, enabling him to look directly into her eyes. They were very luminous and catlike. She was watching him speculatively. The effect was very provocative.

"How's your husband?"

"Still a sleazeball."

"Is he still here in New York?"

"Yes. I'm here on a conjugal visit."

She tucked one leg underneath her. She was wearing a short summer dress and her exposed thigh flashed white when they passed beneath the streetlamps.

"How's your wife?"

He sighed. "She's fine. She's been mad as hell at me, lately, and I can't really figure out why."

"You met her back in Paris after Cannes."

"Yes."

"Did I get you into trouble?"

"I got me into trouble. It's not been a good year."

She lit another cigarette, though the driver had pasted a large NO SMOKING sign on the back of the seat.

"I don't want to go to Billy's. I want to go to your apartment. Why do I know your apartment?"

"You and your brother came to a party we threw there when we first moved back from Washington."

"You have a terrace. I want to sit on your terrace. There's a moon out."

A.C. looked at his watch. It was nearly one A.M. He wondered where Camilla Santee was at that moment.

•

Once inside, Bailey took off her shoes.

"Forget the Tom Collins," she said. "I'll just have gin. A lot of gin. And ice."

She went out onto the terrace, lighting yet another cigarette. She was standing at the railing when he came out with their drinks.

"It's a wonderful moon," she said. "A moon over Dock Street. Did you know I once played Polly Peacham in *The Threepenny Opera*? It was out in L.A. In Pasadena."

He handed her her glass and she gulped from it thirstily, without turning away from the view. She was looking at the city as though it were a new toy.

When A.C. and Kitty had married, they had made at her suggestion a peculiar agreement. They were normal adults. They were marrying for life, and long marriages were subject to many stresses, many strains—and temptations. So they would be rational and reasonable and accept that reality. She was a Catholic, but not a nun. If either of them were to have an affair, it was to be forgiven—like a sin at confession. It was not to ruin their marriage.

More than one affair, Kitty had made clear, would be viewed as something far more serious.

A.C. had never known if Kitty had made use of the license provided by the agreement, though many attractive men had been seriously attentive to her over the years. The closest A.C. had ever come to actually sleeping with another woman had been with Bailey at the previous year's Cannes Film Festival, and Kitty had been furious.

He had been covering the event for the *Globe*. Bailey had been there for the reason most struggling young actresses came to Cannes. They'd met by chance walking along La Croisette one bright, clear morning. What had followed was now only a blur of recollection—the sparkling little city descending steep hills to the sea; the smell of roasted fish, vinegar, and perfume; the crowds of tourists, movie people, thieves, and pickpockets; the indulgent beaches strewn with half-naked women where Bailey had removed the top of her bathing suit as nonchalantly as *une française*.

One day that week they'd driven over to Monte Carlo, descending the Moyen Corniche that had years before taken the life of Bailey's idol, Grace Kelly. Another night, they had just sat in the lobby of the Hotel Majestic, taking in the antic comings and goings of the movie folk and paparazzi.

The final night, they'd ended up in A.C.'s hotel room with some British film people. The drinking had gotten out of hand, as it usually did when Bailey was around. By the time A.C. had gotten rid of the Britishers, Bailey had fallen into a rotten mood. He remembered her biting his ear as they kissed, and her swearing at him.

They'd fallen asleep, fully clothed, on his bed. He'd stirred once, on impulse lifting her skirt and kissing her bare bottom. Then he'd passed out. She was gone by morning. It was the last he'd seen of her. It was the sum total of his infidelity.

In Paris, Kitty had found a woman's comb, a champagne cork, and a hotel message slip with Bailey's name on it in A.C.'s suitcase. The nuptial agreement had ended right there. Ever after that, she was unhappy and disagreeable whenever he was in another woman's company, but her principal problem was the fact of Bailey.

A.C. had never fully understood it, but his wife, despite her money and power, was obsessively insecure over class differences. Though it was her Irish immigrant grandfather who had made her wealth and life-style and position possible, she hated any reminder of his humble origins. She felt awkward and resentful whenever she was in the presence of anyone she feared was a social superior. A.C. was an exception. For all his ancient lineage and Ivy League education, he had no money. None. His parents had quit their upstate country club, and his mother had taken a part-time job in a local village shop to get him through college.

Bailey was everything Kitty resented—and many things she disliked. Bailey was in the Social Register and, on her mother's side, came from one of the wealthiest and oldest families in America. It bewildered Kitty that such a person would choose the disreputable life of an actress. It enraged her that A.C. might have chosen Bailey for his affair.

Nothing A.C. had said made any difference, not even his protest that he had not actually had sexual relations with the woman. Whatever had happened with Bailey, Kitty had concluded she'd been snubbed, in the most unforgivable way.

"I saw a murder today," he said. He was standing at the railing next to Bailey. Their arms were almost touching.

"That black fashion model?"

"Yes. I wrote about it."

"That's what I hate about writers. Everything goes into fucking words."

A thumping sound startled him. It was a taxicab, passing over a loose manhole cover. He looked to the rooftops opposite. He thought he saw a brief flicker of light, but decided it was just his nerves. The man in the sport coat couldn't still be standing there in the middle of the night.

"I don't want to go home to sleazeball tonight," Bailey said. She leaned close to him.

A.C. was feeling reckless, unhappy, and still angry with his wife. He wasn't certain if her asking him to come back home now was a surrender or a summons. He was tired of summonses, and he had done nothing wrong.

"I'm not expecting any other company."

•

The moment of ultimate transgression came upon him in a hazy, dreamlike way. He remembered lying on Bailey's hot, clinging body, raising himself on his arms in hesitation. Bailey's eyes were opened wide, but focused on some inner joyous vision. He came down upon her again, but seemed to float, the last fulfilling burst of passion eluding him. He pressed his face into the softness of the pillow and Bailey's fragrant hair, but she seemed to drift away. In her place, in his weary, drink-wet mind, he saw the haunting, beckoning face of Camilla Santee, felt her long legs and arms around him, heard her voice murmur his name. When fulfillment came, the love that swept over him was all for her. In the final instant, he held Bailey fiercely close, but possessed Camilla.

Afterward, he lay still, then reached to touch Bailey's shoulder as he had Camilla's that afternoon. He remembered Camilla's tears.

He rolled onto his side and sat up, fulfilled, yet wretched—guilty. Now he'd been twice unfaithful—to his wife, and in the same instant, to Bailey.

She sat up as well, and lit a cigarette. "What a fool I was in Cannes to put you off."

The telephone rang. Startled, A.C. reflexively snapped

66

on the light. He picked up the receiver anxiously, the ridiculous notion crossing his mind somehow that it might be Kitty, that she knew.

"Hello?" he said.

There was only a silence, but he sensed the presence of someone on the line.

"Hello?" he repeated.

"Is this United Airlines?" The man's voice was hurried.

"No." A.C. hung up. He knew the airline's number. It was nothing at all like his.

"I'll presume that's not my husband," Bailey said.

"No. I think it was a wrong number." He turned out the light. "Go to sleep now."

He left the bedroom and went out onto the terrace, sitting down naked in one of the wrought iron chairs. The street was empty. Nothing moved on the rooftops opposite, or in any of the windows he could see.

He heard Bailey in the room behind him, pouring herself a drink. She did not join him.

He sat back against the cold metal and closed his eyes. Camilla came back to him, walking toward him down the fashion show runway, her eyes staring, full of murder.

All at once he was beset by a startling and awful realization. It made him feel stupid and foolish—and a little afraid.

Camilla Santee had not been looking at him in that extraordinary electric moment at the fashion show. She'd been looking at the man in the row of seats behind him, the big man with dark hair and glasses, who'd been drinking.

The man in the limousine—the limousine Molly Wickham had been walking toward.

67

CHAPTER

....

4

Lanham went home with his briefcase full of the Wickham case and worked at his kitchen table beyond any care for the hour. The fatigue he felt was the kind he remembered from the war—leaden body and mind pushed along only by habit and a sense of duty and a hatred born of frustration. Like the enemy, any enemy, the murders kept coming. There was always another.

This was a case that downtown and the news media would goad them to solve—the media by keeping it in the headlines and on the nightly news, downtown by screaming every time the story made news. But it was a case they would likely never close. The perpetrator had taken a great risk, but he had done so very shrewdly. His biggest chance of getting caught was in the first seconds and minutes after the shooting, but he had survived them and vanished. Their only real hope of finding him lay in the possibility of his striking again.

It was that very real possibility that kept Lanham laboring over reports and witness statements at his kitchen table. It was not Molly Wickham he was doing this for. It was the next one.

Wickham had already been dead when she'd come into his life. Nothing he could do would change that. She was as long gone as Abraham Lincoln or Cleopatra. In searching through all these reports, he was performing a job little different from a historian's—except that Molly Wickham's killer was still alive.

Sometimes he felt like giving it all up and walking away. Or giving it up and not walking away—just putting in his time and getting his twenty, the way so many in Vietnam had put in their time, shuffling along, just trying to stay alive and get their ticket home. He'd seen detectives who had cashed themselves in early that way, trying to drift through the days remaining until retirement. Mostly they were drunks like Pat Cassidy. A few were dead.

After making a second pot of coffee, he started in on all the fives and unusuals, taking notes where necessary and looking—wishing—for something significant to jump out at him. Nothing had, really. There were no eyewitnesses other than those he'd already talked to, and no description of the assailant better than the vague one given by the newspaper columnist A.C. James.

The man had mentioned two limousines outside the hotel, but at least a dozen had been sighted near the Plaza at the time of the shooting. Someone else had noticed a pickup truck with a horse trailer attached parked just off the roadway in Central Park. Someone else had noticed a parked van.

The horse trailer had had out-of-state plates—Virginia. The van was from New Jersey. He noted this and went on.

"Write that down, it's very important," the King of Hearts had said in *Through the Looking Glass*, when the dormouse sneezed.

They could find absolutely no one who had seen the motorcyclist after he had entered the park. A van like that could hold a motorcycle. So could a horse trailer.

It was too late to look for them now. Whoever he was, this man from Mars, he now had a big head start.

There would be many more such dumb, frustrating, fruitless nights. Lanham's mind and body would grow ever more leaden. His son had once asked him what he did to solve a murder. He'd thought carefully on the answer, and finally replied with one word: "Everything."

All too often, "everything" wasn't enough. No matter how good a case he built against a perpetrator, sooner or later he'd have to turn it over to lawyers. In the end, the almighty law was reduced to a tired jury locked in a room trying to decide between opposing sets of witnesses and lawyers so its members could go home. The best police work in the history of crime wasn't worth a damn if it was put in the hands of a bad lawyer.

He could have been a lawyer, but he'd become a policeman. Sometimes he dreamed that he was a lawyer. The dreams were almost always born out of intense periods of frustration.

He didn't dream the lawyer's dream that night, though. Lanham fell instantly asleep, and awoke too soon.

It was a little after six A.M. He shut off his alarm and put the case out of his mind before it could again take root. He'd start the day with his garden. He'd given over his entire backyard to it, leaving space only for a path that circled between the rosebushes, flower beds, and shrubbery. Lanham had won a third place in the New York Garden Club show with one of his roses, which he'd named the Kathleen Mary, after his mother.

A.C. James had seemed surprised when he'd mentioned his roses during the previous day's interrogation. Lanham wondered if that was because he was black, or because he was middle class—a mere cop. Or both. Maybe black cops shouldn't grow roses. He should have fucking watermelons in his garden.

Lanham had the best-kept house in his section of Queens, which had irritated his neighbors as much as it had surprised them. He was the only black man in that neighborhood. It hadn't helped that he was also a black man who had a white wife.

The house had formerly belonged to his mother, who

70

had been white—Irish white. Except for her peculiar choice of a husband, she was a woman like all the others who lived in the neat bungalows that lined the street. While she was alive, the trouble had been confined to verbal abuse, but after her death it had gotten grim. Windows had been broken and Lanham's garden had been repeatedly vandalized. He'd tried handling matters himself, to the point of punching out a heckler who'd taunted his wife, but that had only increased the hostility of the locals. Finally, he'd given in to the urgings of his captain at the time, and filed charges. Four youths were arrested and one of them did a few weeks' time at a correctional facility for juveniles. Lanham had been let alone after that, and could now even claim a few friends in the neighborhood. They were all cops. His wife, Janice, an arts major and schoolteacher who disliked Queens no matter who lived there, begged him to move, but he stubbornly refused. He wasn't going to give up his mother's house.

He carefully sprayed the rosebushes, covering each of the dew-moist flowers with the thin white powder. Nowadays the only vandals were Japanese beetles, but they were menace enough.

He watched their little bodies drop as they succumbed to the poison and fell—more of nature's infinite multitude of daily homicides. Most creatures died as victims of another. Only man tried to be different.

Lanham was showered, dressed, and ready to leave his house by 7:10 A.M. His wife, barefoot and wearing only an old robe, caught him in the front hall before he went out the door. She wasn't angry, only sleepy. Her red hair was over her eyes. He hugged her and kissed her cheek.

"Gotta go, babe."

"You want some coffee?"

"I had coffee all night."

She stepped out of his reach and looked at him, brushing her hair away from her face. He could hear his two sons upstairs.

"How much sleep did you get?"

He shrugged. "I'll catch up on the weekend."

"This murder is what you would call a big deal, right?"

"It's like one out of the movies."

71

"In the movies the cops always get the killer."

"Some movies are better than others."

She smiled. He'd keep that in his mind all day. With that smile, she'd let him be a cop another day.

"Call me," she said, and she went off to the kitchen.

•

A.C. awoke to hear Bailey talking in the next room, apparently on the telephone. When she was finished, she came back into the bedroom, fully dressed, as much as her simple little summer shift and shoes could be called that. She was carrying a glass of juice. From its pale color, he guessed there was gin or vodka in it—not a small amount.

She seemed upset about something, but smiled for him —an aristocratic little girl's smile, not the Hollywood wanton's he remembered from the night before—and sat down on the edge of the bed, patting his chest. She was still too young and too pretty to look really bad from her night's carouse. Still, she did not look well.

"I'm glad we did that, A.C. I've wanted to do that with you for the longest time."

A.C. did not feel glad. He felt completely rotten, convinced he had just committed the worst act of his life. Adultery had always tantalized him. He'd considered the old laws against it as primitive and as excessive as capital punishment for theft. Now he wondered.

These were not thoughts he wanted to share with Bailey. For all the sordidness he felt, she seemed particularly dear to him on this morning after—someone to be protected, someone he must be responsible for now. Somehow he must care for her with all the pity he could muster. It would keep him from pitying himself.

"You were always a fantasy of mine."

"You were better than a fantasy," she said. She lit a cigarette. "I've got a problem."

Money? Husband? Venereal disease? He pushed the thought away.

"I've got a friend who's in a bad way," she continued. "Drugs. Down in Philly. I've got to get him through it, or

72

into one of those places. He doesn't have anyone else. His wife left him and his family's all dead. I'll be gone a couple of days or more. Maybe until next week."

Before their chance encounter in Mortimer's the night before, A.C. had never really expected to see Bailey ever again. Now he was sad that she was leaving him.

"How did you find this out?"

"I called my answering machine in L.A. He was trying to reach me."

"Can I help?"

"Thanks but no thanks," she said. "This is the proverbial bad scene." She paused. "There's one thing, A.C. Things are really going badly with my husband. If they get out of hand, can I come back here for a couple of days?"

"Yes. Of course. I'll get you a key. I'll be up in West-chester over the weekend. Maybe longer. If you need me, just leave a message at my office."

He rose and fetched a spare from an expensive Russian lacquered Palakh box on the dresser. She held it carefully, studying it as though he had given her something magical. She smiled, but there was much sadness in her eyes.

"Bailey, why did you ever marry that bastard?"

"I'm not really sure. I suppose it was the sex at first. He's rather good at that. And it truly pissed off Mother. She's such an anti-Semite."

"Come back whenever you want. I'll tell the doorman. Just call before you come. Kitty owns the place, you know."

"It's not so good with you two, right?"

He shrugged sadly. "Women. She can't stand all the women in my life, even though they're just part of the job she gave me. I think she's convinced I've been unfaithful."

Bailey smiled. "And so you have."

"Bailey, this was the first time."

"Really? I'm flattered."

"I'm afraid I'm feeling a little guilty."

"You've no reason to. Not because of Kitty."

"What do you mean?"

"Never mind."

"I do mind. Tell me."

"My brother told me he saw Kitty with a man in a hotel once. In London. You were off at the war in Northern Ireland or someplace."

A.C. recalled the time. It was six years before. He'd spent two weeks in Belfast, leaving Kitty to wait for him at the Park Lane. He remembered that she had seemed very cold and distant on his return.

He stared at Bailey.

"What wonderful lives we create for ourselves, don't we, A.C.?"

She kissed him, finished her drink, stubbed out her cigarette, and got shakily to her feet.

"I'll be late for the train," she said. "I hate taking the train. You've got to go through fucking New Jersey. Goodbye, A.C. If you do end up needing a new wife, maybe I'll divorce my husband."

When she was gone, he made coffee and sat numbly sipping it in the living room. He had a sudden urge to call Kitty, as if a chatty, normal conversation with her might help expiate his sin. But he couldn't think of anything to say that wouldn't sound foolish. He didn't know what she would think.

Finally, he began thumbing idly through one of his magazines—a month-old issue of *Town and Country*. On one of the fashion pages, there was a picture of Camilla Santee. He'd paid no attention to it when he'd first seen it. Just another model. She was wearing a sporty summer outfit that looked a little young for her. It showed off her long legs wonderfully, though. And her expression was demure enough to match the clothes. In his brief encounter with her, he hadn't seen such a look on her face.

What if it had been her he'd been with that night? Would he be feeling guilt now, or some sort of rapture? A reckless sense of freedom. To fall in love with Camilla Santee would be like sailing away from his life. He wasn't ready for that.

He stared at the picture for a long time, then tore it from the page and set it carefully on the table.

He had a hangover, but he couldn't bring himself to treat it the way Bailey had hers, the way she probably ministered to herself every morning.

Hung over or not, there was something he had to do,

74

and soon. He looked over at the telephone. He didn't know the nonemergency number for the police department, so he called information.

•

Lanham's first stop upon reaching Manhattan was Molly Wickham's apartment building. The canvass team had been through the building the afternoon and evening before, and the evidence technicians had finished. Two uniformed police officers had remained behind. Lanham would see the reports when he got to the division, but first he wanted a look for himself.

It was a huge, and thereby enormously expensive apartment. When he'd looked up at the building from the sidewalk below, he'd wondered which side the apartment faced. Inside, he discovered it looked east, north, and west as well. It also had a large balcony. Molly Wickham had not been a big-time model for very long, and the movie she'd made sounded like a cheap one. How she'd been able to afford a place like this was a question he wanted answered.

Whatever the apartment had cost her, she apparently hadn't much left over for furniture. There was an antique brass bed in the largest bedroom, accompanied only by a small night table and a not very expensive chest of drawers. A full-length mirror was propped, rather than hung, against one wall. The other two bedrooms were empty. The long and spacious living room had only a couch, coffee table, stereo, television, and armchair in it, plus some African masks and a few museum prints on the wall. A pile of cushions in one corner did for another place to sit. There were faint marks in the thick carpeting indicating that the room had once held considerably more furniture.

In the dining room, there was a small table, the kind that more properly belonged in a kitchen, and four chairs. The kitchen itself had only three counter stools. There were few dishes in the cabinets—no crystal or expensive china. One cabinet, however, was filled with liquor, mostly whiskey and expensive liqueurs.

He could find no books anywhere in the apartment. In the back of a drawer in the bathroom adjoining the master

75

bedroom was a Polaroid photograph. It was of Molly Wickham and another woman—white. Neither was wearing any clothes. They were very busy. Not too many years before, such a photo could have gotten them both arrested.

Lanham looked closely at the picture, his eyes following the curve of body and sheen of flesh to the juxtaposition of Molly Wickham's thigh and a glimpse of profile of the other woman's face. He went out to the living room couch and the full flood of morning light from the window. Taking off his glasses, he cleaned the lenses with his handkerchief and then studied the photograph one more time.

He could be wrong, but he didn't think so. His certainty was like a familiar itch. The other woman in the photo was Belinda St. Johns.

He took out his notebook and jotted down a few remarks to himself, including what the building manager had told him when he had stopped by the man's office on the way up.

The apartment was owned by a French woman, who used it infrequently and apparently lived abroad. Wickham had moved in about four months before as a rental tenant. No doubt the other residents were less than pleased to have a young black model for a neighbor, and were doubtless bent on effecting her removal—but carefully. There was the city's anti-discrimination code to contend with.

Now a man on a motorcycle had ended their predicament for them.

Lanham had written down the Frenchwoman's name— C.C. Delasante, from Juan les Pins, France. The manager said he had never met the Delasante woman, but he had held his job less than a year. He'd heard she was a real looker, and very rich.

The day doorman had never met the woman either, but he had gotten to know Molly Wickham fairly well. He said she had a number of boyfriends and gentleman callers. One of them had come to Wickham's apartment early in the previous afternoon—not very long after the shooting. He hadn't stayed long. He apparently had a key to the apartment, and the doorman had seen him several times before, usually in the early morning. The doorman described him as a big man with glasses, as big as Lanham. He'd been one

76

of a number of men who'd visited Wickham in the past—all of them white.

"You say they finished the canvass?" Lanham asked one of the uniformed men.

"Yes sir. I don't think they learned much, though. She didn't have any friends in the building."

"Did the evidence techs turn up any prints?"

"Yes sir. A lot of prints. Several different sets. And they found a used condom in the bed."

Lanham smiled.

"And there was a piece of a box there, too. A video tape box. It said 'VHS.' "

Now Lanham frowned. "Video tape?"

"Yeah. They took it down to the lab, along with all the garbage."

Lanham looked at the television console. There was a VCR machine at the bottom. He went over to it, turned it on, and hit the EJECT button. Nothing came out.

"What about C.C. Delasante?" he said to the uniformed man.

"Sir?"

"The French woman who owns this place. Did anyone know anything about her?"

"Don't know, sir."

Lanham made a few more notes. Before he left, he put the photo of the two nude women into his briefcase.

•

Vanessa had two surprises for A.C. when he got to the office: Camilla Santee's address and private phone number, and the news that Vanessa was going to another fur fashion show that morning in which Santee might be appearing.

"Her booker said she's supposed to show up, though she canceled the rest of her jobs yesterday. By the little by, chéri, I now owe her booker about ten years' worth of favors."

He kissed her hand. "I'll make it up to you."

"Not that way, sweetie."

The show was for one of New York's major houses, the designer a man whose picture was frequently in W magazine

77

and the *Women's Wear Daily* "Eye" gossip column. A.C. had often seen him in Mortimer's. The show, performed on a stage rather than a runway, was very flashy, with lots of dazzling lighting effects and upbeat music, but Camilla was not there.

A.C. sat morosely pondering that fact. He'd slipped out once to use the unlisted phone number Vanessa had given him, but there had been no answer, not even by an answering machine.

"Dull, dull, dull," Vanessa said. "*Incroyable.* The man simply has no guts. These are coats he could have sold ten or twenty years ago."

"I don't understand," A.C. said.

"The Japanese and Taiwanese bought a lot of pelts last year and now they're flooding the market with coats. It's a soft market. Prices are down and so are sales. So the king of fashion here is playing it safe. These are for the one-coat woman."

"One-coat woman?"

"Women who can only afford one fur coat and want it to last. Not the kind of woman who has a number of furs and buys new ones to keep up with trends. Instead of trying to make a fashion statement this year, the great genius has come out with safe, traditional coats that are guaranteed to sell. It makes me mad. There are a lot of young kids around with some really terrific designs, but the manufacturers stick with people like this. Make a buck, make a buck, make a buck."

"It's a global tragedy."

"Fashion is important, A.C."

"Especially to the animals who die for it."

The word "die" stuck in his mind long after he said it. Molly Wickham had been wearing a fur half an hour before she'd been killed. What had she died for?

Afterward, they stepped out into the milling, Hogarthian swarms crowding along Seventh Avenue, pushing their way to the curb to find a cab. It was another clear, sunny day.

A motorcycle came by, chugging and weaving through the stalled traffic, and they both tensed. It was a messenger.

"Are you going to any more shows?" A.C. asked.

"I've got Bill Blass and Geoffrey Beene after lunch," she said.

"Do you think Camilla Santee will be in them?"

Vanessa gave him a sharp look. "I'm beginning to think Miss Santee has gone back to France. I'm also beginning to think that's the best thing that could happen for you."

•

Lieutenant Taranto had called for a meeting at 10:00 A.M., but it had been delayed by a visit from Assistant District Attorney Rosenbaum. While the other detectives on his team stood around drinking coffee and waiting, Lanham went through the initial evidence report from forensics and returned a few telephone calls. When Rosenbaum finally left, grim-faced and silent, Taranto motioned his men into his small cubicle. There were chairs only for three of them, but it didn't matter. Lanham preferred to stand. So did Tony Gabriel, who took a place to the side of the lieutenant's desk. He was holding a case file, and looking smug.

"The commissioner got an official federal inquiry on the Wickham murder this morning," Taranto said.

"What the fuck do the feds care about a dead fashion model?" said Caputo. He was wearing a light gray suit this morning, with a pink shirt and purple tie.

Taranto shrugged. "Beats the hell out of me. Drugs maybe? What do you think, Ray?"

"I think it's very interesting," Lanham said. "What do they want from us?"

"Everything we got, which is still shit," Taranto said. "It came direct from the Justice Department in Washington, not the local FBI. They said something about Wickham, Marjean Dorothy maybe relating to an ongoing investigation of theirs.

Lanham thought for a long moment. The others watched him. "I think we should run Wickham, Marjean Dorothy through the FBI computer files up here," he said. "And I think we should ask Justice for everything they have on her."

"I'll see what we can get out of them," Taranto said. He looked particularly tired. His eyes were little caves.

"Well, we've got more than shit," Tony Gabriel said. He dropped the case file on the lieutenant's cluttered desk as he might play a trump card. "I got this outta vice this morning. The Wickham broad was on the Deuce. She had a rap sheet."

The others looked as astonished as he did pleased with himself. "The Deuce" was police jargon for Forty-second Street, not the fabled Times Square theater district advertised in the city convention bureau's tourist commercials but the sleazy, neon-lit cesspool and sewer that ran through it between Sixth and Tenth Avenues—the workplace and social center of some of the most troublesome hookers, pimps, thieves, perverts, and wackos in New York.

Like a prosecutor in court, Gabriel flipped open the folder and began to read from the record: "Two arrests for soliciting a police officer and one for lewd conduct. She didn't do any time, though, except for overnights. The last one was four years ago. She gave her age as eighteen, but that was the usual bullshit."

A short but eventful life—from the slums of Jersey City to the Deuce to porn movies to lingerie ads to the big-time fashion runways and Sutton Place.

And a big bullet on the fanciest street corner in Manhattan.

"But get this," Gabriel continued. "Her fines were paid by Chauncey Ellis, Bad Bobby Darcy's shyster."

"So Darcy's a pimp," said Petrowicz. "Who else is gonna pay a hooker's fines?"

"Bad 'Biker' Bobby," Gabriel said. "He used to work the Deuce on the biggest fuckin' Harley in town. And he's a light skinned dude."

"Bad Bobby's in Do Right City," said Petrowicz. "He got two to five in Mattawan for cutting one of his girls."

"Yeah, well two to five's up and he's out," said Gabriel, lighting a cigarette. "I checked. Boss, I think we got a suspect. Bobby keeps his girls working as long as they can turn any kind of trick, and this girl was in shape to do a hell of a lot more than twenty-dollar blow jobs. I think he took her out for quittin' on him."

"How did you get on to this, Tony?" Taranto asked.

"I got a tip from one of the other models. Belinda St. Johns. You talked to her yesterday, Ray."

Gabriel was grinning. Lanham wasn't.

"I think it's bullshit," Lanham said. "When a pimp like Bobby wants to whack a chippie, she turns up floating under a dock with her throat cut and the word gets put out on the street why. He wouldn't pick high noon in front of the Plaza."

"Bobby's a razor artist," Petrowicz said. "I don't think he's ever been caught with a piece."

The lieutenant chewed on his lower lip. "I think we ought to bring him in, Ray. We can't knock him, but we can lean on him a little—maybe get some squeal. Anyway it's something the commissioner can give to the newsies."

"We won't have enough to charge him," Lanham said. "The commissioner will look stupid."

"Again," said Petrowicz.

"Maybe," Taranto said. "But we oughta talk to Bad Bobby. Run his mug shots by the witnesses, too. You want to take him, Ray?"

"I've got better things to do. I'm going back to the crime scene."

"I'll take him," Gabriel said. "Me and Charley. With some help from Vice. Maybe some precinct backup."

"I'll set it up," said Taranto. "Once you get a line on him. Where's Chauncey Ellis?"

"Dead," said Petrowicz. "Last year. Natural causes."

"Enjoy yourselves," Lanham said. He turned to Pat Cassidy. "The CSU got nothing at the scene, but the evidence techs picked up a whole lot of prints from her apartment. Why don't you start running them through records by type? See if you can make any of them. Run them through the FBI, too. All right, boss?"

Taranto nodded.

"That'll take a lot of time, Ray," Cassidy said. "Don't you want me out on the street?"

Out on the street, and into a bar.

"I know it will take a lot of time. That's why I'd like you to start now."

"What about our other cases, boss?" Cassidy said.

81

"What other cases?" the lieutenant said. "You read the morning papers. Unless someone shoots the mayor, there ain't any other cases until we turn up a good lead on this one—and Tony, I don't count Bad Biker Bobby as a good lead until you get him to where he'll need a lawyer, capish?"

"Yeah, yeah," Gabriel said.

The lieutenant's decision to have Bad Biker Darcy picked up ended the meeting. Gabriel headed out to get his car, but Caputo lingered behind, saying he had to stop in the men's room. He paused by Lanham's desk.

"I think you want to empty your pisser, too, Ray," he said quietly.

The restroom was empty except for a sergeant finishing up in one of the stalls. Caputo made a noisy display of washing his hands until the man had gone.

"Something you oughta know, Ray," he said. "Tony got more than that tip from Belinda St. Johns. I'm pretty sure he got a piece of ass."

"Tony gets a piece of ass just going to the grocery store."

"It's bad news, Ray. She's Vince Perotta's slash. We checked it out. I didn't say nothing to anyone else, but Tony's heading for an IAD investigation if he keeps it up. Maybe something worse. Fuck with a wiseguy's broad and you're in bigger trouble than if you turn stool pigeon."

"I don't need this, Charley. It'll screw up the case."

"Fucking A. So I thought you should know."

"Thanks. See if you can keep Tony celibate for a while. Before Vince Perotta deals with his libido permanently."

"What's a libido? Something to do with his fucker?"

"Get going, Charley. Let me know when you're ready to move on Biker Bobby."

"I thought you didn't want to be in on it."

"No. I think it's stupid, and I get nervous when I'm around stupid. But I want to know when it's going down."

•

When Lanham had been in the lobby of the Plaza the day before, it was to take it over as a command post for the initial crime scene investigation. A.C. James and the other witnesses had waited in it almost as prisoners, subserviant

82

to the needs and desires of the police. Now the hotel was back to its aristocratic, normal self, and so was James, dressed in a crisp pin-striped summer suit, seated with elegant ease and poise. He rose to greet Lanham with a cordial smile and handshake—a generous host, a man in charge. Their roles from the previous day were completely reversed.

James looked a little nervous, though. And haggard, as though he hadn't gotten any more sleep than Lanham had.

"It's really good of you to come, Detective Lanham," James said. "I know you must be very busy."

"I am," said Lanham curtly. He still resented the man's condescension about his roses. "But I was going to come back here anyway. And I wanted to talk to you again. So I'm glad you called."

"Good. Let's go in to lunch. I've reserved a table."

"Lunch?"

"Yes. So we can talk. Lunch is the newspaper columnist's M.O. That's the right term, isn't it?"

"Yes. It still is."

"Splendid. And this is on me."

James led him into the Edwardian Room, a restaurant Lanham had never been in before. He was gladdened by the sight of two black men in expensive suits at a prominent table. As he passed, he noticed they were speaking French.

Once they were seated, a waiter was at their table in an instant. They ordered drinks, a Bloody Mary for James, a Heineken beer for Lanham.

"Has your memory gotten any better about the perp?" Lanham said.

"Perp?"

"Perpetrator. The killer."

"Not really, though I've been going over everything in my mind. All I can remember is that the fellow had rather tanned skin, and that in a way he reminded me of a movie actor."

Lanham took a file photo of Bad Bobby Darcy from his pocket and set it gently on the table.

"Is this him?"

A.C. studied the picture for a long moment. "No."

"You're sure?"

A.C. looked again. "Well, no, I'm not sure. But I don't

83

think so. The man struck me as very good looking. Like a male model in a motorcycle ad."

"This guy is handsome. A real ladies' man."

"I suppose there's a possibility it might have been him," A.C. said. "But I don't know. Perhaps if I could see him with a motorcycle helmet on."

"Maybe that could be arranged."

"Is he a suspect?"

Lanham paused. "Not necessarily."

The drinks came. They accepted the menus that were offered, but James set his aside.

"I wanted to talk to you about the man in the limousine I saw, the one at the curb just before the girl was shot," he said. "I was thinking about him last night and something occurred to me. I think he's connected with the models in the show. Probably Molly Wickham, and maybe Camilla Santee. He was at the show. Sitting right behind me."

James went on to awkwardly relate how he had thought Camilla Santee had been looking at him during the show. "I realize now she was looking at the man seated behind me. I should have realized it at the time. She gave him a hard, very direct look. I don't know how I could have thought it was directed at me."

"Wishful thinking, maybe," Lanham said.

"What? Oh. Yes. Perhaps it was. But she was definitely looking at him. He got up immediately afterward. It's very clear to me now. And he was the same man out in the limousine. I'm quite sure Molly Wickham was going to his car when she was shot. I remember him clearly now. When he was sitting behind me at the show, I remember that he smelled of whiskey. He had dark, curly hair. He was a tall man, wearing glasses."

Lanham set his own menu down. "A tall man with glasses? You're sure?"

"Yes."

"And a white man?"

"Yes. I'm sure of that."

Lanham took a sip of his beer. He wondered if he was the only one in the room drinking beer. The two French-speaking black men had what looked to be an expensive bottle of wine on their table.

"This is very interesting, Mr. James. Because a man of that description visited Miss Wickham's apartment shortly after the shooting. He had his own key."

"Well, there you are."

"Not unusual for a man to have a key to his mistress's apartment. The lease was in her name, though, not his. She was renting it from a woman in France. Someone named C.C. Delasante. Ever heard of anyone by that name?"

James shook his head. Lanham reminded himself that he was talking not just to a society gent but a working newsman.

"What I just said is not for quote," he said. "This isn't an interview."

"I understand."

"We got a lot of prints out of the apartment. If your friend in glasses left his there, maybe we can get an ID on him. Maybe you can help us."

"Whatever I can do."

"Mr. James, when you interviewed Miss Wickham about her movie, did she tell you anything about her past?"

"Just what I told you. A cheerleader from New Jersey."

"Would you be surprised if I told you she used to be a prostitute? That she had an arrest record? That the cheerleader story was all bullshit?"

He caught himself, hoping no one had heard the profanity. This wasn't the fucking squad room.

James frowned. "Detective Lanham, a lot of fashion models at this level are pretty top drawer. You know, Grace Kelly used to be a model."

"No black Grace Kellys, are there?"

"That isn't what I meant."

"Sure it is. But I am surprised. How does a black chippie from Forty-second Street get to be a top fashion model? How does that work?"

"Black fashion models are much in demand these days," A.C. said. "If they have the beauty, and the talent, I don't suppose their backgrounds matter that much. And anyway, she made hers up, if what you say is true."

"It's true. I just wonder how she did it."

"All it would take is for the right person, like Philippe Arbre, to see her in action. She had that wonderful walk. You don't see white models, I mean . . ."

"Say what you mean, Mr. James. I'm not hung up about race. I hear the word 'nigger' every day."

James looked embarrassed. "That isn't what I said, Detective Lanham."

"It's funny. I never hear the word 'mick' around me, even though I'm half Irish, half white Irish. I'm as white as I am black. Except in the South. Doesn't take much to be a nigger in the South."

"Are you from the South?"

"Close enough. I was born in Baltimore. My father was a lawyer there. Criminal law. He didn't make very much money, but he was a lawyer."

"But you're a detective."

"I have a law degree, but I'm a cop. When my father died, my mother moved us back to Queens, where she grew up. I went to Fordham, but in New York, it just seemed better that I become a cop. I was a cop in the army, a military policeman. In Vietnam."

"With a law degree?"

"I was drafted before I went to college."

Now Lanham wanted to change the subject. "Have you ever heard of any mob involvement in the fashion business, Mr. James?"

"The crime syndicate? I suppose they may have some money invested in it, as they do in every business. Why, was Molly Wickham mixed up with—?"

"No. Not that we know of. But one of the other models in the show, well, let's just say she has an interesting boyfriend."

"Not Camilla Santee?"

"No." Lanham smiled at James's obvious concern. "Not her."

The beeper in Lanham's pocket began its monotonous summons. He pulled it out and shut it off.

"The office," he said, excusing himself. "I've got to telephone."

When he returned, James was studying the menu. A waiter was hovering impatiently nearby.

"I'm afraid I can't stay to eat," Lanham said, standing by his chair. "They want me to come back in."

"Is there a break in the case?"

"A break? In the Wickham case? We should be so lucky. No, we're just going to pick up one of her former employers, meaning her ex-pimp."

"The man in the photograph?"

"We just want to talk to him, Mr. James, just like we talked to you. Pimps, columnists—we talk to anyone. We'll be talking to you again, too."

"Of course."

After Lanham had gone, A.C. decided to skip lunch, too. He needed to get back to the office. Something the detective had said was worming around in his mind. C.C. Delasante. The initials were wrong, but the rest had to be the same. It was no wonder he'd thought the man in the limousine looked familiar.

CHAPTER

....

5

Peter Gorky's "movie studio" was in the West Fifties, near the Hudson, occupying the second floor of an old brick building with windows so grimy the view didn't matter—especially since it was of another old brick building across the street with windows just as dirty.

Gorky, a big lumberjack of a man, insisted on giving Lanham a brief tour of his premises, pointing out the inadequacies and cramped quarters with something like pride. There were five rooms. In the rear, with no windows, was one used solely for storage—crowded with cabinets and racks loaded with metal film cans, piles of cables and rolls of tape, stacked equipment Lanham didn't recognize and probably wouldn't understand. The next room out was for editing, a girl and a young man each working at a bench, neither paying any attention to Gorky or his guest. Then there were two offices, nearly identical and cheaply fur-

88

nished. The smaller of the two had just one window and belonged to Gorky's absent partner, who he said was out on the Coast. The larger chamber, with two windows, a Museum of Modern Art poster on the wall, and a long, old leather couch, was Gorky's. The poster was of a nude woman and a fiendish-looking man in duster and driving goggles in an open, pre–World War I automobile.

The nicest part was the reception area, which possessed a new couch, three museum posters, and a long-legged woman named Myra, whose eyes and smiles told Lanham she did more at Gorky Productions than type and answer phones.

Gorky led Lanham back to his office and provided him with some coffee from a small machine on a corner table —white plastic conical cup in a hard brown plastic holder.

"That's the whole show," Gorky said, with a gesture toward his office door and beyond. "Cameras and sound equipment I rent. Sound stage I rent. Actors and crews I hire. Deals I do in restaurants."

Gorky was bald and bearded, not quite as tall as Lanham but much more muscular. He wore a plaid cotton shirt, old jeans, and big black leather boots. He wore his shirtsleeves rolled up to his biceps and his shirt front was half unbuttoned. His arms and chest were very hairy. A pair of half spectacles hung from a gold chain around his huge neck. His smile was enormous and easy. Lanham liked him. He felt instantly and completely comfortable in the man's presence. He'd been uncomfortable every minute he'd been with A.C. James in the Plaza.

Lieutenant Taranto had summoned him away from lunch just to sign some paperwork for the arrest of Bad Biker Bobby. The division's interest in Darcy had led to the amazing discovery that he was liable to criminal charge. He was now wanted not merely for questioning in Wickham, Marjean Dorothy. The remainder of Darcy's sentence on his assault conviction was being served on probation, and he had violated the terms of the judge's ruling. To wit, he'd been observed the previous night by two witnesses—Times Square snitches—cruising the Deuce on his bike, and thus consorting with known criminals—that is, his chippies.

"Hell, anyone who stands on the corner of Eighth Avenue and Forty-second Street for ten seconds is consorting with known criminals," Lanham had said.

"Come on, Ray. Bad Bobby is about as known a criminal as you're ever gonna find. What do you think he was doing there, asking directions?"

"I've run Darcy's photo past three witnesses, right? Nothing conclusive."

"They didn't say no, Ray."

Lanham had sighed; then he'd gone back to investigating the Wickham murder case.

"I'm still shook by Molly's getting gunned down like that," Gorky said, gesturing this time at a copy of the morning *Globe* on his desk. "Jeez, right in the eye, right in front of the Plaza. It really tears you up. I mean, shit, she was good kid, Molly. A really good kid."

"How do you mean, 'good'?" Lanham said. He took off his glasses and wiped them carefully, not just out of habit. He wanted to see Gorky's face clearly, and his lenses kept getting misted over from the heat.

"She had the stuff, you know? A lot of actresses are a little dumb; fashion models too. But Molly was really bright. Got it all down quick. Never temperamental, never had to be told anything twice. Got it right the first or second time. Hell, with what we saved in takes, we actually made some money on this picture. If Molly had kept on scoring as a fashion model, and gotten a couple of breaks, she might have gotten into films in a big way."

"Wasn't Molly written up by that *Globe* columnist, A.C. James?"

"Yeah, that was nice," Gorky said. "But no one's going to get famous in my pictures. Not right now, anyway. You know how much I'm going to net on this thing? I figured it out today. $50,701.12. Sure, we got written up in the *Globe—Newsday*, too. And we got some great reviews in L.A. But you know how many theaters we opened in? Fifty, maybe, nationwide." Gorky leaned back, tilting his chair against the wall and folding his hands behind his head. "It's doing good in Europe, though. Especially France. So next year we go to the Cannes Film Festival, right?"

"Who do you know who might want to kill her?" Lanham asked. The question was part of the ritual. He almost never got a useful answer.

"Hard to say. A girl that good-looking, she may have stiffed a couple of guys who were hot after her pants. But that's nothing to get killed over. She was a real good kid. If it wasn't for her background, you might even call her nice."

"Did you know about her background?"

"I knew some of it, yeah."

"Did you know she was once a hooker, that she had a record?"

Gorky thought about his answer, then shrugged.

"I guess I knew that, but so what? I mean, she wasn't sent over by MCA. And anyway, how many actresses do their job-hunting standing up? I was at a party in L.A. once where, except for two stars, all the women there were hired. And what's the difference between a film like mine and the fashion shows and the street? One way or another, the girls are all selling their bodies. Some you look at, some you fuck."

"Did you ever sleep with Molly Wickham?"

Gorky came forward in his chair, placing his hands on his desk.

"We were friends. For a while, we were close friends, okay?"

Lanham stopped to take out his notebook, to consult it, not to write. Unless he was taking a formal statement, he tried to avoid displaying this symbol of the public record. Notebooks tended to intimidate witnesses—not to speak of suspects.

"How did you meet Molly Wickham?" he said.

"You know. Saw her somewhere. Liked what I saw. She was a real looker."

"Molly Wickham did some work for a photographer named Peter Bernstein," Lanham said, eyes on his notebook entries. "Did lingerie ads, girlie-magazine layouts. We get the idea she may have done a porn film or two for him as well."

Gorky's eyes became very serious, but he said nothing.

"We can't find Peter Bernstein, photographer," Lanham said. "He's not listed anywhere anymore."

91

Silence.

"Do you know Peter Bernstein, Mr. Gorky?"

Gorky looked away, toward the nearest window. He tried to grin, but it came out a weak, embarrassed smile.

"Okay, you're going to find out anyway, right? Maybe you already know. I'm Peter Bernstein. I changed my name when I did my first legit film. Are you guys going to bust me for some home movie I made years ago? That's not even illegal anymore. I mean, hell, look at the crap you see on that blue channel on New York cable TV. Jeez, Sylvester Stallone once did a skin flick. Now he's the king. He not only dated that society broad, Cornelia Guest—he gave her the brush."

Lanham reached and snapped open his briefcase, taking out the photo of Wickham and Belinda St. Johns he had removed from Wickham's apartment.

"Did you take this?" Lanham said sharply.

This time Gorky managed the grin. It was far from sheepish.

"No, I didn't," he said. "But I wish I had. Who's the other lady?"

"If it's who I think it is—and we're pretty sure it is—she was on the cover of a fashion magazine last month."

"No shit. Where did you get ahold of this?"

Lanham took back the picture.

"If you see the lady, tell her I'll be happy to work with her anytime," Gorky said.

Vince Perotta would love to hear that.

"Do you ever work with video tapes, Mr. Gorky?"

"Sure. Especially for commercials. I'm shooting a tape next week. Dog food."

"Do you ever do pornographic tapes?"

Gorky spread out his hands. "Detective, hey. This is Gorky Productions now."

"When's the last time you talked to Molly?" Lanham said.

Gorky hesitated. "A couple of weeks ago. She always had trouble with her boyfriends, and she had big trouble with her latest. The feds were on to him for something and they came around to ask her about him. She asked me what to do. I told her not to stiff them."

92

"Do you know this boyfriend's name?"

"She never said. Some guy who lives in Washington and comes up every month or so. Some government type. The feds told her there was a problem about national security. I told her to level with them. I mean, she and this guy didn't spend a lot of time discussing Mideast terrorism or arms control, right? They drank and partied. He mostly drank. I told her to tell the feds everything, because all she really knew was how he liked her to hold his dick, you know?"

"Is that what she told them?"

"I don't know. I never saw her again after that until I picked up the paper this morning. What a miserable fucking way to get your picture on page one."

Lanham closed his notebook. "Okay, Mr. Gorky. Thanks for your time." He paused. "You don't drive a motorcycle, do you?"

"As a matter of fact, I do. It's a BMW. It's downstairs, in back. You want to see it?"

"I'll look at it on the way out. If you think of anything that might help us, let me know. We really want to nail this guy."

"Sure. And if you ever get a chance, see *The Last Round*. It's fucking terrific."

The motorcycle was bright red and the license number wasn't remotely like the one the witnesses had seen. In a way, Lanham was glad. He still liked Peter Gorky.

•

Newspaper morgues are the tombs of secrets. Events, happenings, utterances public and private, reports of arrests, confidential memos, and obscure trivia that might otherwise be lost and buried in the onrush of time are stored away like a pharaoh's treasures, awaiting the future moment when chance and curiosity prompt their rediscovery. A political career rising on a reputation for probity and respect for family values might fall victim to the fact that twenty years before a person of the very same name had been arrested on a morals charge and a reporter had recorded that occurrence in a two-paragraph filler item filed away with all the other published news of the day.

93

In an earlier era of newspapering, when yellowing clips were kept in metal file cabinets and morgue clerks more often than not ran bookie operations on the side and served as whiskey stewards for alcoholic staffers in need of a quick shot to get through a night or morning, a search through this archaeological pile could take hours. Once, when A.C. was still covering politics, he had looked through more than four hundred old photos in the morgue before coming upon the one he needed to prove a presidential candidate a liar.

With the advent of high-tech journalism, newspaper morgues had become "research centers" and the clerks "librarians" or "researchers." The old file drawers of clippings had become computerized data, and the most laborious search could now be completed in a matter of a few minutes.

A.C. depressed the button on the computer console that brought the Pierre (Pete) Delasante file to life. Another button activated the electronic process that allowed him to scan through the entire file, story by story. The first headline snapped into place at the top center of the green computer screen:

DELASANTE TRIAL SET

Pierre "Pete" Delasante, 46, the former White House aide charged with using his administration connections to help clients of his Washington consulting and lobbying firm, will go on trial July 29 before Federal District Judge Samuel Groen, it was announced by the Justice Department today.

Delasante, a onetime Columbia, S.C., college professor and congressional aide . . .

The story went on to relate how Delasante had been indicted that April after charges were brought by special prosecutor Warren Donovan alleging that Delasante had conversations with the White House and the Defense Department while he was representing several American defense contractors and the governments of Guatemala, Chile, and Paraguay.

Delasante had left his White House national security post

the previous September. While he had never been a high-ranking presidential aide on the order of Michael Deaver or Lyn Nofziger, two Reagan administration presidential assistants who'd fallen afoul of federal conflict of interest law, Delasante's was considered a more worrisome case because of his intimate knowledge of National Security Council workings, presidential national security priorities, and other classified matters.

Hastings Bellows Ltd., the multinational media conglomerate, had offered to buy Delasante's firm for a reported $7 million in March, but the offer had been suspended pending the outcome of criminal proceedings against him.

Delasante had admitted to a drinking problem, which had contributed to his leaving the White House, but his attorney, Cyrus Hall, said that would not be an element in his defense, as it was in Deaver's case. Hall said he intended to challenge the constitutionality of the application of the federal conflict of interest law to lobbying because it violated First Amendment rights to freedom of speech. He said a guilty verdict in Delasante's case would be appealed all the way to the Supreme Court, no matter what the financial cost.

Cyrus Hall, one of the most expensive lawyers in New York. Cyrus Hall, showing up at Mortimer's with Camilla Santee.

There were more stories about Delasante's legal troubles. His name also appeared in a short feature section write-up about a glitzy New York charity event he had attended. The only other item in the computer file was a brief sketch written about him in a group of profiles of new White House staff run in the *Globe* after the new adminstration had taken office. Delasante's said he was a graduate of Clemson University and had earned a doctorate at Duke. His Washington career had included serving as a staff aide on the House Armed Services Committee and later with the Severn Institute, a defense-oriented capital think tank. There was no record of military service, though Delasante had been of draft age during the Vietnam War.

A.C. could not recall ever meeting the man during his tour of duty with the *Globe*'s Washington bureau.

He reflected a moment on what he'd read, then pushed

95

the buttons that closed the file and began a printout. The *Globe*'s data search system had no access to any of the Carolina newspapers, whose files doubtless could tell A.C. much more.

What A.C. wanted to look at most were photographs. He shut down the computer terminal and went to the reference room picture file desk, putting down the names Pierre Delasante, Pete Delasante, and C.C. Delasante on the request form. It took the clerk some time, but she came back with five photographs, all of them listed under "Pete Delasante."

Two showed the White House aide accompanying the president as they stepped out of a helicopter on the White House lawn after a conference at Camp David. Another was of Delasante and several other people partying at a charity ball. The last two photos caught Delasante entering the federal court building in Washington for his arraignment. He was not handcuffed, but was flanked by lawyers and U.S. marshals. He'd been immediately released on bond.

The photographs were of a tall, slightly overweight, middle-aged man with dark, curly hair and heavy, black-rimmed glasses. There was a definite resemblance to the man at the fashion show. But A.C. could not be sure—not sure enough to declare them to be the same person in the public print.

There were rules, backed up by a substantial body of libel case law. He could not write in a newspaper column that the mystery man in the Wickham murder case appeared to resemble an indicted former White House aide. If the police said they had noted such a similarity and were looking for the man, he could print that. But he could not say that the police should be looking for such a man.

A.C. took his computer printout and the photographs back to his little office. He decided to save the matter of Pete Delasante for a future column. He certainly had enough for the column due that day—that Molly Wickham had once been a prostitute working Forty-second Street, that police were interested in talking to her former pimp, that one of the other models in the show was apparently

96

dating a reputed mobster. That the glamorous world of high fashion was not necessarily what it seemed.

Lanham had called this information "not for quote." He hadn't told him not to use it.

•

When he finished the column, he gave it the headline THE SECRET PAST OF MOLLY WICKHAM, hit the SEND button, then leaned wearily back in his chair and swiveled toward the broad expanse of window glass that looked out over the hot, shimmering city.

A.C. had always admired his view as one encompassing the magic, elegant world in which he lived and worked— the shining high-rise towers recognizable as the residences of friends and acquaintances, the streets stretching away to the north familiar for their shops and galleries and restaurants. When he looked down at the taxicabs and pedestrians below, he thought only of people he knew. He could imagine Theresa Allenby at that very moment, coming out of the Martha fashion salon on Park Avenue, or perhaps pausing at the Frick Collection on Fifth Avenue after a late leisurely lunch.

Now he saw more. There was every imaginable kind of person out in that jumble, doing every imaginable kind of thing—drunks in bars, derelicts crumpled in alleyways, thieves and pickpockets, drug addicts and panhandlers, prostitutes like Molly Wickham—all part of his shining city. Quite possibly, quite probably, there was someone just then dying on those streets, lying sprawled on the concrete, life's blood soaking into dirty cement, just like Molly Wickham's.

But there would be no newspaper column or screaming front page headlines about any such anonymous person. The death of a robbery victim or a loser in a domestic quarrel or a small-time criminal in harm's way was nobody's concern, as inconsequential as Molly Wickham's shooting would have been a few years and an address change earlier.

His telephone rang, startling him. Bailey Hazeltine would be in Philadelphia by then, playing Florence Nightingale to whatever freaked-out druggie it was who could lay such claim to her friendship. Perhaps she had decided she wanted no part of it. She could be returning home. She could be back by evening.

It wasn't Bailey. It was Kitty. She spoke very matter-of-factly. She sounded grim.

"A.C., I've changed my mind. I'd rather you didn't come up this weekend."

It was as though she had hit him in the face. "Why not?"

"Because I no longer think it's a very good idea."

"But it wasn't twenty-four hours ago that you asked me to come."

"That's not how I feel now."

"For God's sake, Kitty. We made plans. I wanted to take Davey sailing."

"Well, I'd rather you didn't. In fact, I'd rather you didn't see the children again until—until this is all resolved."

"Until what's resolved?"

"I have to face up to the question of whether I want to be married to you or not. I haven't decided exactly what I'm going to do, but in the meantime, I don't want to see you. I want you to stay away."

"I don't understand." It was a lie. But she couldn't possibly know about Bailey. Had the doorman said something to her? Had he been a fool for taking Bailey up to an apartment bought and paid for by Katherine Shannon?

"I don't know what's made you change your mind, but I think we should talk about this," A.C. said. "I thought that was the reason I was coming up this weekend."

"Oh, we'll talk, A.C. I think next week. My lawyer will call you to tell you when and where."

"Why your lawyer?"

"It will all be perfectly clear when we meet."

"But why disappoint Davey?"

"Oh, he can get through a weekend without you, A.C. He's done it enough in the past. And I'm sure you won't be lonely."

"What are you talking about?"

"Goodbye, A.C."

He held the phone for a long moment while the disconnected line made noises in his ear. Then he gently reset the receiver in its cradle.

The phone rang again, a little light in one of its two plastic buttons flashing on and off. It was Pasternak, the city editor, out in the news room. He had read A.C.'s just completed column.

"The *Daily News* says the police are looking for a white man, some guy in a limousine. In your column, you've got them looking for a black pimp."

"I got that from the detective in charge."

"Why don't you quote him?"

"He gave it to me not for attribution. I probably said too much as it is."

"What about the white guy?"

If A.C. told Pasternak about Pete Delasante, the man would set the staff on a reportorial binge, and A.C. would be caught up in it, possibly for days. He wasn't ready for that.

"What about him?" A.C. said.

"That's what I want to know."

"Why do you ask me?"

"Because you've been talking to the police. Because you're a witness to this murder. Because you're an employee of this paper."

"Okay. There was a white guy in a limousine. There were a couple of limousines there. The police want to talk to everyone who was anywhere near there. I don't think Vanessa and I were that much help."

"Well, you're sure as hell not much help to me."

"We have police reporters, don't we? I'm the society columnist. I have the fruitcake beat, remember?"

"I don't like your attitude, A.C."

Before his troubles with Kitty, Pasternak wouldn't have dared talk to him like that.

"Look. I want to help you as much as I can. But everything I know for certain is in that column. If I learn anything more, you'll be the first to know. But for now, let me get back to my art galleries and tea dances, will you? That's what I get paid for."

"Thanks," said Pasternak "for showing so much class."

A.C. locked his office and left the building, leaving a message with the receptionist telling Vanessa where she could find him. It was in a bar on Second Avenue, a shabby Irish saloon Bill Shannon would never dream of entering.

He was starting his second martini when Vanessa caught up with him.

"*Mon Dieu*, A.C.," she said, lighting a cigarette. "Are we going to have to put you in a dryer?"

"I'm just treating a hangover. I went over the edge last night. I'm telling myself it was because of the murder."

"Feeling the creepy crawlies, are you? Well, I didn't exactly dream about sugarplum fairies myself last night. I don't think *la belle* Camilla is doing so splendidly either. Her booker told me she canceled all her jobs today."

A.C. motioned to the bartender, who broke off his conversation with another customer at the far end of the bar.

"Gin and tonic," Vanessa said. She fanned herself with her hand. The moving air violently stirred her cigarette smoke.

"They're running your column on page one again," she said. "But everyone from Bill Shannon on down is a trifle pissed at you. They think you're holding back something to save for your next column and letting the other papers get ahead. The *Post* has a story calling Wickham a Sutton Place sex kitten with lots of boyfriends. The *Times*, bless it, has an editorial calling for increased police patrols in the neighborhoods around the park."

"My next column is going to be about chic new summer resorts, or where Ivana Trump last had lunch."

"Like hell it is. Have you tried to reach your friend the mysterious blond lady? The one who wears other people's clothes for a living?"

Someone had put money in the jukebox. Improbably, it began to play a Ray Charles record: "I can't stop loving you . . ."

"All day. No answer."

"You poor thing."

"Has she ever used another name besides Camilla Santee?" A.C. asked.

"Not that I've ever heard of."

100

"Think about it. Could she have used the name Dela-sante?"

Vanessa shook her head. "Not on any runway I've been next to. Where did you come up with that name?"

"Don't you remember that White House national security aide named Pete Delasante?"

"My dear, national security has so much to do with the fall collections."

"Delasante quit the White House to become a lobbyist. Now he's in trouble. Indicted for influence peddling. I think he was the fellow sitting behind me at the Philippe Arbre show. I think he was in one of those limousines outside the Plaza. And Molly Wickham was leasing her apartment from someone named Delasante."

Vanessa shrugged. Her drink came.

"Delasante sounds a lot like Santee," A.C. said.

"So does Santa Claus. Is it your brain that's doing all this heavy thinking, or the Beefeaters?"

"I think Camilla has something to do with all this. Or knows a lot about it."

"A.C. I think you're on a quick trip around the bend. You don't know anything about her. And even if what you say is true, it would only be all the more reason to stay away from her. Why don't you pretend that yesterday was just another day and Santee was just another pretty face on the runway. Then get on with your life. If you want to get hung up on a woman, why don't you make it a lady named Katherine Shannon James?"

"That particular lady doesn't even want to see me. She called up and canceled our weekend."

"If you're not careful, she's going to cancel more than that."

"You mean my job?"

"It's her newspaper."

"If I weren't a gentleman, there's a word I could use."

"The word is 'shit,' darling."

"I guess that's the one."

"Poor A.C. You've been king of New York all this time, and now it can all come apart with one yank of the string."

"Perhaps. Perhaps not."

101

"New York is an easy lay, sweetheart," she said. "Real easy. But it's got a way of kicking you out of bed."

•

Lanham and Petrowicz sat in Lanham's unmarked Dodge, listening to their police radio as they idly watched the night-life of the Deuce begin to stir and slither. They had parked on Eighth Avenue just south of Forty-second Street across from the Port Authority Bus Terminal. There was still a pale smudge of daylight in the sky, but the slime pit of the Deuce was already overflowing. Two hookers, one fat and white and the other tall and black, were lounging nearby at the doorway of an "adult novelties" store. A few yards down were the lurid posters and blinking yellow marquee of a porn movie theater: SEAR SUCKER! XXXXXXX!

"Ten Twenty-two," said a voice over the radio. It meant a theft was in progress. Another called in a Ten 53—a traffic accident up in the West Fifties. "Ten Seventeen" another car responded. He was en route to the scene.

Intermixed with all this chatter, testament to what passed for a dull night in the city, was the audible manifestation of Tony Gabriel's hunt for Bad Bobby. In language nearly as indecipherable as the Ten code, Gabriel and his assembled group muttered back and forth to one another—summoning each other to land lines when discreet communication was in order, checking frequently back with the dispatcher or with division headquarters for news.

There wasn't much. Bad Biker Bobby might as well have been in Jamaica. Perhaps he was.

"Shit," Petrowicz said, for the hundredth time that evening.

Lanham had called in a Ten—meaning out of the car for lunch—but they had just gotten a couple of burgers and some fries from a McDonald's and were eating in the Dodge.

Petrowicz crammed a handful of fries into his mouth and chewed them.

"I thought you didn't want anything to do with this bullshit collar," he said, his chewing not quite completed.

"Who knows—maybe Bad Bobby's got something interesting to say."

102

Petrowicz wiped his mouth with his balled-up napkin. "You ask me, Ray, I think this homicide is a shitcan. We'll never knock that perp."

"Right now, that's for downtown to say."

"You still think it's the boyfriend."

"That isn't what I said. I said we find the boyfriend, maybe we find out what was going down."

"What did Cassidy get out of the feds?"

"Nothing much, yet. Tony pulled him off the record search to help with this here Manhunt of the Century."

"Checking out the saloons."

"Well, Bad Bobby was known to like his malt liquor."

A black man turned the corner and headed toward them. Seeing them, he spun around and retraced his steps. It was no one they recognized.

"What if the perp is just an E.D.P.?" Petrowicz said, using the shorthand for "emotionally disturbed person."

"What if it's just some freako who has it in for black girls?"

"That's what has Joey T. so uptight. That's what's spooking the mayor. A white perp and a beautiful black victim. Maybe black victims. That's why they're hoping that somehow it could have been Bad Biker Bobby."

"But you think that's bullshit."

"When this Manhunt of the Century is over, I want to lean real hard on turning up the boyfriend."

A barely audible voice on the radio said something neither could understand.

"Ten five," said the dispatcher. It meant *say it again.*

"Ten six," said another unit. *Be quiet. You're tying up the airwaves.*

"G.F.Y.," said the first unit, with perfect clarity. *Go fuck yourself.*

One of the hookers, the tall black one, sauntered over to Lanham, who was sitting on the passenger side with his window rolled down.

"Are you two gen'lemen fixing to fucking bust us, or what?" she said.

Petrowicz gave her a mean look, then bit into another French fry.

"Consider us off duty," Lanham said. "Just having a leisurely meal after a busy day."

"Well, look, honey. Could you go find yourself some other corner to have your little picnic? My friend and I are feeling lonely, and nobody's stopped to talk to us since you pulled up."

She smiled good-naturedly, as though she was someone helping a tourist with directions.

"Get in," said Lanham. "In the back."

"Is this a bust?" she said, her expression wary.

Lanham shook his head. "Get in."

She snapped open the rear door and flopped onto the seat, pulling at the elastic of her tank top in a way that lifted her breasts provocatively. Petrowicz started the car and pulled out into traffic, turning right and heading east on Forty-second.

"If you're looking for a free hose job, shouldn't one of you public servants be back here?" she said.

"We're just interested in a little quiet conversation," Lanham said.

"Ain't you the fancy nigger," she said, making Lanham wonder how many times she'd been arrested. "You look almost like a suit."

"He is a suit," Petrowicz said. "Fordham University."

"Didn't know they had a basketball team," she said.

"You know Molly Wickham?"

"You mean that poor girl got herself in the newspapers the hard way?"

"A.k.a. Marjean Dorothy Wickham," Lanham said. "She used to work the Deuce just like you. You know her?"

"Sheeet. She used to be a working girl? Then there be hope for all of us, ain't there, sugar?"

"You don't want what she got," Petrowicz said.

They were passing the ridiculous billboard façade a previous mayor had erected in front of the Forty-second Street police substation as a symbol of city hall and friendly, neighborly municipal government. Resembling a stage flat, it depicted classical white columns against a blue background. Given its immediate surroundings, the effect was rather like decorating a slaughterhouse with bunting.

"She used to work for a man named Bad Biker Bobby, Bobby Darcy. He was in the joint, but he's back."

The hooker said nothing.

104

"You know Bad Bobby?"

She paused. "Everybody know Bad Bobby," she said softly.

"You work for him? You ever work for him?"

"Shit no. Lucky me."

"He cuts his girls," Petrowicz said.

"Cut? Sheeet, he stuck a couple."

"He was on the street today," Lanham said. "Did you see him?"

"Honey, now that you mention it, I don't think I ever heard of the man."

"Cut the bullshit," Petrowicz said. "You seen him, or what?"

"We just want to talk to him," said Lanham. "He may know who shot Molly Wickham."

"You know, sugar, you're about the tenth cop ask me about Bobby tonight. But I ain't seen him."

"We just want to talk to him, that's all."

"I don't care if you want to give him a million dollars. I ain't seen him. Not since he went to the joint. He ain't been around me. If he come by, I'd be someplace else real quick. And that's no shit."

Lanham handed her one of his snitch cards. On it was printed only the name RAY, and his direct phone line at the division.

"If you see him, just let me know," he said. "Won't bother you any further."

Petrowicz lifted up his hand. They were being summoned on the radio. "Ten Two." Call in to base. On a landline.

They were on Forty-second Street between Fifth and Madison. Petrowicz pulled abruptly to the curb.

"Okay. Out."

The girl hesitated. "Come on, sugar. In this neighborhood, I could get arrested."

"Out," said Lanham gently. "Suddenly we're in a hurry."

They found a public telephone that worked near Grand Central. Lieutenant Taranto wanted to talk to him. Tony Gabriel had just called in with the news. He had found Bad Bobby, or at least where Bad Bobby had gone to ground. A surveillance team was in place and everyone else was

105

coming back into the division. A late-night visit was in the offing, but it had to be planned.

•

The limousine was where he said it would be, parked at the curb on Fifth Avenue just ahead of the entrance canopy of one of the grander apartment buildings facing Central Park. Camilla hesitated. She would sooner have climbed into a vat full of slugs. But she had no choice.

She darted from the corner of the building and quickly slipped into the rear of the car. He leaned to kiss her cheek as she pulled the door closed, but she turned her head away.

"Don't touch me, Pierre," she said. Scarlett O'Hara could not have shown more disdain.

He frowned and eased back. He was dressed in a rumpled white linen suit, a certifiable affectation in New York and, nowadays, even in places like Charleston, South Carolina.

"How many years have we greeted each other that way?" he said. He smelled, as usual, of whiskey and too much cologne.

"Jacques is going to kill you, Pierre," she said. She spoke as matter-of-factly as she could, but her voice was tremulous. It was the boldest thing she had to say. She had rehearsed that line over and over.

"Not anytime soon, darlin'. I've seen to that. We don't need to go over it all again. Death before dishonor, honey. My death; his dishonor."

It was his attempt at a poor joke. His voice broke with the last line. He was scared, and now they both knew it. She could almost smell his fear all mingled with the bourbon and cologne.

The driver pulled away from the curb and headed south down the avenue. His name was Henry and he had the darkest skin of any black man Camilla had ever met. The glass divider was up, but she supposed it didn't matter if Henry heard. He was intensely loyal to Pierre—and very well paid.

"I'm not a man to threaten," Pierre said unconvincingly.

"I'm not threatening you, sir. I'm warning you. You saw

106

what happened to Molly. I'm scared to death myself. He's completely lost control. You've driven him to that."

It was unpleasantly warm in the car and the leather of the seat seemed to stick against the back of her knees and her thin cotton dress. He took off his glasses and wiped his face with a handkerchief, then unscrewed the cap from a large silver flask and drank.

"I am truly sorry for what happened to Molly," he said, finally. His voice was educated and Southern, a gentleman's voice, despite his appearance. But his speech was thickened from drink. "I never meant for anything like that to happen. I loved that girl. I truly did."

Camilla shuddered.

"That bothers you, doesn't it, Camilla?" he said.

"Not in the way you're thinking." She shuddered again, imagining Pierre and Molly Wickham together, seeing her once again dead, missing part of her head. "It's because of you she's dead."

He took another sip of the whiskey, then replaced the cap. The lights of the Plaza Hotel and the high-rises behind it glittered ahead. Just beyond was the floodlit spire of the Empire State Building. Elegant couples strolled along the sidewalk to their left, a few glancing at their long car as they passed.

Another glamorous night in New York. In the dreams of her childhood, she had ridden in cars like this, on nights like this.

She was sweating, and felt sick.

"You introduced her to me," he said.

"I regret it deeply. I regret the day I ever met her. I regret the day you were born. That any of us were born."

He stared hard at her, but she refused to let her eyes meet his.

"Did you bring the money?" he said, almost gently.

She reached into her handbag and pulled out an envelope. She tossed it on the seat between them, as though it were a filthy object.

"I want you to understand something, Pierre," she said, as he slipped the envelope into the breast pocket of his suit coat. "I'm giving you this because you give me no choice.

I'll go on giving you what I can, what you say I have to. But I want you out of my life. I don't ever want to look out into the audience in a show and see you again. I hate Jacques for what he did. But I hate you even more. You brought all this down upon us. I don't know when you're going to die, Pierre. But I will not grieve."

"That's no way to talk to kin, Camilla."

"Don't you dare talk to me about kin. If it weren't for Momma . . ."

"But you'll do anything for your momma, won't you, Camilla?" He patted the pocket where he had put the envelope. "You'll do anything I say."

"I'll pay you the money," she said. "But I want you to get out of New York—and stay out. I don't want you ever to come near me again."

"As a matter of fact, I'm going back to Washington in the morning," he said. "When I come back is my business."

"You just stay away from me."

The driver turned the car onto Fifty-ninth Street when they reached the traffic light at the end of the park. He passed by the Plaza, not fifty feet from where Molly had been killed. She wondered if he had been given instructions to do this—a gesture of bravado, Pierre Delasante, trying to prove that nothing fazed him.

"I think you should get out of the country, Pierre. I'm serious about Jacques. He's got no sense or reason left. He's all hate. He'll kill you in as awful a way as he did Molly."

"You and I will live to dance on his grave, Camilla. That boy is doomed—just like Danielle. If the police don't catch him, he'll get himself killed some other way. It's in his stars."

She covered her face with her hands. She couldn't endure this much longer.

"He killed the old nana, Pierre."

"I know. Poor old woman. But, Lord, she was older than the century."

"He says it was an accident. He was shaking her. He blames you. I think he's worked it out in his mind that killing Molly was an act of retribution. It's all twisted up

108

in his sense of honor. That's why I'm so scared he'll do it again."

"It won't do him any good. It didn't do him any good going down to see the nana, did it? He didn't find anything. I hear he tore the place apart and didn't find a thing. I don't know why he thought he would. Nothin' there but her hoodoo. He was just wasting his time. He killed that poor old nana for nothing."

He spoke very forcefully, with an earnestness that made her wonder if he was telling the truth. She'd known him all her life, but she didn't know him very well.

Reaching a roadway at Sixth Avenue that wound back north through the park, Henry turned onto it, the long car slipping into the shadows beneath the huge, overhanging trees. The headlights picked up a white horse-drawn carriage, plodding along at the side of the road. They swept by. A young man and woman were necking furiously in the back.

"I'm not leaving the country, Camilla. I'm going to see it through to the end. I'm going to win my court case. We have them beat on procedural grounds, not to speak of constitutional ones. The special prosecutor is just trying to make a little name for himself. He's going to be sorry."

"I talked to your lawyer."

"You what?"

"Cyrus Hall. Last night. I took him to Mortimer's. He said he's had enough money from you for now."

"I wish you hadn't done that."

"I didn't tell him anything. I just asked about the money. He said all his fees had been paid and that you'd given him a retainer for the future."

"Is that all he said? All you said?" Pierre was angry.

"All right. I asked him about—about family papers. I asked him if he was holding family papers for you."

"And what did he say?"

"He wouldn't tell me anything. Said he couldn't. Canon of ethics. What a peculiar term to have to do with you, Pierre."

"Well, I'll tell you, darlin', in case you and Jacques get the notion to go ransacking his office. He doesn't have them. All he has is my new will. I have three special bequests, Camilla. There are three letters, all locked away nice and tidy in a safe-deposit box in the Chase Manhattan Bank. If I die, they get sent to the society editors of the Charleston and Columbia papers and *Palmetto Coast* magazine. It's a generous bequest; instructions on how they can get themselves the biggest story they'll ever have in their lives."

"They wouldn't print such trash."

"Who knows what they'd do, honey, after they've seen what there is to see. Even if they didn't print a single little old word, they can talk. My, how ladies like that do love to talk."

"You despicable man."

"Despicable? At any rate, a smart man. And very serious. You get that across to Jacques."

They were all alone on the parkway now. She turned to look out the rear window. No one was behind them.

"I still need money, Camilla."

"Why? Are you just trying to ruin us? Is that what this is all really about? Are you just trying to drag us all down into the gutter with you, to have us begging on the corner of Meeting Street and Calhoun?"

"I need money for another reason, Camilla." He hesitated. A gurgle came from his throat as he swallowed nervously.

"For what? Are you planning to pay for poor Molly's funeral expenses?"

He laughed, a nervous crackle, followed by what might have been a sob. "It's real ironic."

Then the sobbing began in earnest. Camilla wanted to vomit. She clenched her teeth, and waited.

"I'm sorry," he said finally, but he still hadn't regained control over his voice.

"What are you talking about?" she said.

"Someone's doing to me now what I've been doing to you. There's a videotape."

"Videotape? Of you and Molly?"

"Of me and Molly. And Belinda. We had a little party, and things got out of hand. We were all drinking, and someone had cocaine."

"My God, Pierre. You're just a total heap of trash. You are the most indecent man who ever lived."

"There was someone else with us. Jimmy Woody. He's in the tape, too. It was a real long party. Lasted half the night."

Jimmy Woody was a male model. He worked for Philippe Arbre and they were lovers.

Jimmy Woody was black.

"He's in bed with Molly?"

"With all of us. With me. Like I say, it got out of hand." He coughed, and cleared his throat. He was breathing heavily. "I'm not that way, Camilla. Molly could have told you that. But they had the camera out and things were getting wild and Molly thought it would be fun."

"Fun."

"I was drunk, Camilla. You know I have a drinking problem."

"This was in my apartment?"

"Yes."

"Now I hope he does kill you."

"Damn it, Camilla! You're going to get everything back. It's just like I told you. I'm going to make it. I'm going to be back on top again. I still have my clients. They had to drop out of their contracts because of the publicity, but restoring them is just a formality once I get clear. Hell, the Guatemalan ambassador is going to be my guest at the Ford's Theater Gala. We'll be sitting just a few rows from the president himself."

He cleared his throat, and took some more whiskey.

"And when I sell my company, Camilla, I'll be worth millions. You'll get it all back, plus interest. Just like I promised you both. Word of honor."

" 'Honor.' "

"It still means something to me."

"What about the tape? It could ruin you in Washington. Who has it?"

"I'll take care of the tape. Once I get my legal problems taken care of. I'm not the only one who wants it destroyed. Molly was paying. She was afraid it would ruin her career if someone in the business saw the really bad footage. She had enough to hide as it was."

111

"Who has the tape? Belinda?"

He shook his head. His brow was covered with sweat. It glistened, even in the faint light of the street lamps.

"Belinda's paying, too. That boyfriend of hers would kill her in two seconds for something like that. Jimmy Woody's also paying. Philippe Arbre's in love with him. He'll see to it that Woody never works again if he sees that tape."

"Who has it, Pierre?" She sounded like a lawyer in court.

"I'll take care of the tape. You just take care of me."

She sat motionless, her hands folded in her lap. It seemed as though they were the last people left alive in the city as they rolled on through the night.

They pulled up at a red light, stopping pointlessly. There was no other traffic. Pierre was looking at her, much as she had looked at him at the fashion show, just before Molly's murder.

Camilla snapped open the door and got out. She stood a moment in the middle of the road, then hurried into the park, heading east. He called after her, but she said nothing more. She never wanted to speak to him again, to hear his voice again. She wished with all her heart that he would simply cease to exist.

She plunged on through the brush until she could no longer hear him. Once onto an open expanse of grass, she slipped off her shoes and began to run. It was no more than a hundred or two hundred yards back to Fifth Avenue. She encountered only one person who looked like he might have any interest in doing her harm—a young black man in an athletic jacket—but she took him so much by surprise in rushing by that she was well away from him by the time he took full note of her.

She had to clamber through brush again and jump from a fairly high wall to return to the Fifth Avenue sidewalk. She tore her stockings in the process, but it didn't matter. An absurd feeling of liberation came over her, as though she had left all her problems behind her in the park. The feeling lasted for several blocks, until she turned the corner onto her street and saw a man waiting outside her building. It didn't help that she knew who it was. It made it worse.

•

A.C. felt absurd and ridiculous to be lurking on the street at the girl's door, like a smitten schoolboy. He told himself he was merely being professional, that it was no different from the times when he and other reporters had camped out on the lawns of major figures in Washington scandals.

But it wasn't like that at all. His desire to see Camilla again had been with him all day. A.C. had tried her bell several times, having paused in between attempts for a drink at the nearby Stanhope Hotel. He should have left now that it was so late, but couldn't bring himself to do so.

He was surprised to see her coming from the direction of Central Park, instead of the livelier districts to the east. She came toward him like an ethereal vision, her extraordinary beauty rendered somewhat ghostly by the night. When she saw him, she did not slow. Rather, she increased her speed and lowered her head, as though to avoid looking at him.

"Miss Santee," he said, as she drew near. "I need to talk to you."

Her face was as impassive as a store window mannequin's. She kept walking, without speaking, and started up the steps to the door to her building.

"Miss Santee, please."

She was fumbling in her purse for her keys. "I'm sorry, Mr. James. I don't conduct interviews on the street, in the middle of the night."

She found the key and turned the lock. As the door opened, he stepped forward.

"Miss Delasante! Please. I really need to talk."

"What did you call me?" she asked quietly. Her hand was shaking slightly.

"Miss Delasante. That's your real name, isn't it? Camilla Delasante, or C.C. Delasante? You were Molly Wickham's landlord. And you're related in some way to a man named Pete Delasante, from Washington."

She came back down the steps and stood before him, rather defiantly.

"I don't believe I understand what you're talking about," she said. Her strange accent was very strong, its Southernness quite evident.

"I think you do."

Her blue-gray eyes held both fear and fury. They searched his.

"I think you do, Miss Santee. Miss Delasante."

She looked away, glancing down the street.

"And where did you come by this notion, sir?"

"I am a newspaperman. I put things together. That's what I've been doing all day. I don't mean to be rude. I know it must be irritating to find me waiting at your door, but I couldn't reach you by phone. I want to talk to you."

Her eyes came back to his. To his surprise, she put her hand on his arm.

"I'll talk to you, Mr. James, but not tonight, please. It's so late."

"When?"

"Tomorrow. I'll call you."

"Will you?"

"Yes."

"If you don't, I'll call you."

"You won't put any of this in the newspaper? Please?"

"I'll talk to you tomorrow."

Her hand came from his arm as though released by the flip of a switch. She turned from him without speaking. She paused once at the door, then slipped inside. He heard the door click as it closed behind her. He stared at the place where she had been.

At the end of the street, a taxi moving down Fifth Avenue passed along the shadowy darkness of Central Park. Behind him, somewhere in the city, a siren sounded and then was gone. He took a deep breath, reliving the past few minutes. The touch of her hand on his arm had affected him like a kiss.

The first blow struck him in the back of the neck, sending a pain down his spine and making his eyes see white. He tried to turn, but he was hit again—two quick punches in his lower back. He sagged, his knees crumpling, struck a fourth time on the side of his face. He fell forward, scraping his right cheek against the rough pavement. He tried to turn

114

over but was kicked in the hip and then again in his ribs. He wanted to cry out but all he could produce was a hideous moan.

"Leave her alone!" The voice was a man's. The words were uttered separately, and meanly. "Stay away from her!"

The last blow was a kick to the side of his head. A.C. did manage to roll over, but by then his consciousness left him in a drowning roar.

CHAPTER

6

The word had come from the street, from snitches, from people in the neighborhood. Bad Biker Bobby Darcy had taken up residence in a building just off Lenox Avenue north of Central Park. He'd been seen leaving and entering at least twice that day and his motorcycle was now in the first-floor hallway of the building. It was a black machine, similar to the one seen by witnesses at the murder scene, though the license plate bore a different number. License plates could be changed. It was just a matter of breaking the law.

Despite the late hour, a stereo inside the apartment was booming out raunchy blues music, the bass notes reverberating from the door. There was some laughter. The police were waiting for the noise to stop and Bobby and the others to go to sleep. They wished he were not a night person.

Bad Bobby was not yet an official suspect in the Wickham

case. The paperwork they had in hand authorized an arrest for questioning and for violation of his prison release agreement. But the team assembled for the arrest was worthy of a J. Edgar Hoover G-Man manhunt.

Tony Gabriel and Charley Caputo were positioned in the second-floor hallway, on either side of the apartment door, backed up by two detectives from the precinct and several uniformed officers. Pat Cassidy and another precinct detective were on the fire escape outside the window of the apartment's rear bedroom. Two uniformed men were in the alleyway below. More were on the street and one was on a rooftop opposite the building. There were too many cars on the scene and too many kids hanging around. The night was warm and the street was as busy as day. Bad Bobby could afford a telephone.

It was a black neighborhood beginning to go white. The Ninety-sixth Street corridor that City Hall had long established as an unofficial boundary between the affluent Upper East Side and the East Harlem ghetto was quietly and quickly being invaded by developers and speculators who had bought up most of the property along the north edge of Central Park. The high-rises would not be long in coming. In time, Central Park North would be an address to compete with Central Park West and South. It would offer spectacular views stretching the length of the park south to the towers of midtown. Lanham saw the day when luxury high-rises would cover Manhattan all the way up to the Harlem River. Then let the black people complain about substandard housing.

Lanham and Petrowicz were parked a block away from Bad Bobby's building, in sight of some of the backup units, but they were there to observe, not participate—unless something went wrong and their assistance was needed. Lieutenant Taranto had joined them.

"He's going to have ladies with him," Lanham said.

"He's a ladies' man," said Taranto.

" 'This is just for questioning,' you said."

"This is the third time you've reminded me of that, Ray. You could have had the fucking bust. You're the investigating officer."

"You could also call this off."

117

"We've got two guys from the D.A.'s office up here. They don't want to go home with nothing."

"I just want to go home," said Petrowicz.

They all needed a shave. Taranto's growth of beard was dark, Petrowicz's a reddish gold color. Lanham's stubble was already gone to gray, very light in color. If he were a full-blooded white man, he could have gone a couple of days without shaving before much was noticed. Against his brown skin, the beard was a silver sheen in the light from the streetlamp.

Lanham's skin itched. He also needed clean socks and a clean shirt. He was hungry again, though a little queasy from the coffee and cheeseburgers.

"I think we should all go home," he said.

"Cut the bullshit, Ray," Taranto said, lighting a new cigarette. "You can't tell me you'd close this investigation without having a few words with Bad Bobby."

"I'd talk to him, sure. I'd catch him on the street in a couple of days and talk to him. But this? I'll bet you're planning on a line-up and the whole damned show."

"Maybe. Can't hurt."

"Yeah, right."

The car radio crackled. Petrowicz answered it, then summoned Taranto.

"It's for you, boss. A patch from a landline."

The lieutenant got into the car. He spoke, then listened, then swore.

"Shit," he said, handing the microphone back to Petrowicz. "That goddamn *New York Globe* has a piece in tomorrow's paper saying we're looking for Bad Biker Bobby."

"Quoting who?"

"Quoting 'it was learned.' "

In the Plaza, Lanham had told A.C. James "not for quote." What did he think that meant? Where in hell had he been a police reporter, Southampton?

"In a news story, boss?"

"No, in that candy-assed society column your great eyewitness writes. Do you suppose Bad Bobby reads the society columns, Ray?"

"No, I don't suppose he does."

118

"Well, let's fucking hope not."

The first shot crackled and echoed. It was too loud to have been fired from inside the building, yet it had to have been. The echo vanished in a sudden roar and baffle of return fire. Taranto started running. Lanham and Petrowicz looked at each other, then followed.

•

Tony Gabriel was not six feet from the door when the first shot went off. He saw the wood splinter as the round went through and dug itself into the opposite wall with a puff of paint and plaster.

He fired his magnum several times through the door, kicked at the lock twice, then flattened himself back against the wall as the door swung open. He got off two more shots through the opening, then rolled through the doorway. Caputo followed him in, shooting. The two precinct detectives came after, emptying their pieces as Gabriel reloaded his, lying on his back on the floor.

There was movement to the right, behind a couch. Gabriel fired twice, then rolled to the opposite wall. More gunshots killed the stereo in mid-note.

"Tony!" shouted Caputo. "He's goin' out the window!"

Gabriel saw only an instant's black silhouette. It was gone before he could get off another shot. Cassidy and a precinct detective were out on the fire escape. They'd get Bobby. That was the plan.

The room was filled with gunpowder smoke and smell and all the lights were blazing, but it was eerily quiet. Gabriel got up slowly, keeping his back pressed against the wall, his big pistol held pointed toward the window. Caputo moved past him, stepping into the room.

Utter silence, then noise and shouts from out on the fire escape.

"We got an officer down!"

•

The apartment was full of uniformed men when Lanham and the lieutenant entered, Petrowicz following behind

119

them. Except for a sergeant already talking on the telephone, they were standing uselessly and stupidly. There were figures outside the window on the fire escape.

Furniture was overturned and whiskey was dripping onto the floor from a bottle that had been knocked over. There was a moaning coming from behind the couch, and then coughing, a woman's cough. One of the uniformed men was back there, kneeling.

Taranto pulled the couch away. A very tall, very naked black woman was lying curled up against the wall, clutching her knees. Blood was flowing from between them. Lanham could see one gunshot wound above her right breast. It was oozing blood and mucus that ebbed and flowed—what the military called a sucking chest wound. Her eyes were crazy with dope or pain or death. She was staring at them, but not comprehending what she saw.

"I called for an ambulance," the sergeant said.

"Where's Darcy?" Taranto said.

Before the sergeant could answer, Gabriel backed in from the window.

"Where's Darcy?" the lieutenant repeated.

Gabriel blinked. "Cassidy's dead."

"Shit!" said Petrowicz.

"Where the fuck is Darcy?"

Gabriel looked down at the moaning black woman vaguely, as though she were just an object out of place.

"He went up the fire escape," Gabriel said. "Pat took some rounds and a precinct guy got knocked off the fire escape in the alley. He may have broken his back."

"Did you order a pursuit?"

"Yeah. There's precinct guys all over the roof. Charley's up there." Gabriel was shaking.

Taranto snatched up the microphone from the portable of one of the uniformed men. He began shouting into it.

The black woman's arms lost their grip on her knees. Her legs slipped forward and open. The blood was spreading in a widening pool on the wooden floor.

Petrowicz eased past the others and went into the bedroom.

"There's another broad here," he said. "I don't think she's hit."

120

Lanham joined him, turning on a light. It was a white woman, a sallow blonde with long, pendulous breasts. She was also naked, sitting cross-legged on a bed, her back against the wall.

"She's okay," Petrowicz said. "More or less."

She was stoned to brain mush, less aware of the world around her than the dying woman in the living room.

Taranto was at his side. "I called a ten thirty-three," he said. "A ten thirty-three, a ten thirteen—every fucking thing."

Lanham looked back at Gabriel. Taranto did the same.

"They fired first," Gabriel said. "We saw the round come through the door."

Taranto rubbed his eyes and then lowered his hands, gazing bleakly at the giggling blond woman. He shock his head, and then lit a cigarette.

"If you had to wax one of the chippies, Tony, why the fuck couldn't you have taken out the white one?"

Now Lanham felt ill. It was the first time in years.

"Somebody get me the mayor's office," Taranto said. "They got a guy there waiting to hear from me."

•

A.C. heard people speaking. There was an old man's voice, speaking from high above him. More faintly, there was an old woman's voice. They were talking about him, discussing the blood on his face with some seriousness, but also with much detachment. He might have been some object they had come upon, or a corpse in a casket.

Nearer, he heard the tinkle of a tiny piece of metal. When it sounded again, he slowly, painfully opened his eyes and found himself looking into the face of a small white furry dog. Startled by his eyes, it skittered back and gave a quick yelp, then leaned forward again, sniffing and peering. It was on a leash and had a small metal tag hanging from its collar. Behind the dog, A.C. could see a man's legs—highly polished black shoes and gray flannel trousers.

He stirred slightly and felt a hundred kinds of pain in as many places. His head was resting against something firm covered by something soft. A cool hand was touching his cheek, a woman's hand. He could smell perfume, an expensive scent, the kind the women he lunched with wore. He was reminded of when he was a small boy and a friend of his mother's who always wore too much perfume would come into his room to kiss him good night. He had always slept so wonderfully well on those nights. He'd remembered that woman all his life. He closed his eyes, happy with the memory. Sleep came very near.

"Shouldn't we call the police?" the old man's voice said. The man repeated the entire sentence again, as though it were a philosophical question. "Shouldn't we call the police?"

"Haven't had a mugging in this neighborhood for years," the old woman said. "It would be terrible to have all that start up again."

"We should call the police," the old man pronounced.

"It's all right. I'll take care of it. He's a friend."

It was a young woman's voice, speaking very close to his ear. It was wonderfully familiar—the strange, aristocratic accent; the warm, mellow tone.

A.C. twisted his head, wincing, and looked up. There were Camilla Santee's wide blue-gray eyes, full of fear, sorrow, and an intense curiosity. She stroked his bruised cheek with her fingers, keeping the long nails away from his skin.

He wanted to lie there forever, but he slowly sat up, fighting dizziness. He wanted the old man and woman to go away.

"Are you all right?" he heard Camilla say.

"I don't know. I think so." His speech was mushy. His lower lip was swollen.

"I'll take care of him," Santee said. "Thank you for your help."

The old couple hesitated, then began to move away.

"You should call the police, dear," said the old woman. "We can't have this."

"Thank you," Camilla said. "Thank you."

She shifted and leaned to look at A.C.'s face, her eyes searching for serious injury.

"Did you see who did this to you?" she said.

"No. It was a man. Hit me from behind. Kept hitting me."

"Come inside. I want to see how badly you're hurt."

"Said I should stay away from you."

"I said the same thing, sir. Can you stand?"

"I'll try."

With her help, her arm around his waist, his arm around her shoulders, he managed it. He stood a moment, wobbly, his vision a little blurry. His ribs hurt, but he didn't think any were broken. His lower back hurt awfully.

"Do you know who it was?" he asked. "He said I should leave you alone."

"Let me get you inside."

She kept her arm around him until they reached the door and she had to busy herself with her keys. He managed thereafter on his own, hobbling after her into the apartment.

It was small and crowded with too much furniture. The walls were covered with so many paintings it was hard even to see the pattern of the wallpaper. There were bookcases everywhere, all full. It amazed him that a fashion model would have so many books—that she would have any.

Camilla took him to an overstuffed love seat with an expensive floral pattern, gently easing him into a reclining position with his head supported by a large cushion. If he was bleeding, she didn't seem concerned about stains.

"Lie still," she said softly. "I'll get something."

He listened as she moved away, down a short hallway to another room. He heard a cabinet door open and close, and then a drawer. Water was running, and then it stopped.

She returned quickly, kneeling before him, a wet beige towel in her hand. Her face was full of worry.

"Do you think you need to go to a hospital? Do you want to see a doctor?" She hesitated.

He had no idea. When he'd been shot in the leg in Northern Ireland, a doctor had come almost at once. No decision had been required of him.

"I don't think so."

Carefully, she pressed the cold, wet towel against his face. It was painful, but he did not cry out. She began to cleanse the torn skin. When at length she took the towel away, it felt as though part of his face came with it. There was blood on the towel, but much less than he had expected.

"You need something on this," she said. "All I have are Band-Aids."

Holding the towel uselessly, she rose. Noticing the window, she abruptly went over to it and pulled down the shade.

"If you want to go to the hospital, I'll take you. I hope you don't need to, but I will."

"I'll be all right." He said it as strongly as possible.

"I'll get something for you. There's a late night drugstore over on Lexington. Can you wait here till I come back? It won't take long."

"I'll be fine." He sat up. His mind was clearing. She looked so beautiful in the soft light of the table lamp.

"Is there anything else I can get you?"

"I could use a drink."

"Of course. I haven't much. I have some brandy."

"A brandy would be wonderful."

She went this time into the kitchen, returning with a very expensive bottle of French cognac and a large snifter. A jelly glass would have done. He supposed Camilla Santee wouldn't have allowed a jelly glass into her house.

He took a sip. "That helps."

"I'll be back as soon as I can. Don't let anyone in. Don't answer the phone. Just wait for me."

"A hundred years."

She smiled nervously, then took up her purse and left. There were three dead-bolt locks on her door and she turned them all from outside with her keys.

He sipped again. For all his pain, he felt like thanking and blessing his attacker. It seemed so miraculous that he was in her apartment, that she had touched him, that she was worried about him.

A third sip of brandy began to invigorate him. He let memory bring back the moments when she was kneeling by him, the joyous agony of her touch. He took a deep breath and closed his eyes. If he hadn't quite fallen in love, he was sailing away.

Minutes passed, then more. Lexington was a little more

than two blocks away. Had she taken a cab? How long could he reasonably expect her to be away?

Was his attacker her friend, or enemy? Was she safe? He got rockily to his feet, stretching his muscles. They all seemed to work, but with great complaint. He moved slowly about the room, studying her books and paintings.

The books were an eclectic collection. Many of the titles were in French. The paintings—mostly landscapes, one or two modernist—were all originals except for a large lithograph. There was only one photograph on the wall—a copy of a famous Man Ray nude portrait of the artist's favorite model, the legendary Kiki de Montparnasse.

The silver-framed photographs standing on the tabletops seemed mostly to be of friends and relatives. Two on the mantel of the room's small fireplace intrigued him. One seemed to be a family grouping. The other was of the face of a very old black woman. He limped over to it, taking his brandy glass.

The woman's skin was very dark, making the whites of her eyes seem almost luminescent. There were trees in the background, and water, with a man poling a flat-bottomed boat. It was an excellent photograph, worthy of Nicholas Nixon or another modern master. A.C. supposed it had been taken in Africa, or some backwater of the American South.

The family grouping was even more interesting. It was of six people, posed on the side gallery of an old and peculiar-looking house. In the center, seated in a white wicker chair, was a still beautiful woman in middle age, wearing a wide hat. She much resembled Camilla. Behind her was a tall, heavy man with dark, scowling eyes and a large, grimly set mouth, dressed in a white suit. Seated at the feet of the middle-aged woman on the top of the gallery steps was Camilla, wearing a garden party dress but no hat. Just below her was a dark, strikingly handsome man a little older than Camilla and a dark-haired sad-eyed girl, somewhat younger. The man was wearing a blazer and white pants and the girl a summery dress. They both resembled Camilla, but more strongly each other, and there was something of the older man's eyes in theirs.

125

Standing somewhat apart from the others, his hand on the banister, was Pierre Delasante. He, too, was wearing a white suit, but it was quite rumpled and his tie was loose at the collar.

A.C. picked up the picture, holding it toward the light. He studied Pierre Delasante's fleshy face, then looked again at the younger man's.

He shuddered. It was possible. If the detective had shown him this photograph, he might have identified the younger man as the one on the motorcycle. But he might also have picked the older man with the huge mouth. How would any of them look in a motorcycle crash helmet?

He could walk out now with this photograph. He could take it to the police. There was a lot he could tell the police now, and a lot he could tell his newspaper—Kitty's newspaper. His lack of professionalism in both regards was close to appalling. For a reporter not married to the boss, conduct like this could be grounds for dismissal. A week before, he could not have imagined himself keeping back information this way.

But a week before, he had not met Camilla.

A.C. glanced at his watch. She had been gone a little more than fifteen minutes.

He wondered if there was anything written on the back of the family portrait. The frame had swing clamps on the back. Setting down his brandy glass, he opened them, and carefully slipped the velvet backing from the frame.

Nothing was written on the back of the photo, but a piece of letter paper fell out from the backing of the frame. Faint creases showed that it had once been folded in three. The writing that covered most of it was in a woman's hand.

Some traits they had in common, traits springing from the creed of their race. They were brave, and truthful, and manly; to be otherwise would be disgrace. They were formal in address, but in society had the courteous ease of manner that comes from generations of assured position, and of living amongst one's peers.

To women they were charmingly and carefully polite; it was always chapeau-bas *in the presence of ladies. Mothers and wives were queens to sons and husbands;*

126

the slightest offence offered to them was cause of battle.
The men were, it must be confessed, quick of temper,
too prone to resent even a trifling wrong; both proud
and passionate, but generous and liberal to a fault;
faithful in friendship, but fierce in enmity.

The lodestar of their lives was "the point of honour."
A man's word must be better than his bond, because
unguaranteed. A woman's name must never pass his
lips except in respect; a promise, however foolish, must
be kept. If he had wronged any man, he must offer his
life in expiation. He must always be ready to fight for
the State or for his lady. This was the unwritten law
which made "the chivalry."

At the bottom appeared the name "Mrs. St. Julien Ravenel."

He puzzled over the passage, rereading it twice. If it related to the photograph, he could not imagine how. It rather seemed the code of some society, perhaps a secret one; from the sound of it, a very old society.

No one wore white suits anymore—certainly not in New York. The author Tom Wolfe did, but he was a TV talk show eccentric, carefully cultivating the image of a Richmond dandy set loose on the boulevards of Manhattan, though he'd grown up little better than a Virginia farm boy.

Virginia.

The South.

Pierre Delasante was from South Carolina.

A key was inserted in the door. A.C. hastily returned the paper to its place and, with some clumsiness, reassembled the frame. He had only just put it back on the mantel when the last of the dead-bolt locks was turned and the door swung open. He quickly leaned against the fireplace, almost as though striking a pompous pose.

Camilla's eye caught the photograph, then fixed on A.C. He wondered if he had positioned it correctly.

"You seem better," she said.

"The brandy helped."

He pointed to the picture of the old black woman.

"That's a wonderful photograph," he said.

"It's a wonderful face."

"Is that Africa?"

"No. It was taken on one of the sea islands in South Carolina. She's an old Gullah woman. Those people have been in America for three centuries, but they haven't changed much. They're very poor, but very proud. I'm afraid they're in for a hard time, with all the resort building going on down there. It's destroying everything. It makes me so sad."

"Who took the picture?"

She hesitated. "I did. I used to spend a lot of time on those islands. Now sit down." She raised a plastic drugstore bag. "I'm going to fix you up."

There was a hard edge to her voice now. She seemed all business. He had ceased to be an object of concern and had become nothing more than some unpleasantness to be gotten through. Still, she helped him off with his suit jacket. Though it was torn, dirty, and bloodstained, she treated it with great care, as she doubtless did all clothing—as was perhaps to be expected of someone who could completely change clothes in less than a minute without damaging anything.

He seated himself, hunching his shoulders against the pain as he did so.

"Lean back," she said. She shook the contents of the bag out on the side table and then tilted the lampshade, bathing the side of his face in light. "You're a mess, Mr. James."

"It wasn't my idea."

"I know. I'm so sorry." She frowned. "I got the strongest antiseptic they had. You have a bad cut there. It's stopped bleeding, so I don't think you need stitches, but you need something."

"Go ahead."

"It's going to hurt." She first went over the injured skin with a cotton ball soaked in rubbing alcohol, and the pain from that reached all the way to his fingers. By the time she got around to the bandages, his flesh was so numb he felt only a slight burning, as though a cinder had fallen along his face.

He was brave about all this, but she seemed not to notice. She put one last adhesive patch on his cheek, then leaned back, sighing. She studied him wearily.

128

"Where else did he hit you?"

He grinned. It pulled at injured skin.

"It seems like most everywhere. He kicked me in the side. And my back."

"Take off your shirt and tie."

He hesitated, curious.

"I know what broken ribs are like. My brother's had them. He gets kicked by horses. I'll help you."

She leaned close to do so, her hair swinging close, her perfume an enveloping vapor. Her lips were but inches away. He sensed no invitation, but could not ignore the urge or the opportunity. She was startled by his small, simple kiss, but did not resist; her lips, very gently, responded. She pulled back, but not far.

"Mr. James . . ." Her eyes were very wide, mirroring his. He wondered how he must look to her.

Stiffly, he put his hand to the back of her neck, her silken hair flowing over his fingers.

"You're the most beautiful woman I've ever met," he said softly.

She was studying him as closely as he was her. "You don't know me," she said.

"You're in trouble. I want to help you."

"I know you do. You were so nice to me in that bar. I was, I wish . . ."

He pulled her gently forward. Her eyes closed as she came near. Her lips were slightly open when they came to his again. There was pain when her head and shoulder came against him, but he held back all complaint, kissing her softly, over and over.

She moved, slipping even closer, her lips leaving his, her face pressed lightly against his neck and shoulder. He felt her muscles quiver, then relax, felt her breasts against his chest. But she did nothing further. A.C. stroked her hair, then moved his hand to her back, feeling the warm flesh beneath the thin cloth. He hurt like crazy everywhere, yet his head was swimming with pleasure and happiness.

He let his hand slide lower. She sat up abruptly, but carefully.

"This won't help," she said quietly, brushing back her hair. A long strand fell back over her eye.

129

"I'm sorry," he said. "I didn't mean to . . ."

"No, no," she said, touching his face. "You've been a perfect gentleman, Mr. James. I—I needed to be held. I'm really quite alone. I'm awfully scared. I've been through this before. I've seen violent death. It terrified me. I never ever wanted to go through anything like that again, and now . . ."

She eased back and stood up, straightening her dress.

"There's nothing you can do to help me," she said.

"Don't be so sure."

"No. Absolutely. Please. I'm very grateful. I don't know you at all, but you seem so nice. I must confess that, when we were all at the police station, you struck me as, well, you reminded me of the image I used to have of the man I'd hoped I'd meet when I first came here. I think you must be at least a little like that. *Un vrai gentilhomme.* Like your friend said."

"She's a nice lady. So are you."

Her face clouded. "You're married." She glanced quickly at her own left hand. It bore no ring.

"Yes," he said, with a sigh, as though he were admitting some wrongdoing, which it dimly occurred to him he was.

"Do you have children, Mr. James?"

"Yes. A boy and a girl."

A small smile came briefly to her lips. "I'm glad for you. I should love to have children." A frown quickly followed. "You should go home now. Go back to them. And for their sake, for your sake, please stay away from me."

"I can't go back. Not now. My wife and I are . . ." He paused to reach for his brandy and take a steadying sip. "Well, for the moment, we're living apart."

"I'm sorry. But you should leave. It's dangerous for you to be with me, to be anywhere around me."

"Why is it dangerous?"

"Look at you! He might have killed you!"

"Why?" He glanced at the photograph on the mantel. "Who is 'he'?"

She stepped back into the middle of the room. "I don't think you have any broken bones. You would have cried out when you held me."

That he never would have done.

130

"Who attacked me, Camilla? Was it your cousin, Pierre?"

She shook her head, reaching for his shirt. "Get dressed now. Please." She held the shirt for him.

He grunted as his arm went into the sleeve. Mustering his strength, he put his jacket on himself. His tie went into his pocket. He noticed that the knuckles on his right hand were scraped and swollen.

Despite some dizziness, he stood. Nodding toward the mantel photograph, he said, "That young man in the picture. Is he your brother?"

"I'm going to call that cab now." She went to the phone.

"Is he the one who attacked me? Is your family mixed up in Molly Wickham's murder?"

Ignoring him, she dialed an apparently familiar number, ordering a taxi. When she hung up, her hand was shaking slightly. She moved to the door, waiting as he finished his drink. He came toward her.

Her hand went to his arm. "When the cab comes, I'll see you safely into it. I don't want you going out onto the street alone. I want you to go straight home."

He sighed again. "All right."

Camilla held both of his arms now. He saw that tears were coming into her eyes.

"Do you really want to help me?" she said.

"Yes. Of course. Anything."

"Then promise me that you won't say anything to anyone about this. That you won't write anything in your newspaper."

"Of course I won't write anything, but . . ."

"Promise me. Your word as a gentleman."

It was a stern command. "I promise you."

She moved to the door, unlocking the dead bolts and placing her hand on the knob, ready to pull it open the instant the cabbie arrived.

"Will I see you again?"

"Yes," she said, weakly, sadly. "I hope so. Sometime. But not now."

"The police will likely want to talk to both of us again. If there's a trial, we'll have to testify."

"There can't be a trial," she said.

The door buzzer rang, and she pulled it open.

"May I call you?"

"No."

"Will you call me?"

"Please, Mr. James. Just go home."

At the curb, in farewell, he tried to kiss her again, but she turned her head, allowing him only her cheek. In the fashion business, people kissed cheeks when being introduced.

•

Once safely home, he poured himself a glass full of whiskey. He was sick of drinking, but thought he could tolerate one more, hoping it would bring on sleep and push away the pain a little. He was desperately weary. He had to get on with his life the next day, a life that, for better or worse, now included Camilla Santee.

Sleep came quickly, rolling over his jumbled thoughts like a thick sea fog. Sometime later—he couldn't tell whether it was only a few minutes or several hours at first—he was jolted into wakefulness. The phone was ringing. It was after four A.M.

A growly voice on the other end muttered something about the Philadelphia Police Department. He was gone before A.C. could respond. In a moment, Bailey came on the phone. She sounded defiant, but very scared.

"A.C., they've got me in a jail!"

"Jail? What happened?"

"I've been busted. I was with my friend. His apartment was full of junk. Somebody tipped the cops. For God's sake, A.C., I didn't do anything. I was just there! But they busted me. They dragged me out of there in fucking handcuffs!"

The growly voice could be heard again, admonishing her.

"All right!" she said, to the policeman. "A.C., I need money. To make bond."

"Are you okay?"

"Okay? I'm in a goddamned jail! A detention room at some fucking night court. I need to make bond. It's twenty-five thousand dollars. I need, I . . . What? I need ten percent. That's—I need twenty-five hundred dollars."

He gulped some of his drink, coughing.

"Twenty-five hundred dollars," he repeated.

"I can't call my mother. She'd just laugh. My brother's traveling. My husband will kill me if he finds out. A.C., can you help me? Please? It's just bail. I'll get it back after I get all this straightened out. But I've got to get out of here!"

"I'll get you the money," he said. "Where should I send it?"

She asked the policeman, then relayed his instructions. Holding a pen stiffly, A.C. wrote them down.

"I'll have to wait until the bank opens," he said. "I'll be there the minute it does. Just hang on until then. Are you sure you're all right?"

"Yes. God, I love you, A.C. Why didn't I marry you?"

The policeman terminated the conversation.

A.C. hung up and stood quietly, looking out the window at the city. Twenty-five hundred dollars was nearly all he had in the bank.

CHAPTER

....

7

It began to rain just after sunrise, the first pink light of day quickly obscured by a veil of low, gloomy clouds. A growl and snap of thunder left Lanham fully awake.

His few hours of slumber had already been interrupted once that night. There'd been a call from Taranto, who was apparently beyond sleep. He wanted to know how Mrs. Cassidy had taken the news that her husband's torso had been jellified by four or five rounds of .357 Magnum heavy-load ammunition without doubt fired by his fellow police officers. Or so he said. The lieutenant had really just wanted to talk—to a friend. The conversation had wandered. Lanham wondered if Taranto was in trouble. Maybe they were all in trouble.

Lanham did not feel friendly. He needed sleep to the point of happily killing for it, and he had told the lieutenant so. Taranto had kept talking anyway. When Lanham had finally hung up the phone, Janice had risen abruptly from beneath the sheet like a mummy in a horror movie. She'd been listening, and seething. She'd exploded the instant the receiver had been cradled. Janice had been impossibly calm when Lanham had come home with his sorrowful news. She'd given him a beer and then had gone to bed.

After Taranto's call, she'd turned into a madwoman, shrieking and swearing at him, flushing out fifteen years of fear and anger and frustration as she railed at the police lieutenant who dared call a detective in the middle of the night and screamed at Lanham for letting him do it.

Lanham knew what she was really saying. He knew that Pat Cassidy's ugly death had scared her horribly, that she had gone to her pillow with her mind full of bloody images of himself lying in a bloody heap on some fire escape. Their marriage had brought endless trouble into her life and this was the worst of it.

He'd let her rant and scream until she was weak from it. He heard stirrings from his sons' rooms but they had not intruded. They'd been witness to this before.

When Janice was done, she'd thrown herself back onto her pillow and rolled away from him, her stiffened back a fortification.

Lanham had lain there, silent and still, listening to her breathing until it became that of sleep. He'd become sensitive to irony in his job, and there was some in this. Mrs. Cassidy had scarcely reacted to the news at all. She'd been drunk, as she likely had been most every night Cassidy had been alive.

Detective First Grade Raymond Lanham had done a cowardly thing. Having volunteered to bring the dreadful tiding to the new widow, he'd first rousted out the Cassidys' parish priest and brought him along with every intention of sticking the good Father with the entire weepy mess at the first sign of sob or tear.

But all the bereaved Mrs. Cassidy had done was sink back into her chair, mutter some vague word of sympathy for her dead husband, and pour herself another big, sloppy drink. She'd offered Lanham and the priest some of this same solace. Lanham had declined but the priest had not. Lanham left the two of them to it.

He'd gone to sleep with the memory of how shabby Mrs.

135

Cassidy had looked—thin arms sticking out of a raggedy-sleeved old robe; thin white legs and knobby bare feet splayed out on the worn, dirty carpet. He remembered his own Irish mother sitting like that, looking like that, after his father died.

In the morning, Janice didn't speak a word to him. He was just as glad.

On the way in, the rain came and went and came again and stayed. Lanham had a minor accident on the Queensborough Bridge and got soaked arguing with the driver of the car that had hit him from behind—an argument that had swiftly ended when he showed the man his shield instead of a driver's license. The damage to the police car was negligible. Lanham let the man go, leaving him to curse his broken headlight.

The squad room was crowded with detectives who had found in the rain occasion to give sudden priority to back paperwork. Out of habit, Lanham brought a cup of scalding, steamy coffee to his desk, hanging his suit coat carefully on the back of a chair to dry and seating himself wearily. It was jungle hot and he hadn't the energy to pick up the telephone. Petrowicz, seated opposite, was engaged in a conversation on his. He nodded toward Taranto's office, where the lieutenant was talking to two men in big-shouldered suits Lanham didn't recognize. Petrowicz mouthed the initials "I.A.D.," then resumed talking to his caller.

Gabriel and Caputo were not there. Their desks looked untouched from the previous day. A stack of newspapers was on a nearby table—that morning's on the top.

The *New York Times* played the Bad Biker Bobby debacle on the front page of its metropolitan section, using the phrase "gun battle." The tabloids, predictably, were more flamboyant. PIMP FLEES IN SHOOTOUT, said one. TWO DIE IN COP SHOOTOUT, said another. The *New York Globe* had gone bananas: MODEL KILLER STRIKES AGAIN.

Lanham swore. Petrowicz hung up his phone and looked bleakly at his partner.

"What's going on?" Lanham asked.

"Nobody's told me a fucking thing."

"What does the I.A.D. want?"

136

"Just looking for another chance to be assholes. The assholes."

Taranto and the two men from Internal Affairs were still deep in serious conversation. Lanham read through the *Globe* story. He couldn't find the Bad Bobby column by A.C. James that had run in the early editions. It had likely been killed when events overtook it.

The news story that replaced it contained a lot of references to "police said" and "according to police sources," but no police names.

There was much Lanham needed to do in proceeding with the Wickham murder investigation that morning. He'd been compiling a list of skin magazines published in New York that might have bought or been interested in the kind of photo Lanham had found in Wickham's apartment. He wanted to find out how far Cassidy had progressed with his computer records and fingerprint inquiries with the New York FBI and Albany. He wanted very much to talk again with Belinda St. Johns and Philippe Arbre—and with that blond ice princess, Camilla Santee.

But he wasn't even going to speak Molly Wickham's name until he had talked to Taranto.

So he turned instead to the pile of phone messages, reports, and memos that had accumulated since he had left the previous afternoon.

The head to his decapitated "Cuppy" had been found—in a subway restroom. Better, it had already been identified. It was part of a cadaver that had been stolen the week before from a medical lab supply house on the West Side. It was high school graduation time. Maybe some kids had been having a little weird fun.

Another Manhattan cab driver had been shot, but not fatally. The jurisdiction belonged to a different division and there was justification for sliding the taxi murders over to them.

There was good news. A hitchhiker had been picked up on the Connecticut Turnpike who fit the description of a suspect wanted for the murder of a wino found behind the Central Park Zoo earlier that spring.

And there was bad news. An appeals court had overturned the conviction of a Fifth Avenue jeweler Lanham had arrested

137

for strangling his wife. It was one of the cleanest investigations and collars Lanham had ever made, with two witnesses to the man's dumping the body, but the court found that the man was Austrian and threw out the charges because Lanham hadn't had him Mirandized in his native tongue.

Lanham took a sip of the hot, bitter coffee, not minding when some of it spilled on the district attorney's advisory memo. The jeweler had probably hired Claus von Bülow's lawyer.

He was hungry. Janice hadn't even left out a stale doughnut for him. In the past, even when they'd been fighting for days, she always provided him with some sort of breakfast.

The two I.A.D. men stood up, one of them picking up a file folder and putting it in a slim briefcase. They left Taranto's office with minimum protocol and spoke to no one walking out of the squad room. In their world, all cops were potential criminals.

Taranto had closed his door again but Lanham walked in as though invited and took the chair directly opposite the lieutenant. He folded his hands and leaned slowly back, not speaking. Taranto's face was full of sorrowful displeasure, but his voice was calm, even friendly.

"Sorry to wake you last night, Ray."

"No big thing." Lanham paused, then spoke very quietly. "What do we have on last night, boss?"

Taranto raised his hands in an Italian gesture of philosophical acceptance. "We got a lot of hurry-up work done," he said. "The complete ballistics report isn't back yet but the postmortem's done."

"So what do we have?"

"The victim, a female Negro named"—Taranto consulted a notepad—"Joyce Ellen Henry, was DOA at the hospital. The blonde, no ID on her yet, is down at detox in Bellevue, climbing the walls. It'll be a week before she figures out what year it is. The precinct detective, Maurice Stone, he's gonna be okay. He's got a broken ankle and a sprained back, but nothing worse."

"And Pat?"

"Hit four times. One superficial. Three in the heart and lungs. Hamburger."

"Tony killed him."

"Or Charley, or one of the backups. Or all three. We haven't matched all the rounds yet."

"And the round through the door?"

"We got the slug. It's a semi-wadcutter, from a thirty-eight special."

"Police issue."

"Pat's gun had one round fired."

"He got careless or scared, and let one fly," Lanham said. "So everyone came in firing."

"He had a point-one-four blood alcohol, Ray."

"The drink that finally cost him."

"There was an unidentified thirty-eight on the living room floor. No prints. Two rounds fired."

"One of Tony's drop guns."

Taranto shrugged. "No prints."

"So we've got two people dead and all the rounds fired were from cops. Just like that Chicago Black Panther raid in sixty-nine."

"That's conjecture, Ray."

"Conjecture."

"Conjecture's your job. You're welcome to it. But that's all it is."

"Where are the preliminary reports?"

"Already downtown. Including my copies."

"What was that you gave the I.A.D. guys?"

"I gave them what hadn't gone downtown yet and now they're going downtown."

"Are you going to put Tony on restricted duty?"

"What?"

"Automatic procedure. You got a dead civilian on your hands. Are you going to pull Tony's service weapon?"

"We don't know who shot who yet. Anyway, it's not up to me."

The two men stared at each other for a very long time. They searched each other's eyes, but neither found what he was looking for.

"The mayor's holding a press conference at noon," Taranto said. "The mayor, the commissioner, and the chief of detectives. It ought to be a hot one. The captain thinks he's going to chew on the *Globe* for running that column. The big tip-off that blew the collar."

139

"We don't even know for sure that Bad Bobby was in that apartment," Lanham said.

"He's a very wanted man, Ray. We got a citywide, a three-state APB, and an FBI stop."

"I've got some other leads, boss. Good leads."

"I'd be real surprised if you didn't, Ray. But Bad Bobby's got priority."

What friendship there was in their eyes vanished.

"He won't be easy," Lanham said.

"The street'll cough him up. His friends oughta know by now that we're pretty fucking serious about this."

"He won't be easy even if he's on his own."

"Well, we're not social workers."

Lanham drummed his fingers lightly on the edge of the desk, then thumped it, decisively.

"I'll take him," he said. "If there's a draw, if he gets run into a corner, I want to be the arresting officer."

Taranto smiled. His relief was visible. Black on black. The mayor would be pleased.

"Well," said the lieutenant. "It's your case, isn't it?"

"You know how much I think this has to do with my case."

"Whatever you need, Ray. You got it. You got the whole department."

"I want him alive, boss."

"You run the show. Anything you want."

"I suppose you've got the squeeze put on the street, hard."

"We'll have every tit and testicle on the Deuce black and blue by the end of the shift."

Lanham stood up. "I'll carry a portable. Before they call a Ten Thirty-three, they call me."

"You got it. The mayor's press conference is going to be live on the noon news. You want to watch it here?"

He jerked a thumb at the cheap black and white television set on the shelf behind him.

"No thanks." Lanham opened the door, then paused. "Boss, tell me you weren't serious when you said you wished Tony had killed the white girl instead."

"I didn't mean to say it, Ray. I was thinking out loud. It was a screwball thought. I wish Tony hadn't killed any-

140

one, and I sure as hell wish nobody had killed Marjean Dorothy Wickham."

"Or that she was just another hooker."

"What?"

"Just thinking out loud, boss. A screwball thought. Forget I said it."

•

When he got up, A.C. did the bold thing and went directly into the bathroom to confront the face that awaited him in the mirror. It was injured—bruises and crusted blood as extensive as he had expected—but not hideous.

His looks continued to amaze him. Unlike his son, Davey, who had received a bountiful inheritance from his mother's beauty, A.C. had not been a particularly attractive child—too skinny, gangly, and narrow of face, his long, straight nose too dominant. As a young man, he had not much improved, but with the accumulation of years, and the scars, weight, creases, and exposure to weather and experience that came with them, his face had filled and assumed a likability and character that surprised him. The wear of life had added rather than diminished. It had never occurred to him that he would one day come to look like this, that he would become as attractive to women as he had, that he would have such a remarkably satisfactory life—until now.

Kitty was beginning to find small wrinkles gathering at the corners of her eyes, and a few fine lines about her mouth. They were nothing to him; they made her no less dear to him. But they frightened her. She had begun to speak unkindly of younger women.

She would certainly not speak kindly of Camilla Santee.

A.C. got through the rest of the morning on aspirin, a couple of vitamin pills, a quick Bloody Mary, and more strength and forbearance than he'd thought he possessed. The bank people were difficult, treating him as little better than a derelict until he found a bank officer who knew him. The Western Union girl made trouble over the money order, sending it only after he'd shown her three different pieces of identification, spelled out the word "certified" for her as he held the check in front of her face, and asked to

141

see her supervisor. "New York's last gentleman," Vanessa had called him. Now there were none.

Later, it took him several phone calls to reach the right person at the Philadelphia Police Department, but finally the receipt of the money was acknowledged. They refused to bring Bailey to the phone, however. He left a message for her to call as soon as possible.

The city room was a mirror, his injuries reflected in the curiosity, concern, and dismay of the staffers who looked up as he walked through. Vanessa was not at her desk. City Editor Pasternak was at his, and he summoned A.C. over as disdainfully as he might a copy clerk.

"We had to kill your column," he said. "It looked kind of out of date and stupid after the shoot-'em-up."

Stupid? It had been prescient, pointing to the police interest in the black pimp while the other papers had gone with the mysterious white man in the limousine. Prescient, but wrong. Having seen the photograph on Camilla's mantelpiece, A.C. was certain that Molly Wickham's killer was no black man.

"No problem," A.C. said. Those were two more words than he wished to speak to Pasternak that morning. He started to walk away, his step awkward because of his painful ribs and back.

"What can you get us today?" Pasternak said. His voice was almost a growl.

A.C. stopped and turned slowly. He remembered the large pile of invitations on his desk. "There's an opening at the Whitney," he said. "Robert Kotlowitz."

"Kotlowitz?"

"He's an artist. A famous artist."

"This is news?"

"This is a column. Jackie O. may show."

"That's what you always say," said one of the news editors sitting nearby. He smiled to show it was a joke.

"What can you do for us on the Wickham story?" Pasternak said.

Now began a chain of lies. "Nothing. I haven't talked to the police since yesterday. I don't expect to anytime soon. I've told them all I know and I've told you all I know. Now, if you'll excuse me, I've got some work to do."

142

"You're going to write about some dingbat artist when we've got a murder like this? And you're an eyewitness? And you knew the victim?"

"I haven't seen the victim since it happened. And the artist's name isn't Dingbat; it's Kotlowitz. Please. If I hear anything, I'll let you know. If there's any way I can help you, I will. But right now I'd like to get on with my job." He might have added, "While I still have it."

"What happened to your face?"

"I cut myself shaving."

The sarcasm only provoked Pasternak, who couldn't stand not having the last, triumphant word in any confrontation.

"I know you've been putting in some bar time, A.C., but I never figured you for a brawler. They don't have brawls at Mortimer's, do they? They have tiffs."

"What they have, Mr. Pasternak, is class."

He left ignoring whatever it was Pasternak finally thought up as a rejoinder. The two had begun as reporters together, and had even been friends. But Pasternak hated rich people, and had hated A.C. ever since he had become one by marrying Kitty.

Out of habit, A.C. paused at the windows of his little office. The city was unbearably dreary. Clouds obscured the tops of the high-rises and the rain-wet sidewalks were nearly as dark as the asphalt streets. Wearily, he went to his desk and pulled out the invitation to the Kotlowitz exhibit. First, he made phone calls. The Philadelphia police said Bailey had been released, but had left no message for him—adding that they were a lockup and not a message center. There was nothing on his home answering machine. There were no messages for him left with the *Globe* switchboard. Vanessa still had not returned.

He clicked on his computer terminal, staring at the blinking cursor.

A few flicks of the keys and he could have the newsroom in an uproar: "Dead Model Linked to Indicted White House Aide," "Blond Mystery Woman Love Nest Landlord," "Globe Columnist Beaten."

If he put any of this into the newspaper, his attacker might not be satisfied with a mere beating.

143

And he'd never see Camilla Santee again.

He looked at his watch and stood up. Maybe Jackie O. would show this time.

·

She didn't, but Vanessa did. A.C. had left a message for her with the copy clerks inviting her to lunch at the Carlyle Hotel and asking that she join him at the museum. She caught up with him as he stood pondering one of Kotlowitz's abstracts, a plastic glass of white wine in his hand.

"That painting looks like your face, sweetheart," she said.

"I saw her last night," he said.

"Your wife? Kitty?"

"No. Camilla Santee. I went to her apartment."

"And she did this to you?"

"No. She's very nice, as nice as she is beautiful."

"Have you two named the date?"

"I only kissed her."

"The rake's progress. Next you'll be holding hands."

"I'm just trying to help her. In any event, I don't think I'll be seeing her for a while." He moved on to the next painting.

"At last, wisdom. You still haven't explained what happened to your face."

"I was mugged. On the street. It had nothing to do with her." Another lie.

"Is this what you wanted to see me about, chéri? Why you had me come all the way up here? A kiss and a mugging?"

"No," he said. "I really am going to take you to lunch. At the Carlyle."

It was a block away.

·

Rated the best hotel in America, and one of the five best in the world, the Carlyle offered discretion, civility, and old-fashioned elegance compatible with its Upper East Side

144

surroundings and clientele. It served old-money people the way the Plaza did glamour and glitz. When they started shooting fashion models outside the Carlyle, then A.C. would know civilization was in trouble.

Its restaurant was small but had an equally considerable reputation. A.C. was known there, and given his favorite table near the large fireplace that dominated the room.

"This is all very nice," said Vanessa, after they had ordered, "but you'd be doing yourself a lot more good if you were back at the office helping out on this story."

"There's nothing I can do that would help."

"They think there is. They think you have a 'special relationship' with the coppolas in this. I think we're making up half the stuff we're running on this story, but the other papers are still beating us."

"My relationship with the cops is no better than yours is."

"If they find out about your 'special relationship' with the fair Camilla, they'll really be ready to run you through the presses."

"I don't have a relationship. I hardly know her."

"But as you say, *quel frisson*, she kissed you."

"She's in trouble."

"You're in trouble, A.C. Even with City Hall."

"What are you talking about?"

"Didn't you know? The mayor singled you out at his press conference today. You're typical of the irresponsible, sensation-mongering media who'll do anything for a headline, even tip off a wanted criminal that the police are looking for him. You have blood on your hands, he said."

A.C.'s hand went to his injured face.

"They pulled your column because the mayor called up Bill Shannon," Vanessa continued.

"And he wants my help because of my 'special relationship' with the police?"

"Shannon's angry that he had to do that. He's afraid we're going to lose the story now."

A waiter poured a small amount of St. Julien into A.C.'s wineglass. He sniffed it, sipped, and then nodded.

"I almost wish I was back in Belfast."

"Not much haute couture there, sweetheart."

He said nothing. Vanessa took a large swallow of her wine.

"A.C.," she said finally. "I ran into Jeffrey Darlington at a show this morning. He's going to be the editor of the American edition of *Beau Monde*, the magazine they're starting up."

"My felicitations." The wine was excellent. It was the only thing about the day that was.

"He talked to me about writing for them."

"You ought to do it. I'm sure they'll pay well."

"He also asked me if I thought there was any chance you might be interested. A monthly social column. Plus commentary on the arts. Trips abroad."

"Serendipity."

"And I'll bet twice your salary."

"How can I possibly work for a publication Katherine Shannon doesn't own?" He said this with great bitterness.

"It might do your marriage—or what's left of it—a world of good. You were your own man when Kitty fell for you. Become one again."

"I think the only thing that would please her now is for me to become a priest."

"You ought to talk to Darlington, anyway. And when you go up to Westchester this weekend you ought to tell Kitty about it."

"But she doesn't want me to come up."

"Go anyway. Assert yourself. After all, a man who's been kissed by Camilla Santee ought to be able to do anything he sets his mind to, *n'est-ce pas?*"

A peculiar look came over her face. He studied her, but couldn't figure it out.

"Maybe you don't have a special relationship with *les cops*," she said, "but they seem to have one with you."

He turned. Two huge, improbable figures stood at the entrance foyer of the restaurant—Detective Lanham and his partner Petrowicz, the latter wearing a sport coat far more suitable for a Wilkes-Barre Ramada Inn. The maître d' came up to them but they ignored him. Lanham, spotting A.C., nodded once. It was a summons.

A.C. took them back to the lobby, motioning Lanham to one of the red velvet settees that flanked the steps leading to the revolving door and the street outside. There was room only for the two of them and it was crowded at that. Petrowicz stood nearby, arms folded, eyeing passersby as might a soldier of occupation.

"I thought I told you 'off the record,' goddammit," Lanham said. His voice was low and very gruff.

"You said 'not for quote.' It's not the same."

"The fucking result is the same."

"I'm sorry. I was just doing my job."

Lanham paused as two aging blond women in fur coats met at the center of the lobby and embraced. As they swept on out the door, Lanham turned to watch them.

"How did you know I was here?" A.C. said.

"I am a police detective."

"That pimp you told me about. You think he's Molly Wickham's killer?"

Lanham grimaced. "That's bullshit," he said quietly. One of the desk clerks was looking at them curiously.

"I know you know it's bullshit," he continued, turning to lean close to A.C. "But it won't do anybody any good right now to try to put that in the paper, so let's keep it off the record."

"Yes."

"Off the record."

"Right."

"What the mayor said today, about your having blood on your hands, that's bullshit, too. Aggravated bullshit. That woman got killed because of some very bad police work, but also because she made her living and got her jollies being in the wrong place at the wrong time."

"Bad police work?"

"That's—"

"Off the record. I understand."

Lanham looked down at the backs of his hands, then turned them over, exposing the light skin of the palms.

147

"I'm trusting you, Mr. James, because I don't have much choice. I'm in a box on this case right now. My superiors are a little distracted by the events of last night. They're not much interested in my theories, in the things we talked about."

"I'm not as sure about all that as I was."

"Don't jive me, man." The street talk didn't seem to fit him. "What you told me about the man in the limousine makes sense. The feds are sticking their noses into this case and it may have something to do with him, whoever he is. I'm trying to get a lead on him. I made an inquiry through Interpol on that Delasante woman in France, but I've had no reply yet. I think they can both tell us a lot."

"That was just speculation on my part."

"Bull shit." He dragged the two words out.

"Detective Lanham—"

"I need your help, Mr. James. I'm not just talking about your civic duty as a citizen. You saw what happened to Molly Wickham. We don't know why it happened. Until we do, we sure as hell can't just presume that it isn't going to happen to somebody else."

A.C. rubbed his face nervously. "I really can't tell you any more than I have," he said.

"Yes you can. I went through the clips of some of your old columns. You move in this world, Mr. James." He gestured at the lobby. "You live in it. You hear their gossip. You pass a lot of it on in your column. These people talk to you all the time, gladly. I'll bet you can find out a lot about this Delasante woman, things we never could."

"Really, I never heard of her before."

Lanham took out one of his snitch cards. On the back, he wrote down two other numbers—his home phone and the number of the dispatcher's office where he could be reached over the portable. He handed it to A.C. with great seriousness, as though it were the key to something quite valuable.

"If you hear anything," Lanham said, "call me. If something jars your memory, call me. If you get some strange idea about this, call me. I'm going to be busy but you can always reach me."

"Yes sir." A.C. carefully placed the card in his Dunhill

148

wallet. In doing so, he briefly revealed the picture of Camilla Santee he had cut from a magazine and put with his other wallet photographs. Lanham could have seen it, but appeared not to have noticed.

"How did you hurt your face?" the detective asked.

A.C. hesitated. "I had too much to drink last night and got into a fight." It was what everyone thought, so maybe he would be believed.

"It's a rough neighborhood, the Upper East Side."

A.C. smiled. Lanham stood up, and so A.C. did the same.

"Have you . . . have you talked to Miss Santee again?" A.C. asked.

"All I get is her answering machine."

"It's a busy time for models."

"Her agency said they don't know where she is."

A.C. slipped his wallet back into his suit coat pocket. "I'll help you as much as I can."

"Thank you."

The two policemen departed as though in a great hurry. Vanessa was eating her salad, unhappily.

"They're not joining us for lunch?" she said.

A.C. slumped into his chair and drank some of his wine. "No."

"What did they want? More pictures to show us?"

He stared at his plate. He'd lost all appetite for food.

"I've got to find Camilla," he said.

"She can wait until after my entrée," Vanessa said.

•

Camilla spent most of the day avoiding her apartment and its predatory telephone, losing herself in the city and trying to concentrate her thoughts. She went first to Greenwich Village, wandering from bookstore to coffeehouse to boutique, and then moved on to SoHo, poking into new galleries and pretending to be absorbed by some very bad art. Lunchtime found her down at the Battery and its harborfront park, slouched on a bench with her long legs thrust out in front of her, unmindful of the rain that pattered on her hat and raincoat. The sky was low and murky, but she

149

could see across the dirty water to the dark silhouette of Staten Island.

She had grown up near such a battery point; had spent many a rainy afternoon gazing solemnly at a distant island. No island was distant enough.

A tanker was wallowing heavily in the Upper Bay, backing away from the Jersey shore and turning, preparing to follow the channel out through the Narrows into the open sea. Tugs and smaller boats moved around it like pests.

The gray-green water was oily, and dotted with floating bits she didn't want to look at closely. She could easily imagine Pierre Delasante's huge, bloated body floating among it all. Such a sight would not be at all upsetting.

She remembered her father's dead face, drained of blood that had flowed out of a knife wound. Her half sister Danielle had died in an upstairs bedroom of the family house, having put her father's pistol in her mouth and pulled the trigger while everyone else was downstairs at dinner. Camilla could still hear the sound. When Molly Wickham had been shot, it was Danielle that Camilla saw.

Every violent death sickened her after Danielle. Camilla never read murder stories in the newspapers. She never watched the television news or any of the crime shows.

Now, here she sat, contemplating murder quite calmly. It was not only possible and plausible for her to murder Pierre; it was something she devoutly wished to do.

If it would do any good, which it would not. He'd seen to that.

A man farther down the promenade was standing very still, observing her. She couldn't recognize him at the distance. She didn't want to see him any more closely. Rising and turning, she lifted the collar of her raincoat and began walking rapidly away.

On impulse, she headed for the landing of the Pan Am water shuttle, which made almost hourly runs up the East River to LaGuardia. She had a nearly twenty-minute wait upon reaching it, but no strange man drew near.

On the trip upriver, she stood on the forward deck, finding the wind and rain exhilarating and cleansing. The boat made a stop at the Thirty-fourth Street docks. She could have gotten off there, but kept her place, pleased when the

150

engines rumbled and the craft got under way again. By the time they reached the Marine Air Terminal at LaGuardia, however, she was feeling alone and unhappy again. She ran to the head of the cab line, smiling sweetly at a weary-looking older man as she hurried past him and into the taxi that he'd been about to enter. She promised the driver an extra $10 to ignore the ensuing complaints and get the hell out of there. He was content to do so. This was New York.

Once home, she turned on only one lamp in her living room, and then went directly to her answering machine, dropping her hat and raincoat on the floor.

The tape was nearly full. A few of the calls were from the police detective who had questioned her after Molly Wickham's murder. Some were from A.C. James. Most were from the person she feared hearing from most.

Camilla was worried about A.C. James, but the only person she called back was Evelyn Livingston, her booker at the modeling agency.

"Camilla? Gloriosky, girl, where have you been?"

"I'm awfully sorry, Evie. I—I've just gone all to pieces with this murder."

"Well, you're costing yourself a fortune with these cancellations. I even had a perfume commercial lined up. Residuals, darling, lovely residuals."

"I'm sorry."

"I thought you were desperate for money."

"I am. I . . . Evie, I want you to get me an out-of-town booking. I want to get out of New York for a while."

"They'll snap you up in a minute for Paris and Milan."

"No. Not Europe. Nothing in Europe. But anything here. Miami, Chicago. Anywhere. I just have to get out of New York."

There was a long pause, as Evelyn checked booking requests on her computer.

"Well, I don't see anything at the moment, dear. But I'll make every effort."

"You're my only friend, Evie. I'll call you in the morning."

She hung up. There was another call she now wanted to make, but she hadn't thought yet what to say.

Cassidy had left a file folder full of computer printouts for Lanham, the sum total of his labors in tracking the names of Molly Wickham, Marjean Dorothy Wickham, C.C. Delasante, and Robert Darcy through the downtown headquarters and New York FBI computer files. It was a pile of neat but useless paper.

There was a long file on Darcy in the NYPD system. The printout did not contain the entries from the previous night's failed arrest attempt. Bad Bobby's name showed up in the FBI memory bank as well, but routinely—from the occasions when he had been a wanted felon believed to have crossed state lines to avoid arrest and prosecution.

C.C. Delasante did not show up. A short-list of Delasantes appeared in the scan of the federal case–file directory. Cassidy had called up each one—a French general named Antoine Delasante, a New Orleans forger named Louis Delasante, an Iran-Contra witness named William Delasante, a Senate aide named Janet Delasante who had an Arab boyfriend, and a Pierre Delasante.

Cassidy had not been able to call up Pierre Delasante. The federal computer had responded to his request with: L/A USG ST2 LVA FILE NOT AVAILABLE. It had said this the three times Cassidy had tried the name.

There was a cross-reference in the directory listing: "Re: Molly Wickham, Re: Marjean Dorothy Wickham, Re: Jacques Delasante." When Cassidy had tried these names, he had got: L/A USG ST2 LVA FILE NOT AVAILABLE.

"What does this mean?" Lanham said to Sergeant Leander, the division's chief computer technician.

Leander was at his console, but eating a sandwich. A plastic cup of coffee sat dangerously near his computer keyboard. He glanced at the printout, and then up at Lanham.

"What does what mean, Ray?"

"L/A USG ST2 LVA FILE NOT AVAILABLE."

"It means 'File not available.' "

"You mean, there is a file but somebody's using it?"

Lanham was not being funny but Leander smiled as though he was.

152

"It means there is a file but we can't get at it. 'Limited access. U.S. government. Status two. Level A.' It means it's classified and you need a special code for access. High-level stuff."

"There's a wall around it? An electronic wall?"

"A mathematical wall. You've got to figure out the access code, or get it from somebody. It's probably several codes. You've got to be status two, level A, just to know where to start."

Lanham stuck his hands in his pockets, staring at the linoleum floor. There were coffee stains all around Leander's chair.

"Have you ever tried to break into one of those?" he said finally.

"That's not authorized, Detective."

"Could you do it?"

"Ray, I've gotten into the phone company and some hotel chain reservation systems, but that's it."

"I don't believe you."

"Okay. I've scanned some personnel files, all right? Maybe a couple of captains' memo files. But this here's very strange stuff, and I ain't no genius."

"Shit." Lanham took back the printouts. "Okay. Thanks for your trouble."

He wasn't six feet away when Leander spoke once more. "Is this real important, Ray?"

Lanham took a deep breath as he turned. "Yes, it is, Sergeant."

"I know a guy. A certifiable genius. Karl Paulina. Used to be a cop."

"Never heard of him."

"Sure you have. Used to be in burglary until we went over to computers. He helped put in this system. He was the guy who trained me. A great big guy, as big as you. Grew up in New Jersey. Blinked all the time. Kind of a twitchy guy."

"You said, 'Used to be a cop.' "

"He wasn't very good on the street. He was a great thinker, but he was always forgetting his service weapon and going to the wrong address."

"He got pushed out?"

153

"Yeah, but not for that. He's a player. A gambler. He worked up all kinds of systems for figuring out casino odds. He could even figure out how the mob was laying off money at the track."

"He was using department computers?"

"This stuff? Not hardly. This stuff's like Nintendo compared to what he had at home. He's got an Omega—one million megabytes, with a twenty-four hundred baud modem. He can talk to any computer in the world."

"Where is he?"

"Last I heard, in Atlantic City. He was working for one of the casinos. Head of security."

"Head of security?"

"Sure. Outfits like that need a guy like Karl to stop guys like Karl. Not to speak of IRS investigators."

"Do you think he might be willing to help me out?"

"No. But he might help me out. I covered him a couple of times. And I warned him they were going to come down on him. But he wouldn't quit. He had the itch, you know? A player."

"So what do we do?"

"I'll call him."

"Use a pay phone."

"Huh?"

"A pay phone. And not the one downstairs. Use the street. I'll owe you."

Leander smiled broadly this time. "I'll remember."

•

Lanham made some phone calls of his own, on the Wickham case, getting nowhere. He took out some paperwork and put it back. He drank three cups of coffee.

Taranto came in, passed by, then stopped.

"You're supposed to be beatin' the streets for Bad Bobby," he said.

"I'll be out there," Lanham said. He gestured at the slightly crumpled computer printouts. "I'm working on it, boss. I got his computer file."

Taranto nodded, and went into his office. Lanham got up and followed.

"Excuse me, boss," he said. "You said you would check with the feds on Molly Wickham. Remember? We couldn't get anything."

The lieutenant was staring at some reports on his desk. He didn't look up.

"I couldn't get anything either, Ray."

Lanham waited, slouching against the frame of the door.

"My office ain't the street, Ray."

Lanham pulled himself up straight. "Okay, boss."

"Ray." His eyes met Lanham's this time. "I'm putting Tony on restricted duty. It was his rounds killed Pat Cassidy. There'll be a full I.A.D. on it."

"And the round through the door?"

"It was Cassidy's."

"Thank you, boss."

"We still want Bad Bobby, Ray. Prime suspect. Unlawful flight. We want him real, real bad, Ray."

●

The rain had stopped. The night sky was clearing and one or two stars could be seen above the tall buildings. The air was cooler and people were out in the streets.

Camilla hesitated before turning the corner onto Sutton Place, then lifted her head and continued on, her determination manifest in the swiftness of her pace. It would be as if she were simply coming home. It hadn't been that long since she had lived here. She still owned the place. She still had her keys. If she had any luck, Molly Wickham would not have changed the locks. Molly was the kind of girl who seldom changed the sheets.

She slowed again. She was attracting attention walking so fast. She slowed further. If there was a policeman in front of the building, she would just keep on going. If there was one in the lobby, she would pretend she had the wrong address. If she encountered one in the elevator, she would get off on another floor.

The lobby was empty but for a concierge. He looked up from his desk as she swept in, eyeing her appreciatively but curiously.

155

"Good evening," she said, moving on toward the inner doors.

"May I help you, Miss?"

"I live here." She held up her keys. He was no one she recognized. "I've been away. Are you new here?"

"Kinda. Since March."

"Well, I am Mrs. Avenant." It was true. It was also all she could think of saying. The name would not be known to him, or anyone, as he would discover if he checked. She could not stay long.

"Sorry," he said.

There were no policemen anywhere, but she rang the doorbell of the apartment twice and waited until she was sure of no response before using the key.

Someone, possibly Molly but probably the police, had left a light on in the living room. The rest of the apartment was dark.

Fear had numbed her sense of decision. She fought to regain it. She still wasn't sure what she was looking for. She was looking for whatever she found. She doubted the videotape Pierre had talked about would still be there, but she still might come across some clue as to whom Molly and the others had been paying. There might be similar tapes, or pictures. There had to be something.

She started in the master bedroom. Women put personal things with their personal things. Molly loved pictures of herself, loved anything to do with her own body. Camilla half expected to find a mirror installed above the bed. Pierre would doubtless enjoy that.

There was no mirror. There was very little of anything. Molly might as well have been living in a hotel.

Camilla was surprised at how clean the apartment was. She supposed the police had seen to that. They had been through all the drawers, or someone had. No woman, not even Molly, would keep her stockings and underwear in such a tangle.

The searchers had also made a thorough job of the bathroom. The toothpaste had all been squeezed out of its tube. What had they been looking for? Drugs? It had been rumored that Molly was a cocaine user, though Camilla had never seen any evidence of it.

156

It irritated Camilla to find African masks on the living room wall. She took them down, one by one, to look inside them, but she didn't put them back.

She was leaving fingerprints. But this was her apartment, or had been. Her fingerprints must already be here. She was breaking no law. She had broken no law. She had done nothing wrong. There was no just reason for any of this to be happening to her.

Damned tears. She wiped them away and moved along. She was taking too much time.

Camilla was in the kitchen, staring in wonder at all the liquor bottles in one of the cabinets, when she heard the noise—a muffled, distant click. Had something she'd touched fallen down? She froze. There was an exit from the kitchen to the fire stairs and the garbage chute. She was no more than eight feet from it.

Another sound now. Unmistakable. The front door closing. And then a voice, harsh, demanding.

"Camilla!"

She turned toward the doorway, trying to compose herself. She had gone over in her mind what she wanted to do when next she looked into the face that belonged with that voice. In her dreams the last two nights, she had done it—shot him, stabbed him, butchered him. But when Jacques stepped into the kitchen, she could do nothing. All she could manage was to cross her arms and hold them tightly against her chest, as though to keep back her terror.

He smiled, Rhett Butler returned from running a Yankee blockade. He was as handsome as Camilla was beautiful—as Pierre was ugly. But the nastiness in his eyes ruined the effect. She didn't believe in such nonsense, but he looked like someone possessed.

"Why are you here?" she asked. Her own voice sounded like a small child's.

"I followed you. I've been following you all day, darlin'. I never knew you to be so fond of rain."

She backed up against the sink. "How did you get in?"

"The man behind the desk."

"The concierge?"

"He's sleeping now. Under his desk." He held up a ring of keys. "I borrowed these."

"You didn't—He's all right?"

"I think so." Another smile.

"My God, Jacques. The police—"

"The police don't even know who I am. Or do they, Camilla?"

"They'll know soon enough if they catch us in here."

"Why didn't you answer when I called?"

"Why did you beat up that poor man last night? He means no harm. You could have killed him."

"Means no harm? He's a goddamn newspaperman, Camilla! He's the last person in the world you should be talking to."

"He doesn't know anything. He just wants to help me."

"Why? How does he know you need help? You're just a witness. What have you told him?"

"I haven't told him anything, but—"

"But what, Camilla? Can he identify me?"

She remembered A.C. standing by the family portrait when she came in.

"No," she said. "But he knows who Pierre is."

Regret came as swiftly as pain. Why had she blurted that out? Why in hell? What had she just done to A.C.?

"He knows about Pierre?" Jacques said. "He knows about the family?" His voice was very quiet and, consequently, more menacing than if he had shouted the words at her.

"I think he recognized Pierre at the show. He's a newspaperman. Pierre used to work in the White House. Pierre was Molly's lover, for God's sake! It's going to come out."

"Why was he in your apartment for so long, Camilla? What were you talking about?"

"I was trying to fix up his cuts and bruises. You hit him all over, Jacques. You could have killed him."

He snatched at her wrist and yanked her toward him, leaning close, his dark eyes fixed on hers.

"I will kill him, Camilla. If one word about our family appears in that newspaper of his, I'll shoot him down just like that nigger model. Do you doubt me?"

She mustered all her effort to stare back at him, to turn her fear into courage and defiance. All she doubted was whether he meant the "if." Jacques looked out of his mind

158

with frustration. He'd kill again just to relieve that. She'd seen him kill a horse once just because it kept balking at a jump.

Finally, he relaxed his grip enough for her to pull her arm away. Her wrist was red, and beginning to swell.

"He won't put anything in the paper," she said. "He won't do anything to harm me."

"Why not?"

"I think he's attracted to me. A lot."

Jacques smiled. "They're all attracted to you, darlin'. It's the great curse of your life."

Jacques was the great curse of her life. Jacques and Pierre, and their wretched daddy.

He opened his coat. He had a large pistol stuck in his belt. Any patrolman strolling his beat could arrest Jacques just for that.

"You're the biggest fool I've ever known," she said.

He hit her, as hard as he could, striking her shoulder and knocking her violently back against the sink. The pain brought tears. At least he had spared her face.

"I'll kill him, Camilla. And I'll kill that nigger cop if he sniffs around too close. And, by God, I'll kill you, my darlin' sister, if you don't stop playin' flirty-eyes with that damned newspaperman, if you don't start helping me get us out of this."

She rubbed her shoulder, making it hurt all the worse. She had to get away from him—had to get them both out of this apartment.

"There may be a way," she said. "Pierre said there's a tape—a videotape of him and Molly and some others. Doing things in bed."

"In bed?"

"Having sex, Jacques. It's a filthy, awful tape, every kind of nasty, lewd, disgusting thing. Pierre is paying money to whoever has it. He told me last night. He said that's why he needs more from us. The others in the tape are paying, too."

"What others?"

"Another model, Belinda St. Johns. And one named Jimmy Woody. He's . . . he's black."

"Having sex with Molly Wickham?"

159

"And with Pierre. It's on the tape."

"Pierre in bed with a nigger boy?"

"Will you stop using that word? A *gentleman* does not use that word! Nor does he strike a woman!"

His face went blank. She'd finally managed to intimidate him a little.

"Where is this tape?" he asked.

"Do you think I know? I looked through things in here." She shrugged. "*Absolument rien.*"

"Pierre must know where it is."

"I told you. He's paying someone. He seemed very worried. He hopes to have the federal charges against him dropped, and then sell his company—for a lot of money. I don't suppose it would help him much if that tape turned up in Washington."

"Honey, some of his clients would probably ask for that Woody boy's telephone number."

"I mean the federal government. The newspapers. They could ruin him in Washington."

"They surely could."

"If we could get that tape, Jacques, we could put an end to this. Think about it. He'd have no choice."

"We could arrange a trade. Unless I find his cache first."

"You won't, Jacques. He's not stupid. He put it in his will."

"Put what?"

They had been in the apartment too long. She wanted so desperately to get away.

"The directions to where he hid it. He named three beneficiaries to receive certain papers. They're all Carolina society writers. The will is locked up in a bank safe-deposit box. No, Jacques. This tape is our only way."

"Those two models, you said. And Pierre and his black whore."

"There may have been another person, a photographer. His name is Peter Gorky. He and Molly chummed around together. He used to make films like that, dirty movies."

"I'll find him."

"Don't hurt him, Jacques. Don't hurt anyone else. And for God's sake, leave A.C. James alone!"

He stepped close, very much the bully again.

160

"I think you're a little attracted to him, aren't you, darlin'? A nice respectable married lady like you."

"I've only just met him."

Jacques took her chin in his hand, lifting her face to his eyes.

"If I catch you talking to him just one more time, darlin', I'll kill him. Do you understand? Do you believe me?"

"Yes." She closed her eyes. His fingers were still hard on the bone of her chin. "Let me go, Jacques."

He didn't.

"If you're going to kill somebody again, Jacques," she said, as hatefully as she could manage, "why don't you murder Momma? That'll solve everything."

He slapped her face. It sent her reeling, but for a moment, she was free of him. Then he took her arm, pulling her down the hall. He paused in the living room. A great sweep of Manhattan running north along the river glittered and sparkled outside the wide window.

"You go home now," he said. "You stay put until I call you again."

"I'm leaving, Jacques. I'm going to get out of New York for a while," she said. "Pierre's gone back to Washington. You find the tape. But don't you hurt anyone." She hesitated, then folded her arms, standing her ground. "If one more person gets hurt in this, Jacques, I'm going straight to the police."

He pulled the large pistol from his belt and leveled it at her head, slowly pulling back the hammer. She didn't move, except to tremble. If he fired, she would die exactly as Molly had died.

But she knew he wouldn't. As mad and crazed and evil as he was, he still lived by his code. She was his kin, a woman of his house.

He laughed, then returned the pistol to his belt, moving to the front door.

"We'll go out the way we came in," he said. "We'll just act like we belong here."

The elevator was a long time reaching their floor. It was empty.

"The concierge will recognize you," she said.

"No he won't."

Floor numbers blinked on and off in a display panel as they descended. The lobby could be full of policemen. She could shout, "This man killed Molly Wickham." It would all be over.

She looked at his hand. She remembered him caring for a foaling mare. Gentle hands.

"How badly did you hurt him?" she asked.

"That's what I want to see."

The doors slid open like the swift curtain of a stage, revealing a small crowd of people hovering by the concierge's desk. There were others outside on the sidewalk, peering in through the glass of the entrance. Jacques moved them along, gripping Camilla's arm tightly. She pulled away, and hurried up to the others.

The concierge was lying on his back. There was blood running from the top of his head. His eyes were open, blinking. He was muttering something.

"What happened?" Camilla said to a woman. "Is he all right?"

"A robber attacked him," the woman said, as calmly as though they were waiting in a checkout line at Gristede's. "He may be in the building. Someone called the police."

There were sirens.

Camilla looked back at Jacques, but he had vanished. She edged away from the others, then turned and left the building, walking with studied naturalness though every nerve in her body screamed at her to run.

At the corner, she saw two police cars, their rooftops ablaze with light, sweeping up from Fifty-seventh Street. She held her place, scarcely glancing at them as they flashed by. Then, as the traffic light changed, she headed west across the street, more quickly now, seeking the dark.

CHAPTER

....

8

A.C. had a dream of Bailey Hazeltine. It began in a familiar way, with his running after her on a summer lawn. She was laughing and barefoot, in a long-skirted white summer dress. It was night and the shrubbery was lit with floodlights. She leapt over some small bushes, her legs flashing shadows within the gauzy, illuminated cloth of her dress.

Then they were on a beach, a gritty, rocky French beach on the Riviera. All around them, reclining like beautiful sea creatures, were bare-breasted women. There were couples, too, youthful men and girls with arms wrapped around one another, lying very still.

He and Bailey were not lying still. They were both quite naked and they were making love. He tried to get up but she would pull him back, pull him into her. He heard people speaking French, their voices quite distinct. He lifted his head. A fully dressed Japanese man with a camera was sitting just a few feet away, snapping picture after picture of them.

A.C. sat up. His telephone was ringing. He sensed that it had been ringing for some time.

He grabbed up the receiver. "Hello?"

He couldn't quite understand the woman's voice. She was calling him "Mr. James."

"Bailey? Where are you?"

"I'm sorry. Is that you, Mr. James?"

"Yes. James. Who is this?"

"It's Camilla, Camilla Santee."

Another dream? He blinked his eyes against the dark. It was difficult to make out the hands of his watch. He turned on the light.

"Mr. James?"

"Yes. I'm here. I'm glad you called. I need to talk to you."

"I want to talk to you."

It was almost two. "Tonight?"

He waited for her to continue.

"Miss Santee?"

"I'm here. Not tonight. It's too dangerous. Tomorrow." She paused again. "Tomorrow afternoon, at three. Do you know Le Train Bleu, the little restaurant on the sixth floor of Bloomingdale's?"

He had been to a book party there in the spring. "Yes."

"I'll be there. In the back. Spend some time in the store first. Make sure no one's following you."

He'd done that before—in Northern Ireland. "Okay. Are you all right?"

"Yes. But you—you must be in awful pain."

"I'm managing. Your call helps."

"Good night, my dear Mr. James."

After she hung up, he sat still in the darkness for a long time. Sleep did not come until very near morning.

•

Lanham came into the squad room carrying a briefcase and two very heavy shopping bags. He emptied their contents

164

as carefully as possible onto his desk, but they spilled onto Petrowicz's desk opposite and onto the floor as well. They quickly attracted the attention of everyone in the squad room.

"Hey, Ray," said Caputo, dressed that day in a light-blue suit, cream tie, and red and blue striped shirt. "You get transferred to vice or something?"

Everywhere there were breasts, thighs, buttocks, female genitals, male genitals—entwined and engaged in every imaginable position—decorously, athletically, and clinically displayed on the glossy covers and open pages of a pornography collector's wealth of books and magazines.

Caputo picked one up and studied it thoughtfully. "There's something I never tried."

"I don't suppose many have."

"Betcha Tony has."

Lanham took the Polaroid photograph of Molly and Belinda from his briefcase and set it slightly to the side.

"What's this all about?" Caputo asked, perusing further.

"I want to find out who took this Polaroid," Lanham said. "It's got a very distinctive style, very artistic. You see? You can't tell what's up or down."

"You mean who's on top."

"It's not your usual skin mag shot. A professional photograph, even if it is a Polaroid. I'm hoping I might find another one like it."

"Tony could help you. He could tell a Michelangelo ass from a Leonardo ass."

"What do you know about Michelangelo?"

"Hey. I'm Italian."

"Where is Tony?"

"Over in records. Workin' on some old cases."

Lanham pondered the perfect curve of Belinda St. Johns's cheek visible in the Polaroid. "He could tell this one."

Phones were ringing throughout the squad room, as they were always ringing. Sergeant Futterman, Taranto's major doma, was taking most of them. Hanging up from one, he looked over at Lanham.

"Hey, Ray. Mendelsohn over in robbery called. Maybe you should talk to him."

"Something on the taxi drivers?"

165

"On Wickham, Marjean Dorothy. That building on Sutton Place where she lived? The doorman or whatever there got beat up last night. They talked to him this morning. He said some blond woman came in just before he got hit. Said she was a real looker."

"Why didn't you let me talk to him?"

"He didn't ask for you. He asked for the lieutenant."

•

A.C. heard nothing at all from Bailey. He made two innocent calls, one to her brother and one to her mother, but they both said they believed her to be in Los Angeles. He thought of calling her husband, thought better of it, and wondered if she had tried to call him.

He'd found the door to his terrace unlocked and slightly ajar in the morning, but couldn't remember if he'd opened it before going to bed. Drinking his coffee by the railing, he'd glanced down to see a man on the sidewalk staring up at his apartment, then quickly moving on when noticed. His morning copy of the *New York Times* was on the hallway carpet outside his door as always, but there was no copy of the *Globe*. The phone rang—one and a half rings—and then abruptly stopped.

•

He wandered about Bloomingdale's for some time, pausing in the men's department and even buying a tie. He arrived at Le Train Bleu a few minutes early. She was already there, at the last table in the rear, as gracefully posed as though sitting for a formal portrait. She was dressed as though for an afternoon in the Hamptons—navy jacket, white, wide-collared blouse, expensive beige slacks, beige flat shoes. She wore a red silk scarf at her neck.

When he came toward her, her eyes widened a little in recognition and he thought he caught a hint of welcome at the corners of her mouth; otherwise, her somber expression didn't change.

"Don't look so sad," he said. "You're in Bloomie's—the shopper's paradise."

166

"Hello, Mr. James." She gave him a smile. The skin below her eyes seemed a trifle red beneath her makeup.

"Are you all right, Camilla?"

"Yes. You look much better than I thought you would —than I was afraid you would." Her odd Southern accent was once again very strong, a measure of how upset and distracted she must be. He wondered how she must have talked when she'd first come to New York.

He rubbed his face. "I'll survive." He sat down, moving his chair slightly so he could observe the entrance. She had a glass of white wine in front of her. He ordered coffee.

"Camilla. The police want to see you again. Detective Lanham has been after me about you."

"What did you tell him?"

"Nothing. I said I knew nothing about you."

"He's been leaving messages on my answering machine."

"They've been to your apartment. They really want to talk to you."

"I have nothing more to say to them. Aren't they looking for that man, Molly's procurer?"

"The word is 'pimp.' They're looking for him, all right, but Detective Lanham has his own ideas about a suspect."

"Who?"

"I don't know. Not the pimp."

"Lanham is the black detective, the one in charge of the case?"

"Yes. He wants to talk to the man in the limousine," A.C. said. "He doesn't know it's Pierre Delasante, but he'll probably find out."

"You won't tell him."

"I promised you that."

His coffee came in a silver carafe. Camilla reached to pour it for him, setting cream and sugar before him afterward, the Southern lady, offering hospitality to a gentleman caller.

After he had stirred and sipped, she took his injured hand in both of hers, examining the torn skin, careful not to cause pain.

"You said you'd help me, Mr. James."

"Yes. Of course. Anything."

Camilla took a deep breath, and then sighed. "I must tell

you something first. I've put you in great danger just meeting with you. The man who killed Molly—"

"You know who it is?"

"Yes. I did from the beginning. I can't tell you who it is. Not now."

"Why not? This is murder, Camilla."

"I know that! I don't want it to happen again. I'm trying to do something about it. He's already beaten you up. Next time he could kill you!"

He let her anger subside. "How can I help you?"

Her eyes met his. "You've probably guessed. Pierre Delasante is my cousin. He's a very bad man, incorrigible. He's been doing some dreadful, awful things. Molly was shot because of him. I . . . I had nothing to do with it. I had no idea anything like that could happen . . ."

He glanced away. Her beauty was so overwhelming that it was hard for him to look at her and pay attention to what she was saying at the same time.

"Pierre's being blackmailed," she continued. "He and Molly and some others had a party in her apartment, in the apartment I was renting her on Sutton Place. They had what I guess you'd call an orgy, and made a videotape of it. Someone has that videotape. Belinda St. Johns is in it. So is a male model named Jimmy Woody. They're paying, too. They're all being blackmailed. Pierre told me that much. He wouldn't tell me anything else."

"Molly was killed because of that videotape?"

"No. Not because of the tape. You're a newspaperman, Mr. James. You have ways to find out things, better than the police. You found out so much about me." She paused to take a sip of her wine. "I want to know who has the tape. I want you to find that out for me. I'd be much beholden to you."

"You want the tape," he said. "You want to use it against Pierre. Why? What will that accomplish?"

"I want the tape. I'm not asking you to get it for me. God, no. I'm putting you at risk enough as it is. But if you can learn who has it, that would help me very much."

"But why do you want a piece of pornography, especially with your cousin in it?"

"I don't want to look at it, Mr. James."

168

"Belinda St. Johns and that male model must know who it is. Did you ask them?"

"Belinda won't even talk to me. I don't know where Jimmy is. Pierre wouldn't tell me and now he's left town."

A.C. frowned, pondering the problem.

"I'm leaving town, too, Mr. James," she said. "I have to get away from here. For a while, anyway."

"If I can find out what you want, how in hell will I let you know?"

"Call my booker at the agency. Evie Livingston. She'll be expecting your call. She'll tell you where to find me."

"All right. I'll do what I can. I will." He grinned confidently, though he felt no confidence at all. He was agreeing to this mostly as a means of keeping her in his life.

"There's a danger for you, Mr. James. I hate myself for dragging you into this. I—"

"It's all right."

"No it isn't. The man who killed Molly. He's looking for the tape, too. I don't think he'll find it. He'll only cause more trouble. I'm afraid he'll hurt someone again. I wish I hadn't told him about the tape. I don't know what I was thinking."

She took her hands away and rested them on her lap, staring down at them.

"He's made threats about you," she said. "He told me he'd kill you if you came near me again, and here I've lured you to this place."

"You didn't lure me."

"I wouldn't blame you if you just got up and walked away."

"I wouldn't do that. I'll help you however I can. I'm your friend, Camilla."

"You've only known me a few days."

"A lot has happened in those few days, more than happens in most friendships."

"I'm lucky you were there, A.C. James. I'm very lucky." She gently smiled. "You know what you are?"

He shrugged.

"You're my chevalier, my knight."

"That's a very romantic notion."

"I'm a very romantic lady—at least I used to be. When

169

I was a little girl, I'd read about knights all the time. In one book it said that, in the days of chivalry, the looks, the words, and the sign of a lady were supposed to make knights at time of need perform double their usual deeds of strength and valor."

Her words reminded him of what had been written on the folded paper hidden behind her family photograph.

"At tournaments," she said, "the ladies were supposed to have called to the knights: 'Think, gentle knights, upon the wool of your breasts, the nerve of your arms, the love you cherish in your hearts, and do valiantly, for ladies behold you.' The knights responded: 'Love of ladies! Death of warriors! On, valiant knights, for you fight under fair eyes!' "

"You must give me something of yours, if I'm to be your chevalier."

She thought a moment, then pulled the red silk scarf from her neck.

"You gave me your handkerchief in that bar by the police station, and I'm afraid I've lost it. Don't lose this."

He folded it carefully, then, stiffly, slipped it into his pocket. "Never."

Worry crept into her eyes. She looked at her watch.

"I'm going to leave you now, A.C."

With a gentleman's reflex, he rose, bringing pain to his leg and side.

"Stay here, please," she said, rising herself. "Give me time to get away."

"I'm worried about you."

"I'll be all right. Just you be careful. If you were ever in a war, be that careful."

"Very careful." She was near enough for him to put his hand to her waist, and he did so. Her eyes responded in kind to his, but she came no nearer.

"People are looking at us," she said, half whispering.

"I don't care."

She came against him, her hand moving gently to his neck. Her lips caressed his, then she pulled him closer, her cheek pressing his. "Until I hear your voice again."

"Until I see you."

She lingered, but said nothing further. Then she pulled

away, averting her head. There was a brushing touch of her fingers upon his arm, and then she was gone. He didn't look after her. He returned to his seat and finished his coffee, thinking, his hand caressing her red silk scarf.

•

Henry Mohai, the night concierge at Molly Wickham's apartment building, had suffered a deep cut on his head requiring seven stitches and enough of a concussion to be kept in the hospital for twenty-four hours for observation. He'd described his attacker's weapon as a pistol, and he had apparently been struck with the butt. The man had come up to him as though to inquire after one of the residents and then, without hesitation, had pulled the gun from beneath his suit coat and hit Mohai before he could even lift his arms in self-defense.

The assailant had been an unusually handsome, well-dressed man, with black curly hair and a dark complexion. The doorman said he looked like someone who belonged in such a building, which had apartments costing one to two million dollars and more.

No one had reported a break-in. Evidence technicians had gone over Wickham's apartment again and had reported finding fresh prints. They hadn't been able to identify them, except to note that they matched some very old prints they'd taken from the premises on their first evidence sweep.

Mohai's keys had been recovered in a trash basket on First Avenue. They bore no identifiable prints.

The concierge had given two statements to uniformed force from the precinct and been interrogated again in his hospital room by robbery detectives. His wife, a stout, middle-aged woman who spoke English with an Eastern European accent, did not take kindly to Lanham's appearance.

Lanham had a uniformed officer take her outside. Mohai's was a semiprivate room—Lanham wondered who was paying for the extra cost—but the other patient was absorbed by a movie on the television set bolted to the wall. Lanham drew the curtain that separated the beds.

171

He opened his briefcase, first taking out official front-and-profile mug shots of Robert Darcy.

"Is this the man who hit you?" he said.

"No," Mohai said. "Hell, no."

His voice was weak, but clear.

"You're sure?"

"I wouldn't have let that guy get through the door. The guy who hit me was white. A gentleman. This one's a . . . I mean, he's black, isn't he?"

"You have no doubt whatsoever," Lanham said. "This is not the man."

"That's right."

"You said a woman entered the building just before you were attacked. A blond woman."

"That's right. The best-looking woman I've ever seen, and we've got some in that building."

"She said her name was Mrs. Avenue?"

"Avenue, yeah. That's what she said. I mean she didn't say she'd come in from the avenue. She said her name was Avenue, Mrs. Avenue. Well, something like that." Mohai lifted himself slightly higher on his pillow. "She came in like she owned the joint. She had a key and everything. I probably shouldn't have stopped her. But I'd never seen her before."

Lanham took a fashion picture he'd clipped from a magazine.

"Is this the woman?" he said.

"Oh yeah. That's her."

"You have no doubt."

"I'll remember that one a long time."

"She's a fashion model named Camilla Santee. Residents of the building say she used to live there a few years ago —in Molly Wickham's apartment."

"I only been there a few months."

"The owner of Miss Wickham's apartment is listed as C.C. Delasante. Could this be the same woman?"

"I don't know any Delasante."

Lanham took the picture back. Mohai seemed reluctant to give it up. Next Lanham showed him a glossy agency photo of Belinda St. Johns.

"Have you ever seen this woman before?"

172

Mohai studied the picture appreciatively. "Oh yeah. She's been in at least a couple of times."

"To see Molly Wickham?"

"She came in with Wickham. A couple times. Real late at night. I think once she stayed all night. There were some other people, too. You know, fruitcakes. I could smell one guy all the way across the foyer. Some little queen."

"Was there ever a tall man, with glasses?"

"Oh yeah. But he'd come by himself. I guess he was the number-one boyfriend. At first, though, I thought he was a coke dealer."

"Coke?"

"We have a few users in the building. Especially Wickham. Some nights, she didn't need the elevator. You know what I mean? And this guy had a big white limo, a stretch. Not the kind of car you see around here too much. These are mostly old-money people, you know? Not many flashy cars. Only two Rolls-Royces."

"You said it was white?"

"White, or light gray. Something like that."

"This tall man with glasses, he's not the one who hit you?"

"Oh no. He looked like the kind of guy who'd scream if you hit him. Kinda pudgy, and soft. And he was usually half in the bag."

Lanham returned the pictures to his briefcase, clicking the latches shut.

"Thanks for your help," Lanham said, rising. "I hope you feel better."

"Hey, am I going to get some protection?"

"Protection?"

"In case this guy comes back. I seen his face."

"I'll ask my superiors," Lanham said, knowing very well what Taranto would say to a request like that.

•

Belinda St. Johns was working a show in the garment district. It had taken A.C. very little time to track her down, once he had gotten the number of her modeling agency. He had called her booker and simply posed as a policeman

173

wanting to talk to her more about the Wickham murder. Such subterfuge was now a sin in the newspaper business, but he couldn't think of any other way to do it. He was in a hurry.

St. Johns's assignment was a lingerie show—mostly peignoirs, nightgowns, and lounging pajamas—in the showroom of a design house on the fifth floor of a rattletrap building between Sixth and Seventh Avenues. His business card from the *Globe* got him in without difficulty, but all the seats were taken—folding chairs arranged in an oval about the large room—so he had to stand in a corner.

There were only six models—four girls and two boys— all barefoot. Belinda St. Johns had the best figure, and by far the best legs. Intent on her work, she paid little attention to the spectators and appeared not to notice him at all. She was as haughty as before, supremely elegant, a queen among commoners, her beauty almost as perfect as Camilla's. She gave a little skip and tossed her head as she returned to the dressing room.

The two boys, wearing nearly sheer black silk lounging suits that ended at the knee, concluded the show. Designers were now bringing out lines of male clothing strictly for the use of homosexuals.

A.C. trailed the small mob that crowded around the door of the building's lone, ramshackle elevator, lingering at the rear. Then, at an unobtrusive moment, he made his way back through the showroom to the dressing area.

It was also crowded. There were many men there, most of them seemingly involved with the show. One of the girl models was wearing only panties, unmindful of the nakedness of her small breasts. Two others had changed from the designer's underwear into their own. Belinda, in stocking feet, was hastily putting on her street clothes. A.C. started toward her.

"Sir?" said a young man with dirty hair nearly as long as Belinda's, rising to block A.C.'s progress. "Where are you going?"

"I have to talk to Miss St. Johns. It's important."

"The girls are still changing." It came out a hiss.

"That's all right," said A.C., pushing past him. "I'm only going to talk to her."

He caught Belinda by surprise. She didn't seem to recognize him.

"Miss St. Johns, I'm A.C. James. From the *Globe*. We were at the police station together."

"I remember you. Yeah, you were with Vanessa Meyers. Is she here?"

"No. Miss St. Johns, I need to talk to you, about the Wickham story. I'm writing a column. May I buy you a cup of coffee, or a drink or something?"

She eyed him coldly. "I don't want to be in any story. Not about that."

"I don't plan to put you in a story. I just need your help in answering some questions. It's about something I just learned, something the police don't know about."

"Like what?"

He glanced around. The bare-breasted model was putting on a blouse—without brassiere.

"Please, Miss St. Johns. If we could go someplace."

"Are you trying to pick me up?"

"No. Please. I just don't want to talk with all these people around."

"What's this about?" She was very hostile now. He'd have to tell her something.

"It's about a party at Molly's place, a party you attended."

There was a flicker of fear in her eyes, then the toughness returned.

"Fuck off."

"Please, Miss St. Johns."

"Fuck off," she said more loudly. "Beat it."

She began buttoning up her dress, getting the holes wrong in her haste. The long-haired young man returned with a very large woman wearing a black and orange print smock.

"You're not supposed to be in here," the woman said.

"Leave. Now," said the young man, taking A.C.'s arm.

A.C. pulled away, but left them, clumsily tripping over the leg of one of the folding chairs as he crossed the showroom. He'd have to find another way to get to St. Johns. Perhaps Vanessa could help.

There were still people waiting for the elevator, and he

175

was compelled to wait with them. The long-haired young man stationed himself at the doorway to make certain A.C. went away.

It took two more trips of the creaky elevator before there was room for him to wedge in. When they reached the street level, he bolted for the outdoors, taking in a large breath of the street air as though he had just emerged from some oppressive, dark mine shaft.

Before he could move further, he found himself confronted by Belinda St. Johns. In stockings, but lacking shoes, she had obviously taken some back set of stairs. She pulled him a few feet down the sidewalk and then pushed him into a narrow alleyway. Her beautiful face, contorted into ugliness, came almost into his.

"What do you know about a party at Molly's?" she said.

She'd left him no choice. He'd have no other opportunity.

"I know that you were there. So were Molly and her friend Pierre Delasante and a male model named Jimmy Woody. You were all in bed together."

"Where do you get this bullshit?"

"A videotape was made. Someone's blackmailing you with it."

"You're going to put this crap in your newspaper?"

"No. I just want to know who has the tape. I won't involve you at all. I just want to find out who it is. We think that person is involved in Molly's killing."

She shoved him. "Listen up, you asshole! You want me to get my brains blown out like Molly? Are you fucking crazy?"

"I'm sorry, I—"

"Listen to me. If you say a fucking word to anyone about this, if you even dream about putting something in that shitty paper of yours, I'll see you get hurt real bad. I'll get your knees broke. I'll get your fucking balls cut off. This isn't bullshit! I'll do it!"

"Miss St. Johns—"

"I may do it anyway. You came barging into the dressing room when I half had my tits hanging out. I got witnesses. If someone I know were to find out about that, your face would be looking like your ass. It looks like someone gave

176

it a workover already, but that isn't ant shit compared to what can happen to you. Capish? Asshole?"

"I mean you no harm."

"You fucking better not!" She stepped back, glancing behind her to make certain no one had been witness to her tirade. "You stay away from me. Understand? You forget this!"

She was gone. He looked at the cans of refuse around him. He felt as much a valiant knight as the hissing young man upstairs.

•

Taranto was not amused to find such a wealth of pornography in the squad room—or to find Lanham so absorbed by it.

"Come on, Ray," he said, his voice strained and gritty. "Every cop in the city is out looking for Bad Bobby and you're sitting here looking at dirty books. What gives?"

Lanham smiled indulgently, the wise old sage revealing a small part of the great truth he was pondering. "I'm looking for pictures of Molly Wickham. The fairy godmother who took her away from Darcy and the Deuce was a photographer. If I find him, it will help the case."

"Well, get this shit out of here. What if some newsie sees it? Hell, what if the mayor decides to come by?"

"If the mayor was going to come by, there'd be advance men all over the place six hours ahead of time."

"Yeah, well, clean this up before they do. Who paid for it? I hope you don't think this is coming out of department funds?"

"It didn't cost a thing. It was confiscated—except for some magazines I bought at the Waldorf."

"Confiscated? This doesn't look illegal. Illegal is little kids and corpses. Did you get a court order?"

"Not exactly."

"Shit." He slammed his door.

Lanham exhaled sharply, and pushed his chair back from his desk. This really was a stupid idea. He was hoping to find Peter Gorky's name among the skin mag photo credits. He'd save a lot of time if he'd just go out and find Gorky.

He tracked the photographer down on location. He was doing a commercial shoot at the little mall in front of the GM Building, directly across Fifth Avenue from the Plaza. The sequence being filmed was of a model coming out of the building, pirouetting, and opening her coat to reveal some lacy underwear.

Lanham hung back with the onlookers for a time, letting Gorky shoot the sequence twice. Then, when the model paused to have an attendant work on her hair, Lanham moved in, touching Gorky on the shoulder. The photographer turned as though to snap at him, then saw who it was, and became quite polite.

"Hiya, Detective. Out for a stroll?"

"Here to see you. Can you spare me a minute?"

Pained but resigned, Gorky glanced about at his crew and the surrounding spectators, then nodded. "Everybody take a break," he said to a subordinate, a bearded young man in a denim jacket.

"That bench okay?" Lanham said.

"Sure."

"Molly Wickham was murdered right over there, across the street."

"Yeah. I know."

"And here you are."

"Yeah. Great day for a shoot."

They sat down, Lanham turning slightly toward the photographer, Gorky sitting hunched forward, his elbows on his knees.

"What can I do for you, Detective?"

"You told me you didn't take that picture I found in Molly's apartment."

Gorky stared at the pavement. His hands were huge.

"I figure that you did," Lanham said. He added a lie. "It's very artistic. It's like some of your other work that I've seen."

"Okay. I took the picture. I didn't tell you because, what the hell, what would be the point? It didn't have anything to do with Molly's getting killed."

"I don't know what had to do with Molly Wickham's getting killed. I'd like to. That's why I'm here."

178

"I took the picture, all right? A couple of pictures. Po-laroids. I left them with Molly."

"And the videotape? We found a piece of a videotape box. It has your prints on it."

"How do you know they're my prints?"

"Your prints are on file. You were in the army, and you were arrested once for marijuana possession. We made a match." Lanham made up the last part. The evidence techs hadn't come back with anything conclusive on the videotape box fingerprints.

Gorky scowled. "Okay. I shot some tape. We were just fooling around. Having a good time. People started taking off their clothes. It happens in New York, you know. Shit. It probably happens in Iowa."

"What people?"

"Molly, Belinda. A couple of guys."

"And you?"

"I'm not on the tape."

"What guys?"

"Pete Delasante, Molly's sugar daddy from Washington. And a model Molly knows. Name's Jimmy Woody."

"What did you do with the tape?"

"I left it with Molly. Like the Polaroids. It was in the VCR. They were all looking at it when I left."

"There was nothing in the VCR when we looked. No tape in the apartment."

"Maybe she gave it to Pierre."

"Maybe you kept it." Lanham was writing in his note-book.

"Look. I didn't keep it, okay? I got my own tape. What's the big deal, anyway? I'll bet you everyone with a video camera's got some fun and games home movies somewhere. Half the video sales in New York are X-rated. Why are you hassling me? Are you a homicide detective or some moral crusader?"

"What do you mean, you got your own tape?"

Gorky scowled, then sighed impatiently.

"Okay. I shot a couple of tapes. I had one already in the camera when I went over there, and when that was shot up I put in another cassette. It was a long party."

"Where's the one you didn't give Molly?"

"I kept it in the camera. It's around the studio somewhere."

"Did Molly know about the second tape? Did any of them?"

He shrugged again. "They were all pretty far gone."

"I'd like to see that tape."

"You bet your ass you would. That Belinda can suck a dick more ways than the Duchess of Windsor. But it's no Oscar winner. I shot better stuff down in Mexico last year."

"I want to see the tape. I can get a court order if I have to."

"Hey, don't lean on me, Detective. I've been trying to help you. I'll look for it first chance I get. I'll give you a call."

Gorky's crew had gathered near the bench. The model they were using was looking unhappy.

"Is she in one of your home movies?" Lanham asked.

"Are you kidding? Her father's some big wheel at the U.N. and her husband's an advertising executive. Most models aren't like Molly and Belinda, you know. It's not like the movies. They don't have to put out to work."

"You're in the movies, Mr. Gorky."

"Yeah. Can I go back to work now, Detective? It's costing me money every minute they stand there."

Lanham stood. "Give me straight answers from the start and we won't have to talk so much."

"I'll look for that other tape. Have a nice day, Detective."

•

A.C. was able to find out where Jimmy Woody lived from Vanessa, who gave him a peculiar look but said nothing. The address was in Chelsea, a neighborhood A.C. knew well. When he was a young reporter he had dated a girl who lived in London Terrace, a venerable apartment complex on West Twenty-third Street. He and the girl had often gone to local joints, most particularly Mr. Spats, a smoky late-night saloon, and the bar of the Chelsea Hotel, where the girl liked to talk to "the enchanting weirdos."

The girl was as long gone as Mr. Spats. He thought about

her as he walked the old familiar streets. The weirdos were not long gone, and they were not enchanting. One old man, as much a loon as a panhandler, came roaring and raging at him from a doorway, bellowing curses after him when A.C. pushed him aside and hurried away.

Yet apartments here were renting for $2,000 a month or more. Even Chelsea was now chic.

Jimmy Woody lived on Twenty-second Street. His door was answered by a very thin black man. He was middle aged, balding, and wore a floral print short-sleeved shirt over a pair of shorts. He was barefoot. His eyebrows were inordinately dark and large, as though painted. His voice was as soft as it was deep.

"Jimmy is not here," he said. He spoke slowly, uttering each word separately. He put his hand to his face.

"I'm with the *New York Globe*," A.C. said. "I need to talk to him about a story we're doing. It's about a friend of his. Another model."

The man's eyes were dark and staring. "Would you like to come in?"

"No thank you. Can you tell me where I might find him?"

The man paused. "Jimmy has a friend. Uptown." He pronounced the word as though it were a magic, far-off place.

"Can I find him there?"

"Perhaps he will return. He was here two days ago. We dined."

A.C. took a step back.

"Would you like to come in and wait?"

"No. Thank you very much. Good night."

There was a diner around the corner. It was also chic, with flowers in little vases on the Formica tabletops. The counterman, whom A.C. took for an out-of-work actor, knew Jimmy Woody and suggested he might be at the Diamond Head, a bar on Eighteenth Street. Several of the customers had stopped talking to listen to A.C.'s inquiry and turned to watch him when he left.

There were two women in the Diamond Head. It was a small and smoky place, dominated by a huge and garishly lit tropical fish tank. The women's faces, heavily made up, were suffused in pink from that light. One of them, with long and very straight blond hair falling over her eyes, watched him as he came up to the bar, shifting her weight on the stool as though to encourage him to take the empty one next to her. He pretended not to notice.

The bartender eyed him with suspicious curiosity, but answered his questions—all in the negative. He added, finally, that Woody might be in a place on Christopher Street called the Black Bunny.

This time A.C. took a cab, getting out in the sexual no-man's-land that was Sheridan Square. He didn't know the bar, so he made a slow progress along the narrow sidewalk, peering at every sign and doorway and stepping off the curb to avoid the other pedestrians, following Christopher Street almost to Eighth Avenue.

The wooden sign was high and dark, partly obscured by dirt. He paused at the doorway, thinking of the warehouse district that stretched along the Hudson a few blocks to the west. He and Kitty had been through there once in a cab, looking for a late-night jazz joint to which they'd been misdirected. Under the elevated remains of the old West Side Highway, they'd come upon a milling gang of young men—leather jackets and metal and, in their center, some flailing arms.

Kitty had been terrified, speechless until the taxi had reached Sixth Avenue and was rumbling north toward her conception of safety and normality. She hadn't gone with him to Greenwich Village again, not even to friends living in a hugely expensive town house on West Twelfth Street.

He stepped inside the Black Bunny. But for some cheery red and yellow light coming from the jukebox and the glow of candles on the tables, the color tones of the interior were the same as the outdoor sign's, only darker.

It was quite crowded. The heat was palpable, yet the odor of the place was unexpected—a musky smell, laden with perfume. Holding his arms close to his sides, he made his way to the bar. He ordered a gin and tonic, then looked around the room. There was only one black man who looked anything like a male model, but he looked very much like one.

The place was obviously a hangout, where regulars would know one another.

"Excuse me," said A.C. to a man beside him at the bar. "Is that Jimmy Woody over there at that table?"

The man turned. "He's taken, darling," he said.

A.C. moved quickly away. There was no one at the table with Woody, though he looked like he might be waiting for someone. A.C. moved swiftly, pulling up a chair and seating himself before the other man could object.

"You're Jimmy Woody, the model?"

Disconcerted, Woody nodded.

"I'm A.C. James. I write a column for the *Globe*."

Woody reflexively flashed a smile. Normally, he'd likely be pleased and flattered at the prospect of publicity. But, apparently thinking upon his circumstances, he suddenly became very nervous. He was extremely handsome. He could have been the man on the motorcycle, if his features weren't so feminine.

"A friend of yours sent me," A.C. said, talking quickly. "Someone you work with. She said you were in trouble over a videotape, an embarrassing tape."

Woody pushed his chair back a little and looked quickly around the room. "I don't know what you're talking about."

"Yes you do. The tape was made in Molly Wickham's apartment."

"Who sent you? Belinda?" He leaned close now, whispering.

"Never mind who. It's someone who wants that tape destroyed as much as you do. She asked me to help her find it. She said you'd know who has it—that you're paying tribute to this person."

"If it's Belinda who sent you, she knows who has it."

"It wasn't Belinda St. Johns. Please, who has the tape?"

"Are you writing about this for your newspaper?"

"No, no. Certainly not. I'm only trying to help the lady. Nothing will happen to you. Just tell me the name. Please. Two little words."

"I, I . . . oh, shit."

Woody was looking over A.C.'s shoulder, his face full

183

of misery. A.C. turned slightly. Philippe Arbre was coming toward them from the entrance.

"Please go," Woody said urgently.

"The name," A.C. said.

"Go. Go away."

A.C. rose, pushing back his chair with a loud scrape. Arbre looked startled, then indignant.

"What," he said, with much drama, "are *you* doing here?"

"I was just out for a walk and stopped in for a drink," said A.C. He took one of his business cards and gave it to Woody. "If you'd like to talk some more about the modeling business, give me a call."

Woody took the card and set it on the table. A.C. might as well have handed him a cockroach.

"My, my," said Arbre, standing with his arms folded. *"Quelle surprise."*

"So nice to see you," A.C. said, which was not what he wanted to say at all.

He hurried out the door. He didn't slow down until he reached the bright lights of Seventh Avenue.

•

Lanham, bone weary, got home before eleven o'clock, but found his house darkened. Radio music indicated that his sons had gone to their rooms. He wondered if his wife was out, but he found her already in bed. Her back was turned to him, as though she hadn't stirred since morning. She didn't move when he softly called her name, or even, as she usually did, at the noise of his undressing.

He set his telephone beeper on the night table and eased back onto the mattress. It creaked slightly with his weight. She made no sound, though he could tell from her breathing that she was wide awake.

"Jan? You all right?"

There was no answer. He pulled the sheet up to his chest.

"Did they call about Pat Cassidy's wake?" he said.

"Yes," she said finally.

"Can you come?"

"I won't come."

"You won't?"

"I won't come to his funeral, and I won't come to yours."

He touched the warm flesh of her back. He might as well have touched the wall.

.

Camilla had bought the old dress, worn nurse's shoes, and babushka in a used-clothing store north of Ninety-sixth Street. Her elegant, beautiful hands she'd hidden in rubberized work gloves. She'd removed all her makeup and allowed her hair to dry uncombed, but it hadn't helped much for disguise. Still, she had been able to crowd into the office building with the others, the bucket of rags she carried and the scarf and the smudges she'd put on her face getting her past the lobby guard.

One of the cleaning women in the elevator with her had looked at her with much curiosity, but no one had stopped her. Camilla knew a few words in Polish. "*Do widzenia,*" she had said, darting out the elevator when it had reached the floor she sought. It meant "goodbye."

There had still been a few secretaries and others in the law firm's vast suite of offices when she'd entered. "*Do widzenia,*" she'd said again, to the receptionist, bustling by. It had worked.

She'd gone first to the law library, busying herself by emptying several smaller wastebaskets into a larger one and dusting bookshelves with one of her rags. When she'd heard other cleaning women moving into the area, she'd waited until they had finished with a few of the offices and then slipped into the closest, crawling under the desk, curling up into the most comfortable position possible.

The cleaning women, talking in Polish, came and went along the hall, working resolutely but taking a painful hour or more to complete their tasks. Camilla waited until all the lights had been turned out, and then waited endless minutes more. Finally, she crept out from her hiding place and stood, her cramped muscles loosening with as much agony as pleasure.

Her first need was for a bathroom. Those along the corridor were locked, but she found a private one open that

185

served a large corner office, presumably that of a senior partner.

Once she had relieved herself, she set about finding Cyrus Hall's office, which was easy enough. Locating the cabinet that would most likely contain Pierre's file was another matter. She had to turn on the main lights. Most of the file cabinets were locked, including those that seemed to contain the files of Hall's clients.

She had thought of this. A pry bar she had bought in a Second Avenue hardware store was in her bucket under the rags. It took all her strength and two broken fingernails before she got the first one open. She had to break into three more before finding Pierre's file.

It was very thick, most of it having to do with the criminal charges against Pierre in Washington. A separate manila envelope was labeled WILL AND TESTAMENT. She turned off the lights and took her find back to Hall's office, clicking on the lawyer's small, green-shaded desk lamp. Calming herself, she sat down and forced herself to read through the papers slowly.

To her amazement, to the best of her legal understanding, she was the principal beneficiary of the will. Pierre's parents were dead. Camilla's mother and a cousin who lived in Kentucky were each left lump sums of $5,000. Jacques was to receive nothing. Molly was not mentioned.

There were no other beneficiaries. There was no reference to the society editor of any South Carolina publication. There was nothing about a safe-deposit box. Pierre had been lying. The threat he had made to her about what would happen if he were killed had been only a bluff. Like so much in his life, it was made out of whole cloth.

A wonderful suspicion swept into her mind. Did Pierre even have the cache? No one in the family had seen its contents in years. Pierre might simply have been pretending. He was always pretending. They had believed him this time because they were so terrified of what would happen if he were telling the truth.

She went through the rest of the file, reading carefully the catalog of Pierre's assets. He had listed the shares of his consulting company, a holding that the federal courts could render worthless if Pierre fell victim to the charges against him. The rest of the assets seemed quite real. Bank shares in New York. A town house in Washington. An expensive limousine. A sailing yacht. A condominium in Hilton Head, South Carolina. Real property in Tawabaw County, South Carolina.

Wiping perspiration from her eyes, Camilla looked through the attached folio of real estate papers. They were photostatic copies, rendered in legalese—"All that certain lot, piece, or parcel of land with improvements thereon and appurtenances thereto belonging, lying, and being in Tawabaw County, South Carolina, known as Lot 47 . . ."

There was another for Lot 48, and 49, and 50, and more. In all, Pierre owned some eighty or more adjoining pieces of property. Accompanying plats showed surveyors' boundaries—"N 38 o 21′ 07″ E 97.05′." There were numerous descriptions of coastline.

She leaned back in Hall's huge leather swivel chair, pressing her hands against her temples, then relaxing completely, closing her eyes.

The land, quite obviously, was on Tawabaw Island. Her mother owned land there, owned much of the island. It had been in the family for generations. Pierre had been taking it from her—in the same way, no doubt, that he had acquired the use of Camilla's Sutton Place apartment and Jacques's horse farm in Virginia, in the same despicable way he had wrung so much money out of them.

The money, the apartment, the horse farm—all that she understood. He could make good use of these things in the extravagant life he had created for himself. But why the island? Of what good to him was so much swamp and sand and woods? There was nothing on Tawabaw but a small fishing village and some scattered houses and shacks like the old nana's. Those hard-working people were among the poorest in the state.

Pierre's bequest to her included all that land, but he had no intention of dying. The will was an irrelevancy in the present circumstance.

Camilla swiveled in the chair, staring bleakly at the great dark city outside the window. There were a few lights on in some of the buildings. Security guards moved through them at night.

Fear quickened her thoughts. It was time to leave. She had no doubt committed several crimes here this night. She wouldn't add theft. She'd seen enough. Returning the papers to their proper place, she closed the mangled file drawer. Perhaps they'd blame Jacques. She was sure Pierre would.

Her escape meant descending twenty-one flights of concrete service stairs. In the huge basement area, she came across a loading dock. Beyond was a large, truck-size retractable door and, beside it, a small fire exit. It led to a side street. An alarm sounded when she opened it, but she was quickly gone. After she turned the corner onto Park Avenue, the sound stopped.

CHAPTER

....

9

The bright, clear weather had held. The wind had shifted from the northwest to northeast, the breeze about ten knots, rising in gusts to fifteen knots or more, ruffling the surface of the river as far as one could see, the high morning sun glittering on the broken water. There were mountains this far up the Hudson from the city, low and rounded to the west, higher and sharper to the north, the ridges and summit a dark, lush green clearly etched against the clean sky.

A.C. was crossing the river on a starboard tack, sailing on a beam reach and a northwest heading to keep a course against the strong current. Their goal was the city of Haverstraw on the Rockland County shore, by line of sight directly opposite their home above Croton Point on the Westchester side. The crossing was ritual. The lights of Haverstraw were the centerpiece of their view at night, a fixture of their lives. Sailing to it made an afternoon's outing into a voyage. The river here was as wide as a Swiss lake. It was a substantial undertaking for a nine-year-old boy in stiffening weather—even for his father.

It was a rather small boat—twenty-three feet with a rudimentary cabin. Ostensibly, it slept four, but only two with any real comfort. Kitty liked sailing, but only in pleasant, balmy weather. Their daughter, Kathleen, was bored by it. Little Davey considered sailing an essential part of life. He had told A.C. he hadn't been on the boat since A.C. had left.

A sense of cleanliness invigorated A.C., the wind scouring every rancid cranny of his spirit. He had awakened that morning feeling sleazy and sordid from his encounters with Belinda St. Johns and the male model. The impulse to travel up to Westchester despite his wife's admonition not to had become overpowering.

Now he felt calm, even relaxed. He tilted back his head, the sun full upon his face.

A.C. had worn clothes good enough for the train trip from the city but comfortable and hardy enough for the boat—a navy blazer, striped gray and white shirt open at the collar, khakis, white socks, and brown Sperry Top-Siders. He'd left his blazer in the Jeep Cherokee he'd borrowed from the house and left parked at the yacht harbor. He'd rolled up his shirtsleeves. As he held the tiller, he noticed how much the tan on his arms had faded living in the city.

Davey was standing at the forward end of the cockpit, leaning against the bulkhead by the steps that led into the cabin, peering under the foot of the jib at the traffic on the water. He was tall for his age and very slender, giving the impression that he was growing before one's very eyes. He had brown eyes and an incipient handsomeness resembling A.C.'s. His narrow hands and feet were like his mother's. He was very tan for so early in the summer, and the sun had turned his curly, reddish brown hair to a coppery gold.

"Barges coming, Dad."

It was as wide as a Swiss lake but it was still a river. A large raft of coal barges was churning along in the down-

190

stream channel, a large tug pushing from the rear. A.C. calculated its speed and his own. He could cross ahead of it without insurmountable risk, but he was of no mind to take any. He loved this boy as much as he did his wife and had missed him terribly. He wanted nothing to mar this reunion, certainly not any frightening excitements.

"Ready about!"

"Ready!" responded Davey, leaping to the winch that held the jib sheet.

"Helm's a' lee!" A.C. said, thrusting the tiller away from him.

The boat began to swing on its axis, as Davey's arms worked hurriedly on the winch, hauling the jib around to starboard. The boom shifted and the mainsail snapped full, Davey's jib filling almost immediately after. He locked the winch and smiled, the veteran sailor. A.C. smiled back.

They sat idly, watching the barges grow large in their approach, a huge, curling bow wave spreading to either side. As the tug passed, its chugging engine loud, they waved to a crewman. He waved back, a constant part of his job on a waterway strewn with so many pleasure craft.

The heaving wake came at them like a tidal wave.

"Ready about!" A.C. cried.

Davey was at his post again in an instant. They changed tack as swiftly and smoothly as America's Cup racers, resuming their original course under full sail in time to breast the wake effortlessly on the port quarter. The boat heaved up and down, the mast stays and halyards clanking.

When they returned to calmer water, A.C. eased forward along the cockpit seat.

"Take the helm, Mr. James."

"Yes sir," said Davey. He slipped under A.C.'s arm and, sitting close beside him, took the tiller with both hands.

"Heading on the Haverstraw buoy."

"Yes sir."

"Mind the river traffic."

"I will."

A.C. gripped the boy's shoulder briefly, then rose and went below. He found some gin and a bottle of tonic in a storage bin beneath the cabin's small sink and made a drink for himself in a large plastic cup. He poured some warm

191

Coca-Cola into another cup for Davey and brought both back up to the cockpit, sitting opposite his son, even though it caused the boat to heel slightly.

"Thank you, Dad," said Davey, hooking his arm over the tiller as he reached to take the cup. He sipped. "What are you drinking?"

"Gin and tonic."

"Dad? Are you drinking a lot?"

"What?"

"Mom says you're drinking a lot."

"She said that to you?"

"No. To a friend of hers she had over. Mrs. Lambrecht. I could hear her in my room. She was crying."

"No, Davey. I'm not. Not really. I'm sorry your mother got upset."

Annie Lambrecht was Kitty's most frequent golf and bridge partner at the country club—a good friend, but not an intimate.

"Are you all right, Dad?"

"I'm—I'm fine. I was a witness to a murder a few days ago. A woman was shot right in front of me."

"I know. We saw it on television."

"I guess it's getting on my nerves."

Davey was looking at him with doubt, if not mistrust.

"I'm all right, Davey. I really am."

"Are you going to come back to live with us?"

"Yes, of course." He hesitated. His son was not believing him. "Well, I guess that's up to your mother. We're—we're having a fight."

"You never had a fight this long before."

"No. I guess we haven't."

A.C. drank some of the warm gin. He almost never allowed himself spirits when they were in the boat and under way. It was a rule. Only at anchor.

"Dad?"

"Yes?"

"Can I come live with you?"

He and Davey, alone in the middle of the Upper East Side. He and Davey and Bailey, wherever she was. Kitty would kill him first.

"That would be nice, Davey."

"Can I go back with you?"

"Maybe not this time."

"Please?"

"Davey, I'm not really supposed to be up here. Your mother and I, well, this has become quite a fight."

A.C. saw the small powerboat at nearly the last moment, coming upon them in a great noisy rush from the port quarter of the bow. He grabbed the tiller away from his son.

"I've got the helm!" he shouted.

Their boat swerved and lunged to the left. The mainsail flattened and fluttered, then caught the wind on the leeward side, throwing the craft into a violent jibe, the boom swinging wildly to the right, nearly hitting Davey in the head. The boat heeled over dangerously, water slapping up at the rail.

A.C. snapped the mainsheet out of its cleat and let it run out, the boom continuing on far out over the starboard side. The craft righted itself, heading downstream on a run.

Both their cups had fallen and were rolling around the cockpit decking, which was now sticky with their contents.

"Goddamn it!" said A.C.

"I'm sorry, Dad! I'm sorry!"

The powerboat, trailing tails of foam, was racing away from them, a teenage boy at the wheel shouting at them and making an obscene gesture.

"The little bastard."

"It's my fault, Dad. I wasn't looking."

"It's his fault. We had the right of way."

Davey looked very unhappy. He took a seat at the forward end of the cockpit, looking down at his worn boating shoes.

"Take the helm, Davey."

"No, that's all right, Dad."

"You're sure?"

"Yes."

"Okay. We'll get back on a heading for Haverstraw."

"That's all right. We can go back now."

"You don't mean home?"

"Yes. We don't need to keep sailing."

"Davey, it was just a near miss. We did fine. It's all part of sailing."

The boy sighed. "I know."

They were heading downstream. A.C. pointed the bow around to as northeasterly a course as he could manage without slipping into irons. It meant sailing close-hauled and heeling sharply, but he didn't want to have to keep tacking. He wanted to talk.

He began hauling the mainsheet tight, the heel increasing with his pull.

"I could use some weight over here."

The boy clambered over to his side. A.C. put his arm around him. The water was rushing white along the rail.

"Davey, you'll be able to be with me. Either here or there, or somewhere. I'll work it out."

The boy said nothing. On his own, he began to trim the jib to match the angle of the mainsail.

"I love you," A.C. said.

"I know that."

"And Kathleen."

"Yes."

"And your mother."

His son said nothing.

"We'll work it out."

"Dad? How long can you stay?"

"I want to talk to your mother. I'll stay at least until she comes back."

He didn't have to wait. As they entered the harbor on the small outboard engine, puttering through the moorings and traffic with sails lowered, he saw Kitty on the dock, standing with arms folded. He turned into their slip, reversing the little motor to slow their forward movement and steering a little sideways to swing the beam of the boat up against the rubber tire bumpers. As they touched, creaking, Davey leapt onto the dock, grabbing the bow line and securing it with a figure eight on a dockside cleat.

Kitty came forward. She was as picture perfect as the photo on his desk, wearing a pink cardigan sweater, white blouse, loose-fitting khaki Bermudas, and brown loafers.

Her gray hair, slightly windblown, was held back by a pink hair ribbon.

"Do you have the keys to the Jeep?" she asked. Her voice was flat, emotionless, the Westchester accent perfect, but somewhat clipped.

"Yes," A.C. said.

"When you finish with the boat, I want you to drive it back to the house."

"All right."

"Davey, go get in the car. My car."

He could see her gray Mercedes in the parking lot.

"Kitty, I—"

"I don't want to talk to you now. Just put the boat back the way you found it."

Davey was walking up the dock, head lowered.

"Kitty. I didn't mean any harm."

She stared at him for a very long moment. There was something in her gaze that reminded him of nature films of lions silently watching a herd of prey, pondering their choice of victims.

Without a word, she then turned and followed her son to the shore.

A.C. tied the other lines to the dock, coiled the lines and sheets aboard the boat, stuffed the sails into waterproof bags, and stowed them below. After cleaning up the spilled drinks on the cockpit deck, he locked the hatch cover and left the key with the harbormaster, signing the book. Reaching the Jeep, he paused only to put on his blazer, then roared up the roadway to the street above, his wheels spinning slightly as he slid around the curve at the top.

To reach their house, he had to drive to the top of a hill just off Highway 9 north of the village, and then follow their long driveway for two curves down the other side. The view of the Hudson and its valley was as magnificent as he could remember, but his eyes were fixed on the figures standing by the three-car garage.

Kitty had left her Mercedes in the turnaround, but had opened two of the three garage doors. He drove inside, turning off the engine. As he shut the door, he heard her telling Davey to go into the house.

He stepped out into the sunlight. "Now what?"

"Get into the Mercedes, A.C."

He did so obediently. As she got in behind the wheel, he realized this was the first time he had been this close to her in two weeks. She almost brushed his arm. He wished she had.

"Do you want to go for a drive?" he asked, as she turned back onto the road. "Do you want to talk?" She had quite lovely legs and they were very tan. So were her hands and arms. He saw she still wore her wedding ring.

"No. I'm taking you back to the station."

"Kitty. For God's sake. There won't be a train for almost two hours."

"Then go find a bar." She gunned the engine, skidding around a curve.

"Kitty!"

"I told you not to come up."

"You didn't even let me say goodbye to Davey."

"I'll provide you a better occasion. A more memorable one."

"What do you mean?"

"Look. Do you want me to explode? Do you want me to start calling you all sorts of vile names? Do you want to have another big fight?"

"No."

"Then shut up."

She slipped off the road a moment, the wheels chewing up gravel and then bouncing back onto concrete again. He remained silent all the way to the station, staring at her, wondering what might lie within his power to change all this, until they pulled up at the sidewalk fronting the little railroad depot.

"When will I see you again?" he asked softly.

"Get out, A.C."

He sighed, and snapped open the door. Closing it, he sought her eyes, but she was staring straight ahead. When he stepped back, she ground the gears into reverse, screeched into a backward turn, then roared off into the street. Then all was silent. The station was deserted.

There were iron steps leading to the elevated walkway

196

that crossed the tracks to the inbound platform. He climbed them wearily. The station was in a defile, cut off from the wind, and the sunlight was very hot.

On the other side of the tracks, he slumped wearily onto a bench and leaned forward, resting his elbows on his knees. The silent emptiness in both directions underscored the totality of his abandonment. He had asked for this. He'd been doomed to it the moment he'd left his apartment.

Camilla, wherever she was, seemed very far away. She had a home in France. Perhaps she had by now returned to it, and was beyond reach of this horrible mess. When he got back to the city, he could go directly to the police and tell them everything he knew—tell them, and the editors at his paper. He couldn't believe his wife was through with him. Much as he had wanted to, he hadn't taken Camilla to bed. There'd only been a few kisses—as in all of his flirtations. In time, he would forget all about it.

No, he wouldn't. He was lying to himself as much as he'd been lying to his wife. Camilla was now in his system, like some virus. She was in his thoughts as much as his wife and children, sometimes more so. He kept remembering her leaning over him, attending to his wounds; kept remembering her kiss—kept imagining her body without clothes. She had French poetry on her bookshelves and modernist paintings on her walls. He'd seen a CD by her stereo—Shostakovich's *Leningrad Symphony*. She was a Southern lady who had taken a beautiful photograph of an old gnarled black woman, for whom she had felt very sad.

A.C. had never known a woman like Camilla Santee. He wouldn't forget her for a very long time, even if he never saw her again.

He could do nothing that might possibly hurt her. He would talk to no one. Not yet.

He put his head in his hands. Aside from everything else, there was Bailey.

An automobile horn sounded, but he ignored it. Then it sounded again, insistently. He looked up. There was a gray car in the parking lot opposite—Kitty's Mercedes. He saw something move behind the windshield. Then she hit the horn once more.

197

With some slowness now, he reclimbed the steps to the walkway and crossed over. Descending, he went to the driver's side, but did not come near the window.

"What do you want, Kitty?"

"Get in." Her voice was as restrained as before, but her expression had changed. He saw that she had been crying. "Get in. I'm going to drive you into town."

•

Policemen made lousy soldiers. They didn't think like soldiers, didn't act like soldiers. They couldn't be made to look like soldiers. When they tried, they appeared evil and menacing or very foolish. The SS in Nazi Germany pretended to be soldiers, but were really policemen—maybe the ultimate policemen—and it showed. This was true also of soldiers in Latin American countries. They looked like cops—very bad and very corrupt cops, but cops.

The cops at Pat Cassidy's mass looked very foolish. Drawn up in military formation as an honor guard with batons raised as the casket was carried by, they stared straight ahead, lips pursed, shoulders stiff, playacting the guard at the Tomb of the Unknown Soldier. But they were laughable—there was too much belly in view, too many sideburns and woolly mustaches, too much age. Soldiers on parade are trained to rid their faces of all expression. Cops always have expressions. Soldiers are young. Cops are old. Police units had come to Cassidy's funeral from all over the metropolitan area. A few were from out of state —highway troopers in outlandish uniforms, small-town cops from Pennsylvania, New Jersey, Connecticut, and Virginia. The latter contingent roiled the acid in Lanham's unhappy stomach. Bad Biker Bobby was black. Pat Cassidy was dead.

Lanham was a pallbearer. So were Cassidy's two brothers and brother-in-law. Taranto, Caputo, Tony Gabriel, and Petrowicz made up the rest. Cassidy's widow had requested that, even though the fatal shot had been fired by Gabriel.

The mayor made a stock speech full of nonsense, all about war and battles and likening brave men like Patrick Francis Cassidy to the Trojans who stood at Thermopylae. No one had bothered or dared to tell his speechwriter that the heroic stand had been made by Spartans. Mention the name Leonidas to the mayor and he'd think you were talking about someone who owned a restaurant in Astoria.

The commissioner gave a speech only slightly less inane. The chief of detectives got very Irish, and went on about ancient chieftains. Only Taranto delivered a true eulogy—about the days when Cassidy had been a very good cop. No one even hinted that Pat had died because he'd been drunk and afraid.

Mrs. Cassidy sat through it all very stoically. There had been tears that first night. The priest had told Lanham that. They'd come again after the funeral, when she had more to drink; when she was alone again.

Tony had tried to catch Lanham's eye when they had brought the casket to the altar. With the mass said and done, as they came forward to resume their task, he leaned close to Lanham and whispered. "Ray. I gotta talk to you."

"Not now."

"Outside."

"In the car."

"Not in the car. Alone."

Because they were the tallest, Lanham and Petrowicz carried the forward end of the casket. This helped as they descended the steps outside the church, but once on the even pavement, they had to slouch and hunch to keep their burden level. Lanham's shoulder was hurting by the time they reached the black Cadillac hearse and slid the casket forward into the waiting, practiced hands of the undertaker's assistant.

Lanham straightened himself slowly, arching his back. The ceremony was over, but not concluded. The assembled policemen, clubs to the fore, were still at attention, waiting.

"Now, Ray," said Gabriel.

"We've got to go to the cemetery."

"Not yet." He jerked his head toward the mayor, who was talking to a small mob of newsmen.

"All right."

They went down the sidewalk past their car. Petrowicz made as if to follow, but Lanham shook his head. Gabriel stopped by an overgrowth of bushes that badly needed trimming, and lit a cigarette. He looked a little nervous. His eyes were like Taranto's.

"You're after some pictures," he said.

"I guess I made that pretty obvious."

"I got a problem."

"You've got a lot of problems, Tony."

"This girl, Belinda. You know I got something special with her."

"You've got a special kind of trouble with her."

"Give me a break, Raymond. I'll take care of that shit. This is something else."

He took a deep drag from his cigarette, then looked at Lanham hard.

"I gotta ask you a favor," Gabriel said. "I'm going to give you something you can't use."

"You give me a break, Tony."

"All right, listen. That newspaper guy, that rich bastard A.C. James, your great eyewitness. He knows about the videotape you're looking for. He hit Belinda up about it yesterday. She's scared shitless he's going to put something about them in the paper and her old man'll find out. And you know what her old man is like."

"What about you, Tony? Don't you know what he's like? You're sleeping with his woman. Don't you know how wiseguys in his position like to deal with situations like that?"

"I'll worry about me."

"I'm not talking about you, Tony. The outfit isn't going to mess with a cop who isn't in the business. But what about her?"

"I'm trying to help her, Ray. That's why I'm telling you this."

"What does James know?"

"He knows there's a videotape that wasn't shot by Walt Disney and that Belinda was paying off somebody to keep it out of circulation."

"Did you talk to James?"

"No, just Belinda."

"Does he know who she's paying? Do you?"

"That's what he was trying to find out." Gabriel took a long final drag and dropped the cigarette onto the pavement, crushing it with his highly polished shoe. "I know who it is, Ray. Belinda was stupid enough to tell me."

"His name's Gorky, right? A photographer named Gorky?"

"No, she never mentioned any Gorky. It's Molly Wickham's fat boyfriend that she's been paying. Pete something."

"Pierre. Pierre Delasante."

"Whatever."

"But he was in the tape."

"Maybe so, but he's got it. And he's been shaking Belinda down. He's taken her for more than ten thousand so far. Ten fucking large."

"She's not bullshitting you?"

"She's in love with me, Ray. And she's scared to death."

"They're always in love with you, Tony. This one you haven't known a week."

"Things happen, okay? Look. I helped you out here. You help me out. Help me get the fucking tape back. Lean on this guy."

"I'm not much interested in charity work, Tony. Least of all for a police detective who's screwing a witness. But I'll go this far with you. I'm investigating a homicide. I don't give a damn about somebody's dirty pictures unless they're material to the case."

"Thanks, Ray."

"But if they are material, if the D.A. needs a count of every pubic hair in every shot to score some point with a jury, then all bets are off."

"I hear what you're saying."

It was black talk. Lanham didn't like it coming from Gabriel.

"And Tony, I don't want you putting the arm on that newspaper columnist. You'll only make things worse."

"I can't even find him."

"Don't find him. I'll deal with him."

The evil little genie in Lanham's pocket began its insistent squeaking. As he turned toward the church, he heard Gabriel's beeper go off as well. In the crowd, Caputo and the lieutenant were moving. Lanham searched for Petrowicz's face, finding it near the hearse, just above the line of blue caps. He was shouting. Lanham couldn't hear, but could see him mouthing the word.

Darcy. Bad Biker Bobby was about to become very sorry he hadn't taken up honest work. Lanham started running.

•

The state parkway was an old road, designed for pleasure drives in narrower, slower cars of a more leisurely era. The weekend traffic was heavy, but moving fast. It took Kitty's full concentration to keep her place in it.

They had not spoken since leaving the railroad station parking lot. She had something definite in mind to do or say to him, but was fighting herself over it. To intrude upon that struggle would be folly. He guessed she had come near to reaching a conclusion about what was going on between them, and what was to be done. If there was any chance for a last appeal, for one last grasp at saving rationality, he didn't want to destroy it with an ill-chosen remark.

He sat very still, as though pressed back in his seat by the force of the tension. From time to time, when she was preoccupied with shifting gears or changing lanes, he allowed himself a careful glance at her.

Had she noticed, she would have found these most appreciative glances. A man ignores and forgets a great deal about his wife when a marriage endures. She had grown no less lovely, no less endearing, in the accumulating years since their daily lives had become one. Were he meeting her now for the first time, he would be quite smitten. He had a desire to touch the pale downy hairs on her arm, to rest his hand on the tanned smoothness of her thigh. Before the sudden wrench of their separation, he would have done such a thing as a simple, casual, almost careless gesture.

They were nearing the city. These moments with her, spent in painful silence as they hurtled along to the inescapable point of parting, could be their last together. He compelled himself to accept that, to behave well, to do the gentlemanly thing and make it as easy as possible for her, and so for himself. These dwindling minutes would probably be much with him when he was old.

A small red sports car cut arrogantly in front of them,

causing Kitty to slam on the brakes. A.C.'s hand went instantly to the polished wood of the dashboard, then settled on his knee. Kitty tilted back her head and took a deep breath.

"I had an affair," she said. Her voice was calm.

"What?"

She repeated herself, this time spitting out the words. "I had an affair! I slept with another man."

Kitty pushed a windblown strand of hair from her eyes. "I did it several times—many times. For more than a year."

"With whom?"

The words were stupid and unwelcome. He had uttered them as though in reflex, without thinking. He was completely numb. He didn't want to know what naked male had lain sweating and entangled with the mother of his son. He didn't want a name or a face. He didn't want a focus for his pain and anger.

And guilt.

"It doesn't matter really, does it?" she said. As she seemed not to realize, they were slowing. The other traffic was swiftly passing by, as though they were in another dimension.

"I'll tell you this, A.C.," she continued. "He's rich, as rich as I am. He's in the *Social Register*, just like Bailey Hazeltine and all your other lady friends. He's as attractive to women as you are. He's equally charming. His manners are as splendid. He's as sweet, and he's far more thoughtful. He has a job. It's a very important job. But he doesn't let it consume his whole life. I'm not going to go on any more about him, because I don't want you playing detective and embarrassing me any further. I don't want you to find out who he is. But I want you to know this, A.C. He didn't need anything from me. He didn't want anything from me but me."

Suddenly aware of their diminishing speed, she pressed her foot hard against the accelerator, shooting ahead of a station wagon that had been passing her on the left.

"He was in love with me," she said. "He's divorced. He wanted me to get a divorce and marry him. He still does. I had a letter from him last week. He said I've hurt him badly."

Was all this intended to make him jealous? A.C. didn't know how she wanted him to respond, didn't know how *he* wanted to respond.

"Were you with him in London?" A.C. asked, very matter-of-factly.

"London, Paris, New York, Boston, Bedford Village. What difference does it make? What if it were Poughkeepsie? Or Buffalo?"

Bedford Village was an extremely expensive estate-strewn town in Westchester, about twelve miles from their house on the river. A.C. now knew exactly who this man was. But there was no point in uttering his name, unless he wanted to be vindictive—unless he wanted to make a really great mess of this.

"I haven't even seen him in months, A.C. I broke this off a long time ago. I didn't love him. I don't now. I didn't even want to think about divorce. But it was just so wonderful to be loved the way that man loved me. I've never been loved that way in my life."

"That's not true."

She looked over at him, for the first time since they began the drive. Her gray eyes, bright in the sunlight, were mocking.

"It's true," she said.

They were south of White Plains, approaching the city. The suburbs they passed through were old and thickly built.

"In a way, I hated it, A.C. I was scared to death half the time. When I was with you, I felt sick and sordid and dirty. Christ, the guilt. I wanted to tell you at least a dozen times, just to get rid of the damned guilt. It made me feel worse than all of the suspicions I had about you."

She was gripping the wheel very tightly, oversteering enough to make the driver of the car next to them very nervous. The traffic was quite heavy now, though still moving fast.

"That stupid, silly, childish bargain we struck in the beginning. That we'd forgive an affair, I thought, don't you know, that it might somehow keep you from being unfaithful, that you'd never want to squander your only chance to cheat free of charge. But I knew almost immediately it was a mistake. I hated you for agreeing to it. I

204

worried every time you talked to another woman. In the beginning, I think I went with this man just to try to get it all behind me, to get rid of this stupid, dangerous thing I'd intruded on our marriage. Maybe to get the score up on my side, against the day I'd catch you out." She looked at him again. "But it didn't work, did it? There was your part of the bargain, always hanging over me, always there. It was like a power you had over me. I couldn't look at a woman I knew you knew without wondering if you'd been with her. Even Vanessa. Even my friends."

They were passing by apartment buildings now, some old and stately, some weary and drab. Beyond lay housing projects and the burned-out shells that the city would not remove and replace until the poor and the criminals who fed upon them had been swept away.

A green highway sign flashed overhead. She turned right, following a route that took them back to the river.

"Did you talk to a priest?"

"Yes. Of course."

"What did he say?"

"The usual things priests say. It didn't do any good. Priests are not God."

"Why didn't you talk to me?"

"You're not God either, A.C. I thought you'd only lie to me, and that would make things worse. Also, I was a little afraid of you. I didn't know what you'd do."

He reached and took her hand from the steering wheel. She resisted at first, but only for an instant, relenting as he leaned forward and gently kissed her palm. They drove on with him holding her hand in both of his.

"I didn't do anything with any of those women," he said. "They were flirtations, nothing more. I never meant to hurt you."

"Don't lie to me."

She pulled her hand away. They were approaching a toll-booth. He quickly took some change from his pocket and gave it to her, pressing it into her hand.

"I still haven't decided what to do, A.C. Except that everything will have to be different. I don't know how we're going to arrange that, but we have to. We have to try, if there's ever going to be a life for us again."

"I'll do whatever you ask."

"No. You always do whatever I ask. Do what you think will help."

"All right."

"There's one thing, though. And I don't give a good goddamn how difficult it is for you. I don't want you to ever see Bailey Hazeltine again."

"That's all past."

"No it's not. You're seeing her now."

He said nothing. He sensed they were getting to the only thing she really wanted to talk about.

"Bailey just popped up. I hadn't seen her in months. She's in trouble. I just tried to help."

"Are you telling me you didn't sleep with her?"

"She's gone, Kitty. She comes and goes and now she's gone again. Disappeared. I don't expect she'll turn up for a long, long time."

"I mean never, A.C. There's no room in our marriage for that woman."

"All right."

"You promise?"

"Yes!"

They reached Manhattan, following the curves of the West Side Highway. A vague haze had slid over the sky. The river water was gray, but still sparkling in the filtered sunlight.

There was an open parking space just a few doors down from his building. It was illegal, but the police probably wouldn't bother them about it until morning. She turned off the engine, leaning back against the leather seat and stretching out her arms. She let them drop to the tops of her legs.

"It was a long drive," he said. "Why don't you come up for a drink?"

"I don't think that's such a good idea."

"It's your apartment, Kitty."

"Our apartment."

He nodded. "Our apartment."

"All right. For one drink. But just one. The children will be worried."

"If they know where you are, I think they'll be very pleased."

"I'll call them."

They went upstairs without bothering the old doorman, who was asleep. The apartment was just as he had left it— a dreadful mess. Newspapers and magazines were scattered about, including one glossy fashion monthly that was opened to a picture of Camilla Santee. There were several glasses on the tabletops. One of his ties was on the floor.

"Did you fire the maid?" Kitty asked, standing hesitantly in the middle of the living room.

"She doesn't come until Monday."

He began picking up the magazines. She went to a chair in the corner, pulling off her sweater and slipping off her shoes. She was barefoot; her trim, narrow feet were nearly as tan as her legs.

"It's hot in here," she said.

"I'll open the doors to the terrace." He clicked off the locks and pushed the doors open. The outside air was warm and moist, but sweeter than the staleness within, and there was a breeze.

"What would you like to drink?"

"A scotch and water, if you have any left." She glanced around. "I heard about your drinking."

"Not all that much. The murder was hard to take. And then someone beat me up."

"Bill said you were in a fight in a bar."

"That was the office rumor. I was mugged. On the street. Over by the park."

She studied his face. "I'm sorry."

"Life in the city."

He poured scotch, rather heavily, into two glasses, then went into the kitchen with them to add ice and water. When he returned, she was leaning back in the chair, fully relaxed. She sat up and took the drink, making a face when she sipped it.

"Good grief, A.C."

"Just one," he said.

"If that."

They sat quietly for a long moment.

"You could stay for dinner," he said.

"I could."

"There's not much here."

"I'm not exactly dressed for Le Cirque."

"We'll get some takeout."

The front door opened. There was no knock, no call from the lobby, just a turn of the key. Bailey stumbled in, hair hanging over her face, blouse pulled out of her skirt, a large, long run in one of her stockings. If she had been doing drugs, the effect had worn off. Now she was simply very drunk.

She looked at A.C., then at Kitty, a friendly but silly little girl's smile crooked on her face.

"Oh shit," she said quietly. She backed up, then fled out the door.

Kitty got abruptly up from her chair, jamming her feet into her shoes. She slammed her drink down on a table, spilling it slightly, then snatched up her sweater and purse.

"Thank you very much."

"Kitty. I'd no idea—"

"You gave her the bloody key, didn't you? You should have called her and told her you were bringing someone home for dinner."

Her face was very flushed.

"Kitty, will you listen to me, please?"

He reached for her arm, but she pulled away. His hand caught on her sweater. There was a slight ripping sound. It was the final touch.

"I want you out of here," she said, her voice almost a growl.

She went to the door. There was only one elevator. She listened until she heard it close and start its descent, then she stepped out into the hall. He tried to follow, but the anger in her eyes stayed him. He hung in the doorway, wanting to kill Bailey.

Kitty looked down at the floor, her hand pressed hard on the elevator button. He would have done great violence to anyone who hurt her as much as she had been hurt just now.

"This is no way to end it, Kitty. Not like this. Not for this."

208

"I don't know what I'm going to have to do," she said. "I'll have to do what the lawyers say. But I'm going to get you out of my life and I'm not going to let you take anything with you. That includes the children, A.C. That includes Davey."

"Kitty!"

"I can't legally make you leave here until I get a judicial decree," she said. "But I would truly appreciate it if you'd get out just as soon as you can. You, and your lady."

She said the last word contemptuously.

When the elevator closed behind her, he stood staring at it for a very long time.

•

If Bad Bobby Darcy had been smart, which he wasn't, he'd have been out of New York within minutes of the shootout in that apartment up near Lenox Avenue. He might have tarried just a little to pick up some traveling money from one or two of his ladies, but then he'd have been long gone to the first big city that could swallow him up—Miami, Detroit, Philadelphia, Baltimore, any place with enough black people to make his just another black face—until he went into business again, got busted, and had his prints turn up in the cross reference.

Lanham, knowing Bobby was dumb, expected him to hang around. He was a little king in the vast New York scheme of things, but the powers of kingship were not transportable. Lanham was sure he'd holed up among his subjects, depending on the fear of most of them and the love of a few to hide him and see him through. It was what people like Bobby almost always did and it was why they almost always were caught. There would always be someone who didn't fear him enough or love him enough. Lanham had expected to hear from one of them at any time—someone Bobby had beaten up or cut or humiliated, someone looking for a reduced charge from the district attorney's office or for the police to "lose" or "mislay" a file. Someone who just wanted the pressure to ease on the Deuce.

Instead, Bobby had done something both smart and dumb. He'd had his hair cut properly, found himself a

209

courtroom suit, and gone to a rich white man's hotel down near Wall Street and the Battery, a brand new gleaming four-star high-rise palace of a hotel where the police wouldn't have looked for him if he'd shot the mayor in the lobby in front of a hundred witnesses.

In a courtroom suit, especially the pin-striped kind he might have seen on one of his lawyers, Bobby would likely have been given a room without question. The hotel was used by money men from all over the world. It accepted rich white men who happened to be black as easily as it did rich white men who happened to be Japanese or Arab. If Bobby had minded his manners and been reasonably blasé about using one of the credit cards his ladies from time to time lifted from their more inebriated customers, he might have been able to camp out in the hotel for days or weeks, while the police plodded pointlessly through garbage-stewn alleys and urine-soaked unlit hallways all over the city.

But Bobby had been dumb as well as smart. Instead of checking into the hotel, he'd had one of his girls acquire a john and accompany him to his room. Then Bobby had joined them in midtryst and established a temporary ménage à trois. He hadn't been content to heist the man's cash, watch, and cufflinks—as he and his ladies had done to many a visitor to the city. He was apparently interested in serious travel money. It had not been determined what threat Bobby had used to persuade the gentleman to call his company in Houston to request the sum of $5,000, to be delivered to the hotel. If the man's wife was the divorcing kind, especially the Texas divorcing kind, the mere fact of the chippie would suffice. The $5,000 had been sent. It had just arrived at the hotel's front desk.

Bad Bobby was that dumb. He was even dumber. He and his female assistant had moved into the man's room sometime in the early hours of Friday morning. It was now Saturday. The man had been expected home on Friday night. His wife had called the airline and the local police.

Bobby had sent his lady down to the front desk to fetch the money when it arrived. He'd persuaded his Texas hostage to tell the desk clerk over the phone that his "secretary" would be retrieving it.

On a weekday, she might have passed relatively unnoticed, but on the weekend, the hotel was deserted. She might as well have been wearing a neon sign. She hadn't gotten halfway across the lobby before a house detective had stopped her on general suspicion.

She was now being held in the hotel manager's office. She had told a detective sergeant from the precinct everything but her name.

It had been forty minutes since she'd been grabbed and nearly twenty since Lanham and the others had been summoned from Cassidy's funeral mass. The Texan, reportedly quite nervous, had called down to the desk twice asking the girl's whereabouts. Bad Bobby was likely considerably more nervous.

"Shit," said Petrowicz, skidding their unmarked Dodge around a Cadillac limo. "Who'd have thought he'd turn up in Moneyland?"

"Just get us there, and in one fucking piece," said Taranto from the back seat.

They were speeding as fast as practicable down FDR Drive. Other police cars were converging on the area from West Street and the Brooklyn Tunnel. They had orders to keep sirens off and to stay away from the hotel entrance. The cops on the scene had said the Texan's room was on the twenty-seventh floor, and had a view of the street in front of the hotel.

Tony Gabriel and Caputo had been sent back to the division. Taranto wanted them miles away from Darcy when the action closed.

He wanted Lanham as close as possible, but that was what Lanham wanted, too.

Lanham was in the seat next to Petrowicz, leaning forward tensely and clutching the radio mike as though it were a hand grenade with the pin pulled. He paid no attention to the traffic they were careening by. His mind's eye was on the door to the Texan's hotel room. They might have only seconds. Bad Bobby didn't know it, but for the moment he was in charge of everything.

Swearing, Lanham realized he was holding down the mike switch. He was cutting off all reception.

He released the switch. Static and garbled voices filled the car. They were on an emergency channel. Someone was holding down a mike key on the other end.

"What a fuck-up," said Petrowicz.

They rounded a curve so far on the outside the fender seemed only millimeters from the steel guard rail. Lanham expected sparks and an explosive scrape of metal against metal, but it never came.

The radio quieted. Lanham activated his microphone, calling the captain from the precinct who was now the senior man on the scene.

"Ten-seventeen at Twenty-third Street," Lanham said. "What is your present situation?"

"We've got men on the floor, men on the floors above and below," said the captain, a man Lanham did not know. "But the room is directly across from the elevators. Cannot secure."

"Call some shots, Ray," said Taranto, "before we get some downtown heavies on the scene."

Lanham allowed himself the luxury of ten seconds to think.

"Subject is still in the room?" he said.

"Affirmative."

"Have the girl call the room. Have her say she has the money and is coming up."

"Give her the money?"

"Have her call the room and say she has the money and is coming up."

"Are you crazy, Ray?" said Taranto.

"Just want to buy a little time," Lanham said. He wasn't just buying time for the dumb son of a bitch from Texas. He was buying it for himself, so that he could be the man outside the door, so that he would be the one to lay hands on Darcy.

Lanham hit the switch again. "Have you placed the call?"

"Calling now," said the captain.

"Freeze the elevators," muttered Taranto.

"Freeze the elevators," repeated Lanham.

"Affirmative," said the captain. "Already done that. Got a man on each."

"Clear the lobby."

212

"Already done that. Subject responding to call. Subject on line."

"Are you monitoring?"

"Affirmative."

"Ten-four."

Everyone fell silent. Petrowicz had the gas pedal on the floor. The only control he was paying attention to was the steering wheel.

Traffic was thinning. The high-rises of lower Manhattan were very near.

"Oh shit," said the captain.

"What's wrong?" said Lanham.

"She fucked it up," said the captain. "Subject has us made. Subject has terminated the call."

"Let them take him, Ray," Taranto said.

"No, boss. I don't want any more shot-up corpses."

"Ray!"

"You said I could have him. I want him."

"Five minutes," said Petrowicz. "Maybe four."

They were on South Street, passing beneath the ramp of the Brooklyn Bridge. A red stake truck was heaving into view. Petrowicz hit the whooper for a few seconds. The truck jerked over to the side as they whipped around it.

"Why couldn't he have picked Sunday?" said Petrowicz.

They swept into the depths of the Battery Park tunnel. They road curved sharply to the right, leading around the southern point of Manhattan. The tires were in a continuous squeal; the wall lights of the tunnel blurred into a single line.

"Slow down!" said Taranto, "before we pile right through the World Trade Center."

They flashed into daylight again. Lanham was sweating. He held the microphone tightly, but uselessly. He didn't want to speak into it again, not wanting to alter the situation in the slightest degree. He wanted time to stop.

Roaring up West Street now, Petrowicz slid the car across all its lanes, hit the brakes twice, and bounced up onto the sidewalk. Uniformed patrolmen scattered as he skidded to a halt in front of the hotel entrance.

Lanham swung the door open with great violence and hurled himself up the stairs, almost crashing through the

213

revolving doors. There were only police in the lobby, but there were many. No one moved. Everyone stared.

"Get me a floor plan!" Lanham bellowed. He held up his gold detective shield.

Several men in suits came hurrying from an adjoining corridor. Lanham guessed the gray-haired one holding a portable was the captain.

"You Lanham?"

He nodded. "Yes sir. I want a floor plan."

"I thought you had your division commander with you."

Taranto had come up behind Lanham. "It's our case," he said. "Our collar. Give him a floor plan."

The captain snapped his fingers. One of the men with him produced a glossy sheet of paper. "He's in Twenty-seven-oh-one—right across from the elevators."

"There's a stairwell there!"

"Got it covered. Two men."

"I'll use it," Lanham said. "Give me a portable." He turned to Petrowicz. "You're my backup."

"You got it."

"Have you reestablished contact?" Lanham said to the captain.

"Negative."

"Bad Bobby's thinking," said Petrowicz.

"Come on," said Taranto.

"What about the girl?" Lanham said.

"Broke down. She just wants out of here."

"Okay," said Lanham. "We'll take an elevator to twenty-six. Let's go."

It was the longest elevator ride Lanham could ever remember taking. He had never given a thought to power failure or breakdown before. Now he watched the floor numbers flicker by one by one, each number an achievement, each flicker a threat. When the doors finally opened, he took a deep breath before moving.

Then he moved very quickly, Petrowicz on his heels. The uniformed men on the floor were waiting for them. One held the door to the stairwell. Two others were on the landing, flattened against the wall, peering up the stairs with their sidearms drawn.

214

"Detective Lanham from homicide. We're going up."

"Be our guest."

Lanham made a last check over his portable. "Any contact yet?"

"Negative," crackled someone's voice. "He's got the phone off the hook."

Lanham started up, two stairs at a time. He had his weapon still in its holster. He didn't plan to touch it until he got to the hotel room door. He didn't want to use it.

They made the midway turn and started up the final flight of steps to the twenty-seventh floor landing. There was one uniformed man at the door to the corridor. Just as he turned to look down at Lanham and Petrowicz the door flew open, crash-banging against the wall and bouncing back.

Bad Bobby whirled through, eyes white and widened. Someone screamed as Bobby made another turn and flung himself down the stairs. He seemed to be flying, a great dark shape with suit coat billowing. Lanham saw something in his hand—a red razor. Lanham was oddly fascinated by the brightness of the color.

Darcy's arm was swinging. Lanham had his weapon in hand. He brought it up as Darcy's arm came down. Something tore through Lanham's shoulder. The pistol discharged. There was a grunt and a shout. Lanham was turning, falling, his buttocks striking the edge of the stair painfully, as Bad Bobby catapulted by. Lanham felt his finger pull. Another shot exploded, echoing all over the concrete walls. Petrowicz went down. Darcy went rolling, crashing, bouncing, thudding, landing with an ugly sound like a dropped melon.

All sound stopped. Everyone was motionless. Gun smoke hung in the air.

"Son of a bitch," said Petrowicz. He got slowly to his feet, rubbing his elbow. There was running on the floor above.

Lanham grabbed the railing and pulled himself erect. His left arm and shoulder were throbbing and there was blood flowing through the cloth of his suit.

Bad Bobby had landed upside down on his back. His head was turned sideways. One leg was flung up against

215

the wall. An arm was caught under his back. His dark blue suit was rapidly turning purple with blood. Darcy's eyes were closed but his mouth was gaping open stupidly.

Lanham's knee wobbled as he started down the steps. Petrowicz reached to help him.

"You okay?" Lanham asked.

"Yeah. But you're not."

"I'll live," said Lanham.

They both leaned over Darcy. Nothing was moving but liquid.

"He won't," said Petrowicz.

There was shouting from above and urgent, hurried conversation over the portable.

"What's going on?" Petrowicz shouted upstairs.

"He cut the john," said one of the uniformed men at the door. "Real bad."

"Is he alive?" Lanham asked.

"Shouldn't be," said the patrolman. "But he is." He made a slashing gesture across his throat.

"Goddammit to hell," Lanham said.

"You made a good stop, Ray," said Petrowicz.

Lanham knelt next to Darcy, as much from weariness and dizziness as from interest in the corpse. He stared at the long, blood-covered razor lying on the concrete near Darcy's hand.

With two shots of his pistol, he'd done more than end the life of Robert Darcy. As far as the mayor, the commissioner, the newspapers, and the television stations were concerned, he'd probably just "solved" the murder of Molly Wickham. The case would now be as good as closed. He'd been as dumb as Bad Bobby.

CHAPTER

....

10

Sunday came to New York as a day of oppressive heat. It had been carried into the city by winds that had changed to a southerly flow, winds that had died once the thick, soggy, hazy air had settled in. A.C. had left the terrace doors open to the night and now lay listening to the infrequent traffic passing in the street. He'd gone to bed full of drink-inspired important plans for the day, but now he had forgotten just what they were.

He lay there, trying to remember, then finally stirred from his sodden sheets and, after managing some minor washing up, pulled on a pair of old khaki shorts and a clean white dress shirt, leaving the latter unbuttoned.

He was unused to hangovers and this one was gigantic. His head was pounding and it hurt his eyes to look at the windows. He retrieved the Sunday papers from the hall, but he found on their blurry front pages nothing to compel his attention—some sort of screaming police story head-

217

lined in the *Globe*, the stories covering the dull face of the *New York Times* all to do with consequential national and foreign concerns that interested him about as much as the garbage that was piling up in his kitchen trash can. He dropped the papers on the living room floor with a thud and went out onto the terrace, collapsing into the chaise longue at the end.

The street was so empty and quiet he could hear people talking on it. At one point, he heard raised voices and looked to see the woman sunbather from the building across the way arguing loudly with some man who had intruded upon her rooftop sanctuary. The man said something rude and went away. She returned to her towel, and the quiet resumed.

A.C. managed to eat a little something, then attempted a desultory clean-up of the apartment. He removed the accumulated garbage to the disposal chute, but when it came to doing the dishes, he gave up. Tuning his radio to an FM jazz station, he returned to his terrace and spent the rest of the afternoon listening to music and drinking gin.

Sometime during the day, a David Sanborn recording was played, reminding him of his first encounter with Camilla. He tried to think of what he might do about Kitty, but he fell asleep with his mind full of the mysterious blond model.

When he awoke again, night had fallen. The city lights were soft in the haze. He stared at them forlornly. He'd known a mystery writer once who had gone to Hollywood to work on a movie project and had returned hopelessly and helplessly in love with an actress. Their encounter had been transitory as far as she was concerned, but the writer had fallen into an abyss of yearning. When she'd stopped returning his phone calls, the man had retreated to a cabin he had up in the mountains. A.C. had gone there to bring the writer back, finding him dirty and unshaven, spending his days watching the woman's old movies on videotape and, every twenty-four hours, emptying a half-gallon jug of whiskey or vodka.

"This is how I love her," he had said.

He had refused to come back. A few weeks later, it was in the papers that he'd shot himself.

A.C. shuddered. He had fashion magazine pictures of

218

Camilla all over his coffee table. He gathered them together and put them in a drawer. Still bleary, he stumbled into his kitchen and made himself a fresh drink, hoping it would revive him. Instead it pushed him into total drunkenness. In the way of drunks on lonely Sunday nights, he began making phone calls—to Camilla, to Vanessa, to his wife, to Camilla again, to Theresa Allenby. To Camilla.

None of them were home. None. Every time he called Camilla, the recorded message was the only response.

He fell asleep in a chair.

.

Monday morning was announced with a ringing of his doorbell. A.C. staggered to the door, forgetting that he was barefoot and still wearing the same shorts and open shirt of the day before.

It was Detective Lanham, wearing a blue seersucker suit and sunglasses and filling the doorway with his angry bulk.

"It's me," said Lanham, in a growl. "The 'hero cop.' "

"What are you talking about?" said A.C., his words slightly slurred.

"Don't you read your own goddamn newspaper?"

A.C. stepped aside to admit the man, then led him into his disreputable-looking living room. He paused to pick up the copy of the *Sunday Globe*, sitting down on the couch and staring at it. There was a huge picture of an occupied body bag being wheeled on a gurney; above it was a particularly bold headline proclaiming HERO COP KILLS SLAYER OF MODEL!

"That's you?"

Lanham lowered himself into a chair, looking around at the disarray as disdainfully as though he'd just entered some festering slum dwelling.

"Yes. That's me."

"What happened?"

"We met up with Molly Wickham's pimp Saturday. It didn't go down well. He cut up a citizen. He cut me."

A.C. blinked his eyes to clear the blur. Lanham was wearing his suit jacket hung loosely over the shoulder of his left arm, which was in a sling.

"We had to shoot him. I did. I shot him."

The wrongness of the headline suddenly struck A.C.

"But he didn't kill Molly Wickham. I mean, he wasn't the man I saw on the motorcycle."

"That, Mr. James, seems to be completely irrelevant."

"I don't understand."

"Look, I don't have a lot of time. I'm on my way downtown to join our beloved mayor at a news conference. I'm going to receive a commendation. Do you know how many weeks it takes for one of those fucking things to go through channels? I'm getting mine in a day, not even that."

"A commendation for . . . ?"

"For doing what cops do in the South Bronx every night. Bad Bobby Darcy came at me with a razor and I had to use my service revolver to stop him. I stopped him forever. End of story. End of case."

He rose. He looked as haggard as A.C. probably did.

"The case is closed? It's all over?"

"Technically, no." Lanham was looking out the terrace doors. "The district attorney's office is keeping an 'active' file on it. So is my homicide division. But you know what that means. I've got 'active' cases in my files dating back to 1981. This case is going into the files with Bad Bobby as the lead suspect. The presumption is of guilt, not innocence. It amounts to a de facto conviction."

A.C. rubbed his eyes. His hand brushed the harsh sandpaper of his chin.

"But that doesn't mean you have to drop the investigation."

What was wrong with him? What had happened was a godsend. It was precisely what Camilla Santee needed to have happen. Now the police would stop looking for her. She could come out from wherever she'd gone into hiding.

It was Monday. Her booker would be at her modeling agency.

"If some startling new evidence is uncovered, then maybe I can get back to this," Lanham continued. "But in the meantime, there's the press of other business. They found a girl under some bushes behind the zoo last night. Naked, sexually assaulted, strangled. I caught the case. I wasn't up.

I wasn't even on duty. But my lieutenant tossed it to me anyway."

A.C.'s stomach clenched. A shivering chill followed.

"That girl, it wasn't someone named Bailey Hazeltine?"

"No. We got a positive ID. It was a girl named Claudia Schatz. A waitress from one of the clubs on Upper Broadway. I'm supposed to be on a week's medical leave and I worked the case all yesterday afternoon."

A.C. looked down at a fashion magazine at his feet. It was open to a picture of Camilla. He snatched it up and, closing it, dropped it on the table.

Lanham noticed. He was staring at A.C. hard.

"You don't know of any startling new evidence, do you?"

A.C. shook his head. "Can I get you some coffee?"

"No thanks. I don't have time." He hesitated. "Maybe I do. To hell with the mayor."

"I have some instant," A.C. said. He needed to go to the bathroom, but he needed to attend to something first. He went into the kitchen and set some water to boil, then quickly took some tomato juice from the refrigerator and poured it into a glass, adding a slug of vodka.

Lanham was standing behind him. A.C. ignored him, spooning some coffee crystals into a clean cup he managed to find.

"Sugar?"

"Black."

A.C. paused to gulp some of his pick-me-up. "I'll be right back."

He wasn't long in the bathroom, but took time to quickly wash his face and hands and, after a furtive look at the wretched derelict he found in the mirror, to make a hasty pass at shaving. It wasn't a very successful job of it. He cut himself in several places. But it was at least a token gesture toward respectability. He buttoned his shirt and stuffed it into the belt of his khaki shorts.

Lanham had gone back into the living room. The tea kettle was whistling, but the detective had done nothing about it.

"I'll get it," said A.C. "Be right with you."

221

He returned with the coffee, spilling it slightly as he handed it to the policeman. Lanham sipped politely, eyeing A.C. over the rim of the cup.

The fashion magazine was not where A.C. had left it. Lanham had not only looked at it, he wanted A.C. to notice that he had looked at it.

"Have you seen Camilla Santee?" Lanham asked.

A.C. shook his head. "Not in days."

"Not at all? You haven't been talking to her on the phone or anything?"

"No."

"I've been trying to reach her. No luck."

A.C. took a deep breath. "I've been trying to reach her, too. I don't know where she is."

"You talked to Belinda St. Johns last Friday. You were asking about a videotape."

"Videotape?"

"Hot stuff, starring Belinda, Molly Wickham, and company. You asked Belinda who had it, who she was paying to keep it out of the wrong hands."

"How did you know I talked to Belinda?"

"I'm a police detective. Don't ask me how I find out things. How did you learn about the tape?"

A.C. said nothing.

"Did Molly Wickham tell you about it? In your interview?"

"No," said A.C. "Of course not."

"How about Peter Gorky, the great moviemaker?"

"I've never met the man. I never met any of those people until that fashion show, except for Molly."

Lanham drank some more coffee. He didn't seem to like it.

"I'll tell you the answer to your question, Mr. James. Pierre Delasante is the one who has the tape. He's the one who's been shaking the others down. Belinda St. Johns has already paid him ten thousand bucks."

"Pierre Delasante?"

"Was Camilla Santee mixed up in any of that? Does she make movies, too?"

"Certainly not!"

Lanham smiled. "You seem pretty sure about that, Mr.

James, for a man who only just met her, who hasn't talked to her in days."

He set his coffee cup down on top of the fashion magazine. A dark, circular ring began to spread out from the bottom of the cup.

"I asked for your help, Mr. James. And you haven't given me squat. I'd still like to have it. I plan to go on with this. In the meantime, let me give you some helpful advice. The concierge at Molly Wickham's apartment building got beat up last week. It happened just after a woman he positively ID'd as Camilla Santee entered the building. He could have gotten killed. As it is, he's doing some hospital time."

A.C. remembered the rough voice of the man who had knocked him down—remembered the pain of his kicks.

"You've already gotten worked over once yourself," Lanham said. "If you get into this any deeper, it's you who may need my help. And may I remind you that I am a homicide detective." He pronounced the syllables of "homicide" as though each were a separate word.

"Thank you very much for the advice," A.C. said, with exaggerated politeness.

"Have a nice day," Lanham said. "Call me when you come to your senses. Just ask for the 'hero cop.'"

•

A.C. slumped into a chair and pondered all this, coming to the conclusion that, if nothing else, he had better get on with his life—get back to being the king of New York, as Vanessa had so inaccurately put it. He'd lost enough dignity. He was weary of his troubles, tired of drinking, disgusted with feeling sick and frustrated. Kitty had not been so angry, or at least so cruel, as to fire him from his job. He'd go do it, get back on the boulevards, go back to reporting on the delights and amusements of "A.C.'s New York" for his thousands of readers.

He showered for a full half hour, scrubbing himself as though ridding his body of some vile contamination. He shaved again, this time with a new razor blade, and cleaned his teeth as a dentist might. Brushing his sandy hair vigorously—fifty times on each side with his military brushes—he splashed his best cologne all over his face, neck, and chest. Turning on his radio, happy to hear the station playing wonderful 1930s swing, with strings, brass, and drums, he set about dressing his very best—freshly pressed white duck trousers, his nicest blue blazer, his newest striped Guards tie.

His white shoes still had dark, splattered stains on them. He rubbed them off with cleaner and then applied a thick, fresh coat of liquid white polish. While his shoes dried, he made a cup of coffee for himself and read through the *Sunday Globe* carefully. His last column had been stuck at the very end of the feature section, surrounded by liposuction and hair removal ads, but he refused to let that bother him. They were down on him. So be it. Once he had told Camilla what she wanted to know, that her cousin Pierre was the one who was blackmailing the people in the videotape, the Molly Wickham story would be behind him. He could step smartly back into "A.C.'s New York."

A cab came along just as he stepped outside, as though it had been waiting just down the street, especially for him, an encouraging omen.

As he came through the newsroom, no one spoke to him. No one that he noticed even looked up. It disconcerted him slightly, but he forced his ebullience to prevail. The absence of Pasternak's usual bitter asides made it all the better a day. He picked up his messages from the copy clerks' desk and read through them on the way back to his office.

Nearing his door he abruptly halted, looking at his watch. One of the messages was from Camilla. She had called not fifteen minutes before. The message had only her name, and the notation that she had called. There was no request to return the call, nor a notation that she would call again.

"She didn't leave a number?" he said to the girl at the desk. He had almost bounded back to her.

"No, Mr. James. She didn't want to leave her name. She just blurted it out as she hung up."

"Did she say she'd call again?"

"No sir."

Pasternak was watching him now. A.C. returned the look

sharply. The city editor returned to the computer printouts he'd been reading, but a slight, sly smile came to his lips.

A.C.'s door was locked, as he had left it, but his office had not been left unmolested. The photo on his desk of Kitty and his children was missing. In its place was a quart bottle of Gilbey's gin.

Closing his door behind him, he angrily hurled the gin into his wastebasket—a mistake, for it broke and the basket toppled over and rolled, spilling glass and alcohol on his carpet.

A.C. left it there. He began pulling open his desk drawers, looking for the picture, finding no sign of it. Under more normal circumstances, he would have torn into the city room raising the unholiest hell. But, under normal circumstances, no one would have dared touch the photograph.

He sat down, leaning back slowly, calming himself. Bill Shannon was most likely responsible for the removal of the picture, though certainly no Princeton gentleman would have been involved in the bottle stunt. It was a vulgarism worthy only of Pasternak.

A.C., as a gentleman, would not, of course, reply in kind. But he wasn't feeling very gentlemanly.

Stepping over the mess on the floor, he locked his door from the inside and returned to his chair, pulling over his computer terminal. A good columnist always keeps two or three ideas in his hip pocket against the day when no others present themselves. A.C. had a couple in mind. The safari jacket had returned as a "new fashion look" once again. He would write about the recurring ridiculousness of that. He had also talked recently to Kelly McGillis, his favorite actress, who had taken a Broadway role after several years in Hollywood. The conversation had been at a party, but he could easily transform it into an interview.

He set to work. By a little after one o'clock, he'd completed two rather nice columns. With a feeling of triumph, as though this quick and easy manifestation of competence sufficed as riposte to Pasternak's crude humor, he hit the keys that sent the columns into the editing system and then swiveled his chair back to face his desk. His next deadline was not until Friday. He could devote the rest of the week to a far more pressing concern.

His mail was stacked precariously in its usual box. He went through it hurriedly, pulling out only those envelopes that looked to be invitations. Retrieving those from the previous week as well, he tossed the lot into an expensive English leather briefcase—a birthday gift from Kitty—and snapped shut the lid.

Now he'd call Camilla's booker. He had four days all to himself.

An assistant answered when he phoned the modeling agency. She said the booker was out at a fashion luncheon. She did not know where Camilla was or how she could be reached. A.C. said he'd call back.

On the way out past the news desk, he said not a word, but farther on, passing the clipping counter where some of the copy clerks tended to loiter, he summoned one of the dumbest and gave him a twenty-dollar bill.

"I want you to go to the liquor store and get Mr. Pasternak a bottle of Gilbey's gin. Bring it to the city desk. It's to replace the one I accidentally broke."

•

Lanham's phone rang, another in an endless succession of calls that were interrupting his day. He knew it would probably not be his wife, who still was not speaking to him. He wasn't much interested in talking to anyone else.

It was Peter Gorky. Lanham didn't want to talk to him, either.

"You bastards!" said Gorky. "What are you, the Gestapo?"

Lanham felt very tired. "What's your problem?"

"I'll bet you didn't even have a warrant. You just walk in and tear everything apart. I told you I'd find the tape."

"What happened, Mr. Gorky?"

"You know goddamn well what happened. You assholes came in and went through my studio. Shit, you must have looked at everything I've got."

Lanham picked up his pen and made a notation on his message pad.

226

"Someone broke into your studio?" he said.

"You guys did."

"Mr. Gorky, nobody from this department did anything of the kind. No warrants were issued and no searches were made."

"Well, someone was in here. Shit, what a mess."

Lanham sighed. "You've been burglarized, Mr. Gorky."

There was a long pause. "Maybe."

"Well, what was taken?"

"Nothing."

"Nothing? What about that tape you were going to find for me?"

"It wasn't here. I don't have it anymore."

"But you said nothing was taken."

"I . . . Oh shit. Never mind."

"I do mind. You said you had that tape. What happened to it?"

"I gave it to somebody, more than a week ago."

"You gave it away? To one of the people in it?"

"No. To somebody else."

"Who?"

"I—I sold it."

"You what?"

"I sold it to a guy. There's a market for this stuff, you know."

"You made a tape of people at a private party and sold it as a skin flick? Isn't that against copyright laws, not to speak of invasion of privacy? Not to speak of the obscenity laws of the State of New York?"

"It isn't like it sounds. I mean, it won't turn up in video stores or anything. There are private collectors. I sold it to a guy who sells to them. I got five large for it."

Lanham shook his head sadly. Of all the unbelievable stupidity he had encountered in this whole sorry mess, this was without question the dumbest. It was a new world record.

"You sold this tape on the underground market to be resold to 'collectors'?"

"Yeah. What are you going to do about this break-in? Or was it you guys after all?"

"Did you go to college, Mr. Gorky?"

227

"Yeah, Pratt Art Institute. Almost two years. What's that got to do with anything?"

"I'm just amazed, that's all. In my day, colleges didn't accept imbeciles."

"Hey, fuck you, too. What're you talking about?"

"You know very well why you got so much money for the tape, Mr. Gorky. You have two top-dollar fashion models in action, models right off the pages of the slick magazines. Models you see in television commercials. Almost celebrities, right?"

"Something like that. So what? Who's going to see it, a few rich guys. Nothing public."

"A few rich guys, my ass. You've worked in this town long enough to know who runs the pornography business. It's not Twentieth Century-Fox, is it? It's the same guys who run all the big-money businesses on the funny side of the law. I'm sure you know Belinda St. Johns in the biblical sense by now, but do you know anything about her? Did she ever tell you about her boyfriend?"

"Molly did. Some greaseball. So what? Belinda's a greaseball herself."

"The gentleman's name is Vince Perotta, Mr. Gorky. Do you remember the newspaper articles about the family reunion he had upstate last fall?"

"Vince Perotta?"

"I don't know what sort of film fare he goes in for," Lanham said. "He may be one of your biggest fans. But if he sees this little epic, I don't think you're going to like the review."

"Oh shit."

Taranto had come into the squad room. He was looking at Lanham impatiently.

"I'm going to turn this over to a burglary detail, Mr. Gorky," Lanham said. "There'll be some evidence technicians out to get fingerprints, and I'd like you to give them your full cooperation."

"Sure. Anything you say."

"In the meantime, you'd better start busting your ass to get that tape back. And if you've got a sister in Seattle or Anchorage or someplace, I'd begin making plans to pay her a long visit."

228

"You're sure Perotta—"

"Goodbye, Mr. Gorky."

He hung up. Before he could dial burglary, Taranto came over.

"Your arm okay, Ray?"

Lanham flexed it, wincing slightly.

"Okay enough," he said.

"Good. Uniformed force have picked up an eyewitness on that Central Park killing. They've got her at the precinct house. Get on up there. She saw the victim with a guy, going at it under the bushes."

Lanham stood up, reaching for his coat. They'd already talked to the last person known to have seen the girl alive, some East Side kid who was seen picking her up in a late-night fern bar. He'd said he'd taken her home, but that she hadn't invited him in. He'd said he'd left her at her door.

Sometimes life was easy. If you were lucky, you got a case like Molly Wickham only once in your career.

•

A.C. became the most visible man on the Upper East Side. He threw himself into his columnist's job with all the vigor of a green reporter working hard toward a big break. In one afternoon alone, he went to two fashion shows, a benefit tea, a book party, and a cocktail reception.

Camilla's booker got back to him, saying that she had gone to Canada. She said that she didn't know how to reach Camilla, but that she'd relay his message as soon as Camilla called. He took heart from the fact that the booker seemed very friendly, recognition that A.C. was more than a stranger or business acquaintance.

The following day, he stopped for an afternoon drink at his club. It wasn't as powerful and prestigious an institution as the Union or Knickerbocker, but owing to its smaller size and hereditary requirements for membership, much more exclusive. A.C.'s grandfather had belonged to it, before he'd lost his money. Kitty had happily provided the funds for A.C.'s dues, though it was not an establishment her brother could join.

A.C. found the place insufferably stuffy, but he was

happy for a refuge where Bill Shannon could not come after him.

A.C. had a gin and tonic brought to him in the gentlemen's lounge, where he had taken a chair by the window overlooking Central Park. He began looking through the day's newspapers, and was just getting to "Suzy" in the *New York Post* when he looked up to see Cyrus Hall standing before him.

"Good afternoon, Mr. James. May I join you?"

The man looked disparagingly at the *Post*, but otherwise seemed amiable, much more so than he had that night at Mortimer's. A.C. gestured to the leather chair opposite and set aside his paper.

"I do apologize for disturbing you, Mr. James," Hall said with great courtesy, "but I hoped you might be able to help me in a matter—well, a matter of very serious concern."

"Certainly." Members were sworn to come to the assistance of any fellow member if needed, as long as the assistance did not entail any violation of club rules.

"You'll recall in Mortimer's the other night," Hall said, "that I was in the company of a young woman, Camilla Santee. I believe you know her."

"Camilla Delasante. Yes, I know her."

Hall seem startled that A.C. knew Camilla's actual last name, but continued without remarking on that.

"I need to find her, Mr. James. I hoped you might have some idea where she is."

A.C. shook his head. "Sorry. I don't."

"It's really quite important. I've tried to find her everywhere."

"Perhaps if you told me what this is about."

Hall studied him a moment. "It's highly confidential," he said finally.

If one revealed the confidence of another member—indeed, repeated anything uttered within the sanctuary of the club premises—it was grounds for immediate dismissal.

"I'm here as a member," A.C. said. "Not as a newspaper columnist."

Hall leaned close. "We represent Miss Delasante's cousin, Pierre Delasante, who until recently was associated with the White House and is now a consultant in Washington."

A.C. nodded.

"Someone got into our offices this week," Hall said. "Some file drawers were broken into. One of them contained Mr. Delasante's papers."

"Something was taken?"

"No. But they were considerably rearranged."

"Have you gone to the police?"

"No, of course not."

No indeed. It would not do for the clients of such a prestigious firm to learn that their private affairs could be so readily available to intruders.

"We questioned the staff exhaustively," Hall continued. "A receptionist said she'd noticed a new cleaning woman, a blond woman, rather attractive. The cleaning women in our building are all very nice—bonded, don't you know. But no one has ever called any of them attractive."

A.C. was amazed, but perhaps he shouldn't be. There was something very resolute about Camilla Santee.

"I haven't seen Miss Delasante," he said. "I'm looking for her myself."

"Should she contact you, Mr. James, I'd appreciate it very much if you could impart our concern, and our wish to speak to her as soon as possible. As I say, the police are not involved in this matter, and I don't contemplate that they shall be."

"If I hear from her, I'll tell her," A.C. said.

Hall rose. "Thank you." He stood a moment at the window, looking at pedestrians streaming along the sidewalk. "Such lovely weather today."

"Yes," said A.C., finishing his drink. "In fact, I think I'll take a walk."

He found a phone on the street and called Camilla's booker. The woman seemed a little disturbed to hear from him.

"I told her you called, Mr. James," she said. "But she left no message for you."

"Where is she? You said Canada."

"She's no longer in Canada. But I can't tell you where she's gone, I'm afraid."

"Can't? Or won't?"

"I'm not allowed to give out such information."

"Damn it, she told me to call you. She said you'd tell me how to reach her."

"Yes, I know. But she's changed her mind."

"I've found out what she wants to know, and a lot more. I have to talk to her."

"Perhaps if you told me."

"No thank you." He hung up, surprised at his rudeness.

•

For the rest of the day, and on into the next, A.C. went searching for Camilla or word of her whereabouts in great earnest, asking after her at every social occasion to which he'd been invited and a few others to which he hadn't, calling all his friends and acquaintances, calling some he scarcely knew at all, in every case putting out the word: he wanted to find Camilla Santee. Anyone who might help him could consider all past obligations repaid.

No one could. Late the next night, he dropped in at the Café Carlyle in time to catch Bobby Short's last set, happy to be offered an empty table off to the side.

Short and his two sidemen were at their best, bringing forth the old Cole Porter and Noel Coward café society songs from the 1930s as gaily as one might pour tingly vintage champagne.

A.C. sipped, listening to Short sing "Poor Little Rich Girl," glancing at the mixed crowd of out-of-towners and Upper East Side locals and feeling at the center of his universe. He knew he wasn't king of New York, as Vanessa had so hyperbolically put it, but if there was such a thing, this would be the throne room.

When the set was over, Short worked his way through the room, saying his hellos and goodbyes, then finally coming to A.C.'s little table.

"Delighted to see you again so soon," he said. No one could say "delighted" with the effervescence of Bobby Short.

The musician accepted a chair and a drink, lighting a cigarette as they talked a bit about the perfect weather and the unusual pleasantness of the New York summer season. A waiter came up.

"Mr. James, I forgot to tell you," he said, "there was a lady here earlier tonight who asked for you."

A.C. leaned forward. "Not a blond fashion model named Camilla Santee?"

"Very blond and a lady, but not named Camilla. It was Honey Jerome? She's staying here at the Carlyle."

Honey Jerome, née Tutweiler, was from Pittsburgh, where her father had amassed a large fortune in coal and iron and where she had married into even more, keeping a large share of it in a subsequent divorce.

Honey since had lived almost everywhere but Pittsburgh—Miami, Paris, Dallas, Los Angeles, and New York, where she took a suite at the Carlyle for her prolonged stays.

"I'll give her a call," A.C. said.

When they'd finished their drinks and chat, A.C. went to the house phone in the lobby. Honey, as usual, answered at once. She seldom strayed far from a telephone.

"A.C.!" she said, with the kind of exuberant enthusiasm one might hear from a television game show host. "How super to hear from you!"

There was still a little Texas in the accent, a lot of Bryn Mawr, where Honey had gone to college, and a lot more of Southern California, which he thought had become her home.

"Where are you, darling?" she said. "You sound very near."

"I'm at home," he lied. He didn't want to get tangled up with Honey that night. She was a butterfly, always to be seen fluttering near whatever was the center of attention of the moment, but never settling, always off to whatever was next. Her boyfriends had included one of the handsomer roués in the U.S. Senate, an Arab hotel owner, at least two aging Hollywood leading men, a backup Giants quarterback, and the director of one of New York's most avant-garde art museums. Her favored causes and interests reflected the changing front pages and social pages of the *New York Times*—occasionally, even those of the *New York Globe*.

233

She had made a pass at A.C. once, very carefully, as
though to test whether this might prove advantageous to
her social ambitions.

A.C. had declined her offer, though not with any disdain.
She was attractive, though more chic than beautiful. She
was one of the city's more ambitious social hustlers, but
completely open about it. Her modus operandi was friendliness and helpfulness. She did serious favors for people as
reflexively as other hostesses offered refreshment. A.C.
liked her. Kitty detested her. She'd gone to just one of
Honey's "top this" celebrity dinner parties and declared it
enough.

"I was at the Café Carlyle earlier," A.C. said. "Bobby
mentioned you were asking after me."

"Have been simply all day, darling. I called up to Westchester, but I got the most frosty response."

"Kitty and I are—are living apart, for the moment."

"Absolutely everyone's hoping it won't be for long."

She paused. He waited.

"I've been trying to reach you ever since I heard at lunch
that you've been looking for a dear friend of mine," she
said.

At any given moment, Honey's "dear friends" might
range from the head waiter at Le Cirque to the Sultan of
Brunei. A.C. realized suddenly what she was trying to tell
him.

"I've been looking for a fashion model named Camilla
Santee."

"Yes, I know, and isn't she simply the most wonderful,
marvelous, *decent* girl in the world? A true lady. I've known
her for absolute ages. We met just about the time we both
came to New York—at a benefit fashion show. I've forgotten which, but they weren't even *feeding* the poor
models. I had Camilla sit right down at my table and we've
been just the greatest friends ever since."

"Where is she, Honey?"

"Of course, I haven't seen too terribly much of her lately.
Camilla went off to Europe, as I think you know, and I
was in California, but wasn't it just the most marvelous
coincidence? We both turn up back at the same airport this
week?"

"Honey . . ."

"Of course, Bermuda is so terribly near, isn't it. I mean, it might as well be in the Hamptons."

"Bermuda? You were in Bermuda?"

"Yes. A little holiday. It's really not so bad in the summer. And such a lovely place for a fashion shoot. No better place for bathing suits, and Camilla has such a beautiful figure. I mean, I simply seethe when I think of how unfairly I've been treated by my genes."

"When were you in Bermuda, Honey?"

"Why, I got back just yesterday, darling. I was just on my way to the airplane gate when, suddenly, there was my lovely friend. And then to hear today that you were looking for her. Have you become friends, darling?"

"Honey, it's wonderful talking to you, and I'd love to see you again, but I'm afraid I have to go. It's something about work."

"Call me when you're free, darling. I'll be here till the end of next week."

A.C. had no idea where he'd be the next week, but he knew where he'd be the next day.

CHAPTER

....

11

When approached from the air, Bermuda appears as a tiny outcropping of land and it never grows much larger, even as the pilot extends the flaps and lowers the landing gear and touchdown is just a moment away. Every landing seems a possible overshoot, the aircraft whooshing down from one side of the narrow island and hitting the runway bent pell-mell for the other.

When one is finally standing on firm earth, the smallness of the place ceases to matter. A.C. had often gone weeks without straying from an area of Manhattan considerably smaller than this. Here he could abide serenely for much longer.

The air was hot, yet fresh and breezy, smelling of flowers as much as of the sea. There were palm and banana trees, and pines on a distant hillside dotted with pastel houses. The sky was a soft blue between towering billows of cloud.

Rain was doubtless falling somewhere on the island, a gentle shower, quickly come and swiftly gone.

A.C. had first come to Bermuda on a spring break while in college, and had fallen in love with a girl he never saw again after that week, though they'd both lost their virginity in that sweet, long-ago encounter.

His next, and last, visit had been the year after his graduation. He'd come over for a holiday with Bailey and her brother, whose parents had taken a house for the entire season. A.C. had stayed with them nearly a month, and he'd felt miserable upon leaving, wondering when he'd ever come back, and if he would ever be that happy again.

He'd once suggested a Bermuda vacation to Kitty, but she wasn't interested. She knew he'd been there with the Hazeltines, and that his sojourn had produced one of the more enduring memories of his life, a memory she could not share, or inspire.

And now she'd told him she'd been having an affair with Bailey's brother. She hadn't meant to, but the inclusion of both London and Bedford Village in the itinerary of her adultery had given her away in one chilling instant.

Bailey's brother. His friend. The Hazeltines had once been such an important and wonderful part of his life. Now he was paying a bitter price. He'd become quite angry thinking about Bailey's brother and Kitty, but he had no right to it. All he could allow himself was melancholy, with nothing but thoughts of Camilla Santee as antidote.

A.C. had only one piece of luggage—a leather Hartmann overnight bag crammed with three days' clothing. He slung it over his shoulder and hurried to catch the bus to Hamilton, taking a seat in the rear. It was a very large and boxy bus, seeming much too large for the twisting road that was little more than an English country lane.

As they descended a hill, following the road around a long curve, a wide vista of the sea came into view. In its distance, a great white cruise liner could be seen, on apparent course for the harbor. Bermuda was a place of ships, coming from and going everywhere.

At the small Hamilton bus terminal, A.C. bought copies of the local newspapers, looking through the one that seemed the most substantial, calling the telephone number below the masthead. He asked for the fashion editor. The switchboard operator laughed, and then connected him with the social news correspondent, an older woman with a slight British accent. She told him there was some sort of fashion shoot going on that involved Trimingham's department store. The people at Trimingham's, a charming emporium on Front Street across from the harbor quay, directed him from the Elbow Beach Hotel. A.C. was on the next big pink bus heading out to Paget Township and the South Road.

Though the Elbow Beach was perhaps the most British hotel on the island, the young woman in a gray blazer behind the front desk was American, and quite friendly. She said the fashion group had been working on the beach in the morning, but had gone out to Dockyard after lunch for a change of scenery.

He remembered Dockyard from his earlier visits—an old naval base that was now mostly old fort and museum, though the Royal Navy still maintained a repair and supply facility there. It was on the far southwestern end of the island, as it was erroneously called. Bermuda was actually a chain of interconnected coral reefs and smaller islands.

"They're all staying here," she said. "They'll be back for dinner."

"Is there a Camilla Santee with them?"

She consulted her registration book. "Not staying with us."

"How about a Camilla Delasante?"

"No. Sorry."

"She's a model. A blonde. Very beautiful."

"They all look very beautiful, sir. But there's no one registered under that name."

He looked at his watch. He had hours to wait.

"Do you have a room?"

"Do you have a reservation?"

"No."

"Well, I have one available. Not very nice, though. And not with an ocean view."

"I'll take whatever you have."

238

"You can only have it until Monday. After that, we're completely booked."

"That'll do."

He snapped out an American Express card. The bill would eventually go to their house in Westchester, but that was a million light years distant from his present concerns. He began filling out the registration form.

"Is there a bus to Dockyard?" he asked, as she handed him his key.

"Just went by. There'll be another in an hour or so."

"Is there another way to get there?"

"Do you have a driver's license?"

"Yes."

"You can rent one of our bikes." He looked blank.

"A moped. They're fast enough for these roads. Get you to Dockyard long before the next bus."

●

He had always thought of these conveyances as little more than toys, something for adolescents to putt around on until they were old enough to drive automobiles. But, once out on the South Road heading west, he felt quite nervous on the motor bike he'd rented, unused to riding on the left and finding himself regularly passed by the vehicles that came huffing up behind him. On a high stretch that over-looked both the wide, island-dotted Great Sound on the right and the rocky ocean shore to the left, a large Mercedes-Benz garbage truck almost ran him off the road, compelling him to pull over and stop in someone's driveway. He didn't even know if Camilla was here. He was depending on the word of one of New York's most notorious gossips.

He kept on, gaining mastery over the little machine and at length feeling confident enough to remove the helmet he'd been told to wear and drop it in the bike's wicker basket. He had paused in his tiny room long enough to change clothes, retaining the white dress shirt he'd worn on the plane but switching to khaki Bermuda shorts, tan knee socks and a pair of Top-Sider boating shoes. He'd bought sunglasses at the airport. He imagined he looked like an ordinary islander—or at least an ordinary tourist.

239

It took much longer than he'd expected to reach Dock-yard, even though Bermuda was just twenty-eight miles long. Putt-putting past a couple of British frigates tied up along the main dock, he went on to the old fort built around Bermuda's furthermost hill, parking the minibike under a tree and locking it.

There was an admission fee, which he paid, but instead of waiting for the scheduled tour with the others gathered at the entrance, he slipped off by himself and climbed up to the top of the old battlements.

He could see the fashion people down at the end—so many bright colors against the gray stone and turquoise sea. Walking slowly toward them, he recognized Camilla easily by her long blond hair. As he drew nearer still, he saw she was wearing a relatively conservative bikini under a large print beach jacket that the wind kept billowing open.

She was posing—moving quickly and professionally from one stance to another—and did not notice him. He stood off to the side, waiting patiently until the cameraman and the director of the project signaled a break. She went over to the side of the battlement and leaned against it, tilting back her head as though to enjoy the sunshine.

A.C. jumped down beside her, startling her, but only for a moment. To his delight, and surprise, she smiled at him, though a little sadly.

"So you've found me," she said.

"I called your booker, as you told me to do. She wouldn't tell me where you were."

"I'm sorry." She touched his arm gently. "I was going to call you today."

He couldn't decide if she was lying.

"I found out what you wanted to know," he said. She showed no pleasure at the news.

"We can talk about it later. Not here."

The director, a tall blond man wearing a safari jacket and blue jeans, came over.

"Excuse me, sir," he said, not politely. "We're shooting some pictures here. You'll have to go back to your tour group."

"He's a friend, Eddie. It's all right."

"Can't he meet you back at the hotel, Anne? We still have some work to do."

"He won't be in the way."

A.C. nodded pleasantly.

The man went back to the others, less than happily. His concern seemed to have more to do with Camilla's being with another man than with unfinished work.

"How long have you known him?" A.C. asked quietly.

"Since yesterday morning," she said.

"He called you Anne."

"I'm working as Anne Claire. I've done it before. They're both my names. I'm one of those Southern girls who carry the names of all their relatives."

"Camilla Anne Claire Delasante?"

"Something like that."

"And Delasante is your actual name?"

" 'Deny thy father, and refuse thy name.' "

"Sorry?"

" 'O Romeo, Romeo, wherefore art thou Romeo? Deny thy father, and refuse thy name; or, if thy wilt not, be but sworn my love, and I'll no longer be a Capulet.' "

"That doesn't answer my question."

"Yes it does." She smiled again.

"Okay, let's go, Anne," said the director. He had cut the break short.

She slipped off her jacket, handing it to an assistant, and stepped back in front of the camera. Keeping out of the director's field of vision, A.C. moved nearer, observing Camilla's movements as they all were, but far from professionally. Her body was fuller than he had imagined, far from the scarecrow figure that was the fashion model's stereotype. Her breasts were no centerfold's, but were beautifully shaped, round and full enough to swell the bikini top as the designer intended. Her waist was very trim, her legs long and slender but well developed. Her feet, like her hands, were long and narrow. Her flesh was flawless—no moles, no freckles save for a tiny scattering on her upper chest, no blemishes of any kind. Her perfection overwhelmed him. He tried to calculate the odds of such a person being born. How many thousands of short, stout

241

people came into the world for every one as tall and slender as she? How many thousands with long noses or pug noses or wide noses for every nose as wonderfully sculpted as hers? How many millions with ordinary eyes for every face as blessed, as enchanted, with eyes the extraordinary color and size and shape of hers?

The odds in total must be four billion to one. There could be no one on earth as beautiful as Camilla Santee.

The director began complaining about her poses, making her reshoot the takes. It seemed to A.C. he was deliberately dragging out the effort, prolonging matters in hopes that A.C. would tire of it and leave, perhaps hoping to provoke a scene that would justify his demanding that A.C. leave.

A.C. backed up and quietly went over to a wall some distance from the shooting scene, near where a few spectators were standing. A couple of other models were sitting on canvas folding chairs nearby. One of them looked up and smiled. Everyone was friendly on Bermuda. Everyone but jealous directors. Finally, Eddie forgot about him and became absorbed by the task before him. Taking pictures of Camilla, with her eyes mating with the lens so lovingly and yet so mysteriously, must be preoccupying, indeed.

They finished up shortly after four. Camilla pulled a pair of flower print culottes on over her bathing suit bottom, buttoned the matching beach jacket over them, and slipped on a pair of beige espadrilles. When she came up to A.C., she put her arm through his. He imagined she was sending a signal to Eddie: Leave me alone now. I'm not for you to bother with. I'm with him. Stay away.

They didn't speak until they reached the parking lot. She took her arm away, gently.

"I just remembered," she said. "You can't go back with us. We have just those two minis and the van. There's no room with all the equipment."

"I brought my own transport," he said, pointing to his motorbike. "I'll meet you at the hotel."

"No," she said, touching his arm but not taking it again. "I'll go with you." She turned to one of the other models who was coming up. "I'm going back with him. I'll see you later."

The model waved, grinning a little.

242

"It won't exactly be like *Hell's Angels*," A.C. said.

"I'm glad."

She had no choice but to ride close to him, her knees touching his thighs, her arms around his waist, her chin nearly touching his shoulder. When he slowed suddenly, or went over a bump, she'd come up hard against him, her breasts and the warmth of her flesh richly felt through the thin material of his shirt. After thumping over Watford Bridge and zooming up to speed on smoother pavement, he found she was staying close, holding tightly to him, resting her head against his shoulder.

The biker and his lady. It was a silly thing to think, ticking along on the little motorbike, but he enjoyed the image. Until it reminded him of the man now dead called Bad Biker Bobby.

They passed the beautiful Sonesta Beach Hotel, sprawling like a castle keep over its shoreline foundation of rock. Just beyond, the road dipped and swerved toward the waves itself. He felt her hand on his arm and turned to see her pointing to a grassy area off the shoulder just ahead.

"Stop here!" she shouted, into the wind.

He nodded and slowed. With some expertise now, he steered the moped along the shoulder and up onto the thick, matted grass, coming to a rest under a tree near the lip of a rocky outcrop. He turned off the engine. Waves were slapping and sloshing just beneath.

Camilla separated from him quickly, hopping off the bike and leaping onto the rock. She looked about her a moment, then led him on down to a coral mound nearer the water. There were several dry, smooth places to sit. The one she chose had room for him.

Her eyes, taking in the wide expanse of sea, were very serious. He wanted to touch her again, but sensed this was no time for that.

"Who told you I was here?" she said coolly.

"An old friend of yours who saw you at the airport, someone you thought you could count on for anything. I imagine you asked her not to tell anyone where you were."

"My dear friend Honey. She always did talk too much."

"She didn't mean to get you in trouble. She was just trying to get back in my good graces."

"She had incurred your wrath?"

"My wife's. Social climbers are not her favorite people."

"I'd forgotten you were married."

A.C. glanced at his wedding band. "At the moment, we seem to be separated."

"I'm sorry." She hunched forward, slightly away from him. "Tell me what you learned," she said. "About the videotape."

He hesitated. Once this small gift of information was delivered, he would no longer be of any use to her. He'd be an impediment, perhaps even a liability.

"Pierre Delasante has the videotape," A.C. said, sounding as though he were testifying in court. "He's the one who's been asking the others for money."

Her mouth went slack. "You're quite certain?"

"Yes."

"How do you know this?" She was watching the on-coming waves as though one of them might be bearing a message.

"The police told me. Detective Lanham."

"Do you believe him?"

"Yes. I went to Belinda St. Johns, and to that Jimmy Woody. I rather muffed it. I wasn't able to get them to tell me anything. But I think Belinda has something going with one of the cops. That's how it got back to Lanham. He said she'd paid Pierre more than ten thousand dollars."

"She's having an affair with a policeman?"

"I think so."

She sighed and pulled up her legs, resting her elbows on her knees and her chin upon her hands.

"Everything you say, Mr. James, makes perfect sense. Pierre would take money from a bag lady. Belinda has a serious boyfriend—a hoodlum. He'd kill her over something like this. Or he'd hurt her. Have someone cut her face up the way those awful men did Marla Henson. That would scare her as much as death." She paused, brushing her hair away from her eyes. "Belinda's as addicted to sex as she is to everything else she does, but if she's sleeping with a policeman, it must be because he makes her feel safe."

"Not safe enough."

244

"I suppose not."

"Did this hoodlum have something to do with Molly Wickham getting killed?"

Camilla stared straight ahead, thinking, but not about her answer.

"No," she said. "I'm sure he never even met her. He's a very old-school hoodlum. Honor, family, ethnic pride. He has nothing to do with blacks except to make money off of them."

"I don't know what newspapers you've read out here. The police have all but closed Molly Wickham's case."

"Why?"

"They killed the man who was their chief suspect. Bobby Darcy, who used to be her pimp when she was working the streets. He was black, but light skinned. He was a motorcyclist. He hurt his girls when they tried to leave him. The mayor, the newspapers, they've all but convicted him. Lanham and the others have been assigned to other cases."

She looked at him. "So it's all over?"

"Not exactly. Lanham doesn't want to let it go. He knows Darcy didn't do it. He still wants to talk to Pierre. He wants to talk to you. He still wants me to help him. He seems pretty sure that I've been in contact with you."

It suddenly occurred to A.C. that he had done a very foolish thing, bolting off to Bermuda. Lanham might have had him followed. Lanham might be waiting now, back at the hotel.

"This Bobby Darcy could have done it," Camilla said. "He didn't. But it's reasonable for people to believe that he did."

"Yes. But not Raymond Lanham."

"Just what is his problem?"

"He's the officer who killed Darcy. They cornered him in a hotel down by Wall Street. He came at Lanham with a razor. Lanham shot him. He's unhappy about that. Very unhappy."

"Detective Lanham is a black man."

"I suppose it's something to do with that. But Lanham is a very straight cop."

She rubbed at the corner of her eye.

"There's something else," A.C. said. "The attorney you

245

were with at Mortimer's—Cyrus Hall. He thinks you broke into his office and looked at Pierre Delasante's will."

"How do you know what he thinks?"

"We belong to the same club. He spoke to me there about it. All very privately."

"Why would he think I would do such a thing?"

"Someone quite like you was seen there. With the cleaning women."

"I guess I'm not much of an actress."

"I don't know how you could have disguised yourself."

"What is he going to do about it?"

"He said he only wants to talk to you. He hasn't gone to the police. He told me he wouldn't. But the police could go to him."

She sighed again, shaking her head. "So it doesn't go away."

He didn't know what to say. He took her hand. She let it rest in his, then gently squeezed, her fingers curling around his.

"Was Molly the first person you ever saw get killed like that?" she said.

"No. I was a police reporter once. I've seen a few victims." The serenity of the sea seemed so foreign, so out of place. "And I killed someone myself once."

Camilla stiffened. "In Vietnam?"

"In Korea. I was in the army there for a year. A few of us from the officers' club went hunting one weekend in the mountains east of Seoul. We surprised a North Korean infiltrator and he fired at us. It was stupid of him. We shot back. I was the one who hit him."

She was holding his hand very tightly. "Did you see his face?"

"Yes. We went up to the body and turned it over. He was very young, or looked young, anyway."

"Does it bother you? Do you still see his face in your dreams?"

"No. It was a long time ago. I have different dreams."

"All the time I've been here I've been thinking about Pierre, thinking about what it would be like to kill him. Just now I've been picturing his body floating out there in the water, face up. I wonder how long I'd have to live with that."

Her words unsettled him, though he couldn't imagine Camilla hurting anyone, least of all kin. She seemed someone terribly serious about family.

"Where is Pierre?" he asked.

"I don't know. He left New York. He may be in Washington. My brother probably knows where he is—or will soon."

"Pierre's your cousin. Can you hate him so much?"

"Yes, I can. He's my cousin and he is also vile and despicable and scum. What you've just told me is the last piece in the picture. He's lied about everything. He's cheated and stolen and behaved like a pig. I used to tell myself it was just because of the alcohol, but the drinking only brings out what's already there. There *are* evil people in the world, bad people who deserve no mercy. Pierre's one of them."

He held her very close, trying to ease the stiffness of her body. "Camilla. What happened to Molly wasn't your fault. The police will take care of Pierre."

"No they won't. He'll get away with it—all the trouble he's caused. Just like he always does."

"You'll be all right, Camilla. I won't let anything happen to you." He kissed her hair.

"You're a very dear man, Mr. James. You've done everything I asked of you, without knowing why, without really asking why. You've kept my trust, even though I suspect it's gotten you into trouble. You were attacked because of me. You could get killed because of me. Yet here you are. There aren't many like you, at least that I've ever met."

She leaned against him. He lowered his head to kiss her, but she faced away.

"No, please. Just hold me a moment longer."

He put both of his arms around her. Her leg came against his. He fought back a desire that came close to overwhelming him.

"What will you do?" he said finally.

"What will I do? Whatever will I do? I'm going to go back to my life. Somehow. Just as soon as I possibly can."

"You mean back to New York?"

247

"Not that. I want no more of that. I have another life, Mr. James. My own private wonderful life that I made for myself all by myself. I'm going to go back to it, and I'm not going to let anyone take it away from me. That's what Pierre has been trying to do, but I'm not going to let him do it."

"And me?"

"I'm not really someone you want to know, Mr. James."

A tension came between them. He held himself motionless, hoping it would pass, but it didn't.

"I'm very grateful for what I do know about you," he said. "I'm not going to ask for anything more. I've no intention of imposing myself on you, Camilla. I wouldn't do anything you don't want me to do. Please understand that. I really mean it. But you've become a very special person to me."

"You don't belong in my life, Mr. James. And I don't belong in yours."

"I'll help you, however I can. I'll help you get back to your life."

She moved in his arms and lifted her face to kiss him, very gently, very sweetly, but very briefly. She sat up.

"*Merci bien, cher ami,*" she said, her voice very soft, with sadness.

"When are you leaving here?"

"They can finish tomorrow, if the weather holds. Then I must go. They're paying me three thousand dollars Canadian for the shoot, plus expenses. I've received half. Very uncomplicated. Everything in traveler's checks. When I get the rest, I go. Then I must leave you."

She made it sound so final.

"I took a room at your hotel. I hope you don't think me presumptuous."

"I think you're very logical." She found a smile to give him.

"Can we have dinner?"

"Oh yes, please. These Canadians, they're very nice, but I don't want to be with them. I don't want to get involved with any new people now."

"We can go into Hamilton."

"On your little bike?"

"Yes."

"That will be very nice."

He stood up, and helped her to her feet.

．

A.C. chose a restaurant on the second floor of one of the buildings on Front Street. It wasn't particularly fancy, nothing at all in the way of a local version of Le Cirque or any other of the haut monde New York eateries she was used to, but its veranda overlooked the harbor and the menu was full of tasty local specialties.

It was a friendly, cheerful establishment, made all the more so when the lights of the town came on to welcome the evening. Their table was at the veranda's railing, and they could see all the way past the mouth of the Great Sound out to the darker water of the open sea and the Granaway Deep.

He ordered a gin and tonic, surprised to realize it was his first drink of the day. He was more surprised when Camilla chose a strong rum punch, asking for another before A.C. was half done with his.

She had changed into a pretty, short-sleeved dress, much like the one Bailey had worn in A.C.'s dream, except that Camilla's was a pale blue that set off the light tan she had already acquired. He was surprised by that, too. Models in Camilla's league were very careful to avoid that kind of exposure to the sun. The damage that could eventually cause was measured in very large amounts of money.

Their waiter was a young, very dark-skinned black man who, like many Bermudians, addressed them in a well-mannered, deferential way. Somewhat to A.C.'s surprise, Camilla was equally deferential to the waiter, calling him "sir" several times. He lingered a bit after bringing their drinks, departing only when summoned by someone inside.

A.C. leaned against the rail, his eyes fixed on Camilla's face. She glanced at him curiously, but quickly looked away.

"I still have your red scarf," he said.

249

"You're very sentimental."

"Not sentimental. Beholden. I'm your chevalier, remember? How next may I serve you?"

She took a large sip of her rum. "You may serve me by being amusing. By diverting me." She smiled at him, trying to establish a different mood.

"Camilla, I can't help you out of this bloody mess unless you tell me a lot more about what's going on. I know you know who killed Molly. I should like to know why she was murdered."

"Please, no." She was staring into her drink, just as she had the first time he was with her like this, the two of them, in a restaurant.

"You can trust me," he said. "You have to."

"You've helped me enough. You've done more than enough, at great risk. I appreciate it. Please, let's leave it at that."

"Look, Camilla. This isn't simply going to vanish. We have to deal with it."

"Not tonight!" There was the spark of anger in her eyes and a crackly snap of it in her voice.

"I'm sorry."

They sat silently until their dinner came, and hardly spoke through that. Finally, just to draw her out, draw her back, he began talking to her as he would to someone he encountered at a reception or cocktail party, amusingly and inconsequentially—about New York gossip, art exhibitions he'd liked, sailing, silly people who frequented Mortimer's, McMullen's, and other Upper East Side spots they both knew. She responded amiably, but it was obvious her mind was elsewhere. She asked for more wine. They had already gone through a half bottle of an expensive Bordeaux.

"I'm feeling better, Mr. James," she said, when her glass was refilled.

"You have to stop calling me that. We're friends now."

"*Bien sur. J'ai vous baissé.* But not 'A.C.' "

"My Christian names are Arthur Curtis."

"Arthur. Art. No. Perhaps A.C. is best."

She drank more wine. When they were done, night had fully fallen, but it was still quite balmy. She leaned back in her chair and looked up at the dark sky.

"I'd like to dance," she said. "Can we find a place to dance?"

•

There were nightclubs with island steel-drum bands and hotel lounges with small combos playing mostly society two-step music. A.C. was grateful when she settled for the latter.

Camilla did not want to talk. She was content to drink and dance. As she became more tipsy, his own clumsiness on the floor ceased to matter. She danced with great abandon for several numbers, then slowed, clinging to him, her head against his, humming softly to the music. She moved her hand to the back of his neck. As they dreamily made their turns, his leg would slide between hers, her thigh pressing softly against his. For all he knew, she was thinking of someone else as she gave herself so indulgently to his arms, but he held her as though she were his own, a rare and precious possession.

She stumbled. Like most models, she had exquisite balance and caught herself, but he worried now that he might never get her back safely on that little motorbike.

"Time to go home, Camilla."

"Home," she said. "How I should love to go home."

She held onto him somehow, as they rolled along out of Hamilton on Crow Lane. Reaching the rotary just outside the town, he pulled out of the traffic stream, turning onto the little road that followed the opposite shore of the harbor. It was narrow and full of curves, but they encountered few vehicles, the bike's little headlamp poking lonesomely into the soft shadows, the reflected lights of Hamilton twinkling and shimmering in the dark water to the right.

She began to sing: "Sand in my shoes, sand from Havana . . ." She swayed slightly from side to side.

"Camilla! Please! Hold on tight."

"I'm just fine, Arthur Curtis James. No need to worry."

He reached back, gripping her hip, but that only made the machine even less stable. A fall, with the pavement tearing at her flesh and beauty, could be disastrous.

Trusting to the fates, he returned his hand to the han-

251

dlebars, going a little faster now, desperate to get her to the hotel without incident. At length a side road appeared ahead on the left—Chapel Road. He remembered that it led directly across the island to South Road and Elbow Beach.

It climbed steeply, then swerved sharply to the right. He managed that curve, but at the bottom of the following hill, a turn to the left caught him unawares. The motorbike skidded, the rear wheel slipping off onto the shoulder. He fought to regain control, but she was leaning off to the side, pulling on his shoulder.

The front wheel struck something and they went over. He was thrown forward, banging his knee on the handlebar, sailing into the air and landing with a soft thud in the high grass of a ditch. She cried out. Then there was silence.

He sat up. The minibike lay on its side. Its engine rumbled and sputtered a moment, then ceased. The headlamp went out.

"Camilla?"

A pause. "I'm all right. I think."

She was quite near. He got to his knees and groped forward, finding himself suddenly beside her.

"You're not hurt?"

"Just a little scared."

He lay down next to her. "Can you move your arms and legs?"

"Oh yes," She tried it. "Yes. I'm fine."

"Can you get up?"

"I can. But I don't want to. I feel so gloriously comfortable, A.C. This grass is so soft. A.C., look at the stars."

He rolled over onto his back. She moved her head until it was cradled by his shoulder.

I have seen starry archipelagos, and islands,
Whose heavens are opened to the voyager.
Is it in these bottomless nights that you sleep,
In exile? A million golden birds.

"Starry archipelagos?"

"Rimbaud," she said. " 'Le Bateau Ivre.' " She took a deep, happy breath. "A million golden birds."

252

She raised herself and came slowly upon him, lowering her face to his. She kissed him. Her mouth opened slightly and she kissed him again. He pulled her roughly to him, his hand moving down her back, reaching to the warm flesh beneath her dress.

As they plunged into the sweet, mad, delirious experience he had dreamed about a thousand times since the first moment he had seen her on Arbre's runway, an unexpected flurry of unwanted thoughts beset him: fleeting images of Davey on the sailboat, of Kitty behind the wheel of her car, of Bailey drunk and loving in his arms.

He drove these from his mind as their bodies joined. She murmured to him through her kisses, her hair falling over him. Then at once she lifted herself, moving astride him, gently, then with urgency. He kept his eyes closed. Even in the dark, he didn't want to look at her face. She was so very human now. He didn't want to see the goddess.

At the end, holding him closely again, she began to cry, but then, before he could find a way to comfort her, she rolled over onto her back beside him, one breast exposed. Wiping her eyes, she gave a sound of contentment.

"How wonderful, under all these stars," she said.

"More than wonderful."

She took his hand and held it close to her eyes, then kissed it.

"I love you," he said.

"Oh no, A.C. You mustn't say that. Please don't love me."

"Just tonight."

"All right. Just tonight."

•

The motorbike started when he tried it and did not seem seriously damaged. Camilla, smoothing out her clothing, stood somewhat wobbily, but he could not tell if that was due to drink or hurt. She climbed on behind him without complaint, holding onto him with just one hand as, slowly now, he drove them through the dark to the other side of the island.

They left the bike with a sleepy black woman behind the

counter of the rental shed who paid them little mind. As they walked back up the main drive, he noticed Camilla was limping slightly.

"You're sure you're all right?"

"Oh yes. I'm fine. Lovely. Wonderful."

He pointed to the hotel's main building—to the lights at the very top.

"Well," he said. "I'm staying up there. On the other side, actually. Wonderful view of the hotel entrance."

She looked down the hill, toward the sea, and took his hand. "I want to go to the beach."

Her limp seemed more pronounced as they descended. He put his arm around her. There were lights set here and there in the shrubbery and trees. They saw another couple crossing one of the lawns, but there was no one else. The beach club was closed and deserted, though the floodlights illuminating the promenade and the sand below were still shining brightly.

At the bottom of the stone steps, Camilla slipped off her shoes, carrying them lightly in one hand. A.C. followed her example, pausing to roll up the cuffs of his trousers. She moved slowly in the thick, fine sand, and he caught up to her easily.

"The sand is so cool," she said. "It's like walking in silk."

"I love you, Camilla."

She continued on, as though not caring if he followed. The beach was protected by the outlying coral reef and, despite the wind, the waves were small. The underwater slope was gentle, the shallows extending far. She went out until the little wavetops were splashing her thighs, soaking the bottom of her skirt. He sloshed his way to where she was. She turned into him as he put his arm around her, coming close to him. She did not want to be kissed.

"When you close your eyes like this," she said, "standing in the water at night, you could be anywhere. You could be a million miles away in space. When I was a little girl, we used to go to an island where my family owned land. I'd go out at night into the shallows and stand there, listening. I'd close my eyes, and be any place I dreamed of."

He gently lifted her chin, tilting up her face. "I don't want you to close your eyes. I want to look into your eyes."

" 'When I look into your eyes,' " she sang, repeating a line from an old song. "You don't want to look into my eyes, A.C."

They were wide open, staring up into his. The distant light from the floodlit beach reached them, but the crystalline blue was gone. They seemed quite dark.

"You don't know what you might find," she continued. "It could be something horrible."

As must happen to every man with Camilla, he suddenly felt fiercely possessive. He had captured her. She was his and no other's. He slipped his hand over her breast. In all their passion, he'd only glancingly touched her breasts.

She turned away, looking out to sea. A ship's gaily dancing lights were visible to the southeast. It was moving surprisingly fast, crossing to the west.

"I could be on that ship," she said. "Sailing away. I need only walk out to it."

"We could be on that ship," he said.

The night at once became darker. He looked behind them and saw that the lights on the beach had been turned out.

"It must be late," he said.

"I think I'd like another drink," she said. "Yes. Another drink. I'm getting cold."

When they reached the dry sand of the shore, he hesitated.

"The bar may be closed."

"I don't want to go all the way up to the bar," she said. "My room's just there. I have one of the Surf rooms, overlooking the beach. I have things to drink. Rum, gin, too. The Canadians sent it. I thought it funny. Supplying models with strong drink during a shoot."

They started toward the stone steps, crossing the now darkened sand. The ground lights set among the trees on the hillside above were still glowing, like yellow lanterns.

Her limp had become so pronounced he had to help her up the stairs, but when he boldly offered to carry her the rest of the way, she shook her head.

The seaward wall of her room was nearly entirely glass opening with a sliding door. A white table and three chairs were set out on the little patio in front of it. She had him

255

sit down and disappeared inside, turning on a light. A short while later, she returned with two glasses and a bottle.

"This is rum," she said. "I haven't any ice. Did you want water with it? Or tonic?"

"Straight is fine." He poured an inch or so of the liquor into a glass for her, and then an equal amount in one for himself. Seating herself, she took the bottle and half filled her glass.

She was wearing a white terry cloth robe. Her leg was bare, and he guessed she had taken off her clothes. It was warm now here in the shelter of the trees. The night was close around them.

They sat quietly and drank. She coughed, but only once. He wanted to touch and hold her again, but held back.

"Can I still trust you, A.C.?"

"Yes. Of course. Always."

"You'll help me?"

"Yes."

"You'll protect me? You'll keep Detective Lanham from finding me?"

He reached into his pocket and took out the red silk scarf she had given him. He had folded it into a soft, compact square. He shook it out, then brought it to his lips.

"As I promised." He returned the scarf to his pocket. "I didn't mean to frighten you about that. I think I may have exaggerated how serious he is about this."

"No you didn't. I talked with that man. He is a very serious person."

"I don't think his superiors will allow him to go looking for you."

"Unless something else happens."

"What could happen now?"

She took a very long drink of her rum, holding the glass to her lips for several swallows. She coughed again as she set the glass on the table. She had tied her robe loosely, and it fell open. He could see both her small, lovely breasts, and the sheen of her flat belly.

"Drink, A.C. Drink and be merry."

Her voice was cold and lonely. The ship was gone from the sea that stretched before them. The waves sounded close.

"I love you, Camilla. I'll love you forever."

"Forever. What if you had a wrinkled old woman on your lap?"

"But I don't."

"What if I was an ugly woman. A fat, ugly woman, a woman with a big nose, or bad skin."

"You wouldn't have been on Arbre's runway. We'd never have met."

"If I were a woman like that, you'd never even talk to me."

"Camilla. We are what we are. Your beauty is part of you. You wouldn't be the person you are now if you hadn't always been beautiful. You'd be someone else."

"I'd be worthless."

"No. Camilla, if you were to have a horrible accident tomorrow, if you were horribly disfigured, I'd still feel the way I do, because that wouldn't change what you are, who you are. It wouldn't change what's happened."

"I don't believe you."

"Then you don't know me, not as well as you should."

She smiled a little. "Drink."

He gulped the last of his rum. She had nearly finished hers. Eyes downcast, she stood, placing her perfect hand on his shoulder.

"Come inside now," she said. "I want you to make love to me again. For a long time."

There was tenderness and gentleness and caring this time, but no mad passion. He did everything that he thought might please her, thinking only of her, giving nothing to himself. When they separated, he lay beside her, gazing at her sleepy face. She gave him a small, sweet smile, her last of the night. It was almost as though she were ill, and he had administered some soothing treatment. Feeling that his life was now utterly complete, he rolled over and fell into a blissful sleep.

He awakened twice. The first time, it was to a fearful uncertainty as to where he was. He turned and found her naked beside him, lying very straight and very still on her back, like a dead person awaiting the ministrations of burial. She was awake, her eyes wide open, fixed upon the ceiling.

He called her name softly. She said nothing.

The second time, near to the first glimmer of dawning, he panicked to discover the bed empty and cold beside him. But, sitting up, he saw her standing near the opened drapes of the window, her nude form limned by the false light. Hearing him, she turned slowly to face him, standing eerily, like a ghost come haunting.

"I think you'd better go back to your room now, A.C.," she said, her voice low and tired. "They'll be coming to get me in the morning."

"All right." He stood and began to get dressed. He felt clumsy with her watching him.

"When will I see you?" he asked, when he was done.

"Later. Perhaps for lunch. Yes, I'll meet you for lunch at the beach club. About one o'clock."

"One o'clock." He kissed her. She allowed this, but did not embrace him. Her arms hung loosely at her sides.

He slipped outside. In his fatigue and joy and triumph, he felt quite giddy. If he were still a boy, he might do cartwheels on the lawn. Instead, he stretched and yawned and smiled to himself, starting up the walk with jaunty vigor. But something stayed him. There was a whisper of a sound that did not belong. Her voice.

Moving quietly, he returned to the screen of her door. She was talking on the telephone.

"This is all I'm going to tell you," she was saying. "We have nothing to fear from Pierre. It was all a sham. There's nothing in his will. I looked at it. There's nothing in his lawyer's files. He was lying to us. He tricked us. You, me, Momma, God knows who else. I don't think he has any idea where it's hidden—if those things even exist anymore."

The man on the other end spoke so loudly A.C. could hear his voice, though he couldn't make out what the what he was saying.

"Listen to me!" Camilla said. "It's true. He's been lying to us, lying about everything. And he has that videotape. He's the one who's been threatening people with it."

She paused, listening.

"The police know about it," she said. "One of them told Mr. James and he told me . . . No, they don't know anything else. And neither does he. Don't you dare go looking for him. You leave him alone."

258

A.C. heard the man swearing loudly.

"Stop it!" said Camilla. "No. I'm not going to tell you where I am. You're never going to know where I am ever again . . . No, dammit! I mean it. I mean it more than anything in my life. You're dead to me now. Let me be dead to you."

In the silence that followed, A.C. wondered if she had hung up. Then she spoke again.

"I used to love you so," she said. "No, I don't want to hear what you're going to do. You do what you think you must. You find Pierre and you deal with him. I don't care how. I called you because I wanted you to know that it doesn't matter to me, that I don't care what happens to him. I don't care what happens to you. Just leave me and Momma alone. Don't ever bother us again."

There was one more pause, and she spoke again, her voice very low and husky.

"No more. *Rien.* This is the last time I will ever speak to you. Goodbye."

A.C. reached for the door handle, then froze. She would never forgive his intrusion now, never forgive him his listening. He moved away, back to the path, and started up the hill, as sad as he had been happy, unsure of many things. Behind him, he heard her crying, but the sound became lost in the rustle of the trees in the sea breeze.

•

He telephoned her immediately upon awakening in the morning, hoping she might have time to join him for breakfast, but there was no answer. After showering and dressing, he tried again, with the same result.

The Canadians were not in the dining room. He paused only for coffee and juice, then went down to her room, finding it locked and empty, though he was reassured to see her suitcase still in place next to the dresser.

At the beach, he stood on the parapet of the veranda, his eyes sweeping the sands but seeing only tourists. He sat on the railing, waiting, then became impatient and set off on a walk west along the beach, coming at length to a high pile of coral rock and climbing it. The further view yielded

259

no sign of them. Finally, deflated and depressed, he returned to his room. He resisted the impulse to call New York.

He would only be reaching out to trouble, inviting its intrusion. He took a postcard from his desk drawer and wrote a short message to his son, then tore it up. It would be just the same as telephoning Kitty and telling her where he was and what he had done.

Lying back on his bed, he closed his eyes and relived in memory the special moments of the night before as he might examine, one by one, the treasures of a jewel box. He put them back and took them out all over again. Kitty's threats of divorce had left him contemplating a future bleak and empty. It was no longer so.

He resolved not to ask Camilla about her mysterious late-night telephone call. If they could put that behind them, they could put it all behind them.

Camilla was where she had promised she'd be, waiting for him at the beach club at the appointed hour, reading a book at a table near the railing, a tall drink in front of her. She wore a pink blouse and skirt and her espadrilles. There was a supportive bandage wound around her knee. He noticed a mottled bruise on her leg and scratches on her arm. She was reading seriously, unaware of his presence until he touched her shoulder. He was grateful that she smiled, though it was weakly.

"Dear God," he said. "I had no idea you were so badly hurt."

She set down her book. It was in French, a novel by Marguerite Duras.

"I'm all right," she said, in a sad, childlike voice. "My knee's a little swollen. The hotel found me a doctor. It's nothing serious."

"How were you able to work?"

"I didn't. They paid me anyway. I daresay they got their money's worth. I didn't charge them my usual fee."

He pulled out a chair and sat down, crossing his legs. "Your friend Eddie must be furious."

She made a face, bringing unexpected wrinkles to the corners of her eyes. "He'll survive."

260

"I hope I haven't ended your modeling career."

"I don't think there's much left of my modeling career."

"When are you going back?" he asked.

"I haven't thought much about that yet."

"We have the afternoon then."

"The afternoon, the evening. The night." She shrugged.

"What would you like to do?"

"I'm afraid I have a terrible hangover. I'd like another drink. And then something to eat, and then let's do whatever you want."

"I'd love to go sailing."

"Then we shall go sailing."

After lunch, he rented a stout day sailor and took them out into the Great Sound, showing off as he tacked and darted around the big yachts and ships. Circling a few of the islands, he then headed out through the mouth of the Sound to the Granaway Deep, sailing on until the immensity of the open sea began to frighten her.

Returning, they caught a bus to Hamilton and went shopping, afterwards visiting an art gallery. When her knee began to hurt, he took her to a tea room. At first, it was very romantic. They held hands. But she turned abruptly cold and withdrawn, and the mood lingered. Once she left him to use the telephone, returning shortly afterward. A second time, she returned almost as quickly, looking quite distraught and asking to go back to their hotel.

She went to her room, commanding him not to follow but agreeing to meet him for dinner. The hour she chose was barely in time for the dining room's last seating. What little conversation they had was strained and superficial. His attempts at comfort and reassurance produced no effect.

They sat for a long while on the hotel terrace, holding hands again but not talking. Finally, after considerable prodding on his part, she agreed to pass the rest of the evening at the hotel's fancy nightclub listening to the steel-drum music, but instead of improving her disposition, it only provided more opportunity for her to drink.

They drank a lot at the club and more at the little table outside her room. When at length the floodlights were turned off at the beach, he suggested they go for a swim.

261

"No, A.C. Not that."

She put her face in her hands. He began gently rubbing her back.

"I did something terrible last night," she said.

He dared not speak. He feared what he might blurt out about her telephone conversation.

"Because of what I've done, I think Pierre is going to be murdered. I've felt sick about it all day. This afternoon, I tried to undo it, but I couldn't. I couldn't get through. I feel so damned rotten. I . . . ."

"Do you want to tell me about it?" he asked.

She reached and took his hand, stroking it. "Yes, I do. I'd love to tell you everything, A.C., and have you go off and take care of it all for me, as I'm sure you'd try to do. But I can't. It wouldn't do any good. I've made too much of a mess of things. There are no valiant knights, are there? Not even you. There are no happy endings, no happily ever afters."

She lifted his hand to her face.

"The lovely day is over," she said. "Such a lovely day. Such a lovely day. 'Beauty is the scent of roses, and the death of roses.' "

"F. Scott Fitzgerald wrote that," A.C. said.

"It was a sad thing to say. He was a very sad man."

She finished her drink, somewhat clumsily, then reached for the bottle.

He intervened. "Let's go to bed," he said.

Camilla left the bottle alone, but did not stir. "I can't make love to you, A.C. Not now."

"We'll just lie together. I'll hold you."

"All right. We'll hold each other. I'd like that."

He led her to the warmth of her bed. They lay together, face to face, their nakedness a bond. At length, he kissed her, and then again. Finally, they did make love, quickly and gently—and a little sadly. Fulfillment brought relief.

"I love you so," he said.

"A.C. I wish I had known you in another time. In another life."

"We could make another life, a new life."

For a long time, she didn't respond.

262

"A.C.," she said finally. "I don't want you to go back to New York. Not for a few days. Promise me."

"Why?"

"It's dangerous for you. I've told you."

"I'll be all right."

"Promise me!"

"I have to get out of my room. It's booked for someone else."

"There's this room."

"This wonderful room."

She kissed him, and then lay back. In a few soft moments, they went to sleep. Later, at some indeterminate hour, he heard her get up and go into the bathroom. When she did not return after a very long time, he tired of waiting and slipped back into his deep and comforting slumber.

When he awoke again, stirred from a dream, it was to the sound of a strange voice, and a noise at the door. A maid's black face was apparent in the harsh glare of sunlight.

"I am sorry, sir," she said. The door closed.

Camilla's side of the bed was empty. She was not in the room. The bathroom door stood open and its lights were out. Her suitcase was gone. There was nothing in the closet. There was no note.

CHAPTER

....

12

Jacques Delasante hated the dark. He had grown up in a grand Southern house that had always been kept ablaze with light well into the night. He had followed the custom with his own house in Virginia, keeping a lamp on in his bedroom until morning—sometimes through the entire day in gloomy winter. The darkness of A.C. James's East Side apartment oppressed him powerfully, but he endured it, as he had endured so much. The night had become his ally in the task he had undertaken. It was one of many strange and inexplicable things that had happened to him.

He was seated stiffly in a leather chair that faced the small entrance hall of the apartment, allowing him a clear field of fire when James entered, whatever hour that would be. The man kept late nights in his work, but Jacques intended to wait for him no matter how long it took, even if it meant sitting in this chair all the next day.

He had gained access to the apartment with encouraging

264

ease, going first to the roof of the building next door, dropping the one story to James's small terrace, and then quietly breaking the glass of the door nearest the brass lock. He was wearing a pair of the transparent latex gloves all dentists now used as a protection against dangerous diseases, and had been able to move about the flat without fear of leaving fingerprints.

Jacques had turned on lights only twice; once to use James's bathroom and another time turning on the kitchen lights to find the man's liquor and pour himself some whiskey in a cup he'd found. He'd sat sipping it very slowly as the minutes and hours crept by, drinking with his left hand. In his right, he held his pistol, resting the barrel with its long silencer on his thigh. The hammer was cocked. It would take but a second to get off a round.

James was as good as dead. Whatever he was doing— and given the depravity of this New York society, it could be absolutely anything—he would now be consuming the last moments of his life, blissfully unaware of how few they were. Camilla's new flame was a corpse.

James was a snoop, an intruder, a paid violator of others' privacy, a Northern upstart. Jacques could only wonder at his background, this man of consequence in a rabble-ridden city run by Negroes and Jews and Catholics. Back home, such a man could never hope to gain any kind of acceptance—would never dare press a claim to the affections of a woman of Camilla's standing, would never dare kiss her and touch her as Jacques had seen James do in Camilla's little flat.

Jacques's gun hand was trembling. Relaxing his grip slightly, he took a gulp of his drink. Then he set down the cup. He didn't dare fall asleep.

He turned to the French doors at his back. Jacques hated the big, licentious, menacing city that stared back at him through the windows—hated everything it stood for, everything it allowed. New York was the antithesis of his birthplace—of his birthright. He wanted desperately to be on the move, to be hot after Pierre, to return to the South. But he could not leave behind the smoldering danger his damned foolish sister had created with her dalliance with this prying, trouble-making newspaperman. He could not

265

leave this man alive. She would despise him forever for doing this, but that no longer mattered. She no longer understood what mattered. He saw it clearly. As always, he would do what had to be done.

He drank again. When the click of the front door lock finally came, he was on the edge of drowsiness, but the sound snapped him awake as it might a dozing hunting dog. He could see clearly enough in the dimness, but he was too good a shot to need to aim. His hand came up with the gun trained on the archway.

A slash of light from the outside hallway flared against the wall of the foyer, then vanished as the person entering slammed shut the door. It sounded as though James were drunk and fumbling with the light switch. There was a muffled thud as he tripped and fell against the wall, pushing himself away and stepping into the archway.

Jacques fired an instant after, the vague flash from the muffled barrel piercing the darkness. He saw his mistake —and heard the womanly cry—but it was too late to stay the second shot. There was a crash of fallen furniture and breaking glass, then sudden silence. The smell of gun smoke was strong.

Shaking, cursing the perversity of his luck, Jacques rose and went toward his victim, pausing to turn on a table lamp, blinking at the brightness. A beautiful woman lay on her back, her arm caught in the frame of an overturned glass-top table. Her face was contorted; her eyes were staring upward, and were very still.

He swore again, smacking the warm silencer of his pistol against his hand. He'd killed another woman. In the sacred cause of upholding a woman's honor, he'd done it again.

Gun still in hand, he knelt beside her, and lifted her wrist, feeling for a pulse. Beautiful she was, and quite dead, blood soaking the front of her blouse.

The old nana had lived longer than most people had a right to expect. The nigger prostitute was no loss to anyone. But this was a white woman—a lady, from the look of her. There was something familiar about her. Jacques was certain he had never met her, but in some way he knew her. James moved among famous people. This woman might be one of them.

266

It was Camilla's fault this had happened. She had brought this stranger into their affairs. While getting his drink in the kitchen. Jacques had found a picture of Camilla on the table cut out from a magazine. He'd torn it into little bits.

Jacques's bad luck could become much worse. Standing, he quickly switched off the light. He was no coward. There was nothing he would not brave. There were few things he hadn't. But he had to flee this place—flee this city, flee the North.

He went the way he had come. It was difficult—it took two attempts to regain the rooftop next door. But he succeeded. Within a few minutes, he was speeding through the night-empty streets. As before, no one followed.

·

The bullet that ended Detective Second Grade Tony Gabriel's police career never struck him. Had it been fired two or three seconds earlier, it might have. He'd be as thoroughly dead as the beautiful but unlucky woman it had hit, her remains now sprawled with grotesque indignity on the bloody mattress.

Belinda had become so scared she'd gone a little crazy. She'd been doing cocaine before Tony had gotten to her apartment and snorted a couple more lines while he was there, drinking all the while. She asked for sex as though it were another drug, demanding that he make love to her in animal fashion, mounting from behind—screaming at him throughout the act as though it were bringing her pain instead of pleasure. When he could provide her nothing more and withdrew, standing aside to catch his breath, the bullet came through the window with a crack of glass, striking Belinda at the base of the spine and traveling the length of her body, digging a channel that brought violence to every vital organ and exiting near her throat. She looked like a child's beautiful doll that had been dropped from some great height, except for the blood spreading across the white satin.

Shaken, more sick and terrified than he had ever been even in his worst moments as a policeman, Gabriel stood uncomprehending, then leapt back, going to the window

267

and crouching at the side, peering up at the rooftop of the building across the street. The upper ledge was several stories above the level of Belinda's apartment, but the line of sight was perfect for the shot, the trajectory direct from vantage point to the once lovely sculpture of Belinda's naked back.

In reflex, Gabriel's mind began working like a cop's. Nothing moved along the ledge. No one peered from the windows opposite. This was New York, and it was only a gun shot. The windows Gabriel could see that were lighted had drapes drawn across them. If Belinda had not been such a careless exhibitionist, and had drawn her own, she might still be alive.

The perp could have been a weirdo, an E.D.P., some sneakcreep who'd turned from voyeurism to bigger kicks as a sniper. They caught cases like that every year.

Yet it had been such a perfect hit, a one-shot collect. Professional shooters like that did a lot of work for people like Vince Perotta. He and Belinda had given Perotta a lot of reason to make such a hire. She'd been a lunatic to do it. So had he. Every policeman cherishes the hope that no criminal wants the trouble that comes with killing a cop. If it hadn't been for that, Gabriel might have made himself think a little longer and better about romancing Belinda St. Johns. She was just too much to stay away from. He'd never had a woman like that. Life was short, shorter than anyone thought.

The perp could have whacked him along with her. A single twofer shot, or another right after hers. The perp had had plenty of time for either.

Gabriel had gotten off the bed all hot and sweaty. Now he was cold and shaking, but the perspiration kept coming. He crept to the chair that held his clothing and searched for his cigarettes. Lighting one, he sat back on the floor against the wall next to the violated window, feeling for a moment protected.

Maybe Perotta had nothing to do with it. Maybe Perotta was going to be as shocked and angry—and scared—as he was. There was another perp who could have managed this whack, one perp so good, whoever he was, that he had

268

dropped Molly Wickham through the head with a handgun from a motorcycle. The perp who wasn't Bad Biker Bobby.

Belinda was so still, so silent. Gabriel stared at the bottoms of her bare feet, at the twin curves of her buttocks. It was the least attractive view of the human body there was, but he was still held by the sense of her beauty.

She'd been very much like him, from the same kind of neighborhood and the same kind of family. If she'd grown up in his part of Queens instead of Bridgeport, Connecticut, she might never have met Vincent Perotta or been on a fashion runway with Molly Wickham. This might never have happened. Tony Gabriel might be a married man—as much married as he ever could be, as she could be.

Gabriel had been falling hard for her. He wouldn't realize how much for days. It would be the worst part of all of this, the worst part of his life. As soon as they were through with him, he was going to get very drunk that night.

Ashes from his cigarette had fallen onto the carpet. He swore, then rose and ground it out in the ashtray on the night table. After glancing nervously at the window, he got dressed.

He could just walk out. He was a pro. He knew what the evidence technicians would be looking for, what he'd have to do to remove the traces of his presence. He could get it done in fifteen minutes.

Belinda's arm had twisted and her hand lay palm up. Tony leaned and touched it gently. He made a vow. He wasn't going to give this perp a single second more than he already had. His last official act as a police officer was going to be blameless.

He stepped to the phone, and called the cops.

•

They reached Lanham in his car. He and Petrowicz had been interviewing friends of the Central Park victim, getting names of other friends, people who might have known the man she'd left the bar with.

When they told him about Belinda St. Johns, he put the Central Park case out of his mind. They wanted him back

269

at the division. He had taken out his notebook but wrote nothing in it. What could he write? "Tony fucked up." Petrowicz noticed his distress. He ran red lights all the way back to headquarters.

The squad room was crowded, but Taranto wasn't in his office. Caputo said he was still at the crime scene, as were a lot of heavy brass from downtown.

"What a shot," said Caputo. "Right through—"

"Shut up, Charley," Petrowicz said.

Caputo went to get a cup of coffee. Lanham looked through his phone messages, finding one from a detective sergeant he knew at a precinct in Greenwich Village.

"Hey, Ray," said the detective, after Lanham had gotten him on the phone. "We got a double homicide down here. Fag job. Got 'em both ID'd and one of them I think is a witness of yours. In the Wickham case?"

It couldn't be A.C. James. The doorman? A cab driver?

"Arbree," said the detective, reading from something and mispronouncing the name. "Philippe Arbree."

"You said a double homicide. Do you mean murder-suicide?"

"No. They were both clocked by a perp. Strangulation. Well, there's mutilation involved, too, but it wasn't cause of death."

"How do you strangle two people at the same time? Were there two perps?"

"I don't know. The bodies were found in separate rooms. It's a weird one."

"What's the ID on the other victim?"

"Woody. James Woody."

Lanham drummed his fingers on his desk.

"Hey, Ray, I gotta get going. You wanna come down?"

"Have the bodies been removed?"

"Crime scene unit's almost finished. I can put a hold on."

"No. We've got a lot going on up here."

"Yeah, I heard. Real sorry for Tony."

"Right."

"She was a witness, too. That Belinda St. Johns."

A witness, and what else?

"Right. Except we more or less closed the Wickham case."

"You oughta check this out, Ray."

"Yes. I'll get back to you as soon as I can."

"Okay. Good luck."

Lanham gently set the receiver on its cradle. He tapped the desktop again. One of the skin books he'd looked through was still on his desk, half buried by some files and a newspaper. Lanham stood up. He took his weapon out of his shoulder holster and checked to see that the cylinder was fully loaded. Janice was still barely speaking to him.

"Come on," he said to Petrowicz.

"Where we going?"

"The West Side."

•

Lanham had had an itch—a bad one. He'd half expected to find police cars already outside Peter Gorky's studio. He'd given no thought to fire engines.

Petrowicz pulled the car up on the sidewalk to get as close as he could without interfering with the fire equipment. As they came up to the still smoking building, stepping over hoses and oily puddles, Lanham studied the grimy brick façade. The tall windows on the second floor were marked by huge dark water stains around the sills and darker smears left by searing flame and smoke above them. The fire had been fast and hot.

Lanham showed his shield to a fire captain in a white helmet.

"Any victims?" he said.

The fireman turned to bark an order at two men pulling on a hose, then wiped some soot off his face with the back of his hand.

"Victims?" he said. "Yeah, one victim. What're you guys doing here so fast? We haven't even struck the fire yet."

"You found him on the second floor? Gorky Productions?"

"Yeah. He's still there. It was a bad burn. No need for the paramedics."

271

"Thanks." Lanham started for the building's entrance, Petrowicz, a little reluctantly, following.

"Hey!" said the captain. "You guys can't go in there yet!"

Lanham kept going, holding his shield before him as he mounted the stairs, his shoes slipping in the slushy, ashy muck. The smoke was hanging so thickly it seemed to have replaced the air. Lanham held his handkerchief over his mouth, though it made little difference. He was coughing loudly by the time he reached the second floor. It was hard to believe there were cops who griped about how easy the firefighters had it.

A couple of firemen were in the back, breaking out more windows to increase ventilation. Others were moving about the interior, ripping out paneling with pike poles and crowbars to make certain no remaining flames were still flickering within the walls. One of the firemen studied the intruders warily, but then turned away, assuming they had permission.

"Homicide," said Lanham, coughing again. "Where's the victim?"

"In the big room. Through there."

All fire scenes had one thing in common. They were monochromatic. Everything—walls, floors, furniture, glassware—was colored the same black and gray char.

Including human beings. The blackened, charbroiled, skeletal remains of what Lanham presumed had once been Peter Gorky were in the burned-out frame of a swivel chair, the hands still on the arms of the chair, the ashy skull tilted grotesquely over the back. His clothes were gone except for his belt and heavy leather boots, but what made him seem naked was that his beard was missing.

"Is this where you found him?" Lanham said to another firefighter who'd come up.

"What do you think, we sat him there?"

"He was tied in that chair," said Petrowicz.

"What kind of bonds? There's no trace of a rope, unless it was all burned up."

"Wasn't rope," said the firefighter. "Probably used what fed the fire."

"What's that?"

The fireman gestured at the floor all around them. "Film," he said.

As Lanham had not noticed, there were opened film cans and loose, melted tape cartridges everywhere. The storage cabinets had all been opened, their shelves emptied. Portions of some of the reels had not burned. Lanham picked up one coil. The film was brittle, and broke. The frames were all black.

"I gotta get some air," Petrowicz said.

•

When they returned to division, the squad room was as crowded as a subway car, as filled with uniformed force as with detectives. Taranto was in his office, talking volubly with angry gestures to two other men in suits, one of them their captain. Phones were ringing as fast as they were hung up. A reporter, an old veteran known to all the men in the division, had apparently called up enough old favors to get in, and was standing in a corner, taking notes as inconspicuously as possible as he talked to a detective from one of the other teams.

Another detective was using Gabriel's desk and phone. Tony was sitting on one of the wooden chairs along the wall by the entrance, smoking and holding a cup of coffee, staring bleakly at the floor.

Lanham nodded to Petrowicz to go on, then dropped into the empty chair next to Gabriel's. He put his hand on Gabriel's shoulder.

"Don't know what to say, Tony."

Gabriel dropped his cigarette butt on the floor, and crushed it out with the toe of his narrow, highly polished shoe. His eyes were very red, and he badly needed a shave.

"Perotta was in Miami," Gabriel said quietly. "They got him on the phone. He acted like we were fucking taking up his time."

His coffee smelled strongly of whiskey. He'd likely sought recourse to one of the half-pint bottles Pat Cassidy had kept stashed in places they all knew about. Lanham supposed it wouldn't make much difference if he were drinking it straight out of the bottle for all to see.

"There were three other homicides last night," Lanham said. "The designer Philippe Arbre, a male model named Jimmy Woody, and a photographer named Peter Gorky. Would Perotta want to take them out, too?"

"He's a fucking animal."

"No one ever called Vince Perotta a nice guy."

"I'm not talking about Vince. I'm talking about this cocksucker perp. The one that whacked Wickham."

"We'll get him, Tony. But I don't think he's the one who hit Belinda. All these homicides tonight, the time of occurrence was roughly the same. It's not just one guy."

"You won't get this perp. He's got no fucking rules, Ray. We've got rules. I'm going to lose my shield because of our fucking rules. The whole world's got rules. Vince Perotta's got rules. He breaks ours but he keeps his own. But this son of a bitch, this perp, the cocksucker just does what he wants. We don't matter. Nothing fucking matters. He wants somebody dead, they die."

"I don't think he hit Belinda, Tony."

"And you're never going to find out. I'm the only one who's going to pay for this."

"We'll get him." Him? Them? He sounded so foolishly sure.

Gabriel sipped his laced coffee. "Yeah, right," he said, his voice as tired as his eyes.

There was a bustle of movement as a new group of detectives came in. They were heavies—grim-faced, self-important. Taranto had called in the mob crimes unit. Closed or not, the Molly Wickham case had become a small detail in a very big deal.

CHAPTER

....

13

The hotel desk clerk told A.C. what he already had guessed—that Camilla, registered under the name of Miss Anne Claire, had checked out. The clerk had no other information, but people at the airport were more helpful. Camilla had been wearing sunglasses when she boarded her plane, but several airport workers were able to recognize her from the picture A.C. carried in his wallet.

She had not gone back to New York. According to an airline gate agent, she had taken a flight to Baltimore–Washington International.

She had gone after Pierre.

A.C. could not follow—not yet. He had left a wretched mess back in New York—marriage, job, Bailey Hazeltine and her self-destructive problems. He was not the sort of man to walk away from any of that. He'd attend to what duty demanded; then he'd figure out where Camilla Santee belonged in his life.

But she was in nearly his every thought during the flight back. At Kennedy, he ignored the newspapers and bought a fashion magazine instead in hopes of another look at her face. On the cab ride to Manhattan, he went through it carefully, page by page, but there was nothing. Merely models, looking very much alike.

His first stop was the *Globe*. He dropped his bag at the guard's desk by the elevators, then went straight into the *Globe*'s busy city room. No one spoke to him or looked at him, until he reached the center newsdesk.

"I smell cologne," Pasternak said. "Fruitcake cologne."

"I was away for a few days," A.C. said. "Is there anything new on the Wickham case?"

Pasternak smiled, not amicably. There was considerable activity in the newsroom, and a palpable excitement. A.C. saw a copy clerk actually running. Pasternak looked very weary. His shirt was stained with sweat.

" 'Is there anything new?' " mimicked Pasternak. "And this guy thinks he's a fucking newspaperman."

"We got a big story, A.C.," said one of the assistant news editors at the desk. "More murders. Another model."

He pulled a fresh edition of the *Globe* off a stack set at the side of the big desk. Proffering it as he might some rare or important document, he laid it gently in front of A.C.

The headline was a scream in print: NUDE MODEL SLAIN!

Beneath it was a fashion shot of a smiling Belinda St. Johns in a bikini. The rest of the front page was given to smaller headlines and jump heads: "With Cop in Love Nest," "Fashion Sex Ring," "Gays Among Victims," "Mob Moll's Cheating Heart," "Sugar Daddy Is Ex-White House Aide."

A.C. sagged back against a nearby desk, turning to the story about Pierre. Its information was skimpy, identifying Pierre as Molly Wickham's boyfriend and quoting police as saying he attended sex parties with both Wickham and St. Johns. Whatever career hopes the man still harbored for Washington had been ended by the *Globe*, and probably the other papers as well.

There was no mention of Camilla, no reference to her being Pierre's cousin and Molly's landlord.

For now.

276

Another jump story was a profile of Philippe Arbre, identifying him as a designer for European royalty, meaning that some royal cousin might have bought one of his dresses once.

"You have everything in here but UFOs," A.C. said.

"Where were you?" Pasternak barked.

Reflexively, A.C. told the truth. "In Bermuda."

"Bermuda." Pasternak spoke the word as though it were an obscenity. "And did you by any chance leave a phone number where you could be reached, which is standard fucking procedure on this newspaper, procedure followed by everyone from Bill Shannon on down?"

"You didn't need me," A.C. said. "I wrote two columns before I left."

"The hell you did."

"I wrote them, damn it! They were in the system."

Pasternak's voice fell to a very low register. "We found no such columns."

"Then some son of a bitch purged them. They were there. I do my job."

Now Pasternak leaned back and grinned. He might have been Robespierre watching Louis XVI ascend to the guillotine.

"You're right about one thing, Mr. James. We didn't need you. We don't need you. Get out of here. Go to your office."

"A.C.," said the assistant news editor, a friend from the old days, as Pasternak used to be. "Do as he says. Please."

A.C. read the message in the man's eyes. He nodded and, with exaggerated dignity, turned and walked away, pointedly picking up a *New York Times* from the copy desk. Holding back his anger, he smiled at a woman reporter as he passed her, another longtime friend. She nervously looked elsewhere.

The message in the older man's eyes hadn't said enough. What he found at his office said all there was to say. The glass door was locked. Peering inside, he saw that the walls were bare, the desktop clean. The framed photographs from the wall and elsewhere, along with what appeared to be all of his other office possessions, were piled in two cardboard cartons that had been shoved in a corner.

Unable to control himself, he hit the glass door with the side of his fist as hard as he could. A sharp pain stung his hand and ran back up his arm from his wrist. The glass remained intact.

Vanessa was at his side. "Welcome back, A.C.," she said, taking his arm. "Let's get out of here."

"I'll kill that son of a bitch," he said.

"You're not killing anyone." She held up a large manila envelope that seemed very full. "I have your mail. Your check's in here, too. Come on, I'll buy you a drink. This is one time, sweetheart, when I think you really ought to have one."

They went to the bar downstairs. It didn't matter who saw them. The table he took had a view of the street. Bill Shannon's limousine was as usual parked at the curb, the driver reading a newspaper behind the wheel.

He ordered martinis for them both. Vanessa opened the big envelope and poured its contents out on the table, handing him a smaller white envelope bearing the *Globe*'s logo and A.C.'s name, neatly typed.

"It's your severance," she said. "Six months' pay. I checked it, to make sure they weren't doing you dirty."

He started to tear the envelope in half, but she caught his hand in both of hers and then gently took the envelope from his fingers and slid it into the breast pocket of his coat.

"A grand gesture, sweetie," she said, "but it's wasted on me. You're going to need every cent of that. And you've earned every cent of that."

"I can't believe she'd be that vindictive."

"I don't think Kitty had anything to do with it. I think it was dear brother Bill. In any event, they're saying it's for cause. The official story is that you obstructed them on a major story, apparently to protect friends. They also say you were hitting the bottle and shacked up with a woman other than your wife. And you didn't file any columns this week."

"That isn't true."

"That's what they're saying."

"Someone's put a knife in my back."

"Welcome to New York. We have quaint customs like that."

Their drinks came. The cold gin dampened his rage.

"I filed two columns. I put them into the system before I left."

"They say they couldn't find them. Did you save copies in your computer queue?"

"No. I don't think I did. I was in a hurry."

"*Tant pis.* Though I don't suppose it really matters now." She studied him, a little warily. "Where were you, A.C.?"

He sighed, and sipped more of his drink.

"In Bermuda."

"With that actress? Everyone's talking about a cute little vixen named Bailey."

"No, not her. I don't know where she is. I was with Camilla Santee."

"How marvelous for you. The big score."

"It wasn't a 'score.' "

She leaned back, folding her arms.

"I'm your friend, A.C.. Nothing will change that. But you certainly make it very hard."

"I know what I'm doing."

"Look, darling. *The Man Who Loved Women* was a marvelous film. Truffaut's best. But it was fantasy. May I remind you that the hero wasn't married? May I remind you also that he got killed in the end?"

"I'm not living out any fantasy."

"And I am Kathleen Turner." She took his hand, patting it. "You're going to have to make a choice, A.C. You have too many women in your life. It's your curse."

"I made my choice. I married Kitty."

"Oh, really? Heavy action in Bermuda with someone like Camilla Santee is a million light-years out of line. You've no right to expect Kitty to tolerate it."

"Kitty doesn't know about Camilla. No one knows about her but you. Kitty's mad on account of Bailey Hazeltine, and I haven't seen her for days. She's been drinking a lot, and doing drugs, I think. She showed up at the worst possible time last Sunday. If she hadn't, I'd be back with Kitty right now. Bailey's the worst thing that's ever happened to me."

"I'm sure you don't mean that," Vanessa said. "But drop them both. Now. What's the Spanish proverb? 'Take what you want,' said God, 'but pay for it?' Poor Belinda sure did."

"Thank you for your advice."

She patted his hand once more. "I'm only trying to help. Your adoring little pal, through thick and thin."

"I appreciate it."

"You may be in more trouble than you realize, A.C. The police are looking for you."

"Detective Lanham?"

"Yes." She pulled some pink telephone message slips from the big manila envelope and pushed them in front of him. "He's been calling."

He glanced quickly through them. Lanham was far from the only caller. There was a message from Bailey. He wondered if Vanessa had noticed.

"I can't help the police," he said.

"It's probably occurred to them that you knew all those people, Philippe, Molly, Belinda. Everyone but Jimmy Woody. Or do you know him, too?"

A.C. said nothing. He looked through his mail. It was very ordinary—mostly invitations and press releases. One smaller envelope was addressed by hand in large, flowery script. There was an embossed gold drawing of a bee on the back—Honey Jerome's private little emblem.

He stuffed the mail, including Honey's letter, back into the envelope and summoned the waiter.

"Could you throw this away for me?" he asked when the man came up. Puzzled, the waiter nodded and carried away the envelope as though it contained soiled trash.

"Belinda wasn't such a bad kid," Vanessa said. "She was in over her head, is all. Philippe. Jimmy Woody . . ." She shook her head sadly. "I just don't understand."

He noticed that she looked very tired. Her makeup failed to obscure shadowy circles under her eyes.

A.C. drank, looking for the waiter. Vanessa took his glass from his hand, setting it down emphatically.

"All right, A.C. It's time to get off your derriere. You've

no choice but to call *Beau Monde* magazine now. I just hope they haven't hired someone else. I heard they were trying to pirate some people from *Vanity Fair.*"

"I can't go job-hunting now, Vanessa. Not yet."

"A.C. I've talked with my husband. We'd like you to stay with us for a few days, longer, whatever you need. You have to get out of your apartment."

"As soon as I can."

"Please, A.C. Before something else happens to you."

•

A.C. left Vanessa waiting in the cab. He was relieved that she didn't ask to come up to the apartment with him. The telephone number Bailey had left with the *Globe* message desk was his own.

The aged doorman was seated wearily in an old wooden chair by the elevator. He waved weakly to A.C. in salute, but made no attempt to operate the elevator for him.

As he pushed his floor button, he wondered what he would take with him. He'd heard of people fleeing fires or floods madly throwing odd shoes and useless junk into their suitcases. He had only a few minutes. He decided he'd carry away only some working clothes. Two or three of his best summer suits, his best dinner jacket. Enough shirts and other necessities to last him a week.

And if Bailey was there? He'd take her with him, too. She was in far greater need of rescue than he was. He'd find Bailey's brother and have him take her up to his house in Westchester.

The elevator car rattled to a halt. Stepping out into the musty darkness of the hall, A.C. hesitated a moment, wondering if he should just leave. He really didn't want to go to Vanessa's. He wanted to find Camilla Santee.

As he pushed open the door, he immediately saw Bailey's legs and a dark stain. He thought she might have passed out, spilling her drink. Then, as he stepped inside, it became obvious that the stain was not from liquor. Leaving the door open behind him, he stood over her, feeling as numb and helpless as he had when Molly Wickham had died.

He knelt and touched her leg. The flesh was cold, the muscle hard. Her staring eyes ignored him.

"Bailey?" He said her name pointlessly, then repeated it, over and over.

He took her hand. It was cold as well. Dried blood covered her chest. It was so dark and thick he couldn't find any wound. Then he did, a round hole in the cloth near her breast.

She had been shot. But the door had been locked. Had she committed suicide? That possibility had been worrying him. It had worried him and her family for years. She had tried it before, during a very bad year in Los Angeles.

"Bailey?"

He was losing his senses. Where was the gun? He had a gun in the apartment—a .45 automatic he had kept from the army. Had she taken it? If she had, where was it?

Searching over the floor, noting that the blood had seeped into Kitty's expensive Persian rug, he stood up again, puzzled, a little frantic. Before doing anything, he had to understand what had happened. He couldn't think or act logically until this made sense.

The pistol was where he always kept it—in the night table on his side of the bed, wrapped in a chamois. It still smelled freshly cleaned and oiled. It was fully loaded, just as he had left it.

With the pistol dangling in his hand, he returned to the living room. There was no other weapon in the place. No suicide note.

He went into the kitchen. Everything seemed the same, except there were torn pieces of a picture of Camilla on the floor. Had Bailey done that? She couldn't have. She was lying dead by the front door. She must have just come in.

Back in the living room, he found a cup on the table by his favorite chair. He picked it up, smelling whiskey. Bailey didn't drink whiskey. She hated having the smell on her. Her drink was vodka or gin.

There was no gun. If she had killed herself, there'd be a gun. A.C. noticed the door to the terrace. It was open slightly, and a pane was broken out near the handle.

His mind still blurry, he sat down in his chair, holding

the cup and pistol before him. He had to do something. What to do? What had happened?

"My God, A.C., what's going on here?"

Vanessa was in the apartment, standing over Bailey. She looked at A.C., bewildered. Then she saw his gun.

"What have you done?"

"It's all right, Vanessa." What a stupid thing to say. Nothing was right. Everything was wrong.

She was one of his dearest friends, but now she was frightened of him. He could see it in her eyes. She backed away. He rose and came toward her. Vanessa started toward the apartment's front door, but stepped on Bailey's leg. She gave a little shriek and flattened herself against the wall. She put her hands in front of her face.

"Someone killed her, Vanessa. I don't know who. I don't know how. I . . ."

Time suddenly began to move in a big rush. The killer had fled, was getting away. The police would be coming. Vanessa was terrified of him.

He hadn't killed Bailey. He'd wished her no harm. He'd tried to protect her—had used the last of his savings to get her out of jail. His gun hadn't even been fired. His apartment had been broken into. Surely they'd believe him.

But not even Vanessa believed him.

A.C. knew who had shot Bailey. He'd seen the man in the picture on Camilla's mantel. He'd seen him on the motorcycle outside the Plaza.

Don't you go looking for him, Camilla had said over the phone in Bermuda. *You leave him alone.*

But the man had gone looking for him. He'd sat here drinking whiskey, waiting for A.C. to come home—only Bailey had come home instead.

Pierre was probably in Washington, Camilla had said. She'd gone there herself. The man—her kinsman—would be going there, too, to find Pierre, to kill Pierre. Camilla had said she was going to be the cause of that.

A.C. had no real choice. He had to get to that man. He had to find Camilla.

He stuck the .45 into his belt beneath his coat, and, without another word to Vanessa, fled out the door.

CHAPTER

....

14

A.C. awoke in the night dark of his hotel room. For an instant he couldn't recall where he was, and was frightened. He had the odd feeling that Bailey was with him, lying next to him in the bed—that if he were to turn over and look at her she would stare back at him, dead.

He sat up and turned on the lamp. He was alone. Throwing back his covers, he got up naked in the air-conditioned cold and went over to his window. Outside was the broad expanse of Pennsylvania Avenue, a grand boulevard in the European manner quite unlike the cramped, noisy thoroughfares of New York. Far to the left, he could see the great lighted dome of the Capitol. Around the corner to the right was the stately Greek edifice of the Treasury and behind that the White House. The traffic in front of the hotel was light, moving in desultory fashion. Even at this dead hour, it looked hot outside. If he opened the window, the heat would roll in like some poison gas.

He had had a marvelously happy life in Washington, and he and Kitty had had many happy hours in this very hotel. They'd celebrated their anniversary here every year they'd lived in the capital. He remembered her laughing and dancing at an impossibly crowded inaugural ball. He cursed her for making them return to New York.

He forced himself to think about his immediate problems. He'd accomplished nothing in the time since his arrival but to buy a few clothes and determine that Pierre Delasante had probably left town. He was letting time slip away—handing it to his adversaries, known and unknown. He was at the very center of authority in the United States. The District of Columbia's police were undermanned and inefficient, but if they became interested in finding him, they would. He had registered in his own name, unable to concoct any kind of sensible alias or identity—or even to think—when he had checked in.

This waste of time was dangerous. He was known to a lot of people in Washington, and everyone in this city read newspapers. There had been no story yet—Bailey wasn't that famous an actress—but there could be, as early as the next morning's editions.

What time he did have had been bought for him by Theresa. He'd had to gamble on finding an unquestioning friend and, somewhat to his surprise, had chosen well. Theresa had taken him into her apartment even though he'd told her at the outset he was likely to be sought by the police. She'd listened calmly to everything he'd had to say—and he'd told her everything. Then she'd offered without hesitation to help him in any way she could. Ashamed, he'd asked for money. He hadn't dared attempt to cash or deposit his check from the *Globe*. Theresa had gone to her bank, returning within forty minutes with $5,000. He had offered to sign his check over to her. She had taken the check to hold in safety for him, but refused to let him sign it. She'd driven him to New Jersey, putting him on an Amtrak train, leaving him with a hug and all the courage she could inspire.

He went to his phone. After several rings, Theresa's husband answered. A.C. hesitated. Had she told him? Could he trust the man? He'd never had to trust friendship this way before.

"This is A.C. James, George. I need to speak to Theresa."

"She's sleeping, A.C. It's very late."

He heard her voice in the background. Then she came on the phone.

"A.C.! Are you all right? Where are you?"

"I'd better not say. I'm okay. Has anyone tried to reach you about me, Theresa? Is my name in the papers?"

It had always been so easy to put people's names in the public print, for better or worse. Now he was beginning to realize what that could mean, how powerless and vulnerable that could make someone feel.

"It was on the news, that poor dead girl in your apartment. You're wanted for questioning, darling. The police called me. Nothing specific. I think they're calling all your friends. And your wife called. I didn't say anything, but she wants to talk to you right away. She wants you to call her."

Kitty and brother Bill were doubtless working with the police.

"Thank you, Theresa. Thank you for everything. I hope I haven't gotten you in any trouble."

"Don't worry about me. And don't worry about George. You're our friend, A.C."

"I'll call you when I can."

He set the receiver back gently. Sleep was beyond him now. Going to the minibar in his room, he made himself a drink. The little bottles of whiskey reminded him of the cup in his apartment, making him shudder. He poured vodka and some tonic—Bailey's kind of drink. Pulling a chair up to the window, he sat there sipping, gazing sadly at the Washington night.

Memories of Bailey danced by him like spirits. He clung to a special one of Bailey in a white summery dress, on a night of hazy moonlight along the shore of the Cross River Reservoir in Westchester. Warm Bailey. Cool sand at the water's edge.

There were more tears in his eyes than he could wipe away. He had wanted desperately to marry Bailey in those years when he had all but become a member of the Hazeltine family. But she was so very young, still in college, and he was so very poor, with nothing more in mind for his life than to become a newspaper reporter.

If he had married her, she might not have become what she had become. But he had married Kitty. He'd loved them both. And now he loved Camilla. Vanessa once told him that his problem was that he was still in love with all the women he had ever loved.

" 'And cozy women dead, who by my side once lay.' "

It was a line from a poem by Stanley Kunitz called "I Dreamed That I Was Old."

.

In the morning, showered and in clean clothes, he went downstairs for newspapers and read through them in the lobby. As much as he had expected it, seeing his name in print was a shock. The story in the *Washington Post* lumped all the New York murders together, including Bailey's. He was mentioned as owner of the apartment where she was found and as a witness in the Molly Wickham case, which the news account cautiously linked to the others.

"James is being sought for questioning," it said, just as Theresa had told him.

He could not stay in Washington long.

A.C. had located Pierre Delasante's town house in Georgetown late the previous afternoon. As a White House official, Pierre had been listed in the Washington *Green Book*, a local version of the *Social Register*, but with much lower standards. A.C. had gone to the public library and looked through a copy, noting the exclusive address and phone number—which was not listed in the regular telephone directory.

But no one answered Delasante's phone—despite several calls and many rings. A.C. had gone to the place after dinner, finding it locked and dark with newspapers gathering on the front steps. No one answered the doorbell. He'd tried looking through the front windows, then noticed a man in a parked car across the street, a man watching him. A.C. had quickly walked away, then, turning the corner, had fled.

Camilla had come here. She hadn't gone to New York or the Carolinas or Florida or Atlanta or any other place you could reach by air from Bermuda. She'd flown to Baltimore–Washington International, just twenty minutes from the District of Columbia line. Did she know people in Washington, people like Honey Jerome? Hadn't Honey said something about her having worked in Washington?

A.C. suspected Camilla was by now long gone, fled to the deeper South like a rabbit into a thicket. Perhaps she had even fled the country. But she could have flown to all manner of foreign places from Bermuda. She'd come here, where she said Pierre had come after leaving New York.

He had to start somewhere. This was the place.

After a small breakfast, A.C. began making phone calls, mostly to women he had known when he lived here. None of them was of any help—had ever heard of a model named Camilla Santee. One woman he reached had read the story in the *Post*, and became very nervous, asking where he was. He decided to stop calling after that.

Then an idea struck him, and he went back to his phone. There was a woman in Washington who might very well have heard of Camilla, might have known her, as she knew so many women of great beauty. This woman seldom read newspapers, at least those in English.

Her name was Zoé, proprietor of the exclusive and painfully expensive Salon de Zoé in Georgetown. A tall, slender, blond and consumately chic Parisienne, Zoé had come to Washington a dozen years before and almost immediately established herself as the chief local rival to Elizabeth Arden. Zoé did not simply do hair. She and her European assistants specialized in skin care, massage, cleansing, relaxation, and total contentment. Her clients included some of the wealthiest and most sophisticated women in the capital.

They also included a few men. Calculating that Washington's highly stressed, power-obsessed, overworked males would be receptive, and ultimately addicted, to her uniquely soothing ministrations, she opened her salon to men one evening a week and at other times by special appointment. Some wives who found out about their husbands' visits to Zoé presumed she was functioning as the manager of some sort of extraordinarily expensive massage parlor, but there was no sex involved in her services, only the sublime serenity that came from lying under a warmly moist facecloth in a softly lit room, while Zoé's skilled fingers worked the tension from one's neck and shoulders.

A.C. had met her at a party at the French Embassy. On a whim, he'd taken her up on an invitation to try her treatment. He'd become a regular, and they had grown to be friends.

Delighted, if surprised, to hear from him, she immediately arranged a special appointment, bumping a woman customer whom she said she'd turn over to an assistant.

A.C. felt he was at last taking a step on the right road. A salon like Zoé's would have been a vital resource for a beauty like Camilla. He guessed Camilla would prefer Zoé's to Arden's or one of the other salons. Zoé was French.

As he lay in the chair, Zoé's fingers gently working against his temples, he let their conversation follow a natural course, Zoé telling him of business successes and plans for expansion, of a failed love affair and a new man in her life, of a recent trip back to Paris. He told her of his life in New York, of happy things about his wife and children and their house in Westchester, leaving out the dreadful matters of the past week. He did not question her directly about Camilla, as a policeman might. Zoé was his friend, but she was reflexively discreet. People relaxing in her private treatment rooms often felt moved to confession or the sharing of secrets, and it was abhorrent to her to break any confidence, to allow anyone else to pry.

So he approached his goal obliquely, casually.

"I met a woman in New York who I think knows you," he said. "A model, named Camilla, Camilla Santee."

"A model? Named Camilla Santee?"

Her fingers moved to the sides of his neck.

"That's her professional name. She also goes by Camilla Delasante."

289

"*Ah oui.* Camilla Delasante. She's a famous beauty, yes? I saw not long ago a picture of her in *Elle.* Yes, I knew her. She used to come here. But that was many years ago. How is she?"

"Fine. She was just visiting. I think she's living in France."

"France." She pronounced the word with enthusiasm. "France would be a very good place for her. She loved everything French."

"Have you seen her recently?"

"No. Not for some years. She came to me when she was a model here. I was one of those who convinced her that she should go to New York. She was much too beautiful for the work they had for her here."

"She lived here?"

"Yes, for a time. Not in the city. Out in Virginia somewhere. She was a rider. *Equestrienne.* She rode in those races, *les grandes courses,* you know, over fences? And in horse shows."

"You don't know . . . where she lived?"

"Why do you ask?"

"I was wondering if I had met her before. It seemed to me I had, when I met her in New York."

"I don't know. One of those little towns out past Middleburg."

She lifted the facecloth, felt his skin, and then replaced it.

"She's very lovely," A.C. said.

"Yes. You are a little smitten, A.C.? I told her she should give up this riding. It's so bad for the legs. It makes the ankles less trim, *n'est-ce pas?*"

"Her ankles seemed fine."

"She took my advice. She did not like it much living out there, I think. She was with a man—a relative, a lover. I don't know. She left him and went to New York. I was so happy to see her do so well. *Si gentille,* that one."

"Yes."

"But you are still happy in your marriage, yes?"

He paused. "Yes."

"Then you should stay away from great beauties like Mademoiselle Delasante. Your wife will not understand."

He left Zoé with a promise he could not keep, to have lunch with her soon. His next stop was a car rental agency. Out of habit, he took their most expensive available car, a Buick Park Avenue.

In a few minutes he was out of the city, heading west on Interstate 66 into the rolling Piedmont of Virginia's famous horse country.

•

Alixe Lovelace Percy was an essentially attractive woman who had unfortunately become not really fat but too large, as much through constant, vigorous exercise as through her considerable appetite for Italian food and Southern whiskey. She had light brown hair going to gray, brown eyes, sun-browned skin, wide cheekbones, a wide smiling mouth, a hearty laugh, and an Old Virginia dialect, spoken in her family since the first Percys had arrived at the Jamestown Plantations after the Revolution of 1688.

Her horse farm north of Middleburg had belonged to her family since an ancestor had bought the property from Lord Fairfax in the late eighteenth century. Alixe had learned to ride at age four and had owned, raised, trained, and bred horses all her adult life, competing in horse shows and point-to-point races since the age of ten. Her father's family was Old Dominion. Her mother's family was Philadelphia Main Line—very Main Line.

The Washington area was largely a region of the professional upper middle class. Alixe was one of its rare landed, moneyed, hereditary aristocrats. There were horse farms nearby owned by people much richer, but most of them had earned their money in manufacturing and trade and had acquired their Virginia estates as trappings. With the Percys, there had seemingly always been money and always been horses. It was their unstudied and comfortable traditional way of life.

Alixe was not really a snob. She liked or disliked people

291

as they came, judging them by their individual qualities as much as she did horses. But she was keen on blood lines. She could quote listings from the *Social Register*, the Washington *Green Book*, and the membership rolls of the Colonial Dames of America and Daughters of the Confederacy as freely as a fundamentalist preacher might spout verses in the Bible.

A.C. had written about her once in an article for *Town and Country*. He'd been fair but honest, recounting her boisterous parties, free-flowing bar, and taste for the lusty story. She'd loved every word and had become his chum. He'd always suspected that she would like to become more.

She had to meet him at the gate, as she kept it locked. Three nasty Dobermans had the run of her property outside the house proper and the stable area. All of them came bounding and snarling up as soon as he opened his car door. He got back in and shut it quickly, and honked the horn, remembering to slip his .45 automatic under the seat.

Her screen door slammed. The dogs fell silent when she bellowed at them. Then she descended the wide steps of her white-columned porch, striding briskly toward him, hastening her pace when she saw who he was. She was dressed in muddy boots, fawn-colored breeches, and a white shirt with sleeves rolled all the way up. She was very tan.

"God Almighty, it's A.C. James himself. I do own a telephone, don't you know." She undid the gate and swung it open, motioning to him to drive inside.

He obeyed, parking as close to the house as he could. The dogs came up and sniffed his white shoes when he got out.

"I can't stay long. I wanted to see you."

"You can stay long enough for a glass of Virginia Gentleman, can't you?"

She led him up to the porch, shouted instructions through the screen door to a servant, then eased herself heavily into a wicker chair, propping her boots up on the large round table in front of her and lighting a cigarette. The servant, a pale, thin girl with lank blond hair, wearing a billowy cotton dress but barefoot, soon backed out of the doorway with a silver tray bearing a large bottle of whiskey, two glasses, and a pitcher of water. Alixe hated ice. The cold affected the taste of whiskey, she said.

She poured, filling both glasses half way.

"It's damned good to see you, A.C. Are you still married?"

"Yes."

"Heard you're separated."

"You haven't seen me in three years, and you've heard that?"

"Gossip travels faster with horse people than anyone else. I have a friend in Westchester who owns the stable where your daughter is learning dressage."

"Kitty and I are having some problems. I hope they won't last."

"I hope so, too. She's got good form, your Kitty. You two could found a hell of a family. So why are you here? You're not dressed like someone who wants to buy a bloody horse. Or are you selling paintings? That De Glehn nude I bought on your advice? I sold it for two hundred thousand last year. You want a commission, dear heart?"

He shook his head and took a drink of his whiskey, then added a little water to his glass. Alixe was not bothering with that nicety.

"I'm looking for someone," he said. "A friend. Someone I think you might know."

"Man or woman?"

"A woman. Her name is Camilla Santee. She's a model in New York. She used to live somewhere near here. I think she used to ride on the show circuit."

"Camilla Santee, née Delasante. I remember her very well. Hell of a rider. Took two firsts at the Upperville show. You actually know this girl, A.C.?"

"Yes. We're friends. Not for very long, but . . . I know her, Alixe. I need to find her, and soon. Have you seen her, in the last couple of days?"

Alixe squinted at him. "You look alarmingly serious, dearie. She can't be the problem you and Kitty are having?"

"No. She—'s a problem I'm having."

"Well, golly Moses. You're quite the gentleman, to be

293

sure, A.C., and a Van Peet on your paternal grandmother's side, but you're certainly not in Camilla's class. Of course, I've never met anyone who was."

"What do you mean? She's a fashion model."

"She's real bloodstock, A.C. If she were a horse, not even Sheik Maktoum could afford her. She's from what we call 'good family' around here. And we call most people trash."

"The Delasantes are good family?"

Alixe looked at him as though he had said something vastly amusing—or imbecilic. "Not the Delasantes. They've got some very trashy edges, that lot, and I daresay a murky past. No, dear, I'm talking about her mother. She's a Beaugerard and connected to the Hayneses, which makes her very haute Charleston right there. And she's a Wellfleet, and they came to Jamestown before my folks did. But she's also a Dutarques, and that Dutarques blood puts her right at the very top. She's not all that active socially, but she might as well be queen of Charleston—as much worshiped as God and John C. Calhoun. Some like to call her 'the whitest woman in America.' "

"You said Charleston?"

"Yes, love. *Charles*ton." She drawled out the city's name, putting great emphasis on the first syllable. "The most aristocratic city in America. Compared to it, don't you know, Boston is just a city of fishmongers. And New York a den of thieves and money lenders."

"I'm not very familiar with Charleston."

She took a big belt of her whiskey. "Have you ever heard of the St. Cecilia Society, A.C.?"

"I think so," he said. "They hold an annual ball."

"No, A.C. They hold *the* annual ball. I mean, my dear, the Mayflower Ball at the Plaza? Compared to the St. Cecilia, it's a public-school sock hop. Any asshole can be in the Mayflower Society, as long as they're descended from that boatload of antiroyalist religious rabble that landed at Plymouth. Laborers and artisans they were, mostly. Did you know there wasn't a single Mayflower man who could sign 'Gentleman' to his name? Not one."

A.C. shook his head in ignorance.

"The St. Cecilia," Alixe continued, "was founded by

294

aristocrats—Charleston aristos—in the early 1700s. It was started as a concert society, but they began holding balls in the 1820s. The reason you don't know much about it is that they don't want anyone to. They'd sooner let the Reverend Jesse Jackson through the door than any kind of reporter."

"Camilla is a member of the St. Cecilia Society?"

Alixe shook her head. "The members are all men. It's run by men. Very Old South. But once you're a member, all the women in your household are put on 'the list'—the invitation list for the annual ball—and you stay on the list for life. It's the closest thing to being a grand duchess in this country, A.C." She drank again, and lit another cigarette.

"Other women can be invited to the ball," she said, "but only if they're 'off'—if they live away from Charleston—and their family passes a background check. If they move to Charleston, though, they can no longer be invited, unless the male head of household is allowed to become a member. Girls will move to Charleston and then leave after eleven months, so they can still attend the ball. And if a girl should be so foolish as to marry a man who's not a member of St. Cecilia, she can still come to the ball, but her husband and children can't."

"Camilla's father was a member?"

An odd look came over Alixe's face. "Camilla and her mother are on the list because of Camilla's late grandfather. He was a Beaugerard and a Dutarques."

"Alixe, I'm looking for Camilla, not her ancestors."

"I'm just telling you what I think you might want to know, old dear. Shit. Are you sure Camilla's not the problem you have with Kitty? Camilla's the sort of beauty who can make other women hate her just by walking by their husbands."

"I need to find her, Alixe."

"She'd never marry you, you know. I would. Doesn't bother me you're a penniless Van Peet from the Mohawk Valley. But Camilla . . . have you ever heard of the La Ligue de La Vallière? Of course you haven't. But that's my point. A few people have heard about St. Cecilia. *No one* knows about the Vallière League. It's that exclusive."

295

"Alixe, where's Camilla?"

She waved her hand at him, an irritated teacher with an unruly pupil. "La Ligue de La Vallière, dearie, is very, very small. It's members are all Carolinians, all descendants from a group of French Huguenot colonists, who took their name from their leader, a direct descendant of Louise de la Baume le Blanc, Duchess de La Vallière, first maitress of Louis XIV."

A.C. could barely control his impatience. But what could he say? *Hurry up, Alixe, I may be wanted for murder?*

"The Vallière League holds two gatherings a year, one on the anniversary of their arrival at Charleston and the other on the birthday of Louise de La Vallière. No one knows what goes on at them. I don't suppose it matters. What matters is that an invitation to either one of those events would mean more to a Charleston society matron than thirty St. Cecilia balls. I mean, my dear, people would kill for one."

She paused, eyes twinkling.

"Camilla's mother," Alixe said, "is the head of La Ligue de La Vallière."

She sat back with great finality, as though she had just explained everything with that one sentence.

A.C., still uncomprehending, leaned forward. "Are you trying to tell me I should look for Camilla in Charleston?"

"All I'm telling you, boy, is that you shouldn't expect Camilla to marry outside the Vallière League."

"Alixe. I don't want to propose. I just want to find her. Desperately. I think she's in the area. She took a flight to Washington direct from Bermuda."

"I haven't seen her, A.C. Haven't heard from her in years."

"She used to live around here, right? Where?"

"Over in Dandytown. If you don't remember it, it's on the Berryville Road. It's her brother's place. It used to be one of the best farms in Clarke County, but in the last year, he's sold off all his breeding stock. Keeps a couple of jumping horses, but everything else is gone. Money troubles, I hear. Ruinous money troubles."

"Tell me about him."

"Jack Santee? Dangerous son of a bitch. Absolutely

crazy. I saw him kill a horse on a timber jump in the Gold Cup. Got another mount and finished second in the next heat. Handsomest man on the show circuit, and not one of the queers. He's fucked every woman I know, including, if I may say so proudly, me. He has eyes as black as the devil's. Hardly know he was Camilla's brother, except he's so damn good-looking."

"I want to talk to him."

"No you don't, dear heart. You may think you do, but you don't. In any event, no one's seen him around in weeks."

"How do I get to his farm?"

"I'll be happy to tell you, but if you plan to go up there, you sure as hell better have another whiskey. Dealing with Jack Santee's never a pleasant experience, especially if you're someone who's been screwing around with his sister. He'd kill for Camilla, A.C."

•

He had that second whiskey, quickly. He felt no trepidation, not any longer. As he drove out through Alixe's gate, he was ebullient. By the time he reached the Dandytown Road, he was close to euphoria.

His luck had changed. He felt he'd as good as found Camilla, and it had involved nothing more than contacting old friends. He was really rich in friends. Blessed. He would never come to harm, he would not fail, as long as he had such friends.

Dandytown was a small, neat crossroads village appearing suddenly at the end of a long curve in the highway. There was a country inn, a service station, a general store, and a post office, as well as a few tall stone houses of Civil War vintage. It was a village like a hundred others in Virginia, except that the per capita worth of its inhabitants probably rivaled that of Beverly Hills.

On the other side of the town, he took a wrong turning, and then another, compelling him to double back. Finally, he made sense of Alixe's directions, and got himself on the narrow country road that matched her description.

It made a sharp turn to cross a stone bridge, then climbed

a hill. At its summit, he slowed as he saw the house on the next rise.

Alixe had said it would be unmistakable—more an English country manor than a Virginia farmhouse. It was of stone, with high narrow windows and several chimneys. There were stables, almost lost in the trees, and several outbuildings. A stone wall lined the property along the road, with white horse fences extending back to the house and beyond.

A.C. drove slowly down into a shady glen, crossed a narrow creek, then ascended the following rise. The pasture grass was long and uncut. The front gate was open. He turned into the drive, slowing to the pace of a man's walk as he bumped along over the gravel.

The windows were dark. There was a porte cochere in front, sheltering only gravel. A verandah to the side held white furniture, but no human figure. No vehicles were in sight. No living thing moved, except for a large bird in desultory flight toward the stables. He turned off the engine and stepped out of the car. The silence was unnerving, the air damp and heavy and still. He took off his coat and slung it over his shoulder. His white shirt was wrinkled and stuck to his back.

No one answered the door. A heavy brass knocker hung from it and he used it when the bell produced no response. The pounding echoed over the pasture, then silence returned. He had no idea what to do next. It was as though the tortuous path he had followed since meeting Camilla ended here, leading not a step further. It was like the end of life, providing no answer, only silence, only termination.

She had taken a plane to Washington. This was her brother's house. Where in hell was she?

Moving quietly, he started around the side of the house, going up onto the verandah. The white wicker furniture looked to have been recently used, the chairs pushed to odd angles rather than grouped neatly around the tables, but there was no other evidence that anyone had been there—no ashtray or glass. The French doors that ran most of the length of the verandah were closed and locked. Peering through one of them, he saw a large, shadowy room filled with antique furniture, but no movement. Again, there was no testament to any recent human presence—no book beside a chair, no glass left on a table, no odd piece of clothing draped over the back of the couch. On the wall were a few paintings—all of horses as far as A.C. could determine in the gloom.

Mostly there were weapons, antique dress swords and cavalry sabers, antique pistols and muskets, and, over the fireplace, a rifle that looked disturbingly modern.

Their presence stayed his hand when he thought of rapping on the window. He went back to the front, tried the bell and brass knocker again, then walked around the house to the rear. A locked, windowed door led to a sort of pantry. Nothing moved beyond.

As the weight of moisture in the air increased, the sky was turning from hazy blue to darkening gray. His watch reminded him of the approaching end to the afternoon.

The stables beckoned malevolently, the open doors of the stalls a line of black somber staring eyes. Itching with the heat, he started toward them down a wide cinder path.

A.C. stepped cautiously into the first of the stalls. The floor had been swept clean of manure and straw. The feed buckets were empty as was the water trough. It was the same in all the stalls. The tack room had been emptied, nothing hanging from the pegs but one old broken bridle.

In the stable yard, A.C. gave vent to his frustration by shouting Camilla's name. The hoarse, sudden sound silenced the birds, but produced no other response. In a moment, their vague chirping returned.

He went back to the entrance and sat down on the steps. He waited for a half hour, and then another, and kept waiting. A sudden whoosh of wind came through the porte cochere, surprising him, stinging his face with bits of grass and leaves and dust. The sky darkened, and in the distance he could see trees bending like beaten, wailing women. He went to his car to put up the windows, opening the driver's side door just as the first, heavy raindrops struck.

He surrendered. Camilla, her brother, all the mysterious forces at play in this, had won again. He slid behind the wheel, fired the engine, closed the door and windows, and, tires churning in the gravel, angrily drove away. The thundering downpour followed him, making his return trip at first dangerous and then frustratingly slow as he reached the main highway and found it full of traffic.

It was fully night by the time he entered the lobby of his hotel. Recklessly, he went up to the front desk and asked after messages. He certainly didn't expect or want any. If anyone actually knew he was there, he would have no choice but to run.

"Nothing, sir."

A.C. searched the man's face for a sign of untruth or unease, any indication of trouble. He saw only indifference. The clerk was very busy. A.C. thanked him and crossed the lobby to the elevators, glancing carefully around him. No one was paying him any attention at all.

One of the elevators was open and waiting. As he entered, a man stepped in behind him. Turning around, he found himself looking into the unhappy face of Detective Raymond Lanham.

CHAPTER

....

15

They went directly to A.C.'s room, as they might to a cell. The detective, carrying a briefcase in his left hand, trailed worrisomely behind. A.C. had stuck his .45 automatic in his belt at his back, and he feared the bulge might show.

If Lanham noticed, he said nothing. He said nothing at all, except to repeat, "We'll talk in your room," when A.C. had tried to ask him a question.

Reaching his door, A.C. fumbled nervously in his pocket searching for the key, sensing Lanham's impatience.

"Sorry," he said.

"If you take all the keys out of your pocket, you'll find it," Lanham said.

A.C. did so. The door opened to bright lights. The maid had already come by to turn down the bed. She'd pulled the drapes and put on all the lamps. That simple discovery made him feel all the more exposed and vulnerable.

Lanham took a seat in one of the armchairs, sitting stiffly

back and resting both hands on the arms. He watched everything A.C. did.

"Would you like something to drink?" A.C. said, nodding toward the minibar.

"Do you have any beer?"

"Yes. There's Heineken, Michelob . . ."

"Any kind of beer."

A.C. poured the detective a Heineken, then seated himself in a chair facing the man.

"How did you find me?" he asked.

Lanham had obviously been thirsty. He wiped a bit of foam from his lips before answering.

"Like I told you before. I am a police detective. But a four-year-old kid could have found you. I had the D.C. cops make a hotel check on you—told them to start with the most expensive. They got you on the first bounce. And this is the computer age, Mr. James. Amtrak has them; hotels do. Rental car agencies, too."

"But how did you know to look for me in Washington?"

Lanham hesitated. "I put a credit card trace on you a few days ago, and tracked you to Bermuda. Your hotel said a woman of Camilla Santee's description was there, too, under the name of Anne Claire. A Miss A. Claire took a flight to Baltimore–Washington International. I didn't think you'd be too long behind. When you disappeared after Miss Hazeltine was killed, this seemed the most obvious place to look—at least to start."

You'll protect me, Camilla had said. *You'll keep Detective Lanham from finding me.*

"I was alone in Bermuda," A.C. said.

"The two of you were seen together all over the place. A chambermaid saw you crawl out of her bed. If you're going to hide from me, Mr. James, don't stop for a shack job—especially with the kind of woman who can turn heads in the next solar system."

"I wasn't hiding from you, not then. And it wasn't a 'shack job.' "

"She wasn't your wife."

"Am I under arrest?" A.C. said testily, repeating what he had said to Lanham in the elevator.

For a long moment, Lanham didn't answer.

302

"There's an official paper in my briefcase with your name on it," he said finally.

"I didn't kill Bailey, Mr. Lanham. I know how it must look, but, my God, she's an old, old friend. She was very dear to me."

He had almost said that he had nothing to do with her death. But that was quite untrue. He had everything to do with it. If he had taken her to her family that first night, instead of home to his apartment, she'd be very much alive. So many things he now wished he'd done. And not done.

Lanham's eyes were impassive behind his glasses. He continued to study A.C. intently.

"Your denial belongs in an official statement," Lanham said.

An official statement, in front of a witness, and with a lawyer present. The detective hadn't even gone through his dreary Miranda ritual.

"Do you have a warrant?" A.C. asked, crossing his legs. "I mean, do you have handcuffs and all that? Are you taking me back?"

"Not just yet."

Lanham seemed to have relaxed a little, perhaps because A.C. was sitting so calmly. A.C. didn't feel calm. He was desperately thinking of how he might escape from this man.

"I'm also interested in any information you might have concerning the deaths of Belinda St. Johns, Philippe Arbre, James Woody, and Peter Gorky," Lanham said. "You know about those?"

A.C. nodded. "Yes. At least what was in the papers. But I don't have any information beyond that."

"You talked to Belinda St. Johns about the videotape that Pierre Delasante had. Now she's dead."

"I'm not a suspect in that, am I? I was in Bermuda."

"We have a suspect, fat fucking lot of good it will do. His name is Vincent Perotta."

"He's a mobster. Our story said he was Belinda's boy-friend."

"That's about all your paper got right. Mostly you had bullshit. Your editors went off on this cockeyed sex-ring angle. We're pretty sure it's much simpler than that. The old unwritten law." He paused, reluctant to say more.

303

"What unwritten law?"

"Last time I told you something confidential, it ended up in your paper."

"Don't worry about that, Detective Lanham. I am no longer employed by the *New York Globe*."

"Sorry to hear that. Or maybe I should say I'm glad."

"Probably glad. I'm beginning to be."

"The *Newsday* story came the closest. One of their guys has some pals in my division. That videotape we talked about? There were two cassettes. Gorky had the other. The stupid son of a bitch sold it on the underground market. He might as well have sent it to Perotta by messenger."

The pistol was hurting A.C.'s back. He tried to keep the discomfort from showing in his face.

"Our assumption is that Mr. Perotta found the tape offensive. They have a highly developed sense of honor, these wiseguys. Showing them disrespect can be a capital offense. Belinda St. Johns was Perotta's woman. She was one of the most beautiful women in New York and he owned her. Fooling around may be the national pastime of you folks on the Upper East Side, but in his world, you honor that. Pierre Delasante, James Woody, and the others, they fucked with her. So did one of my colleagues, and he's lucky he didn't get his head blown off. Gorky put the whole thing in the public domain. I don't think he liked the way he died at all."

"But why Philippe Arbre?"

"Wrong place, wrong time. There was a tell. A sign. James Woody was castrated after they strangled him. Had his genitals shoved down his throat. Arbre they left intact. Gorky was strangled with film or videotape, probably after they did other things to him. Belinda was shot through the pelvic area. I could be less delicate about it. All nice little touches. These are a great bunch of guys."

"Aren't you going after them?"

"Who?"

"The mobsters. The ones who did the killing."

"I repeat, who? In this country, you don't arrest people on surmise. At least not guys like Perotta. He was in Florida. We got that fact nailed down pretty quick. We've got no witnesses to these killings. We had one of our own on

304

the scene in Belinda's apartment, flagrante delicto, and all he saw was a bullet go by."

"If you're so bloody marvelous at finding people, why aren't you after them? Why are you down here chasing after me?"

"They've brought in the organized crime unit on this. It means a very major investigation. A lot of action. A lot of press conferences. But very little in the way of results. When is the last time you heard of mob heat being put away for waxing anybody?"

"I don't know. I don't follow these things."

"Well, I do. I've been a cop for a very long time, and I've never seen it happen. The downtown brass have also wrapped the Wickham murder into this one. They believe—for the official record, anyway—that she went down as part of this hit. She's now in the big file with the rest of them, which means her case is going to end up in never-never land, too." He laughed, unhappily. "Anyway, we've restored Bad Biker Bobby Darcy's good name. He may have been a pimp, a thief, a razor artist, and an ex-con, but nobody's calling him a murderer anymore."

"You killed him."

"Yes. I surely did. Because a few people had the wrong bright idea, Darcy's dead, one of his ladies is dead, a good cop is dead, and a gentleman from Texas has a very sore throat."

"That's why you're down here, isn't it? The Molly Wickham murder. The case went bad and you want to set it right. All those people are dead for nothing and you killed one of them."

"Line of duty, Mr. James, though it's one I sure as hell would like to take back. Late at night, sometimes, I want to take all of them back. I've killed four people as a police officer. Contrary to what you see on television, that's an unusually high number in the NYPD."

"I'm sorry."

"Shit happens." Lanham took several large swallows of his beer, nearly finishing it.

"And now there are all these new murders."

"There are always murders. Streets and sanitation get garbage and potholes. We get dead bodies. But Perotta's

305

gunsels had nothing to do with Molly Wickham's killing. I know that and you know that, no matter what the organized crime unit has to say at the next press conference."

A.C. got up to get Lanham another beer. For a foolish fleeting instant, standing out of the detective's line of vision, he thought of pulling out his automatic and threatening Lanham with it, holding him off long enough to get out the door and escape.

He was losing his mind. He wasn't going anywhere until this policemen let him—or told him. He lingered at the little bar to make himself a gin and tonic.

"What do you want from me?" he asked, handing the man the fresh bottle.

Lanham, loosening his tie, accepted the beer with a nod of thanks. He seemed all cop now. The professorial demeanor had entirely vanished.

"I want you to help me find your friend in the limousine, Pierre Delasante. He knows what happened to Molly Wickham, and why. So, I think, does your lady love Camilla. Unfortunately, Pierre's whereabouts are very unknown. And I'm not the only one looking for him. Until they get him, Perotta's little bad guys haven't filled out their dance card. He was in Gorky's videotape blue movie. He was in the sack with Belinda and the rest of them. He was shaking Belinda down for serious money. Perotta enforces his laws. He doesn't have to fuck around with trials and lawyers the way we do."

"Do you think Pierre's still alive?"

"Yes, I do. If they'd gotten to him, too, they'd have left him where he'd be noticed—with some kind of tell. I want to get to him before Perotta's hitters do."

"Molly Wickham was in that movie. How can you be that sure she wasn't killed by the mob, too?"

"I want Pierre Delasante, Mr. James. I want his ass, and damned soon. I think you can help me. If you do, we can hold the matter of Bailey Hazeltine in abeyance for a while."

Their eyes met, unhappily. A.C. really wanted to help. He had from the beginning. But there was Camilla.

"I went to his house in Georgetown," A.C. said. "It doesn't look like he's even been there."

306

"I went there, too. I had the D.C. cops open it up for me. I agree. I don't think anyone's been there for many days. I also went to the feds. They've been on him for months but they were about as helpful as the government of China." He gestured at his briefcase. "I've got several yards of computer printout in there on the federal investigation. I broke all kinds of department regulations and I don't know how many laws getting it, but it doesn't tell me shit."

A.C. took a deep breath. He could throw in with Lanham this far.

"I think that's something I can assist you with," he said. "I have a friend in the federal government—a lot of them, actually. But this one could really prove useful. I was thinking of seeing him myself."

"When can we get to him?"

"Not tonight. He's out of town. I checked. But he'll be in his office first thing in the morning."

"He's FBI?"

"Better than that. He's a senator."

"Is this some kind of fucking joke?"

"No joke."

A.C. finished his drink. Lanham remained fixed to his chair, still the inquisitor.

"There are a number of references in the computer printout to a Jacques Delasante, aka Jack Santee," Lanham said. "He's Pierre's cousin. He's also the brother of Camilla Delasante, aka Camilla Santee. Do you have any idea where he is?"

"We've never been introduced."

"Come on. He's the one who beat the shit out of you, isn't he? I want him, too. And I want her."

"I don't know what I can do, Detective Lanham. I haven't seen her or talked to her, not since Bermuda. I'm being perfectly honest. I've been looking for her. I've gotten nowhere."

"They're all from South Carolina. Do you think they might have gone down there?"

A.C. shrugged.

Lanham got to his feet wearily. "Are you going to help me? Or do we go back to New York?"

307

A.C. reflexively rose as well. "Yes. As much as I possibly can." He emphasized the word "can." Because of Camilla, there were some things he couldn't possibly do. He still had her red scarf, folded neatly in his pocket.

"Thanks for the beers." Lanham paused at the door. "What time will your friend be in his office?"

"Certainly by nine."

"I'll be back here at eight. We'll get there early. And I hope you're not feeling any more wanderlust. All that the D.C. coppers know about you is that you're a witness in an ongoing homicide investigation, but they've agreed to baby-sit you. There's a man in the lobby and a two-man detail in a car outside. Mighty nice of them, considering that they've got one of the most undermanned departments in the country. A favor for a 'brother,' I suppose."

"I'm not going anywhere."

"No, you're not. Not without me. Good night."

•

The senator had an early morning subcommittee meeting and was as delayed as the receptionist in his Russell Building office said he would be. A.C. and Lanham waited more than an hour, and then continued to wait, making the receptionist nervous, as they had no appointment. A.C. looked not a little sinister with the remnant cuts and bruises on his face from the beating he'd received outside Camilla's New York apartment. The reception area of the senator's office complex was a very public place, with aides and messengers constantly coming and going. Two men came in— a foreign ambassador and a lobbyist, both in dark pin-striped suits—and took seats on the opposite side. Both had appointments. Both were kept waiting.

A.C. and Lanham were not wearing suits. The detective was in tan pants, a brown lightweight sport coat and a yellow Izod polo shirt. A.C. was dressed in white pants and blazer again, but with a light blue button-down shirt open at the collar. He had removed his tie upon leaving the hotel, taking note of Lanham's casual clothing.

The senator finally entered, striding in a hurry, talking to an assistant who followed. With sudden, practiced af-

308

fability, he greeted the other two callers, shaking their hands and promising to be with them shortly. Then he turned and saw A.C.

"Good God, A.C. James. How are you?" Whatever his smile said, his eyes said, Why are you here? What do you want? Why didn't you call?

"Hello, Senator," said A.C., rising. "This is Detective Raymond Lanham of the New York Police Department. We have to see you."

"I'd really like to talk to you, A.C. But I wish you'd picked a better day. I'm already running way behind."

The foreign ambassador was looking at them with great unhappiness.

"We can't," A.C. said. "It's important. Life or death."

The senator relaxed slightly, allowing his curiosity and concern to show.

"Official business," A.C. said quietly. "National security."

"Okay," said the senator, obviously wanting them out of the reception area. "But just for a minute." His smile returned. "I'll be right with you, Mr. Ambassador."

The friendship between the two men went back to when the senator had been a congressman serving on the House Armed Services Committee and A.C. had been working in Washington as a Pentagon correspondent. As a congressman, his friend had been a leader in the military reform movement, a decorated Vietnam War hero who had taken on the defense establishment over costly, budget-busting weapons systems that didn't work and endangered the lives of American servicemen. A.C. had given him a public forum and backed him up in print whenever possible, especially in the lawmaker's fight against a controversial new armored personnel carrier that many considered less a weapon than a death trap for American soldiers.

In Washington terms, the man owed him, and now A.C. needed to collect. Now that he was a senator, his friend had been made a member of the Senate Select Committee on Intelligence. He was due to become its next chairman.

In his office, the senator motioned them to chairs, went behind his desk, and then looked to his assistant, who had entered and was about to close the door behind him.

"Just us, please," said A.C.

"Okay, George," said the senator. "It's all right."

The man left, obedient but bewildered.

"What happened to your face, A.C.?" the senator asked.

"An accident. Wrong place, wrong time. Nothing serious."

"Glad to hear. All right, let's have it. Be quick."

"Pierre Delasante."

The senator frowned and sat slowly back in his chair, his hands coming together under his chin.

"What about him?"

"There have been a number of homicides in New York City, sir," Lanham said, speaking very respectfully. "People in the fashion industry. Pierre Delasante is involved. He is in the middle of the whole damned thing. We've come down here to talk to him, if we can find him."

"I read the story in the *Post*," the senator said. "What does this have to do with national security?"

"That's what we'd like to know," Lanham took out the computer printout and held it up. "We have the federal file on Delasante. The whole federal government seems to be on him, but it doesn't say why. We'd like to know why. We'd like to know what he's done."

"He's been indicted on conflict of interest charges," the senator said. "It's getting to be routine around here."

"Right," said Lanham. "That doesn't explain all this continuing surveillance. Or why the file is so top secret. Is there an espionage problem here?"

The senator turned to A.C. "What do you have to do with this?"

He obviously hadn't read enough of the story to learn about Bailey Hazeltine and A.C.'s involvement with her. It would have been the first thing he brought up.

"I'm a witness in the case," A.C. said. "I'm helping Detective Lanham."

"If I tell you anything, what will you do with it?"

"It's not for publication . . ."

"Delasante's in a shitload of trouble in New York," Lanham said. "We need him. If he's in a shitload of trouble down here, too, we need to know that. We'd also like some

310

help in finding out just where the hell he is. But the federal government's been stiffing us at every turn."

"This is all off the record?" the senator said to A.C. "Absolutely?"

"Absolutely."

"Your word as a friend?"

"Yes."

"On your oath as a military officer?" Lanham frowned at this. It did sound a little silly, but it was part of the bond between A.C. and the senator that they both took their former military service very seriously.

"My word as an officer—and your friend."

"And you'll tell absolutely no one you talked to me? Not Kitty. Not anyone."

"No one."

"I mean it, A.C."

"I never crossed you in the old days, not once. I helped you all I could. We need your help now. We have to know what this man is all about."

The senator closed his eyes a moment, then opened them, leaning forward, putting his hands down flat on his desk, as though he were on the verge of making an offer in some negotiation.

"Are you involved in this in some personal way?" he said. "I mean, beyond being a witness?"

"Yes. So is a friend of mine."

Lanham looked down at the floor.

"Okay, A.C. The answer to your question is that Pierre Delasante has done nothing. He's not in a shitload of trouble down here at all. That's why the file is top secret. Because there's nothing really there."

"Nothing?"

"Well, nothing that we know of, and we've been looking real hard."

"Why was he indicted?"

"A shot across the bow. The charges are essentially nonsense. The complaint will be knocked down as soon as he comes to trial, unless he commits perjury or gets caught at something else in the meantime. It was just a way to put a leash on him, to derail him a little. The White House

311

is really pissed at him. He's a scary son of a bitch, this guy."

"You're worried about what he might do, even though he's done nothing, is that it?" said Lanham. The detective seemed irritated that the senator was dealing mostly with A.C.

The senator leaned back again. "Delasante left the federal service and immediately set up shop as a lobbyist. He also immediately began spending money, a lot of money—offices in Harbourplace, town house in Georgetown, a big limo, membership in the Army and Navy Club, the Congressional Country Club, a condo on Hilton Head, a yacht, the works.

"He signed up some clients right off, all foreign. Anyone who's worked in the White House could do the same. And as long as you stick to consultation, not personal intercession, it's okay. The problem comes when you have to deliver. Mike Deaver got in trouble because he tried to deliver for the Canadians. Delasante, well, he didn't deliver. Didn't even try. I don't know if he was too smart or too cowardly, but he never made a call to the White House, never took anyone with a security clearance or in a policy position to lunch."

A.C. understood perfectly what his friend was saying. He wondered how well Lanham was following. The detective was still staring at the carpet.

"We"—the senator spread his arms to include the entire federal establishment—"I mean, well, Delasante wasn't appreciated. He was a loner in the White House, a functionary. You know, the burn-bag guy after conferences. But he was privy to a lot—vital military secrets as well as sensitive, embarrassing stuff. I won't elaborate. The attorney general got nervous, I suppose because the White House chief of staff was nervous. The special prosecutor, who had nothing to do, did something. Hence the indictment." He looked sharply over at Lanham.

"He's all right," A.C. said. Lanham's head jerked up. He sat back stiffly, anger visible behind his glasses. This was his investigation.

"As soon as he was charged, his clients abandoned him." He glanced at his watch, doing so obviously. "But other

312

money, pretty big money, kept coming in. He gave up nothing. If anything, he was spending more. It seemed a pretty good indication of espionage, that he'd stored up some secrets and was selling them off. And he started spending a lot of time in New York, which as you know, A.C., is the espionage cesspool on this continent.

"Nothing. No contacts with any foreign operatives, none. A lot of headwaiters, yes. Some pretty girls, some pretty boys. Some drug dealers. But he paid them. No one knows where it's coming from, but the guy keeps getting piles of money. All cash. And he's been spending it like a remittance man. I think there's an IRS investigation, but of course I'm not privy to that."

"Sir," said Lanham. "Do you have any reason to believe that Delasante's social acquaintances—those girls and boys —are involved with any foreign government?"

"No. Which is to say, not that I know of. All I know is what comes to us in regular reports and executive session. But there's been nothing like that. Foreign connections were the first thing we, the investigating agencies, looked for. Do you know of any? Our information is that that black mistress of his—Molly Wickham—was basically just a hooker."

"That's correct," Lanham said. The senator was a Southerner. It occurred to A.C. that Lanham was getting a little edgy.

The senator looked at his watch again. "That will have to be it, A.C. I'm running way behind. I've told you everything I know."

He stood up. A.C. did the same, but Lanham remained sitting.

"Do you have any idea where Delasante has gone?" Lanham asked. "Could he have left the country?"

"Left? Hell, no. He's under federal indictment. He'd be liable to arrest and extradition. No, he's still in the Washington area as far as I know. He was at a reception at the Kennedy Center the other night. Though I haven't seen him since."

Now Lanham rose. He moved to the door ahead of A.C.

"Just one more thing," A.C. said. "He has some relatives, cousins—Camilla Delasante and Jacques Delasante.

They also go by the name Santee. Are they involved in any of this, in anything bad? Their names showed up in this computer printout we have."

"Not that we know of," said the senator. He went to the door and paused, his hand on the knob. "As I recall, they're pretty respectable people. Very respectable. From Charleston, right? I think Pierre is the black sheep of that family."

He opened the door. "How long will you be in town, A.C.? Love to have a drink or something, maybe next week?"

A.C. looked at Lanham, who did not seem happy.

"I'm afraid not," he said. "Thanks for your help. You've no idea how much I appreciate it."

"That's why we're here," said the senator, smiling his affable constitutents' smile and clapping A.C. on the shoulder, a gesture that served to propel him into the short hallway leading to the foyer. "Give my love to Kitty. Love to see her again."

•

A.C. had parked the rented Buick in a permit-only zone to be near the Capitol offices and found a large pink ticket on the windshield when they returned. Despite his unhappiness, Lanham smiled a little.

"Law and order city," he said, as he slid into the passenger seat. He reached into the glove compartment and took out the service revolver he had put there to avoid setting off the metal detectors in the Senate Office Building.

"What now?" A.C. asked, starting the car.

"You tell me," said Lanham, easing the pistol into his shoulder holster. "You came down here looking for Camilla Santee. You must have had some idea where she might be."

A.C. frowned. He made a U-turn and headed the car west on Constitution Avenue.

"I wasn't lying to you, Detective. I don't know where she is."

Ahead of them, rising above the stately federal buildings, the lush green hills of Virginia could be seen just across the Potomac.

"Jacques Santee has a horse farm not far from here,"
A.C. said. "I was out there yesterday. No one was there."
"It's worth another try," Lanham said.
"Let's stop at the hotel. I want to use the bathroom, and get the morning papers."
Lanham sighed. "All right."
There was nothing in the *Post* about the New York murders. The *New York Times* had just one story, in its Metropolitan section—full of pronouncements from the mayor and police commissioner but no new developments or revelations.
While Lanham wasn't looking, A.C. had retrieved his automatic and returned it to the painful place at his back. He'd not forgotten the beating Jacques Santee had given him, or the many guns in the main house of the horse farm. Or Bailey's lifeless body.
They made one more stop at Pierre's Georgetown place, but found it just as deserted as before. Crossing the Potomac over the Key Bridge, A.C. turned onto Interstate 66 at Rosslyn, picking up speed. There was little outbound traffic, and they were soon out into the rolling countryside of the Virginia Piedmont.
The swiftly moving storm front that had brought the rain had pushed it out of the area and the air was very clear and cool. By late afternoon, thermals rising from the sun-heated soil would dot the sky with puffy little cumulus clouds, but now its limitless blue was without blemish.
A.C. drove very fast. Lanham made no objection. In fact, he said nothing at all. Chin in hand, slouched against the door, he stared straight ahead.
"He has a lot of weapons in that house," A.C. said. "Hunting rifles and all that. I looked through the windows."
"I'll keep that in mind."
"You said you've killed four people?"
"More in Vietnam." Lanham sounded a little irritated.
"I killed a man once. In the army."
"You were in Nam?"
"No. Korea. He was a North Korean infiltrator. It was almost an accident. He fired on a group of us. We didn't want to hurt him. I suppose we could have let him go. But

315

we didn't. Stopping people like that was why we were in Korea."

"Don't apologize."

"It wasn't at all like war. There wasn't a real war going on in Korea. It was rather like hunting. I hate hunting."

"Me too."

"I thought I'd put it out of my mind finally. But someone asked about me about it a few days ago and it's come back. When I think about all these killings now, I see that man —the big hole in his back."

"You never get it out of your mind."

"It was Camilla who asked me about it," A.C. said. "It was very strange—as though she knew."

"She's from the South. Killing a slope like that probably raised you in her esteem."

The comment made A.C. angry. He decided against talking about Camilla any more with Lanham. They drove on for many miles without speaking.

"What were you in the army?" the detective asked at last.

"The Signal Corps."

"I mean what rank?"

"Captain. I was a lieutenant in the national guard, and our colonel got me a promotion after we were activated."

"Figures. I was a fucking sergeant."

"I thought you went to law school."

"That was after the army."

In the light traffic, they made very good time, rolling into Dandytown before the lunch hour. There were cars parked outside the few stores at the crossroads, but not many people on the street. Just outside of the village, they came upon a woman in riding clothes, standing at roadside with her dog, as though waiting for someone. She wasn't Camilla. She paid them no mind.

Swearing, A.C. realized he had taken the wrong turn again. He jammed on the brakes, reversed sharply into a driveway, then accelerated rapidly back in the direction from which they had come. On the next rise, he almost collided with a blue sedan speeding toward them in the middle of the road. Swerving onto the shoulder, he hit the horn in anger as the other car flashed by.

"There were two men in that car," Lanham said.

316

"I didn't notice."

"They were wearing suits."

The road behind them was empty.

"Did you notice them before?" Lanham asked. "On the way out here?"

"No, I don't think so."

"They don't belong here."

"Could they be some of your friends from the D.C. police?"

"No."

"I thought you said they were baby-sitting me."

"I lied. When you come to Santee's farmhouse, keep going."

"Why?"

"Just do as I say."

A.C. did. As they went by, he snatched a few quick glimpses of the farm. The front gate was still hanging open. There were no vehicles parked in front. The windows A.C. remembered as dark still were.

"Go on another mile or so," Lanham said, "then do one of those quick turnarounds again."

He kept on, fenced fields and ditches on either side, until at last they came to an intersection with a gravel road. A.C. muffed the turn and had to back up, but they were soon heading back toward Santee's farm.

Nothing came toward them.

"Stop," said Lanham, when the Santee house came into view again.

A.C. did, leaving the car in the middle of the road. Lanham lifted himself slightly and looked around.

"Okay," he said. "Drive in."

Everything seemed the same, just as deserted, just as silent, just as eerie. A.C. started to pull up under the porte cochere.

"No," Lanham said. "Go around the back. I want to put the car where it can't be seen from the road."

Bumping along past the deserted verandah, A.C. steered the car around a clump of bushes and parked on the grass near the back door. By the time he had unfastened his seat belt, Lanham was already out of the car.

A.C. shut the door on his side, then halted. He stared

down the lane at the stables. They looked as undisturbed as before, except for one significant difference.

"Someone's been here," he said. He pointed to the stables. "That big door there, it was open yesterday. Now it's closed."

"It rained last night. The ground's soft. There should be tire tracks."

"Unless they were washed out by the rain."

"Maybe. Maybe the wind blew the door closed."

"I'll go take a look."

"No," said Lanham. "Let's deal with the house first. Go around front and ring the bell."

"What if someone answers?"

"If it's your lady friend, your day is made."

"What if it's her brother?"

"I'll be here to back you up."

"If anyone's in there, wouldn't they have noticed us drive up?"

"I really don't think anyone's here. Go on."

A.C. started walking, then looked back. Lanham was approaching the back door, taking a large pocket knife from his coat. A.C. hurried. No one looked at him from the windows along the verandah. No one answered the bell. He waited, listening to birds calling in the distance. There was mud on the stone steps, but he could not tell if it was old. It might have been there the previous day. He hadn't been looking at mud.

He rang again, three times, sharply. When there was still no response, he went back to the rear of the house. Lanham had disappeared. The screen door was ajar. The wooden door behind it was fully open.

Perspiring despite the cool morning, A.C. stepped inside, finding himself at the end of a long narrow hall. He called Lanham's name, but the detective didn't answer. A boot-scraper and several pairs of riding boots stood along one side. They were quite dusty.

Farther along was a large pantry off to the left. Shelves, fully stocked with canned and packaged goods, ran along three of the walls. Two fifty-pound bags of dog meal, one of them opened, sat on the floor. He moved on, into a large old-fashioned kitchen. Two glasses were set upside down

318

on the drainboard, but no other kitchenware or utensils were in view. The sink was dry.

Hearing a sound toward the front of the house, he pushed through a set of swinging double doors, entering a long, formal dining room with a table large enough to seat a dozen or more people. There were crystal decanters, pewter ware, and antique brass objects set along the tops of a sideboard and cabinets and corner tables. The chamber reminded him of rooms in old colonial plantation houses kept in a state of historical authenticity for the benefit of visiting tourists.

Another set of double doors at the far end of the dining room opened onto a long central hall. Immediately to the right was a sitting room with French doors facing the verandah. It was in the same state of pristine preservation as the dining room.

Along the left of the central hall was the main staircase, descending to the entrance foyer in the grand Southern manner. Opposite the foot of these stairs was the enormous living room he had glimpsed through the windows of the verandah the previous afternoon. Again, it seemed little disturbed, bereft of the little artifacts of everyday life. A.C. picked up a marble ashtray, finding it cleaned and polished. There was dust on the mantelpiece. The candles set in polished brass holders were new and unused, their wicks still white.

Beside the hearth, however, was a large, round woven basket filled with old newspapers. On the top of the pile was a copy of the Winchester, Virginia, paper. A.C. picked it up, noticing that it had been published the day before. He looked farther through the stack, finding a *New York Times* and a *New York Globe* from several days before— the day he and Camilla had left Bermuda. They carried stories of the murder of Belinda St. Johns and the others.

The sound he had heard repeated itself, and then again. Someone was opening and closing drawers. He dropped the papers back into the basket and crossed the hall, entering a smaller corridor that led perpendicularly from it. There were several rooms along it. Lanham had found the one that was the study. He was going through a large desk by the windows, taking papers from the drawers, setting them on the top, examining each carefully, then returning the stack to where he had found it. A.C. supposed he had gone through these motions thousands of times in his career.

"Where have you been?" Lanham said softly, thumbing through what appeared to be a stack of old telephone bills.

"Looking through the house. I found some New York newspapers. Very recent."

The detective folded a sheaf of the phone bills into a wad and stuck them into a pocket of his sports coat. "It was a good idea, coming here."

There were three swords hanging on the wall behind the desk, one of them Turkish or Arabic.

"There are as many weapons in here as there are in the living room," A.C. said.

"I know. The place looks like the fucking Tower of London. The trouble is, a couple of them may be missing."

He nodded toward a glass-enclosed gun cabinet in the corner. It held four rifles or shotguns. There were spaces for six.

As Lanham opened yet another drawer, A.C. went over to the fireplace. There were a number of framed, standing photographs on the mantel, among them a large group portrait similar to the one he had seen in Camilla's apartment in New York—the mother and father, Camilla, a younger, dark-haired girl, and the brother, dark and very handsome. Pierre Delasante was not in this picture.

A.C. stepped closer. The mother looked every bit the aristocrat. It would surprise no one to learn she was the head of Charleston's most exclusive society. Queen Victoria could not have been so self-confident, or so arrogant.

The mother had light hair, though not so purely blond as Camilla's, yet the others in the family were so very dark. Camilla bore a resemblance to the brother and the other girl, and certainly to the mother, but not at all to the father.

There were smaller photographs on either side of the group shot, all individual portaits. A.C. picked up one, staring at it.

"Here's her brother. This is Jacques Santee," A.C. said.

Lanham looked up, a little surprised. "I didn't look at those yet."

A.C. brought the picture over. "I can't think of anyone

320

else it might be. He was in another photograph she had in New York."

Lanham pried open the frame with his knife and slipped the photograph out. The name "Jacques" was written in pencil on the back, along with a date.

"This picture's seven years old," Lanham said.

"He couldn't have changed much. She certainly hasn't."

"Don't you recognize him from the Plaza? The man on the motorcycle?"

"I suppose I do."

"The son of a bitch has nasty eyes." Lanham put the photograph in his coat pocket.

A.C. went back to the mantel. Among the smaller portraits was one of Pierre Delasante and a lovely picture of Camilla in riding clothes. She was as beautiful as in any of the fashion layouts he had seen, but looked nothing at all like a model. He wished he had known her then.

"Since you're collecting photographs," A.C. said, tossing the one of Pierre on the desk, "this has to be the cousin, the man in the limousine. Pierre."

"I know. The lover boy."

A.C. put the one of Camilla into a side pocket of his blazer, frame and all. This was theft. They had broken into her house and now he was stealing her picture. It was one thing for the policeman to act this way. There was no excuse for him. But the compulsion was too strong. This could be the last memento he would ever have of her.

Lanham was removing Delasante's picture from its frame when suddenly his hands stopped. He slowly turned his head toward the door. A.C. heard nothing, and then he did. A creak, a quiet thump, the click of something. Someone else was in the house. Lanham, with great caution, started moving toward the doorway. A.C. stepped ahead of him, wanting to lead the way in case it was Camilla, going down to the end of the smaller corridor. There was another noise, a little louder, but less defined.

Edging out into the main hall, A.C. peered up at the stairs. He heard two quick, heavy steps, coming from the wrong direction—not from the stairs, but from behind. He was turning when the blow struck. There was a sudden numbness. He fell sprawling, hitting the floor with his face.

321

But he was still conscious, aware of his assailant stepping over him, aware that it was a man, wearing thick-soled dress shoes. Light flared between the man's legs. The front door was opening to the sun, the light darkening suddenly with the shadow of another man, who stepped inside.

The nearer figure started to move away. A.C. grabbed the ankle of his trailing leg, pulling and twisting. The man careened to one side, his arm thrust out, seeking balance from empty air. A.C. pulled again, sharply. His victim fell with a crash, the pistol in his hand flying loose, skittering across the polished wooden floor, bouncing off the woodwork and spinning to a halt. The intruder by the door started toward it.

A.C. began to rise, when an enormous, explosive, shattering, deafening roar eclipsed his sense of everything else, followed by a gigantic, crystalline crash and the ping and sting of flying glass and metallic fragments.

A.C.'s forehead was cut. He felt the pain and wetness running down to his eye. Lifting himself, he saw that the man by the door had fallen to one knee. He wavered there, his hands over his head.

What remained of the chandelier at the end of the hall by the door was swinging back and forth. Most of the fixture had been shot away, loose bits of glass flying in every direction, but the bulk of it had struck the kneeling man. Clumsily, almost slipping, A.C. got to his feet.

Camilla stood on the stairs, a long shotgun held expertly in her slender arms. She acknowledged him with a look, but there was no affectionate communion. Her eyes were hard. With a quick motion, she push-pulled the weapon's slide, shoving another shell into the chamber. Her words, spoken angrily, were as sharp and explosive as what had come from the shotgun's barrel.

"Get that pistol in his hand! There's another on the floor. Get it!"

A.C. realized she was talking to him. He quickly did as she asked. The kneeling man had cuts on his face and hands. Bits of glass were stuck like little spears in the shoulder of his coat. A.C. took the fellow's pistol away, noting that it was a Beretta automatic. The gun on the floor was the same model. With both in hand, held by the barrels, he turned back to Camilla.

"Put them on the stairs in front of me," she said.

He did. Straightening up, he realized he was close enough to step inside the shotgun's reach and grab her by the thighs and hips, shoving her back. But why would he do that?

"Step back, A.C.," she said.

"Camilla . . ."

"Back!"

He could not believe this. He supposed she was only frightened. She would know they were on the same side once she calmed down.

Backing away, he saw Lanham crouched in the side corridor, holding his weapon forward in both hands.

"Come out of there!" Camilla said. She turned the shotgun toward the side hall, though Lanham was not quite in her field of fire.

"For God's sake, Camilla!" A.C. said. "Don't shoot him!"

"I won't shoot anyone, sir, if he does what I say. Come out! Now!"

Lanham made a judgment. There was no confusion or fear on his face as he walked slowly into the hall. His eyes were fixed on hers. He held his revolver at his side, barrel toward the floor.

"Set it down gently," she said, her voice more even. She had the shotgun aimed at Lanham's belly, her finger at the trigger. She kept surveillance of the other two men with quick, careful glances.

Lanham placed his weapon on the floor without making a sound. He stood back up and sighed, folding his arms in front of him.

"Where's your brother, ma'am?" he asked. "Where's your cousin Pierre?"

"You never mind my brother. You have no right to be here. None of you. This is private property. You are the ones who have broken the law."

She stood a moment, thinking, centering the shotgun now so it could be aimed at any of them in an instant.

"Is he all right?" she asked the uninjured intruder, nodding toward the other.

"Fuck you," he said.

"Stand up," she said to the injured man. When he had done so, she moved slightly to her left. "Now, all of you. Empty your pockets. Everything. Now! You, too, A.C."

Sadly, he did as she asked. Among the things he carried was her red scarf, neatly folded.

When all of the keys and coins and other objects had noisily fallen, she took a step forward, motioning with the shotgun to herd them closer together.

"Down the hall on your right is a door," she said. "I want you all to walk toward it, slowly, single file."

"I've got to talk to you, Camilla," A.C. said.

"You said you'd keep him away from me, and here you both are."

"Camilla!"

"Shut up!"

The two strangers were moving. Lanham followed. With an imploring look back at her, A.C. did the same.

"Open the door," she said. The first man did so. "Those stairs go down to the cellar. Go on. Move."

She let them get ahead of her, then stood on the landing until they had all descended to the gloom of the lower floor. She spoke no further word and showed no interest in them. With one last glance at A.C., she vanished. They heard a key turn in the lock of the door. Her footsteps clicked and clattered on the floorboards above as she hurried about some business. A.C. was reminded of a woman getting ready to go out for the evening. A silence followed.

Their vision adjusted to the darkness, alleviated only by two slim shafts of sunlight coming from small rectangles of windows near the ceiling. The injured man hobbled over to stacked rolls of old carpeting and sank down upon them. His comrade went to him, removing his tie and daubing at some of his lacerations.

"Are you men cops?" A.C. said. "Federal agents?"

"Fuck you," said the man who'd removed his tie.

"They're not cops," Lanham said. "They're the opposite of cops."

"He's a police detective," A.C. said. "New York City Police Department."

"You're in the wrong place, chump," said the injured man.

A.C. found himself admiring the man's toughness. The pain he was suffering was doubtless outrageous. A.C. pressed his palm against his own forehead and it came away sticky with blood. There was a large swelling on the back of his head. Yet he felt no pain. He supposed it would come later.

"I don't know any doctors around here, but there's a veterinarian in Dandytown," A.C. said. "He can take care of you."

"Forget him," Lanham said. "We've got to find a way out of here." He began to poke around the basement.

"You were in the car we passed," A.C. said to the others. "You were following us."

They weren't interested in conversation. Lanham moved farther away, into another chamber of the cellar. A.C. followed.

"So that's your lady love," Lanham said, with some disgust.

"She's in trouble, that's all."

"We're going to be in worse trouble if that brother of hers shows up."

They were in deep darkness, feeling with their hands. Lanham fumbled along the wall, looking for a light switch.

"Who do you think they are, those two?" A.C. asked.

"If they still had their weapons, we'd be in a shitload of trouble right now. Maybe even dead."

"They're Perotta's men."

"Shut up, A.C."

They had come to a door. Lanham swore, almost happily. Turning the knob, he pushed it open, then felt around the side. A moment later, a light came on, illuminating much of the cellar behind them and revealing a string hanging from a bulb at the ceiling. A.C. pulled it. Another light came on. It was now very bright.

"Ray," he said. "I have a weapon."

"What are you talking about?"

"A forty-five automatic. My old army sidearm."

"Where?"

A.C. patted his back.

"How long have you had that?"

"Since I left New York."

"Well, why the hell didn't you use it?"

"Against Camilla?"

"Shit."

An odd, distant rumble increased and defined itself as an automobile engine, an automobile moving in low gear. Lanham turned and ran back toward the first chamber. He leapt at the window, gripping the sill and lifting himself to look out. A.C. clambered up beside him. The car passed the house, scattering gravel. Its engine sound diminished, and then was gone.

Their finger strength gave out and they slid down to their feet.

"A red convertible," A.C. said. "She was driving. I think she was alone."

The less injured of the two strangers was already moving up the steps to the door. He twisted the knob, to no avail, then lunged at it with his shoulder. There wasn't room or purchase enough for him to have much effect.

"Forget it!" Lanham said. He turned to A.C. "Give me that thing."

"No," said A.C., pulling out the pistol. "I'll do it."

He motioned the other man to come back down the stairs, which, wide-eyed and wordless, he did. A.C. positioned himself on the landing against the wall, aiming the gun at the door lock obliquely. Then he adjusted the angle slightly, making the mechanism the target instead of the latch. Lanham had come up the stairs behind him but halted, watching intently.

"Have you ever done this before?" he said.

"Yes. Have you?"

"Come to think of it, no."

A.C. pulled stiffly on the trigger, jerking the gun slightly, but the powerful round demolished the lock and a considerable section of the wood paneling, flinging the door open. They all rushed into the hallway.

"Son of a bitch," said Lanham.

Their possessions were scattered all over the floor. The pistols were missing. In her haste, Camilla had left their keys.

Lanham and A.C. got to their car first.

"I'll drive," Lanham said. "With the knock you took on the head, I don't feel safe with you at the wheel."

"I'm all right."

Lanham got into the driver's seat anyway.

"What about those two men?" said A.C., settling in beside him.

"Get your pistol ready. I'm going to pull up next to their car."

"You want me to shoot them?"

"I want you to shoot out the front tire." Lanham jammed the Buick into gear.

It took A.C. two shots. The expressions on the others' faces went from surprise to intense hatred. Lanham left them sitting in a cloud of hanging dust.

"Insurance," Lanham said, once they were speeding down the road.

"They can change the tire."

"Not in any great big hurry."

Lanham took a sharp curve too widely, skidding badly as he jerked the car back into the right lane. New York cops weren't much used to winding country roads. A.C. had grown up on them.

"I should drive," he said.

"Later maybe."

"Where are we going?"

"Let's just get a few miles behind us. Then we'll pull over and talk."

They roared into Dandytown well over the speed limit, slowing at the intersection but shooting through against the red. Instead of taking the road that led back to the interstate, Lanham headed south. A few miles farther, they came to an old stone church. There was a parking lot in back. He pulled into it, stopping the car close to the building.

Lanham stretched out his arms a moment and then rubbed his eyes.

"Hand me the briefcase I put in the back, or did Camilla ditch that, too?"

"It's still there." A.C. pulled it over the seat.

The detective snapped open the catches, but left the lid closed.

"We haven't exactly been straight with each other," he said. "I'll go first. You're not a fugitive. You're not wanted for murder. What I've got in here is a subpoena for your appearance at Bailey Hazeltine's inquest next week. That's all. You're nothing more than a material witness. We know you didn't shoot her."

"And just how do you know that?"

"For one thing, we have a statement from Mrs. Vanessa Meyer."

"She saw me standing over Bailey with a gun. This gun."

"According to her statement, she was with you all the time. You discovered the body together."

Vanessa had lied for him, had doubtless committed perjury.

"That's not entirely true."

"I wasn't about to argue with her. We got something else."

He opened the briefcase lid and searched through the papers inside, taking out a manila envelope. "We got a picture of a guy in your apartment. The time it was taken checks out to the probable time of Bailey Hazeltine's death."

He pulled out an eight-by-ten glossy photograph. It was shot with a telephoto lens through A.C.'s French doors and the focus was a little fuzzy, but the man's dark features were clear enough.

"How did you get this?"

"Your wife brought it in. She had a P.I. on your case. He was staked out on the rooftop across the street."

"P.I.?"

"Private investigator. In TV shows like 'Magnum P.I.,' they ride around in helicopters shooting bad guys. In real life, they do scuzzy divorce work like this. He'd been on you for a couple of weeks. I gather he also got some hot shots of you and Miss Hazeltine in the sack, but these your wife did not bring to our attention."

A.C. sank back against the seat, staring at the face in the photograph.

328

"Kitty came to you with this?"

"Apparently she's not so pissed at you she'd let you squirm on a Murder One."

Lanham reached into his pocket. He'd retrieved the mantlepiece picture of Jacques Santee from the farmhouse floor. He held it up next to the one the private investigator had taken.

"Same son of a bitch, wouldn't you say?"

"Yes," A.C. said unhappily, wondering what Kitty must think of him.

"And he's the guy you saw on the motorcycle?"

"Yes. I was pretty sure of that the first time I saw him in a photograph Camilla had in her apartment."

"Jacques Santee."

"Yes. Why didn't you tell me about this private investigator's picture last night?"

"I wasn't sure where I stood with you. More to the point, I wasn't sure where you stood with the Southern blond lady. We're pretty clear on that now, aren't we?"

"Yes. I guess we are."

There was a white frame house next to the church. An old woman was standing on the back steps, watching them.

"So let's go find them."

"Them? We want Jacques."

Lanham shook his head impatiently. "They're all mixed up in this, A.C. Find one, and we're going to find the others."

"When we were in Bermuda, she talked to someone on the phone one night. I overheard her. I could hear a man's voice on the other end. I've no doubt it was Jacques."

"What did she say to him?"

A.C. took a deep breath. "I think she was telling him to deal with Pierre. She said she didn't care what happened to him."

"Like, if he got murdered."

"Yes."

"But he stopped off at your place first. Why would he hit your girlfriend Bailey?"

"I'm sure he went there to kill me. Camilla warned me I was in danger. I'd given Bailey a key to the apartment. She picked the wrong time to use it—again."

"Again?"

"She came in a few days earlier, when my wife was there."

"You've had a hell of a run of luck, haven't you? Let's hope it's going to change. Why would he want to kill you? Just because you were fucking his sister?"

"He was probably afraid she'd told me something."

"Like what?"

"I don't know. There's some bad trouble in that family, some bad blood between them and Pierre. He'd taken over Camilla's apartment on Sutton Place; probably the brother's horse farm, too. I'm pretty certain they were paying him money. At least Camilla was. That's why she was working so hard, why she came out of retirement. She'd been living in France until a few months ago."

"Pierre has something on her—on both of them. Just like he had something on Belinda and the others. Is Camilla married?"

"No, I don't think so. She never mentioned a husband. There were no pictures of a husband. Nothing like that."

"Wedding rings can be removed. Did Pierre know about you and Camilla?"

"Whatever their problem is, it was going on before I met her."

"Do you think it's possible Camilla and the brother were sleeping together?"

"No!" A.C.'s voice carried far enough for the old woman at the house next door to hear. She hurried inside.

"Sorry. I'm just covering all the bases."

Lanham drummed on the steering wheel a moment. He had turned off the car's engine. Returning his briefcase to the back seat, he restarted it.

"I don't think Pierre has hung around Washington for any more gala receptions," he said. "According to the computer printout, he has a condo on Hilton Head, and a yacht moored there, too."

"It's near Charleston," A.C. said. "Camilla's from Charleston. Her family is very prominent socially there. A very old family. Dates back forever."

Lanham shifted the car into reverse.

"Okay," he said. "I'm going south. You want to come

with me, or do you want to go back to New York and face your wife?"

A.C., frustrated, said nothing.

"Look, man," said Lanham. "You're trying to do the right thing. You said the Hazeltine girl was 'very dear' to you. She got whacked because of you. You and I know who did it. I'm going after him. What are you going to do?"

"I'm coming with you."

"If Camilla is heading for Charleston, she has a little head start. If we go back to the hotel to get our bags, she'll have a big one."

"Skip the bags. I have a lot of money on me. We can buy whatever we need."

"If you've got a lot of cash, why didn't you use it at the hotel and the car rental?"

"I thought it would attract attention to me."

Lanham shook his head, then got the Buick back onto the highway. A.C. had a lot of money in his pocket, but he was missing something else. It sadly occurred to him that Camilla had taken back the red silk scarf.

CHAPTER

······························

16

They traversed the state of Virginia on country highways, heading diagonally toward Interstate 95, the main coastal artery leading to the deeper South. The sun crossed over them high in the sky, beginning its slide to the west, the afternoon heat barely noticeable in the breeze from the open car windows.

The little towns they passed through all seemed much the same. Gas stations and fast-food franchises appeared on either side of the road, followed by a jumble of badly painted shacks and small houses with black people on the steps and porches, then square brick buildings as the road became the town's main street, then—often climbing a hill—the grand old nineteenth-century houses of the best section of town. After that, a final stretch of roadside businesses, and then the dusty open countryside again. Sometimes they'd come upon the grand old houses first, and find the black district on the other side of town. Never were they juxtaposed. It had doubtless been like that since the Civil War, when the blacks were first given the right to own their own places.

Except for the addition of the garish commercialism of the fast-food emporiums, these antique communities could not have changed much in 130 years.

Some of the place names were familiar from history books. This sweep of aged farmland from the Blue Ridge Mountains to the Tidewater coastland had been one vast and continuous battlefield throughout the four years of the War Between the States. Historical markers stood in testament to the carnage. Gazing over the undulating cornfields, one could well imagine the limitless swarms of blue and gray and brown, the roiling smoke and din, the ghastly cries, the tilt and fall of flags and regimental colors.

"I hate the fucking South," Lanham said.

"It's changed a lot."

"Yeah, right. I grew up in Baltimore, and that was bad enough. Did you know the Maryland state song still has the words 'Northern scum' in it? And Maryland wasn't even in the Confederacy."

"They have a black governor in Virginia, the first black governor of any state in the history of the country."

"Well, that's a recent goddamned development. They used to have a miscegenation law down here that might as well have been written by the Nazis. If you had as little as one thirty-second black blood in you, you were officially black, and all that that meant. You couldn't be white. That lasted right up until World War II. They changed it to one sixteenth after Pearl Harbor so that some plantation owner in Charles City County—some guy descended from Pocahontas—could be a colonel in the Virginia National Guard."

"The general who's chairman of the Joint Chiefs of Staff now is black."

"I'll bet there's no black general in the Virginia National Guard. I'll bet you we'll hear the word 'nigger' more than once before this is over."

There was a hawk wheeling lazily above a tree line. Some small, furry squeaking creature would shortly die. A.C. was feeling very tired. His head was beginning to hurt.

"You know, I'm mostly white," Lanham said. "I'm half white, because of my mother. But my father had white in him, too. Most blacks do, you know. Alex Hailey, who wrote *Roots*? He had two white great-grandfathers. Both Irishmen. Sometimes I wonder about my boys. They're three-quarters white, but they're still black. If they should marry white women, and have kids, their kids will be seven-eighths white, but they'll still be black. Another generation like that, and my family would be officially white in the state of Virginia. Except they'd still be black. Because of me, because of my father and his family, they'd always be black."

"It doesn't matter anymore, Ray. It certainly doesn't matter with me."

He could think of nothing more to say. Sliding down in the seat, he rested his head against its back and closed his eyes.

"I think I'll get some sleep, Ray."

Lanham looked at him, thinking about the blow to A.C.'s head.

"You all right, man?"

"I'm all right. Just need some sleep."

"Guess you probably didn't get much in Bermuda."

A.C. said nothing.

•

When A.C. finally stirred from his slumber, it was to the dark of night. They were pounding along Interstate 95, a few red taillights visible in the distance ahead. A green highway sign flashed by, its white letters flaring in the glare of their headlights. They were approaching Fayetteville well into North Carolina.

A.C. looked at his watch. It was past ten o'clock.

"You put a few miles behind us," he said.

"I thought I'd let you catch some Z's. You were really out."

"Shouldn't we stop for gas?"

"I already did. You slept through it."

"I need to go to the bathroom."

"No doubt you do. I'll stop at the next service station."

"Pick a place with a restaurant. I'm hungry. Or did you stop to eat, too?"

"No. I could use a burger. Cop food."

They rumbled on awhile, the white lane lines stretching on into an infinite blackness.

"You didn't pass a small red convertible with a blonde in it?" A.C. said.

"No such luck."

"This could be a hell of a wild-goose chase."

"I hate to tell you how many times I've been on one of those. But I've got an itch, A.C. I think they're going home. I think we're going to score."

"We're going to get there in the middle of the night."

"Before dawn, anyway." Lanham glanced up at the rear-view mirror.

"When I was in college, I set the world land speed record from New York to Boston on a night like this. A friend of mine and I left a bar on Park Avenue at one o'clock and arrived on the campus of the Endicott College for Women at four-fifteen, but when we got there we had nothing to do but sit in the car and drink whiskey for three hours. Our dates for that weekend were truly pissed when they found us."

"I have a pint bottle in my briefcase."

"No, thanks."

"The middle of the night is a good time to arrive in a strange town, when you're looking for trouble."

Lanham looked over his shoulder as a car came up on their left to pass them. It was a state police cruiser. Lanham had slowed, but they were still five miles an hour over the fifty-five-mile-an-hour official speed limit. As in all states, there was probably an unofficial speed above that which motorists were allowed to attain without hindrance, but, as in all states, they had no idea what that was.

The trooper slowed to keep pace with them. A.C. could see his young face in the light from his dashboard.

Lanham decreased his speed further, staring straight ahead.

"A black man and a white man in an out-of-state car,"

Lanham said. "And we've got two guns and a bottle of whiskey aboard."

The trooper was talking into his microphone.

"You're a police officer, Ray. For God's sake."

"He could still cause us some considerable inconvenience."

"I think you're getting paranoid."

"I'll tell you about my days at Fort Bragg sometime."

The police car fell back, and trailed them for a while.

"Checking our plates, maybe," Lanham said.

"I don't believe this."

"I've done it myself—for the same reason."

Other cars were coming up behind them. Finally, the trooper made a decision, and shot ahead. Lanham kept to fifty-five until the cruiser had disappeared into the night, into the South.

"When we get to a gas station," he said, "you take over the wheel."

•

A.C. drove much faster than Lanham, and they reached Charleston before one A.M. It was a surprisingly small city with tall trees and church steeples rising above old pastel-colored buildings that glowed eerily in the pale light of antique street lamps. They drove through a run-down commercial section briefly, then A.C. found the street he sought and turned into it, heading for the historic district.

New York, Kitty—all that seemed very far away, as though on another planet.

Lanham rubbed the stubble on his chin. "How far are we from Hilton Head?"

"An hour and a half south of here. At the most."

"You've been here before?"

"Yes. I've covered the Spoleto music festival."

"That's the Gian Carlo Menotti opera thing."

A.C. was surprised—again. "Yes. And I've been to Hilton Head on vacation."

"This will be a little different. God. Look at all the flowers here. This whole city is a garden."

336

"It's the most beautiful city in the South."

"This is where they started the Civil War," Lanham said. "This was the capital of slavery—John C. Calhoun and all those guys."

"He's buried here."

"Not deep enough."

"Not deep at all. This is the low country. Most bodies are entombed above ground."

A.C. pulled the car up before a large columned building on Meeting Street. The structure embraced a garden that opened to the street. A large fountain in the middle of it was quietly burbling water, its soft spray a curtain of tiny flashing jewels in the floodlights.

An elderly black man in a dark uniform coat stirred himself and ambled over to their car, opening the door on Lanham's side.

"This is the hotel?" Lanham said.

"It's the Mills House. You'll like it."

"I suppose you'd think I'd like Jefferson Davis's house, too."

"Ray, this place is owned by Holiday Inns."

The lobby was huge, quiet, and very Southern, decorously furnished and filled with ferns and other potted plants.

Lanham hung back, letting A.C. deal with the sleepy desk clerk. There was no change whatsoever in the young man's expression or manner when Lanham took his turn at the register.

They were given adjoining rooms on the second floor, which they discovered had large French doors that opened onto a wide terrace that ran the length of the building. A.C. strolled out onto it, much taken with the elevated view of the city's rooftops. There was a swimming pool at the other end of the terrace, glowing green in the night.

"If your lady friend's here, she's not going to hang out a sign saying she's home," said Lanham, looking down the street. "Anyway, I want to do a little reconnoitering before we make any big moves."

"Some sleep, then."

"An early breakfast. Maybe seven."

•

A.C.'s sleep was fitful and filled with dreams. At first, they amounted to repeated, vague images of riding in a car—speeding in a car, an automobile over which he had no control, traveling in changing directions, heading he knew not where. Then voices were calling to him; people were yelling at him. Then he was with Camilla. They were naked, making love, over and over endlessly, but without fruition. She was angry with him, and kept averting her face. He tried desperately to look at her, but all he could see was her long blond hair trailing in the wind. She was running away, farther and farther away, becoming a speck of light in a dark night sky. " 'I have seen starry archipelagoes, and islands, whose heavens are opened to the voyager.' Rimbaud."

He sat up, feeling the room close around him. Because the windows opened onto the terrace, he had drawn the thick, heavy drapes fully across, and now they seemed to envelop him oppressively, like some fiendish enclosure in a tale by Edgar Allan Poe. Tearing himself from his bed, he flung them open.

Nothing moved outside. He sat in a chair for a moment, breathing heavily. All his guilt was returning in a rush—guilt over what had happened to Bailey, over what he'd been doing to Kitty, over what might now happen to Camilla.

He wanted desperately to be away from this place, to be away from everything. But even if he'd fled to Brazil when he'd run away from the scene in his apartment, he knew he'd only be in some other hotel room now, suffering this same misery—and fear.

He forced himself to return to his bed. He lay with the covers off, staring straight up at the ceiling. He was stronger than this. He closed his eyes and kept his body very still, relaxing every muscle. Finally, sleep returned.

But so did dreams. He was trapped in his old army dream again. He was in a foxhole on a ridge in Korea at night, all alone. In front of him was a wide, moonlit valley. Its shadows began to stir and from them emerged an infinitely long

338

line of running men. They were shouting and blowing bugles and banging gongs and shooting guns. He fired back, dropping one and then another, killing and killing, but the line came closer and grew larger. The shouting became a din. He pulled himself out of his foxhole and began running. He tripped, and had to crawl. He looked back. The line of soldiers was almost upon him. A single man leapt forward from the others, a long pistol in his hand. He called A.C.'s name. He had a dark, handsome face. He was Jacques Santee.

A.C. sat up. There was a dark figure at the French doors. A tall man. Where had he left his pistol? In one of the dresser drawers. He rolled across the bed and clambered over the floor, clawing for it. The French doors opened. He had nowhere to turn.

"Are you okay?"

It was Lanham.

"What?" A.C. halted, sitting back on his heels.

"I said, are you okay? You were shouting. I could hear you through the wall."

"Sorry. I'm sorry, Ray. I was dreaming."

Lanham, still a silhouette, stared at him. "I'll be right back."

He returned with something in his hand—his pint bottle of whiskey.

"Here. Get you through the night."

"I don't need that."

"In case you do." He set it on A.C.'s night table and went back to his room.

A.C. waited several minutes, then surrendered and went to fill a small bathroom glass with the bourbon. The first drink helped. The second put him to sleep—without dreams.

•

He awoke groggy, but feeling better. A brisk shower and a shave improved things further. He'd been awakened by the sound of children outside. After he dressed, he went out onto the terrace and saw two families already up and using the swimming pool.

A.C. went and knocked on Lanham's door. The detective still had shaving cream on his face when he answered it.

"When you finish up," A.C. said, "come out and join me. I want you to see something."

Lanham gave him a peculiar squint, but nodded. He stepped outside a few minutes later, dressed in the same tan slacks, sport coat and Izod shirt.

"Come see the pool," A.C. said.

"The pool?"

"The pool."

They walked up to the steps that led to the pool's level. On the far side, a blond woman sat idly reading the paper while her children, a blond boy and girl, swam and played with two smaller girls. They were black. Their parents, dressed in bathing suits themselves, sat on the nearer side, talking happily.

"Welcome to the South, Mr. Lanham."

The detective grunted. "Let's eat."

As they finished their ham, eggs, and grits in the hotel's main dining room, A.C. looked down at his shirt. "First thing we do is buy some more clothes," he said.

"Guess you can buy all the white pants you want down here."

"What after that?"

"I'm just going to look around town. Maybe chat up the local law."

"I want to find the mother."

"You want to find Camilla."

"If we're lucky."

"That lady's a lot of things, but she sure as hell isn't what I'd call luck."

Not wanting to wait for the haberdasheries to open, Lanham bought a T-shirt from a local tourist stand, changed into it, then set off on foot. A.C. stopped in the lobby to buy the local newspapers and copies of two Carolina magazines. Taking them to his room, he turned first to the telephone book.

There were no Delasantes listed in it. He tried information, and was told there was a Delasante, but that the telephone number was unlisted. When he asked for the address, the operator told him she was not allowed to give him that.

Exasperated, he looked through the papers and magazines, and then got a better idea.

•

The editor of the slicker-looking of the two magazines was identified on the masthead as a Melanie Bucksworth. A.C. expected an older woman, perhaps a gray-haired lady in picture hat, floral print dress, and white gloves. He got the dress right, but Miss Bucksworth proved to be a girl in her late twenties, wearing tinted glasses and not enough makeup. She'd graduated from the University of North Carolina journalism school, had worked on two small Georgia papers, and then taken this job. A.C. couldn't tell if she liked it or not.

She seemed extremely impressed with the fact that A.C. said he was with a New York paper and had contributed articles to *Town and Country*, but even more taken with his mentioning that he was a friend of Alixe Percy's, whom she said she had encountered as an important personage at Aiken, South Carolina, horse shows and at the fox hunting there.

A.C. had told Miss Bucksworth that Alixe had recommended he do a piece on the old homes and families of Charleston, and this had sufficed for her to agree to meet with him over coffee to talk to him about it. Alixe's name was all he needed for introduction.

Miss Bucksworth was a small, thin woman, with bad legs and a pretty face. Her friendliness bordered on flirtation, but A.C. supposed that had more to do with local custom than any unique response to him. Though he was anxious to learn as much as he could as quickly as possible, A.C. worked hard at being courtly and charming. The girl responded with considerable gush.

"Charleston is such a fascinating story, Mr. James. There's simply no place like it on earth. I've been here more than three years, and I haven't figured it all out. People here are a little slow to accept strangers, don't you know?"

341

Having said that, Miss Bucksworth launched into a discourse on the history and social life of the city intended to impress him with the vast extent of her knowledge. She chattered on endlessly about how well Charleston had survived both the American Revolution and the Civil War, urging him to visit all manner of local landmarks—the Old Exchange and Provost Dungeon, the Powder Magazine, the Edmondston-Alston House, the Heyward-Washington House, the Nathaniel Russell House, the Calhoun Mansion.

"The hurricane was probably the worst thing ever to happen to Charleston, but we all emerged intact," she said. "The same indomitable spirit that stood up to General Sherman prevailed again."

She laughed in a fluttery way, and touched A.C.'s arm the way Camilla had done.

They were in a small, sunny restaurant about four blocks from his hotel. The scars of the hurricane were visible out the window. There were wide stumps where once there must have been great trees.

A.C. then inquired about the famous families of the town, but quickly wished he had not. She began with Anthony Ashley Cooper, Earl of Shaftesbury, who had founded the place as a small colony in 1670 and established the only nobility in the history of America, granting plantation owners noble titles as barons, landgraves, and caciques—a system that had endured another half century. It took her nearly a half hour and two cups of coffee to work her way up to the present. Though inwardly maddened with impatience, he encouraged her, wishing desperately that she'd get to what he wanted to hear.

But in none of this did she mention the name Delasante. A.C. wondered if Alixe had told him one of her enormous fibs, wondering if Camilla's Delasantes were really of no account, or if they were even in residence. There might be no reason to be here at all. He and Lanham could end up making fools of themselves, trying to make a connection between the murder of a one-time Times Square black hooker and this arcane museum of a city.

There was more wish than logic to this thought. Camilla

could come walking along the sidewalk at any moment. So could her cousin or her brother. There was no other place from which they could have come.

"Alixe said something about a family called Delasante," A.C. said. "Are they of consequence?"

"As a family, no. They've only been here four generations. Bought up a lot of land after the War Between the States, and more during the Depression. But Mrs. Delasante, why, yes indeed. She's of the Dutarques and the Beaugerards and . . ."

Miss Bucksworth went on much as Alixe had done. A.C. decided to try a gambit.

"Alixe said there was some trouble in the family, something dark and mysterious."

The girl flushed a little, glancing apprehensively at the other tables in the small room. Only one was occupied, and by tourists—people wearing shorts and boating shoes, with plastic shopping bags set on the wooden floor beside them.

Miss Bucksworth leaned close to A.C., peering at him over her tinted glasses.

"Mrs. Delasante's husband was murdered, don't you know," she said, in a near whisper. "Years ago. The matter was officially listed as an accident, but it's said he was stabbed to death, in Niggertown . . . I mean, in the black section. There was no investigation. It was commonly understood that he had a fancy girl down there, and no one wanted that to become public knowledge. In the days of slavery, that sort of thing was fairly commonplace—with one's own chattel. But since then, consorting with a black girl—it isn't countenanced. Not at all."

"Would you have anything in your files about that, about the 'accident'?"

She sat back abruptly, briefly placing her hand over her mouth.

"In our files? Mr. James, I could lose my job for suggesting such a thing." She came close again. "I'm told there were some at the time who suggested that, well, that the Delasantes shouldn't be welcomed too warmly in some places after the—the incident. They paid very dearly for

343

that suggestion. I mean, Mrs. Delasante belongs to every social club and organization in town, and she runs the most important one. The social community rallied around her and it was those who'd made the suggestion who ended up being cut and snubbed and dropped. After all, it wasn't as though *she'd* slept with a black man."

A.C. smiled with all the charm he could muster, waiting for her to continue as though completely dazzled by her intimate knowledge of her subject.

Miss Bucksworth's voice became even more conspiratorial. "Not that she didn't have a few gentlemen callers of her own in the evening—gentlemen of quality, to be sure—when her husband was off on his adventures. Or so I'm told. He was a very handsome man, Mr. Delasante, but I think she mostly married him because he had so much money. Her own family was in rather reduced circumstances back then. I'm told they'd even considered selling their house. She's been a very tragic figure since her husband's death. Her daughter Danielle committed suicide shortly after. And her other children moved off."

She took a sip of her now cooled coffee, then quickly set it down, somewhat nervously.

"Why are you so interested in the Delasantes, Mr. James?"

A.C. smiled again, and shrugged. "Alixe told me a bit about them. I guess I'm just looking for a little gossip to take back to her."

"You're not thinking of putting any of this in the article you're going to write?"

"Oh, no. Of course not."

She reached quickly for her straw handbag.

"Well, it's been altogether lovely chatting with you, Mr. James, but I have to get back to the job."

"May I walk you to your office?"

"No, no," she said, sliding back her chair. "That won't be necessary. You just sit here and finish your coffee."

"I'll send you a clip of whatever I write."

"That's very kind of you, but please don't bother." She lingered only to say, "Do enjoy yourself during your stay in Charleston." Then she was out the door and hurrying along the street.

Although he hadn't learned it from Miss Bucksworth, it turned out to be easy to get the address of the Delasante house. One of the black porters in the hotel lobby told him, providing careful, polite directions. At the mere mention of the Delasante name, the man became extremely deferential.

A.C. set off again down Meeting Street, walking slowly, respectful of the heat, and savoring the experience. This end of the city was indeed an enormous museum. Were the English governors of the eighteenth century to return from the grave, they would be surprised only by the automobiles.

The porter's elaborate directions took him down some cobbled side streets and then along the wrought iron fence of an old, small cemetery. At its end was the large, yellow house the porter had promised. A number of cars were parked along the street in front of it, among them a very old, highly polished Cadillac sedan—its black driver lounging against a front fender, chatting quietly with two others.

A.C. crossed to the other side of the street, pausing to pretend to study the back of an envelope he took from his pocket, as though it were a tourist's map or guide. The house, set close to the sidewalk behind an iron fence only slightly more ornate than the cemetery's, was fronted by four white columns. A balcony ran along the second floor just behind them. In Charleston style, the house's verandah was at the side, running back to the garden.

The verandah was exactly as it had looked in the photograph on Camilla's mantel. Even the furniture seemed to be in the same place. All that was missing was the people.

Moving quickly, he recrossed the street and stood at the Delasantes' fence. There was movement back in the garden, bright color glimpsed through the distant trellis and adjoining hedges, summer dresses and picture hats, a garden party.

A sudden sound, the opening of a screen door, startled him. He looked up to see a tall woman come out onto the verandah. She wore white gloves and matching hat and a blue and white polka-dotted dress. She paused, and looked at him, with both curiosity and disdain. Her face was fuller than Camilla's, but bore much resemblance. The wide, blue-gray eyes were the same.

"Good morning," A.C. said, with much courtesy.

He might as well have called her a nasty name. She descended the steps quickly and hurried on toward the garden.

A.C. moved on. At the next corner, he turned to study the parked cars from the safety of his distance. None looked like Camilla's.

If he was going to talk to Mrs. Delasante, it would have to be after her guests had gone. He continued walking, heading toward the old Customs House and the Cooper River, following its shore down to the Battery that curved around the point at the end of the Charleston peninsula. High stone steps led to its wide walkway. He felt a slight breeze against his face when he reached the top.

The remains of Fort Sumter were a flat, dark silhouette on the watery horizon at the distant mouth of Charleston harbor. Antique cannon arrayed both along the Battery wall and back among the trees of the adjoining park were still aimed at it, as though the pummeled old installation continued to pose some threat. The barrels of the long guns were stopped with concrete, and most were a century or more old, yet there was something very menacing and powerful about them.

Camilla's ancestors had stood on these ramparts. They had gone north and killed and died. They had lost slavery, but their ancient society had indeed survived, its vestiges manifest in that garden party at the Delasante house.

A.C. moved on. There were many tourists walking about the Battery. One elderly couple asked for directions he could not give. A man and wife with two small, pretty daughters asked him to take their picture for them. He did so, returning the camera with a polite smile, then descended into the park and walked sadly back through the old streets, wishing Camilla had stayed in New York—wishing that he had stayed there.

He'd go back to the hotel. He'd leave it to his detective friend to decide what to do next.

Lanham did not return until evening. He found A.C.

346

out on the second-floor terrace near the pool, where he had gone to have a drink after a nap.

"I could use a beer," the detective said. He looked tired.

A.C. pointed to a telephone mounted on the hotel's exterior wall. "You have to call Room Service. They'll bring it out here."

Lanham did so, then seated himself heavily, stretching out his long legs.

"Where did you go?" A.C. asked.

"Well, I started out at a church."

"Church?"

"The Huguenot church around the corner," Lanham said, pronouncing the French word correctly. "Very historic. The original church on that site was built in 1681. I looked up the Delasantes in the old books they have there. There weren't any, but that other name you told me? Beaugerard? The mother's maiden name? And the Dutarques? There were a lot of those. All the way back to the beginning."

A.C. imagined one of the elderly ladies of the local historical society, in floral print dress and white gloves, playing guide to the New York cop's tourist. He supposed she had been polite, perhaps even pleased at a stranger's curiosity in what they all held so dear—even if the stranger was black.

"Then I went looking at the flowers."

"Flowers?"

"They've got some pretty good gardeners down here. I don't think there's anyone in this town who couldn't win first at the New York Flower Show just by potting something from the yard."

"They'd probably think the New York Flower Show beneath them."

"Then I got arrested."

"For what?"

"For looking at flowers. I thought it was a little park, but I was in someone's private garden. I didn't know. There was no fence or anything. Anyway, someone in the house called the law, and one of them made a stop on me."

"You mean you were handcuffed and all that?"

Lanham shook his head. "I was going to see them anyway. We went for a ride down to the station house, and that's all that came of it, except for some interesting conversation. Did you know this town has a black police chief?"

The police chief was a public servant. All the servants in Charleston seemed to be black.

The room service waiter, an old black man in a white jacket, came out onto the terrace bearing Lanham's beer on a silver tray. Before he left, A.C. ordered another gin and tonic.

Lanham used the cocktail napkin to wipe the foam from his lips after taking a thirsty pull of his beer.

"Mr. Delasante, the old man, died under unexplained circumstances," Lanham said, setting down his glass. "Maybe murder. It was seven years ago, but they still have the case file. He made it back to his house before expiring from a stomach wound. The family said he'd had an accident, but some of the local coppers say they don't believe that because there wasn't any blood on the premises or anything. He got knifed in the gut. Some say he'd been seen down in the black end of town earlier that night, that he got in trouble down there and someone stuck him. The word was that somebody from the family came and got the body so there'd be no talk. But there was no proof of that, no witnesses. No one wanted to pursue it much. At least the mother didn't. So they called it accidental and left it at that."

"I heard much the same thing today, from the editor of one of the local society magazines."

Lanham drank again. His glass was half empty. He refilled it from the bottle.

"There was another daughter, the youngest child," he said. "Danielle. As good looking as your lady love except she had dark hair."

"I saw her in one of the photographs."

"She blew her brains out a few weeks after the old man got whacked. This is not what you'd call a happy family."

"The police told you all this?"

"Most of it. I spent a little time in a couple of shanty bars down in what passes for the ghetto hereabouts. Unlike

348

New York, everybody seems to know everything that goes on around here. They just don't like to talk about it much."

"But they talked to you."

"Yeah. You know, brothers."

The old waiter came with A.C.'s drink. Lanham ordered another beer.

"The feds are here," he said.

"In the hotel?"

Lanham shrugged. "The local coppers know about them. And I saw a couple of white faces come driving by when I was down among the darkies."

"Are they after Pierre?"

"I don't think they know what they're after."

"I found the Delasante house," A.C. said. "I saw the mother."

"Any sign of Camilla and her brother?"

A.C. shook his head. "I went by twice. They were having a garden party."

"No out-of-state cars, anything like that?"

"No. It was just what you'd expect. A typical garden party."

"I've never been to one."

The weary waiter came with Lanham's beer. A.C. signed the check, giving the man a generous tip.

"We'll go there tonight," Lanham said.

•

The streets were amply lit, in an antique way—the house and building fronts illuminated by yellow lamps, the streets themselves blue from tall lights whose tops reached into the hanging branches of the old, leafy trees. This was a city of ghosts—the shades of sea captains, slave girls, old soldiers, unhappy travelers, abandoned wives, and even John C. Calhoun—their fables and legends famous up and down the Carolina coast. With the windows of the car down, A.C. and Lanham could hear dogs barking randomly from yards distant and near, and a few birds still calling to the night. The air had cooled somewhat, converting the humidity to a fine mist. A.C. turned the Buick's radio on and Lanham just as quickly turned it off.

349

"Save that for your room," he said. "We want to hear, and we don't want to be heard."

They prowled down Meeting Street, rolling quietly by the big cemetery next to St. Philip's Church, then turned left and followed the zigzag of one-way streets that took them past the Delasante house.

It looked even larger in the night, its windows lighted at the front and along the upper floors. They saw no one inside as they went by. A large, dark American car of recent vintage was parked by the main gate. It bore South Carolina plates.

"We'll go by again," said Lanham.

A.C. nodded, gathering a little speed. "Do you think the father's death is in some way involved with what's been happening?" he asked. "I've been trying to figure it out all afternoon. Could Pierre have been threatening to tell the truth?"

"What? That the old man was shacking up with a black girl? As many people seem to know about that as know the South lost the war, and it hasn't hurt the mother any. She still seems to be the principal deity around these parts."

"What if he wasn't killed by some black man, by his girlfriend's husband or boyfriend? What if he was killed by his son Jacques? And Pierre just found out about it?"

Lanham stared out the windshield a moment. "I suppose that's a possibility."

"But then why would a man kill his own father like that?"

"Why would he kill some poor girl he didn't even know?"

Because of the pattern of one-way streets, they had to go around several blocks. On the second pass, the Delasante house seemed much the same, but they saw a woman through a window of the front parlor, standing by a fireplace.

"Camilla?" A.C. asked.

"No. I think it's the mother."

A.C. drove on. "Shall I go around again?"

"Go the other way. I want to go down the street behind it."

The cemetery next to the Delasante house ran all the way across the block. They cruised slowly along its rear fence.

"There's an alley there," Lanham said.

"Are you sure that's not a driveway?"

"No. It's an alley. Stop. Kill the lights."

A.C. did so, then backed up slowly. It was an alley, but it was not clear where it came out. A.C. headed into it cautiously. The little roadway was narrow and made a sharp turn to the right, proceeding between high walls. There were two cars parked farther on, pulled up tight against the wall to the left and leaving barely enough room for passage. A.C. inched along past the first, then froze. The second car was a small red convertible, bearing Virginia plates.

"She's here," he said.

"Son of a bitch. Okay, get out of here."

"I'll have to back up. It's a dead end."

"Do it."

"Without lights?"

"Do it."

A.C. swore quietly, then slipped the gear into reverse and slowly began to roll backward, his head out the window.

He managed to avoid the other parked car, but his right rear fender or bumper caught the wall opposite twice, the scraping sound terrifyingly loud.

"Keep going. Get out of here."

Once past the obstacle, he had an easier time of it, though he had to go forward and back twice to get around the sharp turn. Once in the street, he ground the Buick into forward and sped two blocks before turning on his lights again.

"Park here," Lanham said. "We'll go back on foot."

The cemetery's iron fence was easy to scale. A.C. went first, with Lanham standing lookout, then A.C. watched the street as Lanham went over, dropping to the grassy earth with a soft thump. They quickly stepped into the shadows.

The street lamp was flickering, making the shadows seem to move. Half a moon hung in the sky to the northeast, but the graveyard was quite dark beneath the trees.

"I wonder if the father is buried in here," A.C. said.

"I doubt it. They had him cremated."

Lanham led the way, falling into old army habits, moving silently. A.C. followed as carefully as possible, but banged

351

his knee once. He had lost count of the injuries he had suffered, large and small, since first meeting Camilla.

The Delasante house looked immense when viewed from the side. The lights on the ground floor had just been turned off, except for a dim interior glow at the center. All the windows above were lighted. Lanham took them as close to the Delasante property as possible, crouching behind a large crypt, then slipping around to the other side and easing himself to the ground. A.C. did the same.

It was a good choice of place. They were only a few feet from the cemetery's side fence, had the large crypt to lean back against, and had a good view of the entire house. A smaller tomb in front of them kept them in shadow.

"I hear voices," Lanham whispered. "Upstairs."

"I don't."

"Shhhhh. Listen."

Finally, sorting out the night sounds, A.C. heard them, too, but he couldn't discern any words. The conversation was between two women. His heartbeat increased when he realized that one of them must be Camilla.

"Can we move closer?" he said.

"Quiet."

Lights went out in one room, and then another. Two windows stayed bright, the ceiling and a glimpse of the interior visible behind thin curtains. A door slammed. A figure moved past one of the windows. It was a woman, possibly Camilla, possibly her mother. She passed by again. Then the lights went out.

Minutes passed, a few, then many. The stone of the crypt was cold against their backs. A.C. leaned forward, but Lanham kept his place.

A.C. held out his arm in the shaded moonlight, but could not quite make out the time on his watch. Small events marked its passing—a barking dog, a car hurrying along the street to their left, someone coughing loudly in a house nearby.

There was a loud, sudden sound, a door banging. A.C. looked up to the dark, open window above. The lights went on. He could hear the words now, coming in a torrent.

"Go back to bed, Momma! You won't change my mind."

"I won't let you go!"

"You have no choice! I've got to do it, Momma. I've got to end this!"

"Leave it to Jacques."

"Leave it to Jacques? Are you forgetting all he's done? The way his mind is torn up with this, it wouldn't surprise me if he tried to kill all the people on Tawabaw now! I've feared for my own life these past few days."

"He wouldn't harm a hair on your head, Camilla."

"Wouldn't he? There's a man up north, the nicest man I've ever met. Jacques knows how I feel about him, and I think I love him, Momma. Jacques beat him, brutally, and then he tried to kill him. If I hadn't kept him from following me down here, he'd probably be dead right now!"

"What man? I know nothing about him."

"And you won't, either."

"Camilla! What about your husband!"

"Don't talk to me about husbands, Momma! Not you!"

There was sobbing now. It wasn't Camilla.

Lanham was hunched forward, as intent as a night animal in the midst of a prowl. A.C. was stunned, and terribly confused.

"You can't change anything, Momma. We've got to see this through. There's no other way. You made a big mistake, and I've got to fix it. There's no one else."

"It's too late."

"No it isn't. Pierre's got everything hidden someplace on Hilton Head or at Tawabaw. He's going for it. That's all he has left, and Jacques is after him like a hound on a hunt. I'll find them, Momma. I know every place they'll go."

"You've already done so much, darlin'."

"I should have done a lot more. You go back to bed now, Momma. I'll call you from Savannah."

The older woman was crying again.

"Go to bed, Momma. I'll take care of everything."

Those were the last words. A.C. and Lanham waited for more. The night continued as though this were a normal house in a normal time—as though they were not even there.

Finally, Lanham rose on his haunches and leaned near.

"Let's get back to the car," he said quietly. "We'll park back by that street there and wait for her to come out of the alley."

"She said something about Savannah."

"And Hilton Head and some other place. We'll follow her, and this time we won't lose her."

After they'd made their way out of the cemetery and retrieved the Buick, they drove to near the entrance of the alley and turned off the engine, slumping down in their seats.

"Sounds like you made quite a conquest there, sport," Lanham said.

"Shut up, Ray."

Nothing stirred in the street. Nothing moved from the alley.

"In a way, I think I could get used to this town," Lanham said after several minutes.

"And be a policeman here?"

"Something. It's a real pretty town."

"She's certainly taking her time."

"Probably getting her beauty sleep. She'll be out of here first thing in the morning."

They talked, mostly about the South, then took turns dozing. The sky lightened, and then became inflamed with the sun, which went from red to yellow to white, climbing higher. Traffic began using the street.

Lanham sighed. "I think we'd better make sure she's there. Should have done that a long time ago."

"Go back in the cemetery?"

"No. The alley. You go. Better a white man back there at this hour."

A.C. pretended to be a stroller, a man out for a morning walk, taking a short cut. Whistling, he turned the corner of the alley.

The first car was still there, dew glistening on its windshield. The small red car was gone.

CHAPTER

....

17

Savannah was Charleston with sin. It had been founded a
half century after the Carolina city just up the coast, but
seemed much older and wearier, not to speak of wiser.
Charleston had been preserved and prettified, made garden-
club perfect. Savannah hadn't been preserved. It had simply
never changed. Sitting on a bench in one of its many ancient,
tree-sheltered squares on a hot, still afternoon, a visitor felt
time running backward to a century or more ago. And on
hot summer nights, with every street menacing and mysterious and swathed in steamy gloom, there was a sense of
lurking cutthroats and footpads, ghostly and real. Crime
thrived in the heat of this river town like some night garden
bloom. Every solitary figure glimpsed or heard in the shadows of the sidewalk was worrisome, carrying the prospect
of violent, sudden harm.

There were fine ladies in Savannah, in picture hats and
white gloves and floral dresses. But there were women of

a seamier sort as well, hookers in the sailors' bars, Southern girls with daring makeup and mischief in their eyes, strolling along the storefronts of Bay Street on the bluff above the Savannah River. Hard-hearted Hannah, the siren of the old saloon song, would have been run out of Charleston. Here she was queen.

On the drive down, A.C. and Lanham had had an irreconcilable disagreement. The detective wanted to go directly to Pierre Delasante's condominium on Hilton Head, convinced that was where the man and those pursuing him were headed. A.C. could keep in mind only that Camilla had promised to call her mother from Savannah. A.C. had been to Hilton Head several times on spring vacations with his family. Lanham had never been to that man-made island paradise, but was bent on going, convinced it held all his answers. A.C. had different questions.

They had checked into Savannah's Hyatt Regency on the riverfront, taking two rooms. After they had refreshed their once again depleted wardrobes, Lanham left with the Buick, crossing over the Boundary Street Bridge back into Carolina to follow the back roads that led the few miles to the Hilton Head Island causeway—to return or telephone as soon as practicable. A.C. had remained behind, groggy from his lack of sleep but willing enough for the grinding work of tracking Camilla down.

He telephoned hotels and motels throughout the town, then, in frustration, set out on a wander from one to the other, showing desk clerks his model's picture of Camilla and concocting some vaguely plausible story of a runaway wife. None admitted to seeing her. There were no Delasantes or Santees in the phone book, but he found the name of her mother's ancient family—Dutarques.

The listing was for a Juliette Dutarques. An old voice full of apprehension and frailty answered after many rings. She was helpful, however. She politely informed him that Camilla had not yet arrived, but was expected that evening. He had probably stumbled upon Camilla's only relative in Savannah, an aunt perhaps, or an elderly cousin.

He walked over late in the afternoon, finding that the address was an old yellow-brown house with front galleries and two entrance columns set near the street opposite one of the old squares. There was no alley or driveway. There were two dusty, salt-stained sedans parked at the front—both very old and both bearing Georgia plates.

Returning to the hotel, A.C. took time for an hour's sleep, a cool shower, a change of clothes, and a quick dinner in the hotel coffee shop. He left a message for Lanham, from whom he'd heard no word, and then set out once more, feeling refreshed and alert, surprised to find the sun leaving the sky as he stepped outside.

He walked slowly through the heat, pondering his next move should fate and the Delasantes once again disappoint him, but he saw Camilla's red car as soon as he turned the corner of the square. He stood motionless, startled, then eased behind a flowery bush.

A few lights were already on in the house, glowing a warm yellow in the hazy dusk. He had a brief impulse to run and bang on the door and force his way in no matter who answered, confronting Camilla wherever he might find her in the house. Their mistake in letting Camilla slip away during the few minutes it had taken to retrieve their car the night before still stung him.

But he remembered well her words to her mother. She had come here not in flight but in search. She was in pursuit of her brother and Pierre Delasante, and so were A.C. and Lanham. They were all seeking the same thing. Camilla's advantage was that she knew what it was.

There were four benches in the square, each facing toward the center. He took a seat on the nearest, turning to keep the red convertible under observation. If she came out of the house, he could get to it as quickly as she could.

But nothing happened in the house. No one, familiar or unknown, came along the street. Night fully descended, draping the square in a soft darkness.

Lanham might well have called. He could be back at the hotel. He might have found something.

A.C. rose and walked quietly across the street, mounting the steps of the house as might a friendly caller. To the right of the front door were the windows of a formal living room. No one was in it. To the left was a more comfortable-looking sitting room. He edged toward the nearest of its windows, hearing the familiar fuzzy sound of a television

357

set. Its screen glowed brightly behind the curtain. He could see an old woman in a chair very close to it.

He rang the doorbell twice, then stepped back. She was a fair time coming.

The woman peered at him over the tops of a pair of half-glasses. "Yes?"

"Good evening," he said. "I telephoned earlier, for Camilla. I was hoping to meet her here."

"Oh yes. Yes. I told her you had called, but you failed to leave your name."

"A.C. James," he said. "I'm a friend from New York."

"Yes. How do you do." She hesitated, as though wondering whether to admit him. "Camilla's not here. She went for a walk. I expect her back soon. I expected her back before this." The woman glanced behind her. "I'd invite you in, but . . . Is there a number where she might reach you?"

"Not really. I'm out for a walk myself. I won't be back to my hotel for a while."

The woman began to close the door. "I'll tell her you called on her, Mr. James."

She seemed too confused and unsure to be lying. A.C. moved back from the door. "Thank you very much, Mrs. Dutarques. Good night."

"Oh, it's Miss Dutarques."

"Yes. Well, thank you. Good night."

He walked down the street a way, in case the old woman had lingered at her door to watch him, then returned to the square and his bench. His view included the sitting room window. He saw the woman go back to the television set.

It was only a few minutes afterward that he heard the sound of high heels coming along the street. She was walking quickly, her blond hair bouncing slightly in the air behind her, catching the light from the streetlamp.

A.C.'s white buck shoes had rubber soles. Making little sound, he slipped from his bench and circled around a bush to get behind her. He could simply speak her name, or do something more forceful. His automatic was again at his back in his belt.

She was almost to the gate of the house. A.C. took a few bounding steps and grabbed her by both arms. She strug-

358

gled, but did not scream. She wrenched one arm free and then whirled around to face him. Her recognition was instant but her expression didn't change. It was a mixture of fear and defiance, and a touch of something gentler.

"I have a gun, Camilla."

"You don't need that, A.C.," she said.

"Why? Because you don't have a shotgun aimed at me?"

"Let go of me."

"I only want to talk. I'm not going to do anything to you."

She was trembling. "All right," she said unhappily.

"Let's sit in the square."

She glanced about warily, then nodded. Holding her arm at the elbow, he led her across the street to the bench. She sat at some distance from him, facing away, across the square. He sat sideways, watching her every small movement.

"Why did you come to Savannah?" he asked.

"You must know if you're here. I'm looking for Pierre and my brother."

"Why?"

"I'm going to stop the killings."

"How do you intend to do that?"

She bowed her head. Her hands clenched into fists on her knees. She was fighting some impulse.

"What do you want of me, A.C.?" she said. "Why did you come down here after me? Why can't you leave me alone?"

"One of those people killed in New York was a friend, a very dear friend."

She looked puzzled.

"Her name was Bailey Hazeltine. An old friend. She was killed in my apartment. By your brother. He was waiting for me and killed her. The police have a photograph."

"The police? Are they with you?"

"Only Detective Lanham."

"Where is he?"

"I'm not sure. Not far."

She looked at him closely now, her eyes more as he remembered them so well from Bermuda. They glistened in the dim light.

359

"Please go away, A.C. Go on back home, and let me do what I have to."

"I'm doing what I have to. Lanham means to take your brother back with him."

"It's much too late for that."

He took her hand, holding it softly, remembering her words of the previous night to her mother. She did not resist. After a moment, he felt a responding pressure from her fingers.

"What is this all about, Camilla? What does your brother want from Pierre? What has Pierre been doing to you?"

"That's something you can never know. It's a *family* matter." There could be nothing more serious or sacrosanct for someone from Charleston, South Carolina, than family.

"Pierre is a swine. Your brother is a maniac, a murderer. Why are you protecting them? Just because they're family?"

"Pierre's not family. Not blood!"

It was something she had not meant to say.

"He's your cousin."

"No he's not. He's my brother's cousin, not mine. I'd kill myself if I had such vile blood in me."

He pulled her to him. She came stiffly, but let herself be enveloped by his arm.

"I'm your friend, Camilla. More than that. Trust me. I want to help you. That's all I've ever wanted to do since this started."

She hesitated, then turned toward him.

"Whatever happens, you should know this," she said. "Pierre is not my cousin. My brother is only my half brother."

"But you're a Delasante."

"I have a different father."

"I didn't realize your mother was married before."

"She wasn't."

"I don't understand."

"I'm a bastard, A.C. Illegitimate. *Illégitime.* The man who is my father is not the man my mother was married to when I was born. Not Robert Delasante."

"Does this have anything to do with all these murders?"

Silence.

360

"I won't tell anyone, Camilla. I wouldn't."

Her voice took a hard Southern edge. "It's been common knowledge in Charleston for years that I'm illegitimate. Under the circumstances, I am quite proud of the fact."

A car drove slowly by behind them, an almost sleepy sound.

"Robert Delasante," she continued, "the man my mother married, the father of my brother and my poor darling sister, was a most despicable man, A.C. He was a drunkard, a philanderer, a thief who stole from his own kin. He was a brutal man, who used to beat us all when he could. If you think Pierre is scum, you should have met Robert Delasante. He was a pillar of the community, but if someone else hadn't killed him, I probably would have done it. And I hate him as much dead as I did living."

"He's been dead a long time."

"He was a liar. He had no honor. He lied to my poor mother in the most despicable, horrible way. And his lies have lived on after him."

"And your real father?"

"He's dead now, too. He died last year. He was a lovely man, the man my mother should have married. But he had very little when they met, and he was from off."

"Off?"

"He wasn't from Charleston. He was a Northerner originally. From Louisville. The Delasantes were Carolina."

"I don't understand."

"How could you? You're a New Yorker."

He leaned forward, turning sideways to see her better. In so doing, he caught the movement—two men in dark suits running toward them down the sidewalk. The larger trailed behind; the smaller was carrying something in his hand, something metal. A gun? A knife? A badge?

A.C. stood up, pulling Camilla up, getting her behind him. The small man was moving very efficiently, coming directly for them, despite the barrier of the bench. He had decided exactly what he was going to do. A.C. saw the knife clearly as the man made his leap, his foot reaching the top of the bench and springing him forward.

Shoving Camilla aside, A.C. took a step back, then hurled himself toward the small attacker, in his fear and

361

fury swinging his leg up high in a brutal kick that caught the man in the groin.

They both went sprawling, the man crying out and swearing obscenely as he hit the ground on his shoulder and rolled. A.C., lying on his side, got to his knees.

The larger man had hold of Camilla, his arms wrapped around her; she was kicking at him with her heels, accomplishing little. Still she did not scream, as though this were a family quarrel and she didn't want the neighbors to hear. The smaller man, in pain, was attempting to rise. He still held the knife. The larger was the one who had been cut up by the glass from the chandelier at the Virginia farmhouse, which explained why he had chosen to take on Camilla.

A.C. moved toward the other, his ankle strangely numb. He tried to kick the man again but his foot didn't work right. The man caught it and twisted, the knife blade scraping A.C.'s shin. Wobbling, A.C. pulled back and then came down hard with his other foot on the man's neck. He tried for the head, like squashing an insect, but missed.

It didn't matter. The knife dropped. The man, coughing and burbling, clutched at his throat.

His partner was dragging Camilla away. A.C., hobbling, came after them, pulling out his pistol. Startled by the action, the large man took his hand away from Camilla's waist, as though to reach within his own coat. She turned, clawing at his face. He clutched at her hair, but she got free, ducking under his arm.

"Run, Camilla!" A.C. shouted.

She did. The man, deciding between her and A.C., lunged after her. A.C. stopped and raised the gun. He had a clear shot at the man's back, or did he? Camilla was just ahead, her heels clattering as she ran.

Bailey dead, because of him. Not Camilla, too.

The man on the ground behind him had stopped his horrible sounds. A.C. looked back and saw that he was moving, trying to get up. Camilla and the heavy man were drawing away, crossing the street diagonally, toward where Camilla's red car was parked. She was perhaps ten feet ahead, but he was gaining.

362

A.C. fought his indecision. He'd have to catch up with them, or shoot.

There was the roar of an engine off to his right, and then a bright flare of light as a motorcycle with its headlamp blazing swung around the corner of the square. A.C. thought it must be the police, but it wasn't. There were no markings. The driver was only a silhouette as he flashed past, something in his hand.

The driver steered deliberately toward the man chasing Camilla, accelerating. A.C. saw the man stop and turn, saw the swarthy frightened face, two arms flung up.

Camilla's pursuer fell over backward as the motorcycle came by. The cyclist sped on, braking only for an instant to make the approaching corner. Then he gunned the engine again and continued around the square.

Camilla was facing A.C., her hands at her face. She studied the lumpy mound that had been her attacker for a fleeting moment, gave A.C. one quick last look, then was at her car.

A.C. called her name. The car door slammed. The engine growled into life. The headlights flashed on as she pulled away from the curb. A.C. stood helpless as he followed the car's swift progress around the square, watching as she disappeared into the darkness to the west, her car chasing the echoes of the motorcycle.

The man in the street remained a motionless heap. A.C. went up to him and saw that he had been shot, the sound of the gun drowned out by the noise of the motorcycle engine. He turned back and saw that the smaller man had staggered to his feet, the knife gripped clumsily in his hand. He had no pistol. He no longer posed a threat and knew it. Dragging his leg slightly, he was trying to get away.

Several lights had come on in nearby houses. Whether this signified that someone had summoned the police, or that people had simply been disturbed by the speeding vehicles, A.C. could not tell.

The man with the knife had tried to kill him. If he got away, it might be to find comrades. A.C. had to stop him. He told himself this just as his colonel had told him the infiltrator had to be stopped that long-ago cold afternoon in Korea. After that shooting, A.C. had sworn never to kill any living creature again.

But the man could not be allowed to escape. A.C. remembered his time in Northern Ireland, recalled how the IRA Provos used to discipline their own.

Taking a deep breath, he walked quickly up to the man and as calmly as possible fired a single shot from the .357 Magnum into his right knee. He went down like a bridge collapsing, and began to scream.

Hobbling down a side street, A.C. looked back just once to see lights going on all over the square. Now the police would come. They would find themselves preoccupied for some time.

A.C. entered his hotel at the lower, riverfront level to avoid having to walk through the lobby. He was limping badly from a sprain and his shin was bleeding through his white pants from the scrape of the knife.

He got to his room without anyone noticing him or his injuries, then soaked his ankle in ice-cold water run into the tub, washing the abrasion with soap. Drying off, he poured Listerine over the ragged skin, then wrapped it with a clean handkerchief as a bandage. Then he changed clothes yet again.

While he waited for Lanham, he had a long, slow but very strong drink, using the time to study the street map of Savannah he had bought.

On the reverse side was a map of the overall metropolitan area, showing a section of the Carolina coast to the north. He was familiar with those coastal waters. He had sailed in them on vacation.

It was nearly one A.M. when Lanham finally knocked on the door. He looked very hot and tired, and a little surprised. A.C. was sitting with his leg propped up on a table. His ankle bulged.

"Something happen to you?"

"A lot. I found Camilla, and then Perotta's men found us. One of them's dead. The other's wounded. I shot him through the leg."

"You killed a guy?"

"No. Make yourself a drink while I explain it to you."

He told Lanham everything in great detail, leaving out

only Camilla's revelations about her family and the circumstances of her birth.

"You let her get away again," Lanham said, when A.C. had finished.

"I had no choice, Ray."

Lanham rubbed his face. "Maybe you didn't. If you'd tried to stop her, that fucking brother of hers probably would have come back and blown your head off. I'm surprised he didn't do it anyway."

"What did you find on Hilton Head?"

Lanham shook his head. "Not a hell of a lot. I had trouble getting in to Sea Pines Plantation, where Pierre's condo is. I had to lift a windshield card from a parked car to get through the gate. Pierre wasn't there. His condo was locked tight and there was mail in the mailbox. The maid said he hasn't been there for weeks. The feds are there, though. I don't know what Pierre was privy to in the White House, but they must think he's got real potential as a turncoat. I spotted a couple of agents in a car in the condo's parking lot. And there was a guy at the pool who didn't look like he was on much of a vacation."

"Where in hell can Pierre be?"

"The computer printout said he had a boat moored at Hilton Head but I couldn't find it. I looked all over the marina. The kid in the harbormaster's office there didn't know anything."

"What kind of boat?"

"Some sort of cabin cruiser. Probably a seagoing version of his limo."

"You said the harbor master's office. Which harbor did you go to?"

"The one down the road from his condo. It's on the southern tip of the island."

"There's more than one yacht harbor in Sea Pines. The one you went to is for shallow-draft boats. The channel snakes up a creek and it's impassable at low tide. If Pierre has a big cruiser, he'd likely keep it up Calibogue Sound a ways at Harbour Town. It's a deep-water marina."

"Is there any of these rich man's playgrounds you haven't been to?"

"I've never been to Campobello. But I've sailed in Calibogue Sound before. That's the stretch of water between Hilton Head and the mainland. I was just potting around in a day sailor and I never paid any attention to the names of the other coastal islands. But look what I've found now."

He pulled his map up on the table between them, spreading flat the folds.

"When she was talking to her mother, Camilla mentioned three places; Savannah, Hilton Head, and someplace called Tawabaw. I've found Tawabaw."

Lanham wiped off his glasses with his handkerchief and leaned over the map, looking like a scientist studying some specimen.

"Hilton Head isn't very far from here," A.C. said. "Not by water. See." He pointed to the mouth of the Savannah River. "This bit of headland here is Tybee Island. Across the river mouth from it is Daufuskie Island. Across the Calibogue Sound channel from Daufuskie is the south end of Hilton Head—Sea Pines Plantation."

Lanham nodded. A.C. pushed the map closer.

"This little island here," A.C. said, "just off the coast of Daufuskie? That's Tawabaw Island."

"Is there a bridge to it?"

"Probably. It's a narrow enough channel. But Pierre has a boat."

Lanham looked at him quizzically.

"I think we should rent ourselves a boat," A.C. said.

CHAPTER

18

In the morning, they took an early breakfast, using the time at the table to go through both the local and the Charleston newspapers. There were stories about the incident in both, the longer article in the Savannah paper, under the headline GANG-STYLE SHOOTING IN OLD SAVANNAH. The account was sketchy, attributing the violence to drug trafficking—the official police surmise. The dead man had not been identified. The man A.C. had shot was refusing to talk.

The injured man was in the local hospital. There was a vague reference to the Drug Enforcement Administration having been called into the investigation of the shooting.

"Do you think they'll leave us alone now?" A.C. asked, sipping some of the excellent coffee.

"Mr. Perotta has more than two employees."

"But they won't keep on after Pierre, will they? You said there were federal agents around his place. They wouldn't risk running into them, would they?"

Lanham shrugged. "Somebody was given a job to do, and it didn't get done. The penalties for failure in their line of work are considerable. Vince's honor is still bent out of shape. Every wiseguy in New York is probably trying to get a copy of that videotape. They must be laughing their asses off—Vince getting cuckolded for all to see in a cheap skin flick."

He finished his coffee, declining more when the waiter quickly appeared at his side.

"I'm more worried about the brother," he said. "He knows we're here now."

"Are you going to call your department's mob crimes unit? Tell them what's happened?"

"I don't think so. They're frying their own fish. The two jerkoffs you tangled with last night—I doubt they're the perps who whacked Belinda and the others anyway. Those guys did their jobs. They're probably in Vegas by now, spending their hard-earned pay. Unless Vince has covered his ass by sending them into early retirement. In which case, the mob crimes boys are going to have to use up a lot of shovels finding them."

He pushed back his chair. "Come on, A.C. Let's get this boat trip over with."

They stopped to buy some sailing clothes and change into them, hoping to look a little less conspicuous, then headed for the docks, making three stops before they found a marine service operator who was willing to rent them a boat.

He offered them a twenty-three-foot O'Day sailing cruiser, with a small cabin and outboard engine, which they took for a week's charter with a $500 deposit. The manager required A.C. to demonstrate his seamanship with a brief run across the river and back, and was sufficiently impressed to let them go without further question.

When they were at last on their own, chugging downriver, Lanham came aft and took a seat in the cockpit opposite A.C.

"Was all that crap because of me?" he asked.

"No. A lot of people say they can sail when they can't. It's not like renting a car."

"I can't sail."

"I'll teach you a little something. Make you earn your

368

passage. For starters, when we get out into open water, I'd like you to work the jib sheets. They're those ropes that lead back from the forward sail. When we change tack, the jib has to be pulled from one side to the other, and then you'll have to cleat the sheet to hold it tight."

"I don't have the faintest goddamn idea what you're talking about."

"You will. You'll get lots of practice. The wind's out of the northeast, in the general direction we'll be heading. We'll have to tack our way up."

Lanham looked at him balefully.

"Tack."

"Tack."

They passed the old remnants of Fort Pulaski on the right, crossing the channel of the Intracoastal Waterway. There was some traffic in it, mostly powerboats.

"Where are they all going?"

"North. That's the Intracoastal, a sheltered boat highway that runs all along the coast."

"Does it go anywhere near where we're going?"

A.C. looked at the chart on his knee. "Yes. It runs behind Daufuskie and comes out in Calibogue Sound."

"Why don't we take it?"

"It's the long way around. We'd have to run on the engine all the way down the side of Daufuskie to get to Tawabaw. And I don't want to use up all our gas."

Lanham accepted this glumly.

"Don't worry," A.C. said. "We won't be in the open sea long."

The wind began brisking up before they were even clear of the river. Leaving Lanham to hold the tiller steady, A.C. killed the motor and went forward to hoist the sails. After both were in place, he clambered back to the steering.

"Hold on," he said, steering off the wind.

Pulling and cleating, he drew the boom back until the boat was sailing close-hauled and heeling over at a sharp angle, the running foam coming close to the rail.

"The wind's a good fifteen knots," he said. "We'll make good time."

Lanham clutched the woodwork tightly.

"You do this for fun?"

"It gets a lot more fun than this."

"Shit."

A.C. missed his son. He'd find a way someday to have Davey sail a boat with him again. He could see him aboard right then, showing Lanham how to work a jib.

Lanham would like him. Davey was a very brave boy.

"You're heading straight out to sea," Lanham said, as calmly as he could manage.

"Don't worry. We have to sail forty-five degrees off the wind. The further out we go, the less we'll have to tack."

The water was choppy, the bow tossing up spray at every wave. The wind had blown all heat out of the air. They seemed at a far remove from the sultry Savannah square where he had last looked upon Camilla's face.

She had said she loved him, had told her mother that. But she hadn't said it to him. What would he do if she ever did? What could he do?

Husband. Camilla was married. It had angered him terribly to hear that, but by what right?

"What are all those boats out there?" said Lanham, freeing one arm to point off the port bow.

"Fishing boats, most of them," A.C. said, speaking above the wind. "This is a big area for deep sea fishing."

"Rich guys?"

"A lot of them. Some are just fishermen making a living."

"Look at them all."

A.C. did, his gaze traveling the hazy horizon. They could have been an armada of warships, they were so many.

"I wonder if there are any drug runners out there."

"Could be. Nowadays you never know."

"So much coastline. So many boats. It's no wonder nobody can stop them."

A.C. nodded, letting out the mainsheet a little to allow for a sudden strong puff of wind.

The flat green sliver of land to their left that the chart said was Tawabaw Island was visible now directly abeam. A.C. made the boat fall off a little farther, evening their heel.

"I'm going to come about now," he said. "Here's what I want you to do."

He showed Lanham the procedure, then retook the helm. "Ready about!" he shouted. He gathered in the main sheet, pointing the bow up, then shoved the tiller away from him.

The O'Day spun, the boom slapping smartly into place to port. Lanham was too slow on the jib sheet, and it flapped wildly for a moment until he finally brought it under control.

"Not too bad," A.C. said.

Lanham grinned. "It was fucking terrible."

"We didn't capsize."

The island was flat and covered with trees. As they approached, moving fast on a beam reach, a thin line of brown appeared beneath the trees, widening and becoming yellow in color as they came yet nearer.

Sailing parallel to the shoreline, they could see a few gray buildings between the trees and undergrowth. A glimpse of red proved to be the body of a pickup truck, though for a moment A.C.'s heart leapt with the hope that it might be Camilla's car.

"Can't we get closer?" Lanham asked.

A.C. shook his head. "These are shoal waters. I've bumped the bottom twice already. We don't want to get stuck in the mud."

"Who lives on this island?"

"Mostly Gullahs, I'd guess. Descendants of slaves brought over centuries ago. They have what amounts to their own language."

"I know about them," Lanham said. "I took some black history courses." He smiled, to show it was a joke.

A.C. guessed at the conditions they'd find ashore. Shacks and sheds, unpainted houses, chickens wandering the muddy paths that did for roads. At a clearing in the trees, they saw two figures standing motionless, watching them.

"I can't imagine what interest the Delasantes would have in this place," A.C. said, "unless they owned it."

The sailboat glided on. When they rounded a small headland, they could see surf breaking on the sand. The habitations disappeared in the hanging greenery. Beyond the next point, the larger mass of Daufuskie Island emerged.

371

"I don't think we're going to have to get any closer," A.C. said. "I don't think any of the Delasantes are there."

"Why not?"

"There aren't any boats."

"You said there might be a bridge. There were vehicles on the island."

"Pierre has a boat, and brother Jacques is after Pierre."

"Maybe you're right."

"We'll check out the channel on the other side. There's probably a landing there."

Rounding the point, A.C. threw the boat into a careful gybe, a tricky maneuver involving a turn with the wind aft, in which the suddenly swinging boom almost clipped Lanham's head. Then A.C. headed on a near run down the channel, until the island screened off the wind and the sails began to flap. He started the engine, and in a moment their speed picked up again.

"There are some boats along there," Lanham said, holding onto the boom to keep it from swinging back and forth.

"Rowboats and skiffs. Locals."

There was an old, long dock, with several tired little work boats tied to it. Ahead was a rickety-looking bridge. A.C. slowed the motor, then carefully turned the O'Day, feeling the keel dragging through the muck.

On shore, a number of people had come out to look at them, standing amidst the hanging moss. They all looked to be black people.

"I don't think the Delasantes are here," A.C. said. "Not today."

"Okay," said Lanham, assuming a leadership role again. "We'll come back later."

"You want me to make for Hilton Head?"

"Yes. I want to find Pierre and his goddamn boat."

A.C. increased the little motor's speed, heading back up the channel. Lanham was facing away from him, still looking at the shore.

"Are you in love with her?"

"What?"

"With Camilla Santee?"

"That's a gentleman's own business."

"Fuck the gentleman shit. I want to know how deep your feelings run. I want to know what I can count on from you when we get to where we're going."

"My feelings run deep. Very, very deep."

"I thought so."

"But you can count on me. You can count on me to do anything but hurt Camilla."

"Fair enough. Do you still have that gun?"

"I've got it. I only have about a dozen rounds for it, though. I left the box in the car."

"I have what I used to carry around as an ankle pistol. It's accurate up to about two feet. Let's hope we won't need them."

They caught the breeze from the sound. The jib began flapping, then the mainsail. A.C. remained on the engine, holding course.

"You never told me where your partner was—Detective Petrowicz?"

"He's working other cases."

"They couldn't send anyone else down with you?"

"The trip was my idea."

"You don't want to call in the locals?"

"Do you? You want to explain Camilla to them?"

"No."

They were clear of the channel and in full view of the open waters of Calibogue Sound, the long green mass of Hilton Head on the distant shore. To the north, along its coast, pricking up above the trees, was the tiny, white stick that was the lighthouse at Harbour Town.

"Then let's go see what there is to see," Lanham said. He moved to the starboard jib sheet, awaiting A.C.'s command. A.C. killed the motor, letting the boat fall off and gather speed as the mainsail filled.

"We'll have to tack all the way across," A.C. said.

"Whatever it takes."

•

The channel at Harbour Town was wide and deep. Some very large yachts were tied up at the outer quay. Powerboats and sailcraft of smaller size were crowded along the main wharf. The town had a very artificial look, a children's-book illustration of a seaport. In a sense, the place seemed a foreign country, a far off, isolated land in which the inhabitants wore T-shirts and shorts as a form of native dress. Crowds of people milled and swarmed about the waterfront—a number of children waiting in line to ascend the lighthouse, a tourist attraction that provided a background for snapshots but appeared to serve no real nautical purpose.

With the sails dropped and furled, A.C. putted through the harbor traffic, making a full, slow circuit and carefully reading the names on the sterns of the moored boats. None struck him as significant.

Leaving Lanham at his own request to prowl through the crowd along the dock, A.C. went to the harbormaster's office to acquire a tie-up for the night. He was treated as just another yachtsman, his wealth and business there presumed. He asked after Pierre Delasante casually. The attendant was busy, but took time to quickly glance through a registry book, informing him that Delasante's boat was named *Floride* and that it had not left its slip for weeks.

He found Lanham sitting idly on a bench not far from the *Floride*. A.C. took the place beside him, copying Lanham's slouching posture.

"How did you find his boat?" he asked quietly.

"I didn't," Lanham said. "I found that mope over there in the straw hat with his shirt hanging out. He looks so tired I'll bet he's been out here all day. And I'll bet that lump under his shirt holds eight rounds in a clip."

"The fourth boat down is Delasante's. The *Floride*. The man has a sense of history. That was the name of John C. Calhoun's wife."

"It's big."

"Not so big. No more than fifty feet."

"It's got its own rowboat. I never even owned a rowboat."

"It's called a dinghy. I don't think there's anyone aboard. They told me at the harbormaster's that it hasn't been out in weeks."

"I'd like to look it over. But let's wait awhile."

374

"What can we find that the FBI or whoever hasn't already looked for?"

Lanham shrugged. "We might find something they don't know they're looking for."

"And if we don't find anything?"

A growly sigh preceded Lanham's reply. "A.C., I'm so fucking tired of this case I'd just as soon give it up and go back home right now. I'm really just going through the motions. But I want to go through all the motions, so I can at least tell myself I did everything I could when I ask myself years from now why we never caught the son of a bitch."

A.C. stared down at the gray-green water, watching it rise and fall in oily slopes against the side of the nearest boat.

"You've had lots of unsolved cases."

"This one is special."

The man in the straw hat was watching them, pretending not to.

"Why is Petrowicz working on another case?"

"Because the newspapers are on the mayor's ass and he's turned around and kicked ours. Petrowicz was transferred to another division. Caputo was suspended pending the outcome of the I.A.D investigation into the shooting of Bad Bobby Darcy's girlfriend. My boss, Taranto, is on administrative leave. Detective Gabriel has left the department."

"And you?"

"I'm fine."

They sat uncomfortably for some time longer, feeling futile and nervous, as closely observed as Delasante's empty boat.

"What if we just went aboard?" A.C. asked.

"There's at least a couple of feds hangin' around here. They might do something stupid. Let's get your boat tied up where it's supposed to be and then get something to eat." Lanham stood up. "Maybe there's a store where we can buy some penlights and a couple of knives."

"Knives?"

"You're a sailor. Knives can cut boatlines, if you're in a hurry."

They took dinner in a tourist café overlooking the harbor, then returned to their boat after sundown. The mooring A.C. had obtained was on the opposite side of the harbor. As the advancing night cleared the dusk from the sky, they sat in the cockpit of the O'Day, waiting, tired of waiting. There was a yellow glow from the streetlamps set around the harbor. The streets and public ways were still full of people. Loud shouts and laughter indicated the presence of teenagers, and the probability of beer.

"If Jacques shows up, there could be shooting," A.C. said, seating himself by the tiller. "There are all these people around."

"Santee only shoots who he wants to. You can say that for him."

"I'm not sure you can say that about federal agents."

"The first thing they learn is how not to shoot bystanders," Lanham said. He was staring across the harbor. "Our friend has either been relieved by someone new or he's dog tired. Either way, we've got a little more edge than we did this afternoon." He leaned forward. "You see that rowboat tied up behind the sailboat there?"

"It's a dinghy."

"Whatever the fuck it is, see if you can get aboard it and cut it loose. Then bring it over here. I feel like a ride across the harbor."

A.C. climbed up on the dock, walked a short stretch of its length, then doubled back and hopped on the other sailboat, moving swiftly aft. Telling himself simply to act as swiftly as he might in a sudden storm, he cut the line with three slashes of the knife and slipped into the dinghy. It had two small plastic oars.

"We'll use them as paddles," he said to Lanham, as the other got clumsily in, nearly capsizing them until he centered himself on the rear seat. "It'll be quieter."

They were nearly hit by a passing fishing boat, but managed to reach Delasante's yacht and get aboard without prompting any alarm. There were two fishing chairs facing aft in the rear, and a seat forward by the steering and instrument console. There was a glass-windowed door to the left of the console, leading below.

"Get behind me," Lanham said, kneeling. "I need the penlight to pick the lock."

He had it open within a minute. They inched their way down a short flight of steps, then stood in the main cabin. Keeping his light below the level of the windows, Lanham flicked it about.

"Shit," he said. "Somebody's torn the place apart."

"The federal agents?"

"Them. Perotta's creeps. Santee. Maybe all of them. What's that over there?"

"That's the chart table."

"All right. You know boats. Check it out. I'll go up forward."

Lanham worked quickly. He was back before A.C. was done.

"What did you find?" A.C. asked.

"A hell of a lot of booze. Not much else. How about you?"

"A hell of a lot of charts."

"Great."

"The one on top is of Daufuskie Island. And Tawabaw Island."

They heard sudden shouting. Lanham had his small pistol in hand by the time they realized it was from the teens they'd heard earlier.

"Now's a good time to go," Lanham said.

They returned the dinghy to its parent boat, then crept back to their own.

"Does this boat's cabin have a light?" Lanham asked.

"Yes. Of course."

"Well, turn it on for a while. I want our friends to know we're here."

They talked, fell silent, then talked some more. Finally, Lanham asked A.C. to turn off the interior light.

"You want to turn in?"

"No. I want to go to Delasante's condo. How far is it to the south end of Hilton Head from here?"

"A mile. Maybe two."

"Good. We'll walk."

"Weren't you there before?"

"Not inside. Anyway, who knows? Maybe your lady love will be there by now."

It took much longer than A.C. had expected, because they kept to the side of the blacktop road and leapt away from it whenever headlights approached—at one point cutting into some woods, getting their feet wet. Near the last group of buildings, there was a car parked improbably on the shoulder. They gave it wide berth.

There were floodlights on the grounds of the condominiums, especially near the parking lots, but large areas remained in shadow, or screened by trees. Lanham led A.C. to a building hard by the beach, pulling him down behind some bushes.

"Last time I was here, they had two guys in a car in the parking lot, another by the pool, and another idling around near the elevator. The guy by the pool has probably moved over by the beach or somewhere, but I don't imagine the setup has changed much."

"How are we supposed to get to his apartment? Just walk right up?"

"No, Mr. James. We climb. We'll go around to the ocean side, dodge the lookout, and then use the balconies. Don't worry. They're almost like steps on a ladder. You just want to be careful you don't wake anybody up."

"I'm not sure I can do this."

"You'll have to. It's our only way."

Delasante's condominium was on the fourth floor, in the middle of the building. They climbed the balconies on the far end, Lanham twice having to catch A.C. when he slipped, then worked their way across. In one apartment, a couple was noisily making love. In another, an older man was sitting watching television, his back to the open sliding door. He never noticed them.

Lanham had said that if Delasante's balcony door was equipped with a horizontal jolly bar, they'd be stymied. If it was held closed only with a catch lock, he thought they might get in quickly. To their surprise, the glass door was wide open, and only the sliding screen barred their entrance. It was not latched.

The screen made a slight scraping noise when Lanham

moved it. He opened it only a short distance, just enough to slip in sideways. A curtain had been drawn across. He pushed his way through gently.

They stood motionless a moment, listening. The refrigerator was humming, and there was a sound that might have been water dripping from a faucet. Another faint noise could be heard, but A.C. could not identify it. He supposed every modern habitation made such sounds in the dead of night, if you listened for them.

Lanham clicked on his penlight and made a slow sweep with it, illuminating a scene much like the one they had found on the boat—drawers removed, the carpet pulled back, upholstery slashed, pictures taken from the wall, papers scattered on the floor. The kitchen had received similar treatment, to the point of food cans being emptied into the sink and flour spread out over one of the counters. Small insects were crawling over the mess.

They backed out and started down a hall, stepping over clothes that had been pulled from closets and thrown on the floor. The hallway made a right-angle turn, passing the open door of a bathroom strewn with the contents of the medicine chest. At the end of the hall was the doorway to a darkened bedroom, a tangle of sheets and torn carpeting visible just beyond.

A.C. followed Lanham into the room, watching as the detective played the little light over a tumbled pile of dresser drawers at the foot of the bed. Lanham abruptly halted, as though hearing something, and then all at once the lights in the room went on.

"Well, well, well. More visitors. Only this time I'm at home to properly receive them."

Pierre Delasante, grossly rumpled and drunk, lay on the bed, propped against the headboard like a wounded soldier left against a tree on a battlefield. He wore a creased and wrinkled beige summer suit, a sweat-soaked shirt hanging out of his pants, and a black tie pulled askew. In his left hand was a whiskey bottle; in his right, a long-barreled revolver, which was pointed waveringly at Lanham, though his bleary eyes flicked back and forth at both of them.

"I remember you," he said to A.C. "You're the pretty fellow Camilla met at the fashion show. You were there when Molly was killed." His eyes moved. "And you're the police detective who's been such a pest. Gentleman of color, at that. Clever of you to come looking for me here. Unfortunately, everybody seems to have been that clever. I fear even Jacques has been that clever. You know who he is, don't you? Jacques Delasante? Of course you do. That's why you're here. Well, take note of his calling card."

He waved the hand with the bottle at the disorder, then fell into violent coughing, the pistol barrel shaking with each spasm. When the attack subsided, he cleared his throat painfully, then took a long drink from the bottle, wiping his lips on the back of his hand. His finger sparkled with a large ring.

"Do you know where the fair Camilla might be, sir?" he said to A.C., pushing himself up higher on the headboard.

A.C. simply stared. Delasante steadied the aim of the revolver.

"A civil question, sir. A civil answer, please."

"No," said A.C.

"Northern manners," grumbled Delasante. "Did she tell you about my little retreat here? Is that how you found it?"

"This place was listed in the federal computer files," Lanham said. "Along with all your other assets."

"Ah, yes. My federal friends. Grateful to have 'em. Yes I am. Follow me everywhere. But I'm glad to have 'em. I expect some callers from New York, don't you know, and I do not believe that they are going to be very well behaved."

He laughed giddily, but more coughing was the result. He sat up, swinging his legs over the side of the bed, holding the revolver crosswise over his lap.

"I only hope the federal gentlemen can recognize them. I fear they're expecting Russians or Cubans or some damn thing. I think perhaps the FBI has the mistaken notion that I've engaged in spying—sold secrets, trafficked in drugs, compromised the White House. Damned stupid. Never did anything of the kind. Never broke the law. I've done nothing to the New York gentlemen, either. I've done nothing wrong, sir. Committed no crime. This is just a family matter. Just between kin."

"Molly Wickham wasn't kin," said Lanham, quietly.

"Wonderful girl, Molly. Real pussycat. The African body. Magnificent, wonderful girl." He got to his feet, wobbling slightly. "Gentlemen, let us move to the other room. I don't plan to leave here until morning, and I don't wish to spend the night on a bed with you two looking down at me. Just move ahead of me slowly. Move along."

When they were in the hallway, Delasante flipped on a light switch. At the end of the hall, he pushed another. Two lamps in the living room came on.

"Seat yourselves, gentlemen," he said. "I'll bring glasses, and we can all have a nice, pleasant drink. At least he didn't pour out my liquor."

"Is it wise to have these lights on?" Lanham asked, lowering himself carefully into the slashed remnants of an armchair.

"Oh, why not?" said Delasante through the wall opening above the breakfast bar. "The federal agents know I'm here."

He returned with three glasses and a fresh bottle. The way he was holding his gun, A.C. feared it might go off, but Delasante managed, setting his burdens down on the coffee table. Removing the cap of the bottle, he filled his own glass, then shoved the bottle to the center of the table.

"Take your pleasure, gentlemen," he said, easing his bulk into a lounge chair and propping his moist, stockinged feet up on the table edge. "It's going to be a long night. Sorry there is no ice. My refrigerator was emptied of everything."

A.C. poured himself a small drink. Lanham didn't. The detective sat with his arms folded, assessing Delasante from behind his thin-rimmed glasses, the lenses a little misty from the heat.

"Why was Molly Wickham killed, Mr. Delasante?" he asked.

"Totally unnecessary," said Delasante. "A gesture of contempt, directed at me. A threat of future violence, also directed at me. But totally pointless. Altogether ineffective."

"Though here you are," A.C. said.

"Here I am, but not at all intimidated. Not a bit. I am not deterred."

"Deterred from what? What do you want? What have

381

you done to make Camilla and her brother hate you so much?"

"As I say, sir, a family matter. But you're interested in family matters, aren't you? You write a society column for one of the New York papers. Very gossipy stuff, as I recall. Well, sir, I suggest you commence reading the Charleston papers. You might encounter something interesting in the next few weeks, perhaps in the next few days."

He began his wheezy laughter again, drowning his chortles finally in more whiskey.

"You're in love with Camilla, aren't you?" he continued, when he could. "Of course you are. They all fall in love with Camilla. I did, you know. Madly. But all she was ever willing to give me was trouble. She's the devil's own unholy work, that woman. Brings trouble to every man. To fall in love with Camilla Delasante is to curse yourself."

"Jacques Delasante killed Molly Wickham," said Lanham, a question uttered as a statement, asked as though the answer was to be entered into some record. "You were a witness to it."

"Yes. Of course. I was there. I watched him do it. Extraordinary shot, that man. Extraordinary shot, extraordinary rider. Jacques Delasante would have been quite a legend, if he'd been around to fight in the War Between the States. Instead, he merely became a murderer. Jacques began killing a long time ago. He thought it would solve all the Delasante problems. So wrong, that boy. He hasn't solved them yet."

A.C. started to ask the man about Tawabaw Island, then thought better of it. It served no good purpose to reveal to Pierre what they knew, or were guessing at.

"Would you be willing to come back to New York?" Lanham asked. "To testify to the grand jury?"

Delasante laughed, the sound grating on A.C.'s nerves. "My business is here, sir. You find Jacques. That's your business. You take him back. I'll be much obliged."

"You could be subpoenaed."

More laughter. "I have already been subpoenaed. I have in fact been indicted. I'm to stand trial in Washington City. But I intend to be in neither place. I'm ruined, gentlemen. Jacques and you newspapermen accomplished that. But it's

I who will do the final foreclosing. I have only vengeance left. But I shall have it. You just read the Charleston papers. There'll be something of interest to you soon enough."

There was a sudden snap of a sound outside—a gunshot, and then another. Then shouting. Lanham pulled out his pistol. A.C. let his be. Delasante dropped his feet to the carpet and leaned forward, his eyes fearful and glassy, his mouth hanging slightly slack.

"Is it Jacques?" A.C. asked.

Delasante took a last slug of whiskey, then stood. "Sounds much too clumsy for Jacques."

He was sweating profusely. His overblown aplomb now seemed so much affectation.

"Put down that silly little pistol," he said to Lanham.

The detective only stared. Delasante raised his huge revolver, the sight level with Lanham's head. A.C. realized he could do nothing, not yet.

"Put it down! On the table!"

Lanham did so.

"Now walk ahead of me. Both of you. Down the hall."

They caught each other's eyes. Lanham's offered no counsel. A.C. moved ahead, with Lanham following. All Lanham had to do was reach beneath A.C.'s coat to get the .45. But he did nothing—perhaps out of fear, perhaps out of wisdom. For the maneuver to succeed, he'd have to kill Delasante, and no one wanted to do that. Delasante had all the answers. Delasante was immortal.

"My apologies, gentlemen," he said. "I'd hoped to spend the night. Good drink. Good conversation. Sitting around the table. A very Southern evening. But now I think it best that I move on. Alone. Get into the closet."

He pulled open the door, giving Lanham a slight shove. The closet was deep, and the shelves in the rear had been emptied. Linens and the remains of cardboard boxes were all jumbled on the floor. A.C. stumbled over them, reaching to the wall for balance. Lanham bumped up against him. They tried to turn around.

"This is the storage closet," Delasante said. "It's for keeping personal things out of the hands of vacation renters. The door is stout; the lock's strong. You'll be here for some time. Someone will find you, have no fear."

He shut the door hard and everything went dark. They heard the lock turn.

"Nice fellow," A.C. said.

Lanham clicked on his penlight, flicking the tiny beam to the door, then to his watch.

"We'll give him five minutes," he said. "You still have bullets in that thing?"

"Yes."

"Give it to me."

"No. I'll do it. I've had the practice."

In the enclosed space, the sound of the gunshot was deafening. Bits of metal struck A.C.'s hand and chest. Lanham must have been hit by them, too, for he swore.

The door swung open, gun smoke eddying out into the hall.

The apartment was deserted. Delasante had departed in such haste he'd left Lanham's pistol on the living room coffee table. Lanham snatched it up and headed for the door.

"Come on, Captain. We gotta hustle. I think Perotta's people have arrived on the scene and the feds have noticed. Let's get the hell out of here while we can."

The hallway was open to the air at the end, a railing running to the elevator housing. They paused momentarily to look down at the beach where they saw in the shadowy moonlight three figures fighting in the sand. None looked to be Pierre. He had disappeared.

"We'll take the stairs. Quick!"

On the ground floor, they leapt down some wooden steps to the Bermuda grass, then hurried along the back of the next building, cutting through a cool passageway that led to the parking lot.

"We have no car," A.C. said.

"Astute."

"Can we steal one?"

"Never learned how to steal cars." Lanham looked around. There was a bicycle rack, with a half dozen or so bicycles standing in it.

All were locked. Two were held fast to the rack with a single chain.

"Give me that forty-five now!" Lanham said. "I don't want to take chances with this one."

A.C. handed him the heavy pistol. Lanham placed the barrel flush against the lock's combination dial and fired. An instant later he was pulling the chain loose through the spokes.

"Where are we going?" A.C. asked.

"We're going where he went. The only place he can go." He yanked one of the bikes around and clambered aboard. "Hurry up, before they see us, if they haven't already."

Apartment lights were going on all over the complex. Some people were shouting.

The bicycle left to A.C. was a women's model, slightly smaller than the other. He had to pedal furiously to catch up with Lanham, who seemed eight feet high rising on the pedals.

Once out of the parking lot, they followed the curve of the entrance drive out to the road, then veered off onto an asphalt path. The vague moonlight allowed them to see ahead, though not well enough for the speed at which Lanham was traveling. Rushing through one grove of trees, A.C.'s bike slipped off the paving into bushes, sending him tumbling. Ignoring the scratches on his arms and face, he righted the cycle and pressed on.

They lost their way twice and ended up having to use the road, but they reached Harbour Town amazingly fast, almost as quickly as a car could have managed. Delasante had had a considerable start, however, and he had a car. Leaving the bicycles at the edge of the quay, they slipped into the shadows of a building for a moment, peering through the yellow glow of the decorative streetlamps. There were some people cleaning up in a nearby bar, and a couple necking down by the water's edge, but they could see no one else.

Lanham tossed him back his automatic. "Lag behind a little and cover me. I'll go first."

Hurrying along the moored boats, they came at length to Delasante's slip. It was empty. The murky water it encompassed was still sloshing somewhat at the pilings. A.C. jumped up on some stonework, looking out at the channel.

He could see a dark shape moving just beyond it. The craft showed no running lights.

"Why did you have to rent a sailboat?" Lanham said.

•

Once clear of the breakwater, A.C. turned the little engine to full power and steered for the middle of the sound. Standing up in the cockpit, his hand on the boom of the mainsail, he swept his eyes along the horizon in a long, careful circle.

"I can't find him," he said. "Not enough moonlight to make out his silhouette."

"Could he have gone north?" Lanham asked.

"The intracoastal cuts through here to Port Royal Sound, but there's a causeway across it to the mainland. There's a drawbridge, but you can't get anyone to open it at night."

"What's south?"

"The open sea, Savannah, and the channel behind Daufuskie. And Tawabaw Island."

"Where he's going."

"Maybe not tonight. That's a big boat, too big for that little channel behind Tawabaw, and too big to get very close to the island on this side. He might try, but he could run aground in the dark."

"He's got that dinghy."

"That he does."

A.C. throttled down a little, steering now more to the south. The lights of Savannah were a bright yellow on the far distant horizon.

"We don't have a lot of gas," A.C. said. "But if I raise the sails we'll stick out like a neon sign in this moonlight."

"All right, Captain, what do you suggest?"

"The tide seems to be running out. I think we should just cut the engine and drift with it."

"And listen."

Myriad small sounds came at them once the engine was silent; the splash of a fish breaking the water's surface, some night birds calling from a distant marsh, a channel buoy tinkling and clanking, a far-off muffled thump, unexplained. To the south, the insect hum of a boat motor could be heard. It was a faint but steady sound, moving away.

"Is that him?" Lanham asked.

"I don't think so. It's too small a boat."

"How far away?"

"I couldn't say."

"But it isn't him?"

"I really don't think so. It sounds like a speedboat, or an outboard. He's got two big diesels in that thing, and they're inboard. You wouldn't hear that much."

"Maybe we can't hear him because of that speedboat."

"Maybe."

"Maybe that speedboat is after him."

CHAPTER

....

19

The tidal current took them south and east, till they drifted below the southern tip of Hilton Head and passed from Calibogue Sound into the ocean. The boat lifted and fell in heavy swells. At their height, A.C.'s view took in the distant, twinkling riding lights of boats far out in the deep water, which he thought to be fishermen working the night. None of them was moving and there were no lights moving toward them. He judged Delasante still to be somewhere in the sound. Fearing that he might be drifting too far out, A.C. finally hoisted sail. Lanham, who'd been dozing, looked up.

"I'm going back in and find an anchorage," A.C. said. "The moon's going down."

"Back in where?"

"To the other side of Calibogue Sound. We're dead straight off Daufuskie."

The wind had fallen, but there was breeze enough to maintain headway, the boat spreading a small wake that glimmered in the fading light from the moon, until its half circle vanished into the murk on the southeastern horizon. In its last gleaming, A.C. had been able to make out the treetops of Daufuskie, and held course for them. The breeze was from the sea, and he set the sails for a run, securing the jib sheets with both port and starboard cleats to keep the foresail from flapping. The boat would, he knew, simply plow into the sandy, muddy bottom off the Daufuskie shore, but the tide would shortly lift them again. With the wind low, it would be an easy anchorage.

The boat hit bottom with more force than A.C. expected, the keel catching hard, twisting the boat sideways.

"We all right?" Lanham asked.

"I think so. We'll know in a little while, when the tide comes back."

A.C. went forward and threw out the anchor, paying out a fair length of line before affixing it back to the cleat. He could hear the water washing against the shore, quite near. He listened a moment longer for other sounds, then lowered his sails and secured them.

"Get some sleep," he said. "I'll stand watch."

"All right," Lanham said. "Good night."

"Almost 'good morning,' " A.C. said.

Sliding down to rest his back against the other side of the cockpit, he folded his arms for warmth. It was quite humid, but the air had turned clammy.

It wasn't long before he felt the keel lurch and shift, and then the boat lift. The tide was beginning to return.

The O'Day turned and pulled on its anchor rope, rising and falling gently. They were secure for the night. Further wakefulness proved impossible. A.C. slipped into sleep.

•

They awoke to a dawn's first light heavily filtered by fog, its faint glow seeping through a mist that lay all around them. A.C. could see the nearby shore clearly enough, tall trees and some huge, gnarled, upended stumps. There'd

389

been bulldozers here, clearing the beach. Houses or a resort would not be long in coming. A few birds had begun chirping, but the sound was faint and muffled.

"Now what?" said Lanham, relieving himself over the side.

"There's a portable toilet below," A.C. said.

"Sorry. Like I told you, I never even owned a rowboat." He stepped down into the cockpit. "Now what?" he said, seating himself.

"We'll head down for Tawabaw."

"In this fog?"

"It'll burn off eventually. We've got a good quarter-mile visibility."

"You're going to sail down?"

"No wind. Don't worry. I think there's gas enough."

It took three pulls before the engine caught. There were still several inches of gasoline in the tank, enough to get to Tawabaw and back to Savannah.

Not enough if they needed to go anywhere else as well, especially in a hurry.

A.C. cranked up the engine speed sufficiently to make headway against the tidal current, then swung the bow completely around, steering south.

The shore came and went in the fog. He steered out into the sound a little to make sure of deep water. There was a rosiness to the gray in the east, yellowish at the top. The rising sun was beginning to eat through.

A.C. rolled up his sleeves, slipping the automatic into his belt at the front. When he decided they had gone out enough, he turned to starboard again, steering due south. The shore had slipped from their view; when they approached the Tawabaw headland, it seemed to jump at them through the mist.

Rounding it, they could see nearly a mile now. Just at that reach was the gray silhouette of a power cruiser lying motionless just off the Tawabaw shore.

"Ray. If Camilla's there, leave her to me."

"Yeah, right."

"I mean it."

"I know you mean it."

As they came closer, A.C. reduced speed to lessen the

engine noise, but it still seemed to be making a crashing racket. He swung out into deeper water again.

"I'll come at it from astern," he said.

As they shifted course, the gray silhouette seemed to lengthen, and then divide. There was another boat with it —much smaller—tied to the larger craft's stern.

Lanham wiped his glasses, then crouched up against the cabin bulkhead, squinting over it.

"It says *Floride*, all right," he said.

Holding the speed now down to near idle, A.C. putted slowly past the stern of the smaller boat. There was nothing inside but gear. It had shipped some water, and a plastic cup was floating near the rear seat.

A.C. moved the sailboat to the other side of Delasante's cruiser, cutting the engine just short enough to allow the two craft to slide gently together.

Lanham climbed up over the side, turning once he was on the deck of the cruiser to catch the line A.C. threw to him.

"Fasten it to anything," A.C. said.

Lanham held a finger to his lips, but did as instructed. In a moment, A.C. was up beside him.

The cabin window curtains had been pulled closed, and the interior was dark and gloomy, but there was light enough to see the splayed, shoeless feet and sprawled legs in their light-colored pants, jutting out from the small doorway forward. Lanham yanked back two of the curtains, then knelt beside the body. A.C. knelt on the other side.

"You're not a cop," Lanham said. "How come you never throw up?"

"I was a police reporter."

Lanham leaned closer to the still form, gingerly touching with a finger the bloody mass of what had been the head.

"Goodbye Pierre," he said. "Whoever did this sure must have enjoyed it."

"You mean Jacques."

"I guess. I've never seen anyone shot up this much."

It looked as though Delasante had changed into a red shirt and jacket, but they were the same clothes he'd been wearing on Hilton Head. There was an eye and the mouth visible in the face, but the rest was puffy crimson mush.

Lanham reached and carefully pulled the shirt up over the man's large belly. It took some effort, for the blood was still moist and sticky.

"He must have had a gun emptied into him," Lanham said. "Twice. He's real dead."

A.C. sat back on his heels, then leaned all the way against the bulkhead, closing his eyes a moment. He hadn't noticed the rank, damp, sweet-sour smell before. Now it overwhelmed him. "God."

"You all right?"

"Yes."

"You sure?"

"Fine." A.C. rubbed his eyes, then opened them. He rubbed his temples, looked around the cabin, then got shakily to his feet and went over to the chart table. The Tawabaw chart had been pulled separate from the others and spread out. He picked it up, but it told him nothing. He knew where they were.

"Why now?" A.C. asked. "After all this time?"

"Whatever Jacques Santee has been looking for, he must think he's pretty near it. He must think Pierre has led him to it."

"On Tawabaw. Camilla said Hilton Head or Tawabaw. So it's Tawabaw."

"This isn't over," Lanham said. "There are two boats here."

Without another word, they crept back up to the cruiser's afterdeck, crouching down behind the steering, not wanting to expose themselves now. Lanham lifted his head slightly, looking up the mist-shrouded shoreline.

"Can you take our boat up the shore a little? Into the fog?"

"All right." A.C. squinted up at the sky. "It's burning off pretty fast, though."

"I'm going to cut these two boats free. Meet you on the beach."

"I'll be there."

Lanham tapped his shoulder. "You'd make a good cop, Captain."

"Not as good as you."

A.C. rolled over the side, dropping into the sailboat and

392

hunching down. In a moment, the line to the cabin cruiser came loose. He pulled it in out of the water and then started the engine, quickly throwing it into reverse. The O'Day swung backward, bumping against the smaller powerboat. Shifting into forward, he pulled away, veering toward the shoreline for a moment and then out into deeper water. Once at a safer distance, he shifted his course, skimming alongside the island into the mist, keeping low until the other two boats had disappeared.

.

Camilla knelt in the muddy grass, the mummified, patchy remains of a long-dead, gutted raccoon lying on the ground beside her. The thick oilskin pouch had been in the rotted animal. It had been there all the time. Jacques had killed the poor old nana woman and torn the shack apart, and found nothing. He'd ripped open some of the hideous dead creatures she'd hung about the place, but had missed this one. It might have been just a few feet from his hand.

The nana might have told him that. Had he asked her? Had he given her that much chance at a few more moments of life? Or had she been aged beyond reasonable speech? Perhaps he was afraid of her hoodoo. Everyone else had been—the villagers, the local police. They had taken the old woman away but left everything else as Jacques had left it, the dead animals hanging from the trees, full of death and vermin, and evil magic.

Camilla had gone to them first. The raccoon was one of the larger creatures and in it she'd found the nana's cache. Pierre's buried treasure, its contents as vital to the Delasante clan as the treasures of the pharaohs were to the ancient Egyptians. The oilskin was dark and greasy, and small, sluglike insects crawled upon it, but inside, once un-wrapped, it was pure and new, just as it must have been when Pierre had bought it.

Camilla's hands were filthy and her nails were clogged with grit. Her white skirt, stockings, and white shoes were spattered with mud. There were dirty spots on her arms and face where she had slapped at insects. Her neck and underarms were oily with sweat. The perspiration had dripped in runnels into the divide between her breasts. Her hair was damp and matted. She had never been so soiled in her life, but she felt just the opposite. The act she was performing, the dreadful thing she had already done, these were cleansing acts, purging acts. She was engaged in purifying destruction, the purification brought by flame.

She must start a fire in this watery, spongy place. There was old, dried wood enough in the weathered shack, wood torn asunder by Jacques's violent hand, as though he had prepared it for her, with this conclusive morning, this ultimate moment, in mind. She gathered it together and arranged it into a pile, a miniature pyre.

But the wood would not ignite by itself. She needed tinder—little twigs and paper. The few twigs she found were damp, and there was no paper. The old nana had kept none, had no use for it. Camilla sat back on her haunches, knees high, looking around, a little dazed by her futility.

It came to her almost as a revelation. The answer was at hand. In the objects of destruction was the source of destruction. What she had come to burn would start the healing fire.

She knelt forward again, and reached into the oilskin pouch, pulling out the old Bible. It had been preserved for generations as carefully and purposefully as Pierre for his dark reasons had kept it safe and hidden for the last several months in this place. The pages were limp, but had been made in a century when book papers were intended as permanence, when all printed words were meant to last.

The pages would burn. It would be God's word that would be burning, a sacrilege as provocative of fate as violating the old woman's hoodoo. But Camilla decided to presume a divinity in their sacrifice. The holy words would perish for the greater good of destroying evil words, erasing with flame and char and curling smoke the passages that had been written in this book not by God but by culpable mortals, words that had been used by Pierre for the basest purpose, words, names, that had brought this horror down upon them all.

She tore the pages out at random, reading their headings as they came to hand: Corinthians, Proverbs, Matthew, Luke, John:

Think not that I am come to destroy the law, or the prophets: I am not come to destroy, but to fulfil.

But the children of the kingdom shall be cast out into outer darkness: there shall be weeping and gnashing of teeth.

As he spake by the mouth of his holy prophets, which have been since the world began: that we should be saved from our enemies, and from the hand of all that hate us.

And the light shineth in darkness: and the darkness comprehended it not.

She crumbled the pages one by one, setting them with gentle care among the pieces of piled wood. Satisfied that there were enough, she picked up the matchbook she had brought from the car, looking with sad amusement at the name on the cover: "The Carlyle." Where was A.C. James now? To what fate had she left him on that street in Savannah?

She struck a match. It flamed and glowed and went out. Leaning closer to the pile, using more caution, she struck another, holding it carefully until the flame caught the cardboard stem. Then she moved it gently toward the nearest edge of holy paper. The flame spread along it, climbing. Soon, it was all touched with burning, a smoky, smoldering fire, but a relentless one. If God were opposed to her deed, he did not prevent it.

She opened the Bible again, at the beginning, turning to the first of the front flyleaves reading over the carefully penned old-fashioned writing—some of it practiced script, some of it crabbed scrawl—all names and dates, births and deaths. There were dozens and dozens of long-dead people here, some of them buried on this island. At Camilla's hand, they were dying once again, vanishing forever—as though they had never lived.

•

A.C. set his anchor, let the boat pull out the length of the anchor line, then, holding his pistol high, jumped into the water, surprised by its depth. He found solid footing, however, and pushed forward, ascending the slippery, sandy slope till he was at last able to gain dry land. He paused to empty the water from his Top-Siders, then put them back on and started back down the shoreline to where he had left Lanham, staying close to the trees.

The policeman had moved away from the boats, and was crouched at the tree line in the shelter of a sandy hummock, his pistol in hand. A.C. came up quietly and knelt beside him.

"No one's come out," Lanham said. "There's a house on the other side of these trees. I saw a chicken. No people."

"What do we do?"

"It's not a big island." He stood up slowly, looking both ways down the beach, then stepped up into the woods, moving as carefully and quietly as an Indian. He waved A.C. back and to the side, the veteran sergeant leading a patrol. A.C. had never led troops in the field in his army time, but he remembered his training. Squad tactics. Keep an interval. Stick to cover. Stay off the paths.

A.C. held the heavy pistol straight before him. He'd reloaded it in Savannah, and it was ready for more violent harm. He'd destroyed a man's leg with this weapon. The paper had said it had been amputated. What power, to take a man's leg so simply and easily.

Jacques Santee had killed that easily. He'd be ready to do it again. He could be bringing a gun to bear on them at this very moment, waiting for them to clear the trees.

Lanham moved on, relentless. They were so near what they all had come to find.

They reached the edge of a clearing. There were several houses, all rudely painted—most of them an odd, eerie blue—strung out along either side of a grassy, sandy lane. Wide boards had been laid out on top of some concrete blocks, forming a crude table. Some old laundry tubs were set on the ground beside it. Fishing nets were hung over the low limb of a dark, mossy tree. A rusted car, lacking wheels, was set up on concrete blocks. Another, just as old and in nearly as bad a condition, sat serviceably on muddy tires. The red pickup truck they had seen was farther along the lane, canted slightly to the side.

In the middle of the clearing, brightly red, was Camilla's car.

A.C. looked at Lanham, who ignored him, his eyes searching the farther woods.

A chicken appeared from behind the concrete blocks, moving in a slow, arch, antic strut. A large dog lay on its side by the steps of a small house, only a flick of his stringy tail indicating life. Birds flew and swooped and called. Insects buzzed.

A sudden movement, a flash of pink, caught A.C.'s eye and he turned with his pistol. It was a little black girl, skipping barefoot from between two houses, singing to herself. She failed to notice them, and kept on down the lane to the right.

Lanham was watching her, his gun lowered. Moving quietly, A.C. went over to him.

"There are people here," Lanham said softly. "They're all here. They're in their houses."

"Should we try to talk to them?"

"They'll be scared shitless." Lanham turned to the left. "I think we should look down that way. We'll take either side of the path. Just keep the noise down."

He moved off, slipping from tree to tree. Reaching the path, he crouched down, hesitated, then hurried to the other side. A.C., with some struggle, set forth through the brush, moving sideways to slip between the grasping brambles and twigs.

The ground was mucky, and sucked at his shoes. A bramble tore at the skin of his calf. Some of the insects bit and sweat began to trickle down his back. He ignored it all. They were hunting, and his thoughts were cold. His attention was fixed ahead.

He saw Lanham suddenly raise his arm. A.C. halted.

Ahead, around a slight bend in the path, was a small, crude footbridge with a single wooden railing. Just in front of it was what looked like a pile of dark rags.

Lanham continued now, very slowly. A.C. kept pace, creeping forward. It was a person there, lying as though in wait, close to the ground, a military ambush.

A.C. raised his pistol, keeping the sights near the prone

form. It had to be Jacques. Camilla had long blond hair. If the figure moved, he'd fire. He wouldn't wait for Lanham. It could cost him his life—both their lives.

He hated this. He was furious with himself for being here.

The form remained motionless. At last, Lanham stepped out into the path, motioning A.C. to join him.

The pile of rags was a man, lying sprawled on his back, his arms flung back toward them, his eyes staring upward, motionless. He'd been facing the other way. There was a huge, ragged hole in his dark blue shirt, the flesh of his chest beneath all blackened and bloody.

Flies buzzed around the dark, handsome face. One perched on the lower lip. It flew off as A.C. knelt close, next to Lanham.

The man's dark hair was very curly. On impulse, A.C. touched it, then drew his hand back.

"It's him," he said, finally. "Jacques Delasante."

"The man on the motorcycle."

"Yes."

In Jacques's belt was a large, ungainly automatic pistol with a square-edged receiver. Lanham gently pulled it free, holding it by the seat of the barrel.

"It's a machine pistol," Lanham said. "German. A war relic."

"It looks like it works."

"It worked."

Lanham set it on the man's chest, then rose, studying the marshy woods across the bridge. "You said you'd handle Camilla," he said.

A.C. moved on ahead, sticking his pistol back into his belt and walking down the middle of the path. As far as he was concerned, the combat patrol was over. If Lanham wished to be more cautious, that was his option. If he wished to do her violence . . . A.C. had trust enough in Lanham to believe that he would not. The policeman had had a chance to shoot her in Virginia, and had not taken it. A.C. could not imagine Detective Raymond Lanham wanting to add another death to this long trail of killing.

They found her in another clearing, a very small one, in front of a sagging, weathered shack so decrepit it seemed more a work of nature than of man. Camilla had built a fire in the grass, and was kneeling over it, as though for warmth. Then A.C. noticed the objects around her, and that she was tearing pages from a book.

He stood quietly, near the heat of the flames, waiting for her to take note of him.

"Camilla?" He spoke her name gently.

She looked up sharply, as though startled from a dream. Her eyes widened, and then became questioning.

"What are you doing, Camilla?"

She stared at him, as though thinking of what to say, or do. Turning her head, she saw Lanham standing near.

"Camilla?"

She went back to her strange work. He saw that it was a Bible she had. The pages she was tearing and setting carefully into the fire were covered with handwriting. He wondered if in the course of all this horror she had gone mad, if all the Delasantes were lunatics.

"Camilla!"

Her eyes were very sad now as she lifted her head again, almost imploring. He wished Lanham were not there. He wanted suddenly to help her, though he was far from certain what it was she would desire him to do.

She closed the Bible and dropped it into the fire. The flames flattened and retreated from it, then curled back.

"Every family in the South has its Bible," she said, her voice very weary, almost ghostly, but at least sounding sane and rational. "Noble or poor. White families, black families. They hold the names of the born and the dead, generation after generation. This is the Bible of the Hingham family. A black family. They lived here, but now they're all dead."

She took a packet of letters from the ground beside her. The envelopes had aged to a pale brown, the old-fashioned handwriting on them faded to a brown of a darker hue. Camilla snapped the frail ribbon holding them together, tossing it into the fire, and then began throwing in the envelopes, one after the other. The paper was so very old it disintegrated as much as burned.

The letters might well contain what a court could construe as significant evidence in these murders, but A.C.

399

didn't care, even though the evidence might bear tellingly in a trial concerning the murder of Bailey Hazeltine. Camilla seemed to be explaining herself. He would let her do so, unhindered.

Lanham was standing stone still, watching patiently, his pistol in his hand, but lowered.

"Before the War Between the States," Camilla said, "the Hinghams were slaves. They were owned by the Tramore family, which owned the entire island. But the Tramores were driven out by the Union army. The plantation was burned. They lost everything. They never came back. The land was cut up into small plots, and sold for nominal sums to the former slaves."

Though she spoke so strangely, and her clothing was dirty and torn, she reminded A.C. of the elegant Southern ladies who served as guides and docents at historical houses, reciting their speeches and answering questions with well-mannered reverence for their subject. This was no tourist guide's tale, however.

"The Hinghams had been the most prominent Negro family on the island. Many of them could read and write, though it was forbidden by law. One of them served as the Tramores' majordomo. Another had been sold to a Tramore relative in Virginia and he had bought his freedom. He had moved north and worked for the Abolitionist party. He wrote tracts and lectured and even wrote a book. I believe it's in the slave museum in Charleston. His name was Samuel Hingham."

Lanham had sat down, holding his gun on the ground beside him. A.C. still stood. Camilla was looking up at him, though she continued to feed the envelopes into the fire.

"After the war, he came back to Tawabaw. He was elected to the U.S. Congress and served a term there. For a time, he served as minister to Liberia. When Reconstruction ended, all that ended. He lived on here at Tawabaw, where he was a man of much consequence. Even the white people on the mainland thought well of him. These are his letters, what's left of them, and some letters that were written to him."

Another went into the flames, and then another.

"With Reconstruction, some of the Delasantes from up in the Piedmont came down here. They bought up or took most of the best land on the island from the Negroes. They worked it for nearly ten years, but never made much of it. They tried rice and sea cotton, but it didn't take. Tawabaw was good only for oystering and crabbing, and growing roots like elephant ear. They kept some of the land along the coast, but sold the rest back to the Negroes and left. Many of the blacks left, too, especially after the last World War. The poverty was very bad here, and the people ended up not much better off than when they had been slaves. But they kept up the old life here. They're very proud and independent. Their biggest fear has been that the white man would come and make this into another resort island like Hilton Head. Pierre was buying up land on Tawabaw. He was negotiating with developers. I found the papers in his lawyer's files."

"Is that why Jacques killed him?" A.C. said quietly. "Is that it, that Pierre was selling out to resort people?"

She ignored his question as though it had not been asked, reaching into the oilskin pouch and pulling forth some photographs. The smaller ones, brown images on white, were mounted on cardboard, and had probably been taken around the turn of the century. Camilla tore each in half before adding it to the fire.

"These are relatives of Samuel Hingham. The Delasantes took most of these pictures. This is one of his daughters. He had many children, not all by his wife."

The daughter went into the flames. Camilla picked up a larger object, an old tintype showing a handsome black man, wearing a high collar and old-fashioned cravat.

"This is Samuel Hingham. A fine-looking man, wasn't he? He had fairly light skin, and that was rare in the sea islands."

Gripping the tintype on both ends, she leaned back slightly and brought it down hard on her knee. When it remained intact, she brought it down again even harder, a slight cry escaping her lips when it broke into three pieces, cutting the skin of her hand and her knee. The metal fragments went into the fire, blackening swiftly.

She picked up the last photograph, holding it gingerly,

401

staring at it with some fascination before turning it for A.C. to see.

"This is one of Samuel Hingham's sons. His name was Robert. Very handsome. He looks white, doesn't he? He was raised as white. His mother was a Delasante. Some of the letters here are hers, written to Samuel after she had moved away from the island."

She placed the photograph on top of the other burning objects with great care, as though this was the last act in a religious ritual.

"This Robert Delasante was my stepfather's father. He was Pierre's grandfather, and my brother's grandfather, and my sister's. They were all part Negro. They were Negroes. My mother never learned the truth until it was far too late, but she had married a Negro. Do you understand what that means? She married a Negro."

She sat back and took a deep breath, her eyes fixed on his.

"Now you know," she said. "The proof is burning up. There is no other proof, but you know."

A.C. came nearer to her. "Did it matter that much to you? That's all I want to know, Camilla. All that's happened, all that you've done . . ."

"Matter to me? I would have been proud to have had Samuel Hingham among my ancestors. I doubt that you believe that, but it's true. My mother, though, my poor mother. This would have destroyed her. Jacques killed his father because of this. My sister Danielle committed suicide, because of this. My mother, she's the family. She's all that's left of us in Charleston."

She looked down at her hands, at the blood on the one. She rubbed it off on her skirt, then slowly, stiffly got to her feet. A.C. noticed that Lanham did the same.

"Up in Washington, Pierre had a taste of being very rich," she said. "When he got in trouble, he wouldn't give it up. He took money from me, from all of us. My brother sold his horses. My mother gave him jewelry. This"—she pointed to the fire—"this was the only reason we did it. This is all that kept Pierre alive."

She turned and looked all around her, as if the little

clearing and the shack and the island offered some final explanation.

"I'm glad that Pierre is dead," she said. "In the end, I'm glad Jacques did that. But the people on this island. They're related to Samuel Hingham. These poor people . . ."

"Your brother would have killed them," Lanham said, his voice weighty, as though rendering a judgment.

"I'm so sorry, A.C. But I've been sorry for such a long, long time."

She turned away. He sought words to stay her. The ones he found were unwanted, but they had to be said. At least once.

"Camilla. Who killed your brother?"

She hesitated, head down, then continued on, going to the door of the shack and stepping carefully inside. A.C. glanced at Lanham. He had not moved.

Camilla came back out into the light, holding a shotgun. She gripped it by the barrel, carrying it stock down in front of her. Moving around the fire, she came before A.C. and held the weapon out to him, as though it were a gift.

As he took it, she looked away from him, then started walking slowly toward the little wooden bridge, her head down, her hands held together. When she reached the bridge, she stopped and gazed back at them, waiting.

Neither man moved. A.C. stared at Lanham. He looked back, though A.C. could see only the glare of sunlight on his glasses.

"Do you want to go with her?" Lanham asked quietly.

"What?"

"Do you want to go with her, to wherever she's going? This is your chance, your only chance. After this, you'll never find her again. Do you want to take it?"

"Just go? No questions asked? You'll let me?"

"No questions asked. I have all my answers."

She was starting across the bridge, still walking slowly.

"No," A.C. said.

She had come into his life in the fantasy of a fashion show. Now she was leaving him in a fantasy of black magic, having brought him to this place of witchcraft and death. If he let her go, if he did not follow, all she would ever be to him again was a fantasy. Little wisps of memory of her would come to him in old age—the color and scent of her hair, the haunting magic of her eyes when she had first looked at him.

"No," A.C. said again, firmly. "I want to, Ray. God, I want to. I'll always wish I had. But I can't. I can't leave what I'd have to leave."

"Well, Captain. Sometimes the choices are hard."

She was gone. Both of them looked to where she had been, but she had vanished, like a fantasy. Black magic.

Lanham muttered something A.C. could not quite hear, rubbing his shoulder. Then the detective put his pistol into his pocket and went over to the fire. It had diminished slightly. He pushed some charred end pieces of wood into the flames with his foot, rekindling them. One of the photographs had fallen out of the fire, most of it unburned. Lanham pushed that back in, too.

He went to the oilskin pouch, picking it up and peering inside. Then he reached and pulled out one final package, removing the rubber band that held the plastic wrap around it in place.

"The videotape," he said, pulling out the cassette. "Pierre and his friends in Molly Wickham's apartment." He held it up for A.C. to see—as if the entwined naked bodies recorded within were visible.

"Trash," he said, and dropped it into the fire, adding the pouch. There was some sudden crackling, and the smoke turned quickly black.

"Can you believe it?" A.C. said. "All those people dead, just because . . ."

"I can believe it," Lanham said. "That's why I came down here."

He led the way over the bridge and back up the path. To A.C.'s surprise, when they came to Jacques Delasante's body, Lanham stepped carefully around it and kept going. A.C. grasped his arm.

"What about him?" A.C. said.

"Jacques Delasante? He's dead."

They hadn't heard the engine start, but Camilla's car was gone from the village. The inhabitants had come out of their houses and were standing around in little groups. An older man, gray beard and spiky hair bright against his dark skin, came forward.

"It's all over," Lanham said. "You have nothing more to worry about."

"Dey be gone?"

"All gone. All over."

The old man pointed to where Jacques's body lay behind them. "'E something for dead."

Lanham nodded. "He something for dead."

A.C. nodded also, as though all were explained, all understood. Then he turned and followed Lanham into the woods.

They lingered a moment on the beach, near where the dinghy from Pierre's boat had been pulled up on the sand. The two powerboats had drifted out into deep water.

"We won't need to get wet this time," A.C. said.

"No."

"Pierre's boat has a ship-to-shore radio. Do you want to use it?"

"What for?"

"To call New York. The Coast Guard. Those federal agents."

Lanham shook his head.

"You just want to leave all this?"

The detective went to the dinghy and gave it a shove, moving it several inches closer to the water.

"Someone will come along," he said. "Today. Tomorrow. There must be a sheriff's office on the mainland. We'll let this be their case. I really do think this is a matter for the local authorities. Maybe they'll get around to talking to that thug you shot in Savannah about it. Our mob crimes unit can put it in the case file with all the others."

•

The winds were light but steady from the east, and, once the sails were set, A.C. was able to cast off and get under way without recourse to the engine. He steered toward open water, giving wide berth to the shoals to the south of Tawabaw. Lanham trimmed and cleated the jib for him, then sat down on the seat beside A.C. He looked very tired. A.C. was so weary the ache went to his bones. He let the mainsheet run out a little, holding the tiller loosely in his hand.

Lanham clasped his hands together, looking down at the bright white cockpit floor. "This is my last case," he said. "I'm turning in my shield as soon as I get back to New York."

"My God, Ray, why?"

"I'd face disciplinary action anyway. I'm supposed to be working a Central Park sex murder. I wasn't authorized to come after you, or anyone. Mob crimes has those other cases. Another detective has Bailey Hazeltine. He's a good man, but he was working the wrong lead. He got all excited about the drug trouble she got into in Philly."

"But you have that subpoena. Aren't you supposed to bring me back for the inquest?"

"I lifted that when another guy wasn't looking. They'll issue another. Paperwork. I'd show up, if I were you, but I wouldn't worry about that inquest changing your life any. Unless you want to identify the man in the photograph your wife provided us as Jacques Santee."

A.C.'s silence answered that question.

"What will you do?" he said, after a moment. "You've been a cop all your life."

"Not quite all my life. I've got that law degree. I was thinking I might take some refresher courses and have a try at passing the New York State bar exam. It would be nice to work in the law and be able to call some shots."

"Cops call shots, don't they?"

Lanham smiled. "Cops are just cops. They catch cases. They close cases. They bring criminals to the law. But that's all. The rest is up to the lawyers. What people call justice, it's all just lawyers. One of them might as well be me. Anyway, it's about the only way I know I can get straight with my wife again. She quit the cops a long time ago, if you know what I mean."

A.C.'s eyes drifted to the water, now all aglitter in the hazy sun. Distracted, he let the helm slip in his hand, inadvertently pointing the bow up into the wind, the sails pinching, beginning to flutter and flap, as though the wind and the boat were trying to attract his attention to some-

406